THE MUSEUM OF BROKEN THINGS

Lauren Draper is a Melbourne-based writer and marketing professional. She is a graduate of RMIT's Professional Writing and Editing program and now works in children's publishing—she loves nothing more than a story infused with magic, hijinks and a touch of nostalgia. *The Museum of Broken Things*, her debut novel, was shortlisted in the 2020 Text Prize. Her work has also been longlisted in the 2019 Richell Prize and has appeared in various non-fiction publications. She grew up in Western Australia, mostly on land but often in water. She now lives in Melbourne with one struggling coffee machine, a moderately behaved golden retriever and her partner.

laurendraperauthor.com

THE MUSEUM
OF BROKEN THINGS

LAUREN DRAPER

TEXT PUBLISHING MELBOURNE AUSTRALIA

The Text Publishing Company acknowledges the Traditional Owners of the country on which we work, the Wurundjeri people of the Kulin Nation, and pays respect to their Elders past and present.

textpublishing.com.au

The Text Publishing Company
Wurundjeri Country, Level 6, Royal Bank Chambers, 287 Collins Street, Melbourne Victoria 3000 Australia

First published by The Text Publishing Company, 2022

Book design by Imogen Stubbs
Cover illustration by Adèle Leyris
Typeset by J&M Typesetting

Printed and bound in Australia by Griffin Press, part of Ovato, an accredited ISO/NZS 14001:2004 Environmental Management System printer.

ISBN: 9781922458537 (paperback)
ISBN: 9781922459831 (ebook)

A catalogue record for this book is available from the National Library of Australia

For my mum, who always believed this book would happen.

1

I DIDN'T ALWAYS live here. Not so long ago I was living in a thriving metropolis with more than one coffee shop on each block and four full bars of reception. I went to Heathmont High School, home to one thousand students, my two best friends, a deeply average orchestra, and one cursed statue. Well, allegedly.

I don't know who started the rumour, but it goes something like this: sometime in the 1950s, the school board erected a bronze statue of a mystery woman known only as M. A. B.—the letters are all worn off, so you can't actually read the plaque anymore. More affectionately, she's known as Queen Mab, Mabby G, The Real MAB and so on.

Mab is located at the school gates, holding out one hand as though to welcome arriving students. Supposedly, every student in the graduating class has to touch her outstretched arm on the first day of school, or the entire year level is cursed with bad luck.

The general consensus is that she was a famous teacher,

maybe a writer—someone important forgotten by time and crappy records. According to the more macabre rumours, Mab was a student who died in her final year. Cause of death always varies, but they're all fairly bad ways to go, so I prefer the first theory.

But the point is this: on the first day of school, I was running late for class and I forgot all about old Mab. I rode my bike straight past her and didn't realise my mistake until lunch. I clapped her arm three times to appease everyone's superstitions while Willow and Nina watched, taunting me that it didn't count anymore and Queen Mab would send a plague on all our houses, et cetera, et cetera. I never used to believe it was real.

Now I think I cursed myself.

Nan's funeral is nice, but it's still a funeral and I have to excuse myself to have a meltdown in the courtyard afterwards, when everyone is grabbing my hands and trying to emphatically ask if I'm *doing okay*. I don't even know most of these people; they're all my parents' friends or people from Nan's nursing home. They all approach with watery smiles and kind eyes, telling me how special I was to her. Not to play favourites, but I kind of *was* her favourite grandchild. I mean, she only had two to choose from, and my brother, Theo, is a hormonal fifteen-year-old jock who spends too much time in the bathroom and doesn't read, so it wasn't much of a competition. But all their platitudes are too much, and too soon.

The courtyard of the church is small and dark, not

much more than two bench seats and a sad little ficus with browning leaves. I double over in the shadows, heaving a sob that echoes in this bleak chamber. My fingers clench the black fabric suffocating my ribs, a dress that's too tight and too formal, a skirt that billows around my feet and gets stuck every time I move. I want to tear it off and throw it in the bin. I'll never wear it again—it smells like cloying incense and disinfectant, the smell of hospitals and nursing homes and death.

My breath hitches, and I place a hand on my chest, just to make sure I'm still breathing. I think of Nan's stethoscope, her most precious possession, and how she gave it to me after I broke my arm when I was little—I'd cried and cried until she'd finally placed the headpiece gently in my ears, put the bell to my chest, and said: *Listen: hear that? That's your heartbeat. That's all you need, a beating heart and air in your lungs. You're all right. You're going to be all right.* I'd watched her wrap my arm, piece me back together again, and decided I wanted to be a doctor one day, just like her.

My lungs heave, stuttering back to life. *Be all right*, I tell myself. Just hold it together for another hour; then I can go home and fall apart in private.

A door opens behind me and I swipe my cheeks. 'I'm coming,' I say, facing the tree for a few more moments, waiting for my lip to stop trembling.

'You okay?'

I roll my eyes as I face Theo, brushing down my skirt. 'I'm fine. Having a great day, actually.'

He rolls his eyes in return. 'You know what I mean.'

'Yeah,' I grumble, conceding. 'I know what you mean.' I blink a few more times to make sure the tears stay on the right side of my eyeballs. 'You all right?'

He shrugs. 'Yeah. I mean, we weren't that close. I know you...'

There's a pause. 'She loved you too,' I say quietly.

'I know. It's okay that she liked you better though.'

I laugh a little and he punches me gently on the shoulder, then makes his fist explode and wiggles his fingers in my face. 'Come on,' he says, messing with his suit pants. 'Mum's gonna flip.' He puts a hand in his pocket as if that's more discreet and wiggles around.

I whack his arm. 'Can you stop *adjusting* yourself for two seconds. We're in a church.'

'Yeah, but it's one of those all-faith kinds. It doesn't count.'

I gag. 'God is judging you.'

'You don't even believe in god. You always say god is a woman.'

'And she's *judging you.*'

A figure steps around the corner, eyes narrowed on Theo and me. She's tall and elegant and our faces match: high cheeks, freckled nose, eyes blue and red-rimmed. She looks tired. 'Would the two of you *shh!* These walls aren't soundproof.'

'Sorry, Mum,' I say. Theo echoes it back, looking down at his shoes, face burning red.

She reaches a tissue to her eyes, snuffling quietly. 'It's fine. It's fine. Are you okay, Clarissa?'

'Mum, I'm fine. Are you okay?' My parents are worried this is the thing that will push me over the edge. I don't think they realise that it doesn't feel *worse.* Nothing is worse than The Terrible Thing That Happened. The thing we don't talk about anymore, the thing I'm supposed to fold away into the deep recesses of my heart and deal with in a functional way. Deal with and move on. I never quite managed that last part though.

Mum hiccups in response. I hold her hand and guide her back inside. 'It's all right, Mum, it's nearly over. Let's find Dad.'

A car comes to take the casket away, and a lady in a daggy three-piece suit comes to collect the flowers. Everyone shuffles out, having consumed all the available snacks and emotional turmoil, and suddenly it's just the four of us. Dad drives home while Mum tries not to cry in the front seat. It's so quiet even Theo has nothing to say.

But it's the house that's the worst. Mum stops in front of the pamphlets and photos she's left scattered across the benchtop. There was so much planning, I think she almost forgot Nan was gone—the distraction made it easier to pretend for a little while. She shuffles up the stairs without saying a word, and we hear the bedroom door closing quietly behind her.

'You kids okay for dinner?' Dad asks, struggling to loosen his tie.

'Yeah, Dad,' I murmur. 'You can go. We're good.'

He nods, eyes rheumy and grey—Dad loved Nan too. I think he feels like he's not allowed to miss her as much as the rest of us. He nods again and trails upstairs.

Theo jumps on the couch and flicks on the PlayStation controller. Teenage-boy resilience.

'You want kebabs?' he asks. 'Or Chinese?'

My hand lowers to rest on a photo propped up on the counter, taken when Nan was about my age. Smiling demurely, chin tilted at the camera. She looked so different in the end—so small.

I feel like I'm about to peel out of my skin. I don't want kebabs. I don't want to go upstairs and cry. I don't want to hear Mum sobbing when she thinks we can't hear. I don't want anything at all except to be far away from this house and this town and all the horrible things I try not to think about when I'm stuck here. 'I'm going for a run,' I whisper, and turn away before Theo can reply.

I don't even bother to change; I just kick off my heels at the door and then I'm gone—sprinting down the empty street, past weeping gum trees and golden fields, my feet slapping against warm concrete and rough bark. I run until my dress is filled with sweat and my chest feels like it might explode. I run with bunches of fabric in my hand, not caring if I look half-crazed or if anyone sees. I run until I hit sand, rounding on the empty beach, the wind blasting my cheeks, and suddenly realise where I'm headed.

That stupid pier, too long and half-broken. I don't even know how deep it is at the end—deep enough not to break my neck, and that's all that matters: I fling myself off the edge, dress billowing behind me, and plunge into the water.

It's so cold it knocks the air from my lungs. I sink down,

air bubbles and arms trailing above. For a moment I can just float, feet paddling, heart slowing, the day washing away. I imagine the water cleansing my invisible wounds, the ones that fester with regret.

I hold my arms out, keeping steady below the surface. Everything above the water glows, fragments of sunlight and sky. It's quiet here: not the quiet of loaded silences, or the dreary hum of country towns, but something more peaceful—just me and sea, the way I've always liked it. The only thing I really like about Hamilton.

I wait until my chest hurts and I need air before kicking up and bursting through. I tilt my head, squinting at the sun and slicking wet hair away from my face, and arch back until I'm floating. Waves nudge my shoulders, pick up my fingers. The dress weighs me down a little, but I pull it up to my waist and it's not so bad. I stay like that for a while, fabric pooling around my hips and sun on my face. I can feel my arms shiver as goosebumps flush across my skin, but I don't mind so much.

A throat clears.

'Are you, uh…do you need a minute?'

I sit up so fast I sink, head dunking below the waves. I splutter, coughing salt water, and look for the voice. My legs kick out, treading water while I spin around, eyes cast out over the empty horizon. *Oh god, I'm going crazy, I've actually lost it.* I turn back to the pier and finally glance up. When I see a face staring back at me, I consider ducking back under the surface and staying there until either I sprout gills or he leaves.

If there *was* a god, she'd strike me down now, because Gideon Hawthorn is staring down at me.

Gideon is something of a legend at Hamilton High School. Tall and blonde and, objectively, has a very nice face. He exists in a little bubble of perfection: the teachers love him, he seems to know all the answers without ever paying attention and with one earbud always wedged in his ear, and he's always surrounded by people offering high-fives or party invites. He also has the current record for number of school pranks resulting in full evacuations, and upon one occasion, the fire brigade being required to corral a number of sheep back to their fields (or at least, that's what I over-heard one day eating my lunch, alone, in a library carrel and eavesdropping on people who actually *have* friends). Need-less to say, we have never spoken, because I am fairly certain that, until right now, he didn't know I existed.

'I'm—I'm fine, t-thank you,' I stutter.

'Okay,' he says, resting his chin on his hand. 'Cause, you know, you're wearing a dress.'

I glance down and try to smooth the fabric so it no longer balloons around me. I wonder if he saw my under-wear because I might die of embarrassment if he did—it has little Superman logos and the band isn't really elasticised anymore. 'Yes. I noticed.'

'Cool. Just checking. You're the new girl, right?'

My cheeks are aflame. Of course he has no idea what my name is. 'Clarissa. Reece, I mean. Only my mum calls me—never mind.' Where's a good riptide when you need one? I take a breath, squinting at the sun. 'Reece,' I manage to say, coherently. 'I'm Reece.'

He grins, taking a seat at the end of the pier, legs dangling off the edge. 'Oh yeah, that's right. I'm Gideon.' *Oh, fuck off.* He has dimples. Of course he has dimples. They're so deep I could stick my fingers in them. I want to drown myself just to get away.

'So you know there's no ladder, right?' he asks, idly kicking his legs and watching the waves.

'What?' I twist in the water, looking at each of the wooden pillars. Oh my god. How have I never noticed there's no ladder? I've been coming here all my life and I finally know why they don't let you bomb off the end. I squint at the shore: it's a one-kilometre swim, and I'd really rather not do it in formalwear, but I guess that's where this conversation is headed. 'Um, that's fine. I'll just…swim back.'

'Swim back?'

'Yep.' I start paddling away to prove my point. Seaweed grabs my ankle and I cringe.

Gideon seems very amused by this, and starts to walk along the pier to keep pace while I swim. I get stuck on an armful of tulle and have to bat it away. 'Want me to hold your dress?' he asks, eyes twinkling with mirth.

'No, thank you.'

'Right. So you're just okay then? You're all good? You don't need a hand?'

'I said I'm fine,' I say contritely. 'You can go now.'

He shrugs. 'Okay. Just keep an eye out for Bruce on the way back.' He watches me for a moment, head cocked to the side, then he turns away.

I last all of three seconds. 'Wait! Who's Bruce?'

He smirks over his shoulder, entirely content with himself. 'Resident shark. Don't worry, he's pretty chill.'

I suddenly feel the need to yank my feet out of the black water and plant them back on safe, dry ground. Instead I nod, chin raised defiantly. 'Right. Of course.'

'Of course you knew, or of course he's chill?'

Of course I'm trying to pretend I'm not shit-scared of a man-eating beast because you're very attractive and I look like an idiot floating in the ocean like an oil spill in a black dress. I hesitate until I have something more intelligent to say. 'Uh…both?'

He grins even wider and runs a hand through golden curls. 'All right, well.' He gives me a two-finger salute. 'See you at the other end. It was nice meeting you, Reece.'

He starts to walk away and I can feel my toes tingling—a feeling of dread rushing through my body. Why do I watch so much Shark Week? Why didn't I just say, *Sure, Theo, I'd love a kebab,* and go cry in the shower like a normal person? More importantly, why did I fling myself off a ladderless pier in my nicest, heaviest dress? Oh *god*, my pride is going to be flushed away with the tide. 'Wait! Okay, okay. Can you maybe, you know, give me a hand?'

He turns, dimples fixed firmly into his cheeks, and spreads his arms. 'I thought you'd never ask. Here, swim round this side.'

I paddle over to the edge, where there's a slightly lower platform that fishermen usually sit on to keep the boardwalk clear. I realise Gideon must have been sitting down here, which is why I didn't see him when I sprinted past. He leans over the edge and reaches an arm down. I take a breath and reach up, kicking until my fingertips barely brush his own. I realise that if he hadn't been here, it truly would have been a very long swim back to shore.

My fingers are ice-cold in his warm hand, but he doesn't seem to mind. He just waits until I have a good grip then wraps his other hand around mine and hoists me out of the water like I don't weigh anything. The muscles in his arms twitch as my dress clears the surface, and I have a split second to wonder if we're both about to tip in before I manage to heave myself onto the wooden slats and flop down like a dead fish.

'Well, that was humiliating,' I say, closing my eyes and trying not to let my breath sound too ragged. He's not even puffing and he did all the work. I shiver in the sunlight, the wind on my skin now numbingly cold. I rock up to hug my knees, eyes fixed on the squid-ink stains and the splintered slats—anything but Gideon, who has now witnessed a serious low point in my life. I wonder if he can tell I've been crying or if he'll assume my red eyes are from the salt water.

I dare a glance up, and find him grinning again, sincerely amused. I usually stare at the back of his head in English, and now that I'm so close to his face I take it all in: the tilt of his lips, the brown flecks in his eyes, the little bump on his nose. I'm vaguely aware that I'm sublimating my grief, but also, I'm okay with it for now.

'Speak for yourself,' he says, sitting beside me. 'I had a great time.'

I groan, hiding my face behind my hands. 'What are the

chances I can bribe you to never tell another soul about this?'

I crack an eye open and see him crossing his heart with one finger. 'Scout's honour,' he says. 'I'll take it to the grave.' His eyes wander a little lower before they flick away, and I realise my dress is very tight and slick from the water, and I am also very cold. I stand up, trying to kick the sopping fabric away from my feet. I'm dripping everywhere. Maybe I should just jump back in again: at least I looked more graceful in the water.

I start backing away with my arms crossed over my chest. 'So, ah, thank you, and all. For saving me from Bruce. And a very long swim home. I'm going to—uh, I'm going to go home now.'

He bites down on his lip, trying not to laugh. 'Can I give you a lift?'

I can feel my cheeks heating up as my bare feet stumble on the uneven planks. 'No, no, I'm okay, I can walk.'

'You have no shoes.'

'Yep.'

'And you're soaked.'

'Uh huh.'

He sighs, shrugging out of his jacket. It's fleecy and a badge is stitched on the right-hand side: *Hamilton Beach Lifeguard*. Oh great. I'm not even a damsel in distress, I'm an occupational hazard. He drapes the jacket over my shoulders and I shudder into it without protest. The material is so warm—it feels like it's come straight from the dryer. 'You sure you're okay?' he says.

'Yep. Peachy.'

'Okay.' He reaches out and tugs the zipper up to my chin. 'That looks cute on you, but I do need it back at some stage.'

In the corners of my fuzzy, grief-fugued mind, the thought takes a few extra seconds to unfurl: did he just call me cute? Just casually? Like *oh yes nice day also nice face you got there*? And does that mean cute like little-kid-smothering-their-face-in-chocolate-cake cute, or Gideon-Hawthorn-has-dimples-I'm-going-to-dream-about cute? This seems like an important distinction to make.

'I'll give it back to you at school,' I say instead.

'Don't fall in on the way back,' he says, then ambles back up the pier. I feel like I should say something else but I'm so cold and tired that my brain short-circuits. So instead I turn towards town, grateful for the jumper against my frozen skin, and wondering if he'll keep his promise not to tell anyone about my impromptu swim.

It takes forever to get back home, since the tulle skirt has soaked through and I have to drag it up to my knees to walk properly. The sun slips below the horizon, and nocturnal things wake from their daylight slumber and start to call from the canopy above. The dusk brings a sigh of cool air, carrying a sea-salt breeze off the ocean. This is the only time I ever turn off the ceiling fan in my room: when it's the perfect temperature outside, the air still warm and sweet from the day, kissed by the ocean and heavy with hope. I dawdle a little, not minding the wet dress so much anymore.

Theo's still on the couch when I get home. He barely looks up from the screen, but double-takes and jolts from the cushions when he does.

'Jesus, what happened to you?'

'I fell off the pier,' I say, wringing my hair into the kitchen sink so I don't drip all the way up the stairs.

He leaps over the back of the sofa. 'Oh shit, are you okay? You know there's no ladder, right?

Does everyone know that except me? 'Yeah. Someone pulled me out.'

'Lucky. Who was it?'

'Just a guy from school,' I say, my voice tight and an octave higher than it needs to be. 'Gideon.'

'Hawthorn?'

I nod and he whistles. 'Oh damn. He's hot.'

'I noticed.'

He snorts. 'You have panda eyes, by the way.'

Our ceasefire is over. I throw a pillow that connects with his head. He fends it off with one hand. 'Chill out, woman.'

'I am chill. Super chill. And don't call me woman.'

'Whatever you say, sis.'

'Please leave me alone, *bro*.'

He rolls his eyes. 'Sorry for giving a crap. Also, do you want kebabs or not?'

I take a breath to stop myself from shrieking. Instead, in very measured words, I reply, 'No, Theo, I do not want a kebab.'

'Well, I already ordered, so I'm just gonna eat yours then.'

'That's fine.'

'Whatever you say,' he repeats, going back to his game.

I trudge up to the bathroom, hesitating a moment at Mum's door; I can hear *Charade* playing in the background—it's her comfort movie—and my parents talking quietly. I hurry down the corridor so her evening isn't further ruined by discovering a very damp, eavesdropping daughter, and turn on the shower. I strip out of the dress, letting it pool on the tiles, and sink under the hot water, my skin stinging and red from the spray that bounces off my shoulders. The sting of the hot water feels so good that I shiver, sliding down the glass until I'm sitting on the floor. The muscles in my legs feel like jelly, and I'm not sure I could stand even if I wanted to.

I sit there until the water runs cold and the bathroom is fogged with steam, and finally wrap myself in a towel and twist my damp blonde curls into a pinecone on my head. I end up rinsing my dress in the bath, since I feel like a jerk that Mum paid for it and now it's all crusty from seawater, and hang it over the towel rack to dry.

Back in my room, I tug on my comfiest trackpants and jumper and flop down on the bed. I'm so tired I feel like I might fall asleep on the covers. But I'm not warm enough now that I'm not directly under the boiling-hot shower, and although I *could* finally find and unpack my winter clothes, my eyes drift to my dresser, where I've left Gideon's jacket. I wonder what it smells like—I didn't really notice on the way home, and that now seems like a wasted opportunity. Does he wear that bitter body spray Theo drenches himself in? Or does he smell like cookies and sunshine? *Don't be a creep*, I tell myself. I bring it to my nose anyway, and his jacket smells like summer and sunscreen and salt water. My face is buried in the fleece when the door bangs open and Theo walks in.

'Your kebab is here. Hey, what are you—'

'*Theodore Blackwell, I do not want a fucking kebab.*'

'God, *fine*, you could have just *said that*.'

He slams the door behind him and I think it may actually, scientifically, be possible to die of embarrassment.

That night I lie awake, watching the ceiling fan spin round and round, counting the seconds, minutes, hours that I can't sleep. My skin itches and my limbs are restless. All I want to do is run down to the beach and dunk myself under the surface again, just for a moment of peace.

I never slept well, but at least I used to have someone to share the time with. Willow and I were night people, haunting the midnight hours long after the rest of the world was asleep. Nina could sleep through a nuclear blast, but Will and I liked the evenings.

Loneliness hits me now. I blink away tears, not bothering to catch the ones that fall onto my pillowcase, spilling down my cheeks to pool in the hollows of my ears. It's too much, suddenly: realising that Nan is gone, and she might have been my only friend left in the world; and that the only other person who has witnessed my mental breakdown was a near-stranger who had to haul me out of the ocean.

When I can't stand the loneliness anymore I call Willow's phone, waiting breathlessly until her voicemail picks up. She hasn't answered in a while.

Heya it's Will, leave a message.

With the receiver close to my ear, I stare at the sliver of moonlight splicing the room in two. Waiting a minute, just in case. She doesn't answer.

'Hey, Will. Sorry I keep calling. I don't really have anyone else to talk to, I guess.' I pull the covers over my head and pretend for a minute that she's on the line. 'Nan died this week. I mean, we knew it was coming, but it still sucks, you know? And I miss you guys so much. The funeral sucked. Everything sucks. I know that's what every teenager since the dawn of time has said, but…' I pause, feeling my heart thumping in my chest. The beat of every moment I regret. It never stops, on and on and on. I should have said goodbye. I should have fought my parents harder not to move here. I should have been on time to school that first day. And now it's too late, and the two people I care most about in the world are out of reach. 'It's not the same anymore. I needed you guys today and I know I can't…' I sniff, running the back of my hand across my face to catch the snot and tears. 'Anyway. I miss you guys. Bye, Will.'

I click *End* and stare at the phone. The wallpaper is still set to a photo of the three of us: me, Willow and Nina. Willow's smiling the widest, her orange curls spilling out of the frame. Nina's mouth is open to yell something, though I can't remember what it was. I'm squished in the middle, eyes closed, laughing at both of them. It's a truly terrible photo taken on a wonderful day.

I swipe to my texts, clicking on Nina's name. I think about messaging her, but the stack of one-sided texts are already embarrassing and I know she won't ever answer them now. She was so angry when I left. She even resorted to calling Theo just to force him to hold out the phone while she yelled. And then, like a matchstick drenched in kerosene, she flamed out. All the anger burned away, all at once.

She hasn't said a word to me since.

I guess that's what happens when you skip town without telling anyone.

2

MUM LETS US have all of two days off school before she sends us back again. Theo spends his forty-eight hours glued to the couch, playing a variety of loud and obnoxious video games that someone would usually object to, but no one quite has the energy. Dad and I clean the whole house and cook enough food to last for the next month—because dealing with our emotions would have been a bit of a stretch.

Mum spends a lot of time whispering to her friends on the phone, or napping in her room. She comes out occasionally to give us a thin smile, and I know she's trying to project resilience but mostly it just makes me want to run off the end of the pier again. She talks a lot about how she knew it was coming and that at least Nan wasn't in pain for long. If she says it enough, she might believe it.

But on Wednesday morning she claps her hands and declares a return to normalcy. 'Life goes on! We must take these tragedies in our stride and use them to grow stronger. Loss begets new growth.' Mum's a physical therapist. I'm pretty sure she has that phrase embroidered on a pillow somewhere.

Theo leaves without me, because he's not a total social pariah and actually has friends to meet before class starts. I end up riding my bike past Nan's nursing home. Although I guess it's not 'her' anything now. Just a room we've already cleaned out, ready to be given away as soon as someone else needs it. I nudge the kickstand out, propping the bike between my knees. It's nice, as far as nursing homes go. It's painted minty green and there's a rose garden some of the residents look after. They have an old-fashioned brass door-bell that tinkles when the wind blows. But it's not the same, knowing she's not inside. Now it's just another building, the same as any other on the street. I blink back tears as I cycle on.

It takes me ten minutes to reach the school gates and in that time I have almost convinced myself that today won't be especially heinous. I'm worried about running into Gideon, but he breezes into English class late, and I resume my habit of staring at the back of his head. At one point, he turns in his seat and his eyes scan the back of the room. When they land on me, he grins and gives me a wink, then turns back when the teacher tries to spring a question on him. My cheeks burn with embarrassment, and I spend the rest of class with my eyes fixed studiously on my notebook, doodling nonsense in the margins.

When the bell rings, I purposefully dawdle so we don't have to walk together and make awkward small talk. What would I even say? *Seen any good sharks lately?*

But I shouldn't have worried, because Gideon packs his things so quickly he's the first one out the door.

The rest of the day is uneventful, except for one particularly bleak lunch period when I excuse myself to go snot into a wad of toilet paper in the girls' bathrooms because I suddenly remember that I never gave Nan her birthday card this year—it's sitting on my desk, still bare inside.

I cycle home.

I do my homework.

I wake up in the night and stare at the ceiling fan.

The rest of the week passes in a blur. I sit in class without hearing what's being said.

Watching Gideon becomes my favourite distraction.

I become intimately familiar with the three freckles on the back of his neck. I can recognise him in a crowd by the slump of his shoulders, like he can never be bothered to hold himself upright. When I feel a pinprick of tears, a memory of Nan washing over me, I blink furiously and concentrate on his fingertips tapping on the table—I try to match the rhythm to a song. Sometimes he looks up from his locker and sees me in the hallway and beams, tips his head and says *hey*. I mumble something back and cringe all the way to my next class. At least it seems like he kept his promise: no one whispers about the strange girl who jumped off the pier without a plan.

When Friday night finally comes, I collapse on the couch with a groan, tugging the throw blanket over my legs even though it's too hot to be under the covers. I miss the cold. I miss *seasons*. Hamilton is just hot and dry, an endless parade of bright sunny weather and cloudless skies: it's a terrible backdrop for moping.

Dad brings home takeaway and Mum sits at the table with us. Her eyes are puffy and her skin is pale, but she laughs when Dad talks about his day and his co-workers, and tuts at Theo when he burps after gracefully chugging a whole can of soft drink. It's like her edges are fuzzy, but she's still there: hanging on even though it hurts. She notices me watching and leans over to squeeze my hand.

'How are you doing, honey?'

'I'm good, Mum,' I lie, shoving a spring roll in my mouth to avoid answering any more questions.

Theo, desperate for both attention and normalcy, demonstrates a backflip that topples a lamp and scuffs the floorboards in the living room, and then rambles about the upcoming swim races. His hair flops to one side, and in his dinosaur pyjamas he suddenly looks much younger: not the tough, flippant teenage boy he projects at school, but a kid who is sad that his family is sad, who knows something is wrong but not how to fix it.

'I'll race you,' I say, just to see him smile. 'It'll be good practice.'

He holds out his hand across the table, a smirk breaking on his face. 'Oh, you're *so* on.'

'Only at the beach,' I add. I used to swim competitively. Used to love it. But I haven't done it for a while, and I don't want to be *totally* humiliated by the school squad.

'You know you can't doggy-paddle though.'

'Hey,' I object. 'Bet I can still lap you twice.'

'That was *one* time. And I was *six*.'

I laugh, inhaling flakes of pastry.

'Loser buys kebabs,' he says, making me shake on it.

'Gee, I think I'm good for the whopping amount of twelve dollars.'

He has to help me clean the dishes after dinner, but he's eager to go to his room and…do whatever teenage boys do in the evening. Honestly, it's a mystery. Sometimes we hear him screaming at the computer screen and talking to friends on speaker, and sometimes he's silent for hours on end. He rushes through his plates and then thunders upstairs, leaving me to dry.

When I've set the last dish on the rack, I notice Mum and Dad at the table, holding hands and watching me. Giving me *the look*.

'Reece, can you sit down with us for a minute?' Mum says.

Oh no. *No no no*. I know that voice; I recognise that piteous look, the guarded set of her shoulders. 'Has something happened? Are you okay? What's—'

'No, no, we're sorry, we're fine,' says Dad. 'We didn't mean to scare you.'

'It's Nan's will, honey. The reading is tomorrow.' She takes a breath. 'We'd like you to come with us.'

I look between them, not quite understanding. Nan didn't have much in the end; Mum already let me take a necklace from the nursing home and packed up everything else. It didn't even occur to me that there might be more, that her life wasn't quite done lingering in this world yet.

'Why?' I manage, voice breaking. 'Why do I need to go?'

Mum's hand slips into mine. 'Because you're in it.'

'What? *In it?* In the will?'

'We don't know what it is,' she continues. 'They have to ask everyone who's named, even if it's something small. I thought we could make arrangements, if you didn't want to come, but...'

'I didn't mean—I don't want her money or anything.' This feels strange—like somehow I'll be stealing something precious.

Mum's hand comes up to cup my cheek, smoothing back the hair from my face. 'We know. We just wanted you to be prepared. It might just be a letter or an old knick-knack. But she wanted you to be there, so whatever it is, it meant a lot to her.'

'What about Theo?'

'He's a minor,' Dad says gently. 'Legally he doesn't have to go, and he's let us know that he'd prefer not to.'

I can tell they're both stressed about my answer. Dad's mouth is downturned and he's rubbing small circles on Mum's back, just enough that she knows he's there.

'Okay,' I say. 'I'll come.'

Their bodies slump at the same time. 'Thanks, darling.' Mum kisses my cheek and Dad smiles at me, nodding. He gives my hand a squeeze, and I have to excuse myself because I know he's proud of me for being strong for Mum's sake, but I'm about one minute from falling apart.

'G'night,' I murmur, tugging myself out of their arms.

I stand outside Theo's door a minute, listening to his

muffled voice. He's laughing and talking to someone, loud and carefree. I think about knocking and going in, sitting on the floor and building a fort, like we did when we were little. Then he lets out a giggle, lowering his voice to a conspiratorial whisper.

I'm suddenly exhausted. It's not until I'm slipping under the covers that I remember Gideon's jacket is still folded on my chest of drawers, and I crawl out of bed to tug it over my head, falling asleep wrapped in the smell of salt water and sunscreen, too hot in the fleece but not caring as long as I can dream of the ocean, and hang on to the sound of silence.

3

THE LAWYER'S OFFICE is an old cottage with a wooden sign out the front, paint peeling away from cursive letters that read *Hall & Scott Law Firm*.

Mr Scott is a rotund older man who has already sweat through his checked shirt but nevertheless insists on keeping his sleeves buttoned around his wrist. He introduces himself as Kenneth, though nobody seems to be calling him that, and he ushers us into a small, dark room where dust coils in sun traps near the blinds.

He apologises for a precariously stacked mountain of files, shifting them so that we might actually be able to see him parked behind the enormous desk. He offers us tea, which everybody refuses. Mum is clutching her purse, fiddling with the zip as she waits for him to start. Dad reaches out to calm her bouncing knee, and she looks up long enough to catch his fingertips.

Nobody looks at me, which is just as well because I think I might be sick. It's not that I don't want anything of Nan's.

Maybe some photos or letters, but the thought of inheriting Nan's money feels wrong—to take something from her, something of value that she might have kept for herself. I remember the sparse furniture in the nursing home, how she longed to return home to her trinkets and comforts. She could have sold so much more and been comfortable, but she didn't like the idea of giving those things away.

'Well then,' says Mr Scott. 'Shall we commence? I know this is difficult for all of you.'

Mum nods, and he shuffles a sheaf of papers, fixing his glasses as they slide down his nose. He clears his throat and begins with all the *final will and testament* preamble. 'This document was witnessed by a Mrs Jane Andersen.' He glances up to verify this information.

Dad nods. 'Head nurse at the home. They were close.'

Mr Scott seems relieved as he continues. 'To my daughter, Olivia, and her husband, Nicholas, I leave my home in Hamilton, at 38 Kemp Street, which they may sell or retain depending upon their wishes. The arrangements for the bungalow at the rear of the property are to remain in perpetuity until the current occupants give notice to vacate.'

'Is that unusual?' Mum interrupts, frowning a little.

'Not especially,' says the lawyer. 'Sometimes it's a condition of contract. Is that an issue?'

She blows out a breath. 'I guess not?' She looks at Dad but he just shrugs.

Mr Scott resumes. 'To Olivia and Nick, I also leave the remaining contents of my savings account. Should I not have the chance to say these words myself, I give my daughter all my love, and hope that I have provided you the strength and guidance to build your future without me. I am sure it will be a bright one.'

Mum drops her head and covers her face in her hands, her shoulders shaking. I reach over and she grabs my hand, clutching it close to her chest.

'To my grandson, Theodore, I leave my 1972 Volkswagen Beetle, which he has not-so-subtly coveted all these years. It may be held in estate until his eighteenth birthday if I am to pass before this occasion. It is my express wish that nobody mentions it is, in fact, a pile of rubbish, and the exact colour of snot. Nevertheless, I hope it brings him joy and inspires adventure.'

Dad laughs, and even Mum gives a little hiccup.

'And finally to my granddaughter, Clarissa, I leave my collection of rare and valuable medical texts, so that she might pursue her passions with my guidance, if only in memory. I am so proud of you, my clever girl, and I would have dearly loved to be the one to help you on this journey.'

Mr Scott clears his throat. 'She also requested this item be delivered to you directly,' he says, sliding something across the table to me. 'She had it secured in one of our safe-deposit boxes.'

I reach out, fingertips brushing against the cover. It's an old book I've never seen before. Although Mum and Dad look at me expectantly, I have no idea why she's left this to me. I frown, trying to read the title, but it seems to be hand-painted in gold calligraphy, and has faded to the barest whisper of crooked letters. The leather is worn soft, with two buckles securing the cover. It's heavier than I expect, nearly tumbling from my hands when I lift it.

My chest constricts, so tight I think I might suffocate right here. I try to breathe past the lump of bile in my throat, but all I feel is dread flooding my lungs, chilling my veins. There are three pairs of eyes on me. The room is silent.

'Excuse me,' I whisper.

I make it to the back door before I heave the contents of my stomach into a flowerpot.

The ride home is silent and awkward. Mum is riffling through the papers that the lawyer let her keep, and I can see her fingertips brushing against Nan's handwriting, as though some small part of her might be stored in these words. I tuck my body into the side of the car, closing my eyes and pretending to sleep, though I'm sure nobody is buying it. The book sits in my lap, heavy and unopened.

I never told Nan about The Terrible Thing That Happened. I never told her that it destroyed so many lives. I never told her I didn't want to be a doctor anymore.

When I was little, I'd beg Nan to let me leaf through her records and photo albums, and I'd marvel at the small, well-dressed woman within. At first she was always in the back row, but nevertheless demanding the camera's attention as she stood shoulder to shoulder with a group of men. Those first pictures are black and white, and you can barely see the top of her permed head and pillbox hat, peeking over a shoulder that blots out the rest of her body. But as the albums went on, year after year, she started to claim the centre row. Somewhere in those albums was a newspaper clipping, declaring *State's first female surgeon*. She was a force, Mum would say. Every *no* became a *yes*; every doubt galvanised her iron will. She worked right up until she couldn't hold a scalpel anymore and, even then, she still saw patients at home.

'It wasn't about saving lives,' Nan told me one day. 'It's about making people feel heard. Validating their pain is often the first step to healing it.'

It seemed like everywhere she went, little miracles followed Nana Blackwell. She still had a box full of baby photos and thank-you cards, stuffed full to the brim with grateful notes.

Eventually she got annoyed at being called 'just a lady doctor' and ended up becoming head general surgeon at the city hospital, just because someone told her she couldn't. Those thank-you cards are full of smiling faces, adults on crutches or kids grinning at the camera, displaying their arms and legs proudly.

Anyway. I wanted to be just like her. I even put an application in last year to do a summer internship program for Doctors Without Borders.

But that was then.

The car pulls up and Dad whispers, 'We're here,' playing along with the ruse.

Mum turns in her seat. 'Clarissa...'

I gently push the door open. 'I'm fine, Mum.'

I hear her sigh but I'm already gone, running up the stairs to my room. Theo calls out but nobody answers, and I end up locking the door behind me. I shove the book under my bed, then pace the room aimlessly, until I give up and flip open my phone.

Heya it's Will, leave a message.

My words are thick and jumbled. 'It's me. I just—I'm sorry, I just need someone to talk to and Nina's so mad and—' I bite my lip to trap a sob. 'She left it all to me, the books, and I'm so angry and so embarrassed because I never told her, and it's all a waste—'

There's a knock at my door. I hang up. Mum's voice calls out quietly from the hallway. 'Clarissa, honey? Do you wanna talk about it?'

I don't want to talk about it. I don't want to talk to anyone. So I throw the phone down on the bed and do what I do best: I run.

Except it's no small feat sneaking out of a second-storey window, and I'm sure I manage to bang every part of my body against the splintered weatherboard on the way down. Maybe my parents are just indulging me and letting me have this moment, because it's not exactly a subtle exit. I hit the ground with a groan, my feet skating across loose gravel as I land on my butt. I allow myself a twinge of embarrassment, then get up and grab my bike.

I don't really know where I'm going—there's nowhere *to* go. I don't have friends to call. No other family to visit. I pedal past the second-hand bookstore, but it's closed.

So I head to the same place as everyone else in this tiny town.

The main beach is crowded with a parents' club and

little nippers flinging their tiny bodies into the ocean with unmasked glee. There's a tourist bus rolling in too, so I keep pedalling until I've circled half the town and hit the back beach.

I don't know what its actual name is, since everyone just calls it the Swells. My feet sink into the sand as I step over thick brush, winding my way down the trodden path to the water. It's a locals-only beach, with a series of alarming yellow signs set into the dunes reminding swimmers of the strong currents and rocky outcrops. It's mostly surfers here, out on the break, so far from shore they're hardly dots in the distance. It's not really a swimming beach, since the water is usually a little too rough for casual paddling, but it's quiet enough that sometimes I come down here and swim laps between the headlands, which jut out to create a private cove.

The sun is starting to dip below the horizon and the beach is abandoned except for a few bags lying by the life-guard tower, waiting to be retrieved.

I wander away from it all, inhaling salt air until my blood seems full with it, and end up dragging my feet in the water. It's a balm against the heat on my skin, and if I'd had more foresight before wiggling down the drainpipe, I would have grabbed my bathers.

Someone jogs up beside me, and I think they'll pass by but they slow down instead. A familiar blonde head bobs beside my shoulder. 'Are you stalking me?'

I turn to him, sighing. '*Why* do you only show up on my bad days?'

Gideon smiles. He always smiles. 'Like a bad omen?'

'Exactly. Turn around, I want to make sure you don't have a pentagram tattooed on the back of your neck.'

He laughs as he obliges, showing off a perfectly bare neck devoid of Satan-worshipping tattoos. I wonder what it feels like to put my hand right there, over those three little freckles. 'See?' he says. 'Not cursed. That I know of.'

That makes one of us, I think.

He keeps pace beside me, feet splashing in the water. 'So what brings you to the Swells?'

For a second I think about telling him. Instead I shrug, careful to keep my eyes down. 'Needed to get out of the house. You?'

He tugs the corner of his jacket and I notice the familiar logo. 'Kinda my job,' he says with a lopsided grin.

'Oh my god,' I say, dropping my head into my hands. 'I'm an idiot.'

He laughs again, and it's such a nice sound. 'Wanna jump in?' he says. 'I'll rescue you if you drown.'

I glance at the crashing waves and think, *yes*, I really would like to sink for a moment. But I shake my head. 'I didn't bring bathers.'

'So? Just, you know.' He waves a hand over his body and wriggles a little to suggest I could jump in with undies on.

'Thank you, but I think I'll spare us both that particular humiliation.' I think of the *Tuesday* underwear I threw on this morning even though it's Saturday and die a little on the inside.

'It's the same thing.'

'It's really not,' I say. 'But you should get in. I'll keep an eye out.'

He seems to think about it, but then drops down onto the sand. 'Sit, if you want,' he says. 'My shift is over in five minutes. I'm feeling pretty good about the odds of no one drowning in that time.'

I ease down beside him on the sand, watching the horizon: a murky red-blue, smudged in mottled patterns with the sun dipping low. 'How concerned should I be about Bruce over here?'

Gideon glances at me beneath his mop of messy blonde hair. 'He doesn't get snacky until at *least* six o'clock.'

'That sounds very made up.'

'It's too warm for the big sharks down here, so you don't need to be too worried. Mostly just the reefers. You know, less teeth.'

'Mostly?'

He grins again. 'Yeah, mostly.' He kicks at the sand with one foot, his eyes locked on the surfers paddling in. Occasionally they dip under a wave, and I hold my breath for the few seconds until they resurface. Again, I wish I *had* brought my bathers. I want to be underwater, with the rush of currents washing over my skin, the shock of icy water on sunburnt shoulders.

I sigh without meaning to, and rest my chin on my knees, wishing I had learnt to surf when I was younger and less afraid of toppling off the waves.

'So,' Gideon says. 'Want to talk about your crappy day?'

I close my eyes, letting the evening breeze cool my hot

cheeks, imagining that the wind carries my grief to some faraway land. 'My nan died,' I say. I think I've needed to say it for a while. The words were stuck in my throat, needing to escape, and I guess Gideon is the first one to ask so he's going to be the first one to hear.

He starts to say he's sorry but I cut him off. 'It's okay, it's just that she left me some stuff and I feel weird about taking it.' I lower my gaze and fiddle with the zip on my shirt. 'Sorry, this is kind of a downer. And you hardly even know me. We can talk about something else.'

He gently bumps my shoulder with his own. 'Hey, it's fine, don't worry. My grandparents died a couple years ago, it's rough.' He gives me a small smile. 'Your nan was Mary Blackwell, right?'

'Oh. Yeah, how did you…?'

'Theo mentioned. We're on the swim team together. Plus, you know, small town…'

'Oh, right.'

'So, what did she leave you? A treasure map to untold riches? A chest full of haunted diamonds?'

I laugh, in spite of myself. 'Nothing as exciting as that. Just…personal stuff, sentimental. It feels like someone else should have them, I don't know why she would leave it all to me.' Well, I do know. What I really mean is, *I wish she* hadn't *left it all to me*. I never told her; I never had the chance. I didn't want to disappoint her.

Gideon is a good listener. He lets the pause sit, waiting until he's sure that I'm done, and even then he thinks for a minute before he answers. He doesn't ever waste words: I've noticed this in all my hours of watching him this week—he's so careful with them, using them like he's worried they might run out one day.

'She wanted you to have it?' he says, after a while.

I nod, glad that the waves are kicking up droplets when they break, hiding the tears on my face.

'Well, even if you don't want it, your nan must have loved you a lot to leave you something like that. Maybe it doesn't even matter what it is—maybe it just matters that she was thinking of you. And maybe her loving you that much is more important than what she left behind.'

My spine straightens with a shiver, and I surreptitiously swipe at my cheeks. I turn to look at him, surprised to find him so close, leaning in. He's very *pretty*, I realise—long lashes he probably never notices, high cheekbones and a soft cupid's bow on his lips. But also tired in a way I never noticed at school: a purple blush under his eyes, skin a little too pale under his freckles. The wind tousles his hair and tugs at the edge of his jumper, but I'm shielded here, on our quiet patch of sand.

I clear my throat. 'That was actually...very insightful, Gideon Hawthorn.'

He graciously bows his head. 'Thank you, Clarissa Blackwell. Do we say each other's full names now?'

I laugh, shaking my head. 'Sorry. Weird week.'

He shoulder-bumps me again. He's so easy with people. Is it supposed to be this easy? Have I just forgotten how to be human?

'So am I ever getting my jumper back?'

I cringe in horror. 'Sorry, I forgot. I'll bring it to school.'

'It is my *favourite* jumper,' he says solemnly.

I tug the sleeve on his yellow jacket. 'This one is identical.'

'Oh no,' he continues in mock horror. 'This one is new. I had the other one worn in the way I like it. You know how new jeans are always horrible and too tight? This one is all stiff and itchy. The old one was stretched out and ratty and coffee-stained. It was perfect.'

'Okay, okay,' I concede. 'I promise I will return your filthy old jumper.'

'Hey. It's not filthy. It's *fashionably distressed.*'

'Mmm, I'm pretty sure there's a sauce stain on the sleeve.'

He grins at me, and I worry I've said too much. Look, here's the thing: it's actually a really great jumper. He's right—it's perfectly crafted to hug your body and cradle your limbs like a divine heavenly cloud or whatever. Which, of course, I know because I have taken to wearing it at night. Like a creep. Like a pervert. No wonder I've forgotten how to be human.

I shiver as a gust whips over the shoreline and flicks sand onto my bare legs and cheeks. The sun has nearly slipped away, and the air has turned, *at last.*

'Come on,' he says, noticing the goosebumps that race across my arms. 'My shift's over and it's getting dark—let me drive you home.'

And so I let him drag me up and over the grassy sand dunes, and I let him drive me home, my bike tossed in his boot, with yet another borrowed jumper draped across my shoulders. We sit in the driveway for a long time, and eventually he sticks out his hand. His fingertips are smudged with black, probably from messing with a car engine or bike chain.

'So it's official. Friends?'

I ignore the small voice in my head that says, *More*. 'Friends,' I say. 'Thanks for the lift.'

'You should get your licence, if you can. Small-town problems—the only places worth going are far away.'

I smile, but I don't answer. I have my licence already—I just never plan on using it again.

As he drives away, I trudge up to my room, thankful that everyone seems to be politely ignoring my escape.

Maybe it doesn't even matter what she left you, I think. *Maybe it just matters that she cared*. I summon all of my remaining bravery, sit on the floor beside my bed, and drag the book out of its hiding place. With shaking hands, I undo the twin buckles that hold the pages closed, and try to open the cover.

Nothing happens.

I frown, tipping the book sideways. *Huh*. There are two locks hidden beneath the buckles—and the book is sealed shut. I pull and tug, but it's useless. After ten minutes of trying to prise it open with bobby pins and pen lids, I give up.

'Sorry, Nan. Guess you forgot the key.' I push the book back under my bed, telling myself I didn't want it anyway.

4

I WILL NOT be awkward, I tell myself. It's just school. It's just English class, the same as always. Except I can no longer stare at the back of Gideon Hawthorn's perfect head because now he might stare back. Because he wants to be *friends*.

I groan, yanking the handlebars of my bike to glide right past the school gates and circle back to town. *Chicken.*

I say *town* but it's really just one road that leads straight to the ocean. Entertainment includes Country Target (which sells enormous frilly knickers, old DVDs and almost nothing else), a second-hand bookstore that only opens when the owner feels like going in, and a particularly riveting maritime museum detailing three hundred years of various thermometers, coastal erosion patterns, and one cannon (never fired). And then there's the Beach Bean.

I push my way through the cafe's beaded curtain and wave to Mrs Kostakis. It's pretty busy but she stops what she's doing to make her way to the till, wiping smudged hands against a home-stitched apron—this one is embroidered with *kiss the coffee-maker.* I like Mrs Kostakis, even though her coffee is awful. She chats to me in the mornings, and only occasionally berates me about my caffeine intake. Sometimes she's the only person I talk to all day, apart from my family.

She also knows everything about everyone in this town.

'Reece! Come in, come in. Oh darling you poor thing, I heard about your grandmother.' She reaches over the counter to pat my cheeks. 'How are you doing?'

Maybe it's because I know she really cares, but I suddenly feel very ill and my hands start to shake. I want to tell her that I miss Nan, and that I should have gone to see her last weekend but I was too tired from watching zombie movies all night and I missed visiting hours. I want to tell her that it's my fault Nan died alone, because I was always there on every Saturday except the one when she needed me. I want to tell her that I feel especially terrible because the week Nan died is also the week I developed a ridiculous crush on a boy who pulled me out of the ocean, and it feels like a gross betrayal to her memory. 'I'm okay,' I say instead.

Her eyes crinkle in the corners, lifted by a sympathetic smile. 'You poor thing. Come on, I'll get you a coffee. You want a pastry?'

'No, that's okay—'

She waves a hand. 'Of course you do, you're too skinny. Sit down, I'll bring it over.'

She sets about making a coffee (the quality of which is not kissable) and brings me a blueberry muffin. Then she pulls out a chair and sits opposite me. A few customers in line look perplexed at the lack of service, but she doesn't seem to mind their pointed throat-clearing.

'Now, shouldn't you be at school?'

I pick at the muffin with my fingertips. 'Would you believe me if I said I had a free period?'

She considers this. 'Today, yes. Tomorrow, no.'

'I'll go in a minute. I just didn't want to…you know. Go alone.' I feel my cheeks start to blush as I realise I've admitted the very sorry state of my personal affairs to a middle-aged woman who has a business to run. Mrs Kostakis has better things to do than console me about my social life. Nevertheless, she leans forward and tucks a few curls behind my ear, much like my own mother would. 'Ah Reece. Such a pretty face and no boy has caught your eye? Or girl. Whatever works for you.' She winks, lips spreading wide and showing off the white of her teeth.

I laugh and she pats my hand. I feel better for a moment, but then she cocks her head and I see her calculating. 'You know,' she says, far too casually. 'My son goes to your school.'

The smile drops off my face. 'Oh no, please, it's okay. I'm fine.' I don't need the humiliation of an eighteen-year-old playdate.

'You know, you say you're fine an awful lot. "How's the weather, Reece?" It's fine. "How's school?" It's fine. "How's the coffee?" Fine, fine, fine.'

'That's not true,' I say. 'Your coffee is terrible.'

'And yet you keep coming back.'

'Mum won't let me get a machine,' I admit.

'Good! I've seen how much you drink, it will stunt your growth.' She stands up with a flourish and shoos me away.

'Now go on, get to school. Come back tomorrow and tell me something good, not just *fine*.'

She waves me out the door, wiry black hair bouncing on her shoulders as she makes sure I actually get back on my bike and head in the general direction of an education.

The thing about small high schools is that everybody knows everybody, and nobody wants new friends. No one's interested in the weird city girl who doesn't talk enough, doesn't play sports and doesn't party. I tried talking to a few girls on my first day—they were nice, I guess. But they were nice in the way that's polite, and nothing more. No one spits on me, but no one says hello either. Sometimes I think it's worse. Although after The Terrible Thing That Happened, it's not the worst kind of pain. Mostly, it's just boring. Sometimes I go the whole day without speaking and the words feel strange on my lips when I get home.

I make my way to the lockers and give mine an affectionate nudge to pop the lock open, and brace for the avalanche of junk. Out of the corner of my eye I spot Theo by the foursquare courts, talking to a blonde girl with legs longer than my whole body. He laughs, reaching out to high-five one of the guys sliding by on a skateboard. Theo is like a golden retriever puppy; he's so persistent and yappy you can't ignore him. He just kind of flops right into your life. He had more friends on the first day than I've made all year—though it's not exactly difficult to top *zero*.

'Yo, are you Reece?'

A very tall boy is standing in front of me, with tan skin,

dark curly hair, and familiar green eyes. The knot in my stomach twists.

'Uh, yes?'

He nods, and his hair bounces. 'I'm Miles. My mum texted me and told me I have to be nice to you.' He leans against my locker and watches me collecting my books.

I wait a moment in case the earth decides to split open and swallow me whole, saving me from this conversation. Unfortunately, no such miracle is forthcoming. 'Oh, um, you know what, that's okay, just uh—tell her thanks.' I will never go to the Beach Bean again. I will revolt. I will buy instant coffee from Country Target and learn to love it.

I turn to walk away and he grabs the strap of my backpack. 'Whoa there, Reece's Pieces, I don't think you know what's at stake here. I have been promised a fresh tray of baklava for being your best bud for the day, and I fully intend on making that happen.' He swoops down and whips out his phone. 'Smile,' he says, grinning maniacally as he immortalises my stunned face in his camera roll. 'See? Easy. I'll even share a piece with you.'

'You know, that's really okay, I'm sure your mum won't mind—'

He looks at me like I'm crazy. 'Oh, she'll *mind*,' he says. 'Come on, walk and talk, we're already late.'

'Late?'

'Yeah, you're in my bio class, right?'

I frown, mentally checking a rolodex of faces from my classes. I really need to pay more attention to people at this school. 'I...think so?'

'Cool, well, I'm gonna need you to be in my group assignment. Numbers aren't my thing, you know?'

Curiosity gets the better of me. 'What is your thing?'

'Baklava, obviously.' He laughs, bouncing on his feet as he waits for me to catch up. He's so *tall*. 'Nah, I'm kidding. Music.'

'Music?'

'Yeah, music. You know, notes, beats, words.'

'You sing?'

'Oh, *hell* no. I play piano.' He flutters his fingers through the air, long and lithe. His good cheer is infectious, and I find myself laughing.

'Are you any good?' I ask.

He whirls on me, a hand over his heart in mock-hurt. 'Am I any—am I any *good*? The nerve of some people.'

'I take that as a yes.'

'I take that as a I-don't-go-to-the-school-concerts.'

'Sorry. I'm new.' Pause. 'Well. Sort of.'

'Oh yeah. Hey, you should come to the next one, it's just me and that dweeb Ava.'

I tilt my head, trying to follow. He talks almost as fast as Theo after three Red Bulls. This is the most I've ever spoken at school, and I'm out of breath. 'Is she…not good?'

His whole body goes slack as he groans. 'Urgh, I wish.' He cocks an eyebrow at me. 'So what do you do?'

'Oh, I—I mean…' I stumble for anything to say. I have no list of interests, nothing to rattle off. Nothing to fill the spaces in conversations like this one. Not anymore. 'I used to swim.'

'Used to?'

I shrug like it doesn't bother me. 'Not so much into team sports anymore.'

'I hear you. Like, I wanna be the best all by myself, you know? That's why I don't play string instruments—you gotta play in an orchestra, and *damn* some of those morons test my patience.' He starts humming a tune that I'm fairly certain is Beethoven. Or Mozart. Some old dude with a piano.

He glides through the corridors like he's in a slipstream; any object in his way moves around him, stepping away just quickly enough to avoid collision. I'm sweating by the time we make it to our classroom.

Miles flips open a textbook and a mostly empty notebook, where he's scrawled a few bars of music, alongside some video-game titles and little towers of cubes all connected in the margins—everything except actual notes. He talks through most of the class and I can barely focus on the work and his voice at the same time. The teacher shushes him a few times, but it's only half-hearted and mostly he whispers quietly enough to only annoy me, except when Ms Atwood asks us to draw partners and he screams out '*I dibs Reece!*' loud enough that the whole class titters.

'You must really suck at biology,' I whisper, red-faced.

'You have no idea. Mitochondria is the powerhouse of the cell though, right?'

'You read that on the internet.'

'It's *literally* all I remember,' he says, face crumpled and despondent.

'Well, that should be helpful the next time we're in *year eight*.'

He groans, eyeing the whiteboard with suspicion. 'You wound me. Hey, do you like coffee? I can hook you up for the rest of the year.'

I snort. 'Yeah, you still have to do half the work.'

Being with Miles is like being in a spotlight. People smile at me, glance at me covertly. A few of the girls in the front row twist around, curious, as though they've just noticed my sudden appearance in their world.

I can't tell if Miles is being nice to me because Mrs Kostakis told him to, or because he's just nice to everyone. Either way, I still expect him to abandon me at the end of the class and go wherever people go when they have friends to meet for lunch.

He seems to notice I'm dragging my feet and turns back. 'Come on, move those tiny legs. If we're late all the good toppings will be gone.'

'You really don't have to hang out with me,' I blurt, eyes fixed on the ground. 'It's super nice of you and everything, but I don't mind if you have people to meet. I can just go...' I trail off, since I don't actually have anywhere to go and can't think of a lie fast enough.

He hustles me along. 'Don't you count as people? Come on.'

At the cafeteria, where most of the senior students sit whether they have lunch or not, Miles deposits me at an empty table and briefly abandons me before returning with two heaving serves of frozen yoghurt.

'Oh, thank you,' I say, genuinely surprised. 'I can pay you back.'

'Nah, you're good. Just seriously don't let me fail bio because my mum will *kill me*.'

I laugh and scoop up some of the toppings—fresh fruit and caramel syrup, which is an interesting choice—and pop them in my mouth. The sweet and salty flavours melt on my tongue and it's possibly the best thing I've ever had. 'Oh my god,' I say, shoving down another spoonful. 'This is amazing. How did I not know about this?'

'It's the only good thing in the caf, don't get excited. One of the kids has a dairy farm—his dad bought the machine as a joke, but we keep using it and they keep stocking it.'

'I want to eat this, and only this, forever.'

'The sugar makes you twitchy,' says a girl, plonking a bag at the table and slumping down. 'Trust me, I tried. Worth it though.'

I try to place her face. I'm sure I haven't seen her before but there's something familiar about the tilt of her lips and the jut of her chin.

'I'm Ava, by the way,' she says kindly, giving me a half-wave.

I glance over at Miles, confused. He rolls his eyes. 'My sister,' he explains. 'Queen Dweeb herself.'

'Your sister...' I start to ask, before I realise it's probably none of my business. I'm about to tell Ava she looks almost exactly like her mum until I realise high-school students don't want to hear that.

'I'm Reece,' I say instead.

'Oh right, my mum mentioned you.'

'Oh *no*,' says Miles, waving a hand in her face. 'I got here first—that is my baklava, you tiny little traitor. Don't you have people your own age to hang out with?'

She gives a very dramatic roll of her eyes. 'I'm waiting for Sally.'

Miles grunts, then looks at me to clarify. 'Sally plays percussion,' he says, in the same way people might say *Sally eats babies for breakfast and sells meth to retirement homes.*

'You're such a freak,' Ava says happily. She waves at a blonde girl dragging an enormous cloth bag across the courtyard and springs out of her seat. 'Bye, dork,' she says to Miles, flicking him in the ear as she leaves. 'It was nice to meet you, Reece! You should come to the party this weekend!'

She races off to join her friend, and Miles sighs, slumping onto the table. 'There is some mild sibling rivalry.'

'I see that.'

The bell goes and he pushes away from the table. 'Hey, you really should come on Saturday,' Miles says. 'You ever been to a paddock party before? Come—I'll introduce you to people.'

I feel my eyes fly wide and I panic. I *so* do not want to go to a party where I know exactly two people, but I can't think of a good reason to say no. 'Oh, that's okay, I have, um—'

'No way,' he says as he gets up. 'You're coming. Meet us at the Bean! Seven o'clock!'

And then he's gone, and I'm left staring, mouth agape. For the first time in three months, I have plans this weekend.

Theo has swim practice, so I ride home without him, pedalling fast as black clouds gather low on the horizon. A summer storm is brewing, and when it rains here, it *rains*, bucketing down for hours until the riverbanks swell and branches crack off the trees. I barely make it home when fat droplets start to fall. I dump my bike near the door (since, obviously, no one here would dare steal it) and holler out to make sure nobody's home, then grab a packet of banana chips and flop on the couch to watch *Ghost Hunters*. I could be working on a mountain of overdue homework, or unpacking boxes in my room, but neither of those things offers the blissful mindlessness of watching grown men pretend to be scared of shadows. A crack of thunder rumbles the glass panes in the kitchen, and a bolt of lightning flashes blindingly white against the cheery yellow wallpaper. I'll never tell anyone, but I love the storms here. The storms and the ocean—that's it, I swear.

When I can't hear the TV anymore over the rain, I peel myself away to shower and change into the only clean clothes I can find—a wrinkled button-up shirt and old flamingo pyjama shorts. I'm eyeing the hamper full of dirty washing in my room when the phone rings. 'Hello?'

'Dad's late,' says Theo.

'Oh, I had a great day, thank you for asking. And how are you?'

'Cold. And wet. And did I mention *cold*. Can you come pick me up?' he whines. His voice is extra pathetic, with that pleading tone he only uses when he's truly desperate. And I do feel bad for him—the roof sounds like it's going to cave in at any moment.

I groan. 'Theo, no, I hate these roads. Especially in the

rain. And the kangaroos come out of nowhere.'

'Come *on*, Reece, you haven't driven in ages.'

'Yeah, there's a reason for that. I hate it.'

'Urgh. Did Mum at least leave the car?'

I glance outside. The black Jeep is parked in the driveway. Rain starts to spittle on the windows, coming in sideways. 'Nope.'

'Please, Reece. *Please.* I know she left it, she told me Dad gave her a lift today.'

'Dunno what to tell you, kid. Better start pedalling.' I'm pretty sure he's not that stupid, though. Dad's coming to get him eventually, and he's already wet. What's the rush?

'Can you at least tell Mum—hang on.' He pulls the receiver away to talk to someone, the conversation too muffled for me to hear anything. 'Never mind, I got a lift.'

I'm pretty sure he mutters *thanks for nothing* as he hangs up.

Guilt settles in quickly, so to make up for abandoning Theo I pull out fresh pasta sheets and a few bottles of passata—fifteen-year-old-boys are generally placated by lasagne, and he's always ravenous after swim practice. He once ate two whole chickens while I watched, then washed it down with a protein shake. He should be twenty kilos heavier but I think the hormones and sexual repression burn the calories right out.

When the tray is in the oven, I settle back on the couch and resume *Ghost Hunters*. The rain is now coming down so hard the tin roof sounds like it might split open. I glance around at the doors, worried they might blow off their hinges.

The front door bangs open behind me and I hear a pair of shoes scuffing on the doormat.

'Don't be mad, I made pasta,' I yell.

'I love pasta,' replies a voice that isn't Theo's. I whip around so fast I'm pretty sure I strain a muscle in my neck.

Theo is grinning as he whips damp hair off his face. 'Hey, Reece. This is Gideon. I think you guys know each other.'

My mouth gapes open for all of two seconds before I remember to snap it shut. 'A little,' I manage to stutter, mostly through clenched teeth. Gideon is grinning too. He and Theo are wearing matching jackets with the school crest stitched on the side, and they look sort of similar except that Theo is wide where Gideon is long. They're both soaked through, even from the short run up the driveway.

Nevertheless, Theo seems incredibly pleased with himself. 'So that lasagne is for me?'

'Not anymore.'

He laughs and bounds up the stairs to shower, pausing at the top of the landing to smirk down at me. 'By the way, I told Gid to stay for dinner. You said so yourself, the roads suck at night. It's, *like*, not even safe for him to drive home.' He does a ridiculous head-bobble that I think is meant to be an imitation of me.

The bathroom door slams shut and Gideon and I are left staring at each other in loaded silence. He's smiling, I'm mortified, and neither of us are saying anything. I now regret changing into my tiny flamingo pyjama shorts: I'm reasonably sure a considerable amount of my butt is visible. I really need to do laundry. Or go shopping.

I give in first, rising slowly from the couch. 'Can you just…hang on a minute?'

His gaze has wandered to the family portraits on the walls. 'Sure,' he replies as he examines the photos: baby Reece and baby Theo tottering down the beach; tween Reece with braces, grinning on a Ferris wheel.

I spin away and swipe my phone off the counter, tapping out a rapid text. *Get back downstairs before I come up there and strangle you myself.*

Theo responds with a shrug emoji. I start to text back a string of expletives, but my phone keeps suggesting he go *duck* himself.

'So,' Gideon says from behind me. 'What are the chances of getting my jumper back? Or are you attached to it now?'

I close my eyes and count to five. I take a deep breath, and turn to face him with a mostly pleasant smile fixed on my face. This is *fine*. This won't be awkward. And he's probably not going to tell my entire family about that day at the pier. But maybe I should try to hustle him out of here before there's even a chance to bring it up. 'Sure. You can have your jumper back. Wait here.'

He, of course, ignores me and follows me to my room.

'Do you have any particular issues with boundaries or is this a special occasion?' I ask, voice lilting with nerves.

'I would wait downstairs but *Ghost Hunters* gives me the heebies.'

'Then change the channel.'

'I'd rather snoop, but thanks,' he says.

I sigh and push open my door, revealing the sea of boxes

and clothes strewn across the room. He whistles. 'No wonder you needed clothes,' he says sarcastically. 'You clearly do not have enough.'

'Ha ha, very funny. Here.' I snatch up his jumper from the vanity and hurl it at his face. He catches it, looking around, and I stand there not knowing what to do with my hands.

I don't know why he sets me so on edge. It's not like we ever talked before that day on the pier. I just, you know, ogled him from the back of the classroom sometimes. It wasn't even a crush, it was just...visual appreciation. And he's been nothing but nice to me, especially after he drove me home the other night. So I really need to calm down. People have friends who are boys all the time. *I* used to have boy friends who were not *boyfriends*. Before this. Before everything.

He spies something on the other side of the room and glances at me. 'May I?'

'I mean, you're already here. Please continue, violate my privacy.' It was supposed to be a joke, but it falls flat. He doesn't move until I roll my eyes, waving a hand. 'Knock yourself out.'

'I did save your life,' he reminds me, stepping around the flotsam on the floor.

'You saved me from a swim,' I correct.

'And a shark.'

I cringe. I had forgotten about Bruce.

He lifts a finger to the edge of a photo. It's the same one on my phone screen. 'Are these your friends back home?'

'Mmhmm.'

'Do they have names?'

'Yep. Good ones.'

'Will you tell me what they are?'

'If you ask nicely.'

He picks up Nan's stethoscope, placing the bell on his chest and holding out the headpiece. 'This is cool,' he says. 'Where'd you get it?'

'It was a gift,' I answer, stepping towards him to thread the earpiece over my head and brushing his hands aside to shift the bell into place. I listen to the thud of his heart, and wonder if I'm imagining the way it seems to speed up.

'What's the news, doc?' he murmurs, though the sound magnifies in my ears.

Tick tick tick.

'Congratulations,' I say. 'You are, indeed, alive.'

He grins, pleased with this diagnosis. I roll my eyes, and gently fold the stethoscope back onto the shelf. Nan gave me the stethoscope when she retired. It's the same one she'd let me use when I broke my arm. My hand drifts unbidden to the scar near my wrist, the rough ridge left behind. I push the memory away and sit on the edge of my bed, covertly stuffing Mr Snuggles under the pillows.

Gideon continues to prowl around, almost as though he doesn't realise he's doing it. He picks up a book, flicks through the pages, sets it down. Looks at a photo frame. Gently nudges a half-empty box full of old trophies. 'What were these for?'

'Swimming,' I say, struggling to remember if I'm annoyed at him or not.

He looks up in surprise. 'Well, that explains a lot.'

'I don't usually leap off piers,' I clarify. 'For what it's worth.'

There's no trace of amusement in his eyes now. 'That's good,' he says, voice quiet. Then he brightens again. 'Plus you ruined a perfectly good dress. So, do you talk to them much?

'What?'

'Your friends.'

'Oh.' I hesitate too long. 'Yeah. All the time.'

He walks to the other side of the bed and flops face down into the pillows. I feel panic rising in my chest and leap off the mattress. 'What are you doing?' I ask, voice rocketing up an octave.

'I'm tired. I need a nap.'

'You can do that downstairs. Or in Theo's bed. Or on the floor.'

He points a finger in the vague direction of the clutter strewn across the room. 'False, Clarissa. I would not fit on the floor.'

'Well, I'm *sorry*, I haven't exactly got around to unpacking. And don't call me Clarissa.'

He mumbles something I don't understand, then rolls over. 'Five minutes,' he bargains. 'Swimming knocks me out.'

I'm about to tell him to get up, but there's something in his face—maybe it's because he looks so tired with the deep-purple bruises under his eyes, or maybe it's because his dimples show when he smiles—and I hear myself say, 'Urgh, fine. Five minutes.'

His hands dart under the pillows. 'And I get to cuddle this little dude.' He pulls out Mr Snuggles and holds him tight, eyes closed but lips curled into a smile.

'Excuse me,' I say, turning towards the door before he can see my beet-red face. 'I need to go die of embarrassment.'

Theo is standing in the corridor when I emerge, his eyebrows raised into his hairline. He's staring at Gideon's too-tall figure squished into my double bed.

'Not a single word,' I snap.

He holds his hands up in surrender. 'Hey, no judgment. Dude's hot.' He follows me back to the kitchen and grabs the banana chips I abandoned earlier. He watches me as I set the table, and he's clearly weighing up his next words.

'Spit it out,' I say.

'What? I'm just standing here.'

'Speak now, or forever hold your lasagne.'

'Just, you know. Gid's cool. He seems kinda bummed lately. You could be a little nicer to him.'

I narrow my eyes at Theo. 'I *am* nice.' But in the back of my mind I think: *Has he? Seemed sad?* Gideon always smiles so easily, offering them like he has an endless supply.

Theo shrugs. 'Whatever. None of my business.' And then: 'So are you guys friends or what?'

I don't actually know the answer to that question. 'Not really,' I end up saying. 'I barely even know him. We only talked at the pier the other day. And once since then, I guess.'

'Huh,' he says, eyeing me as banana crumbs fall out of his mouth and spill down his jumper.

'Huh *what*?'

'Nothing.'

'Theo—'

The front door sweeps open and Mum and Dad come in, heads ducked low under enormous raincoats.

'Smells delicious,' Dad says, dropping a kiss on the top of my head.

Mum glances at the table with its extra place setting. 'Do we have company?'

'Oh yeah,' says Theo, jumping up to sit on the kitchen bench. 'Some guy's asleep in Reece's bed.'

My mouth drops open in shock. I can't seem to remember any words, or how to use them. Dad is studiously inspecting the cornices on the ceiling.

'Clarissa?' Mum says, waiting for an explanation. 'If you're going to have company—'

Then Theo laughs, punching me in the arm. 'Nah, just kidding. Gideon's here. He's on the swim team, remember? He drove me home.' He gives me a look, like, *See? I own you now*, and I give him a look that says *I'm going to put Nair inside your shampoo bottle until even your eyebrows fall out*, except that's a fairly complex concept to convey and I'm pretty sure all he picks up is seething anger.

'Would you like to go get your friend?' Dad says, starting to pull out knives and forks to serve.

'Sure,' Theo says, bounding away to wake Gideon.

Mum catches me by the shoulder, murmuring in my ear. 'Is this the boyfriend?' she hisses. We're pretty sure Theo has some kind of secret special-friend he's keeping from us, because he's been 'studying' at the library a lot and coming straight home to shower. And he washes his sheets, like, *a lot*.

'No, Mum,' I say. 'He's in my year. I'm pretty sure he's the captain or something.'

'Oh good,' she says, relieved. 'Because I don't know where the good plates are.'

'Mum, I don't think Theo's theoretical-boyfriend cares about whether or not we set out the good china.'

Dad's ears perk up. 'Who has a theoretical boyfriend?'

'No one,' we say at the same time.

The boys appear in the lounge room, and Gideon holds out his hand like a grown-up. 'Hi, Mrs Blackwell, I'm Gideon. Thanks for letting me stay for dinner.' His hair is all mussed and his cheeks are red, as if he really did fall asleep for a few minutes.

I can see the cogs in Mum's head turning. Her eyes slide towards me before she gives him a kind smile and takes his hand. 'Please, it's Olivia. And you know Nick?'

Dad greets him warmly, and I realise they must have met at some stage over the past few weeks. Theo joined the swim team as soon as we got here. I joined a new streaming TV service.

Dinner is quick and awkward, with Dad and Theo doing most of the talking. Mum pushes the food around her plate and Gideon inhales his food too fast to talk. He has two platefuls and I'm pretty sure the only reason he doesn't ask for a third is because he doesn't want to be rude. I sit in the middle, poking at the lasagne sheets, trying not to look at either of them.

After dinner, Gideon tries to help with tidying up

until Mum shoos him away, stuffing multiple Tupperware containers in his arms.

'You're welcome to stay a while longer,' Mum says, trying to bribe him with offers of biscuits, hot chocolate and ice cream. I swear he glances at *Ghost Hunters* on the TV and cringes.

He shakes his head. 'I have to get home, Mum'll be worried. Thank you though.'

'Next time,' she says.

'Sure.'

'Reece, will you show Gideon out?' *Betrayed*. Mum doesn't miss much, and the amusement is written across her face. She challenges me with a single raised eyebrow, and I pull a face at her when Gideon isn't looking.

'Come on,' I say, putting on the emergency gumboots we leave by the door. 'I'll walk you up the driveway and protect you from dropbears.'

We walk in silence to his beaten-up four-wheel drive, and he loads the leftovers into his passenger-side seat.

'So. Thanks for dinner,' he says.

'I'd say it was my pleasure but I'm sure Mr Snuggles would object.'

He barks a laugh, crossing his arms across his chest and leaning back against his car. 'So,' he continues, face becoming sombre. 'Did you work things out? About your nan?'

The question takes me by surprise. 'Oh, I…I haven't thought much more about it.' This is a half-truth. Last night I took out the book again, checking the back cover for words I might have missed the first time, something that might explain what's inside. But then I heard Mum coming up the stairs and shoved it back under my bed.

'Why did you come here?' I blurt.

Now surprise registers on his face. 'Your brother needed a lift,' he says slowly, like maybe my memory isn't so good.

I roll my eyes. 'Next time, let him walk.'

He laughs, and then it's quiet. His lashes brush against his skin, and I can't help but notice how long they are, touching his cheeks when he smiles. *He literally said he just wants to be friends—stop thinking about his eyelashes, you nit.*

I back away, conceding several steps and many more heart-beats. 'Well, goodnight, then. Drive safe and…everything.'

He stuffs his hands in his pockets, rocking on his feet. 'Goodnight, Reece.' He hesitates in the open door, half in and half out, before slipping away.

I wait until his tail-lights disappear around the corner then stomp back inside, scraping the mud off my boots in the doorway. Mum and Dad are sitting at the counter, strange expressions on their faces. Mum pats the seat beside her. 'Come sit, Reece. Your dad and I want to talk.'

Theo snorts from the couch. 'Pretty sure she knows what a condom is, Mum.'

Dad chokes on his coffee. 'Theodore Blackwell. Go to your room.'

'*Go to your room,*' mimics Theo, but he slinks away anyway, already typing on his phone. I think my parents are yet to realise that sending him to his room isn't a punishment.

'I think it's nice that you've made a friend,' says Mum, full of false cheer. 'Takes your mind off things.' She cringes, as if realising that reminding me of *things* will make it worse.

I give her a thin smile to let her know it's okay. 'Thanks, Mum. How was work?'

She gives a dramatic sigh, waving her wine glass through the air. 'That hospital is hopeless. Not a patch on what it was when your grandmother ran the place. I only went in today because I had two patients who would have lost their appointments otherwise.'

Dad leans over to rest his arm on Mum's shoulder. I heard my parents talking this morning, when they thought I couldn't hear. Mum is technically on leave for another week, but she didn't want people suffering after they had waited so long to see her—and, as she'd explained, she didn't feel any worse being at work. At least she had a distraction there.

'Mary was a force,' Dad says, smiling down at the table. I caught him in the pantry one night, turning over a box of caramel chocolates in his hands before hiding it behind some dusty bottles of wine on the tallest shelf. He used to slip Nan sweets in the nursing home, even after she wasn't supposed to eat them anymore (*something else will kill me first* were her exact words). His own family aren't close anymore—they had some kind of falling-out a few Christmases ago. I remember Theo and I were half-asleep in front of the TV after midnight Mass—their tradition, not ours—and pretending to watch cartoons with the volume turned low, when really we were both trying to eavesdrop on the furious whispers coming from the kitchen, our grandparents' voices, stern and strained.

We were supposed to stay for lunch the next day, but Dad shook us awake early in the morning, the house silent and cold, wrapping-paper shreds still stuck to the carpet. He packed us in the car, and that was it: we never went there again. Now they only send a birthday card once a year.

Dad's voice jolts me out of the memory. 'That book she gave you,' he says. 'What was inside?'

'Oh. It's locked,' I tell him. 'And there was no key. I tried to crack it open but I didn't want to break it.'

'I wonder if we missed something at the nursing home?' Mum says. 'Maybe she left a few things with that nurse— Jane? She might know.'

Dad nods. 'They did keep a few valuables locked up for residents. Some wobbly memories in there, so they'll hold on to the really sentimental stuff sometimes.'

They're both looking up at me with such hope that I find myself saying, 'Sure. I could swing by on the weekend.'

'Do you want me to come?' Mum flinches as she says it, so I shake my head. We've been in there only once since Nan died. It took us less than an hour to pack everything: a blanket, a few cardigans, a book she never finished. She hadn't been in there long and she'd kept a lot of stuff at her old house, hoping she'd get well enough to go back. That's a whole other issue we need to deal with soon.

'It's okay, I can go, I don't mind,' I lie.

'I'll come with you,' Dad says, giving me a sad wink. 'Jane said we should check over Mary's room one last time before the next person moves in on Monday. Think there's a bottle of gin hidden in the bathroom cabinets we forgot to clear out.

Don't want the staff thinking she was a booze hound.'

Mum quirks an eyebrow. *'Well...'*

Dad laughs, and they turn to each other, cocooned together: Mum still tucked under his arm, leaning her head on his shoulder.

'Thanks, Dad. I'm gonna head upstairs, I'm tired.' I fake a passable yawn and mumble *goodnight* as I hug them in turn.

Something thumps in Theo's room as I walk past, and a roar of indignation follows a second later. He must be playing a game with his friends online—they still talk, even get the train down sometimes to visit. The thought makes me feel even more lonely.

I sigh, suddenly exhausted. It's not until I'm slipping under the covers that I realise Gideon's jacket is laid across my bed, a crumpled post-it note stuck to the collar. *It looked better on you anyway.*

I always liked Saturdays at the nursing home. The car park is full and laughter echoes in the hallway. Staff make cookies in the mornings for visitors and pick flowers from the garden for the dining tables.

But today it just makes me sad that Nan isn't waiting for us, with her smear of pink lipstick and hot rollers in her hair. Dad jokes with the nurse, Jane, as she leads us to Nan's old room. I stand in the doorway, not wanting to venture inside. It feels empty, like when you walk into your house sometimes at the end of the day and you *know* that no one is home; that the air is too still, that you've somehow ended up alone. It's just...vacant.

Jane pauses in the doorway. She was here every weekend. Used to bring me cups of tea and the Scrabble dictionary when Nan declared I had cheated.

'How are you doing, doll?' Jane asks, squeezing my shoulder. I like Jane; her voice doesn't drip with pity, or brighten with false cheer. She never intrudes, but she always asks the right questions.

'I'm okay,' I say. 'We're okay.'

Jane nods. 'She was real proud of you, you know? Always telling anyone who would listen that you were so clever. The next great Blackwell doctor.'

My stomach twists.

I clear my throat, watching as Dad disappears into the small bathroom beyond. 'Did she...leave anything? With you, maybe?' I pull out my phone to show her a picture of the locked book, and enlarge the photo to show Jane the binding. 'She left me this, but there's no key.'

Jane frowns, leaning closer to the screen to get a good look. 'Hmm, haven't seen that before. Honestly, sugar, your nan didn't keep much here. She still had the old house, right?'

I nod, shoving the phone in my back pocket.

'Check there,' she says, eyes drifting to a pager clipped to her waistband. 'If you can't find anything, you can always come back.'

I try to hide my disappointment but Jane sees it on my face. The pager clicks off. 'You know what?' she adds. 'Let me look in the pigeonholes, maybe something has snuck in.'

She hustles down the corridor, calling out to old Mr Pritchard on the way that the Germans are *not* coming, and if he would just sit down for a minute she'd be right back.

Dad emerges from the bathroom, holding a half-empty bottle of gin, shaking his head. 'Sorry, Reece. Nothing else in there.'

'S'okay,' I say. 'I'll meet you in the car, Jane will be back in a sec.'

He kisses my head and slips out the door, making sure the keypad beeps closed behind him.

I wait with two ladies who are often in the sunroom; Helen and Mhari, I think their names are. They fuss over my hair, and make small talk about the weather and the terrible coffee. Helen seems to drift off to sleep before Jane returns, holding an envelope. 'No key, but I know she was waiting for this; just came yesterday, good timing.'

Beaming, she hands it to me. There's a return address in the top-left corner: the hospital Nan used to work at, in the city.

'Do you know what it is?' I ask, nervously running my fingers across the seal.

There's an echo of Nan's pride etched on Jane's face. 'It's a letter of recommendation—for that internship program you mentioned. Your nan wanted to help, if she could. Still has a few friends who practise.'

Doctors Without Borders. God, that was so long ago. I had only mentioned it once or twice—how had Nan remembered? It must have been more than a year ago. Before everything...just *before*.

'Right,' I say, managing to smile. 'Thanks, Jane.'

Mr Pritchard has wandered into the lounge room, eyeing

Helen suspiciously. Jane rushes after him, calling over her shoulder: 'Good luck, kid!'

I crumple the letter in my pocket as I slip out the door.

Luck be damned. I was already cursed.

5

THEO AND I usually spend Saturday nights watching zombie movies, taking turns to pick the scariest, most twisted ones we can find in a never-ending effort to gross each other out. Once he made me watch some creepy eighties movie called *Flesh Eaters* and then waited in my cupboard for two hours just so he could jump out and scream 'I WANT TO EAT YOUR BRAAAAINS' at one o'clock in the morning. I screamed so loud Mum banned him from ever going into my room again.

But this Saturday, after the disaster at the nursing home and the long swim I'd taken afterwards, I walk in the door with ocean-damp hair, and sheepishly ask Mum if I can go to the stupid party. She's so shocked that she not only agrees, but offers to blow-dry my hair with her fancy curlers.

Which is how, impossibly, I end up at the Beach Bean at exactly 6.55 on Saturday night, my hair bouncing around my shoulders and gold glitter drying on my eyes. I'm clutching my phone in my hand, waiting for Mum to drive away, and half-planning to call the solitary Hamilton taxi service so I can run away, when a window above my head pops open and Ava's head sticks out. 'Hey! Come round the back and we'll let you in.' Then she disappears inside and I have no choice but to do what she says.

Miles comes barrelling down a corridor and greets me by yelling, 'Reece! You came!' and sweeping me into a bone-crushing hug. Surprisingly, Miles and Ava stuck by me all week. If I didn't come to lunch, one of them would find me and drag me to their table, introducing me to their friends. People were nice to me, and I was nice back. For the first time since we moved to Hamilton, I stopped dreading school every day. Gideon, on the other hand, I haven't seen for a few days. When I asked Theo he mumbled something about Gideon being sick.

'Come on, come on,' Miles says. 'Mum'll have a connip-tion if the food goes cold.' He leads me up a metal staircase to their apartment; it's warm and bright, overlooking the ocean. There are two comfy-looking couches facing a piano wedged in the corner, and sheet music coats every surface—so many pages you could bind them up into a fat book.

Mrs Kostakis gives me a warm smile when we enter the kitchen. 'Hello, Clarissa, how are you today?' She kisses me on both cheeks and shoves a tray of ham and cheese crois-sants into my hands.

'I'm good,' I say, and mean it.

'I'll leave you kids to it. Let me know when you're ready to leave.'

Ava comes bounding out of her room, wearing a tight

black dress and laced-up boots. 'You came! I'm so glad!'

I look down at my own outfit—black jeans and a tie-up shirt. 'Uh, am I under-dressed?'

Ava waves a hand at me. 'You look great, don't worry.'

Miles rolls his eyes. 'Dweeb has a whole *vibe* going on.'

'It's called style, Miles. Some of us have it.'

'Yeah? The nineties called and said even they don't want the goth look back because it was a mistake the first time around.'

'It's *vintage*,' Ava bristles. They bitch at each other until it's time to leave, with a little more venom than Theo and I might have. But when Mrs Kostakis waves them out of the car and tells them to be safe, they share an identical look and answer '*we will*' in unison.

We're standing at the end of a very long driveway, and by the time we arrive at the actual house Ava is complaining that her shoes hurt. It's already dark, so it takes me a few minutes to blink at the lights ahead and realise that Miles wasn't joking about the paddock. Sure, a few people are lingering inside, fiddling with the music that jumps every time someone changes the song, but mostly everyone has spilt out into the adjoining paddock, dancing and drinking and running around, depending on how inebriated they seem.

'Okay, so the rules,' says Miles, suddenly serious. 'Stay in the light—it's all farming land around here, and if you get lost you're staying that way till morning. If anyone offers to take you down the lake, say no. Unless you wanna get all *Dirty Dancing*, and that's your own freaky business.'

Ava nudges me in the ribs and points at a few groups.

'Those girls are super nice, those ones aren't, and see the guy doing a keg stand? Yeah, he's an idiot with a one hundred per cent chance of projectile vomit. Stay clear of the splash zone.'

'And there's no reception out here, so if you wanna leave, grab one of us and we'll walk down to the main road together,' says Miles.

'And don't get the paddocks mixed up. Left is the party. Right is Bertie the Bull.'

'Right is bite, right is bite,' Miles says, repeating the rhyme a few times, a pained look on his face. 'Damn that beast is nasty. Almost took a finger off last time.'

'You tried to *pee* on it.'

'It was dark! I couldn't see!'

Ava scoffs at him and then they both turn to me. 'Hey, are you okay?' says Miles. 'You look kinda wigged.'

'I just—that's a lot of things to remember,' I say, blinking in confusion. The parties I went to back home weren't so complicated.

'You'll be fine,' Miles reassures me. 'Come on.'

And then we're in the middle of it all: people writhing to loud music, friendship groups clustered in circles and giggling, girls waving and people passing me cups, which I mostly refuse except for one Ava promises me is just soft drink. I mean, I'm eighteen. I *could* drink if I wanted to. But after the long list of things to remember, I don't exactly feel like letting loose. We do a lap of the party, and although a few guys try to pull Miles away he waves them all off and stays beside me. Ava occasionally flits away to chat to her friends, but she always comes back, like a gravitational star. She complains that she's cold and we wander over to a fire pit someone's built, with a few logs around it for sitting. I squint at the dark cracks in the bark, but I'm shivering and decide the warmth is worth the risk of bugs.

Ava whispers in Miles's ear and he glances over his shoulder and groans. She gives him an evil grin and he hisses something back.

'What's going on?' I ask, suspicious. I start to turn my head but he grabs my face in panic, smooshing it in his palms.

'Don't look, *don't look*, but—'

Ava stands up and waves. 'Hey, Connie!'

One of the girls huddled around the speakers waves back. She walks over and plonks herself beside me on the log. 'Urgh, the mosquitos are killing me. You were smart to wear stockings. Oh, hey Miles, didn't see you.'

Miles squeaks something in reply, his face dropping. Ava leans back and mouths the word *loser* at him then reaches into her purse and tosses the girl some bug spray.

'Here. Mum makes me carry it everywhere.'

'My hero,' the girl says, squirting some on her knees. 'Sorry—I'm Connie,' she says, smiling at me. 'I think we have chem together.'

She has long blonde hair and long tan legs. I remember her because she's kind of hard to forget. Miles looks like he's about to have a stroke and falls uncharacteristically quiet.

'Reece,' I answer, giving a little wave.

'So you're from the city, right? You must miss it.' Connie folds her legs under her, getting comfy.

I pretend the question doesn't bother me. 'Sometimes. I like the beaches here though.'

'Do you see your friends back home much?'

'Oh, it's—um, it's a long drive.'

'I'll bet. I can't wait to get out of here. Kinda sick of paddock parties.'

I laugh, and her eyes crinkle. 'I've never been to one before,' I confess. 'It's...different.'

'Honestly, gumboots are your friend. Don't even bother looking cute, it's too dark anyway.'

My eyes slide to Miles. This girl is next-level. Blue eyes, perfect teeth. She is indeed wearing gumboots with her cut-off shorts, which isn't an outfit I could pull off and yet somehow she looks like an off-duty Instagram model. Someone calls her name again and she stands, brushing dust off her butt. Miles looks away, his cheeks turning pink.

'Anyway,' Connie says, 'it was nice to meet you, Reece. Come sit with me in class next week!'

'For sure,' I say. When she's gone, my eyes cut to Miles. Ava cackles with unmasked glee.

'So, weirdo. What the hell was that?' I ask.

'I'm in love,' he groans. 'Oh my god, she just—the smile and the legs and she's so *nice*.'

'She *is* nice,' says Ava. 'You should try, I don't know, talking to her sometime.'

'I just—she just—I get all tangled, you know? Like in my brain.'

'Like in your pants,' I quip.

They both go slack-jawed. 'Oh my god, did you just

make a joke?' Miles stands up with his arms spread wide. 'Ladies and gentlemen, she *does* have a sense of humour!'

I smack Miles's shoulder. 'Shut up. I'm not done making fun of you yet. Wait your turn.'

'Making fun of Miles for what?' Gideon appears out of nowhere and takes Connie's place beside me. My stomach churns, and I'm too nervous to even look up at him.

'Connie,' supplies Ava. 'We had an encounter.'

Gideon grins at Miles. 'Hey man, I'm so proud of you. Did you say actual words to her this time?'

'You know I absolutely did not.'

'Maybe next time.'

'Shut up, I hate your big ugly face and your ogre-like personality. Also, have you met Reece? This is Gideon Hawthorn, my former best friend. Gid, this is Reece Blackwell, my new best friend. Sorry man, you've been downgraded for the purpose of obtaining piping hot baked goods.'

Gideon nods. 'Seems like a fair trade.'

'Hi,' I say, feeling sheepish. I don't know where we stand after his visit last week.

'Hi yourself,' Gideon answers good-naturedly.

'Have you guys met before?' Ava says with a suspicious quirk of her brow.

Gideon kicks her lightly on the shin. 'Her brother's on the swim team, I drop him home sometimes.'

I feel my cheeks burning, noting he didn't say that *we* were friends. Which I guess we aren't. Even though we shook on it. But still. It stings a little to know he thinks of me as

Theo's sister. Not *Reece*, wholly separate person with whom one might want to spend time.

'How are you feeling, man?' Miles asks, thankfully changing the topic. 'You've been out all week.'

Gideon gives him a strange look that I can't quite read. 'Just a cold,' he answers. 'You know, the usual.' Then he smiles down at me. 'Think I saw you this afternoon at the Swells, but you were too quick to catch.'

I feel a flush rising in my cheeks. I had picked my way across the rocky outcropping, intentionally avoiding the life-guard hut because I hadn't felt like talking. 'Just swimming away from Bruce,' I joke, wondering if Gideon had jumped in the water to come find me.

Ava watches us, her eyes narrowed, and I think she's a bit more clued in than her brother.

'Miles, I have to pee,' she says. 'Come with me and help me carry drinks back.'

He rolls his eyes and stands. 'Yes, ma'am. What do you guys want?'

'I'm driving,' says Gideon. 'Just Coke.'

'Me too, please.'

'Sure thing. Urgh, I'm coming, *Jesus*,' Miles says as Ava drags him back to the house, leaving us alone.

'So,' Gideon says. 'Feeling better?'

'Yeah. Sorry. Weird week. Thanks for, you know...'

'Snooping through your bedroom and providing sage life advice?'

I laugh. 'Sure.'

'So, how's your first paddock party? Has anyone taken

you cow-tipping yet?' He's leaning towards me, his hair freshly washed and still wet, dripping against the edge of a blue collared shirt that's rolled up to his elbows.

'I'm sorry, did you say "cow-tipping"? What does that even mean?'

'You know, when you sneak up on a cow at night and tip it sideways. They can't get up again until morning.'

'What? No.' I shake my head, trying not to laugh. 'No way. I don't believe you.'

His eyes twinkle and I can't tell whether he's joking. 'Just don't try it in the next field.'

'Right. Bertie the Bull.'

'You're a quick learner,' he says with surprise.

'Miles and Ava were very thorough.'

'Did they tell you about the lake?'

I nod. 'For drunken groping.'

'And there's no signal on the hill.'

'Only at the main road.'

'How quickly they grow up,' he laments, mock regret in his voice. 'You don't even need me anymore.'

'Uh, excuse me, I never *needed* you.'

'Oh, that's right. I swore to pretend the pier never happened. I stand corrected: you, Reece Blackwell, are a strong independent young lady who has never required the assistance of a passing stranger to—for instance—rescue her from a ladderless pier and possible shark attack.' His lips have curled at their corners.

'That's not true,' I huff. 'You weren't a stranger.'

He raises his eyebrows. 'I wasn't?'

'I mean, not exactly. I had seen you at school.'

He smiles as he takes a sip of his drink. 'Interesting.'

'What's interesting?' I ask, peevishly.

'Nothing at all, Clarissa.'

I'm about to shoot back another retort, but someone turns up the speakers and we both cringe as a bass-thumping techno song comes on. A bunch of guys start leaping around the dance floor, doing their best imitation of literal head-banging, which is amusing and nauseating all at once. The crowd around us starts to rise, joining in the dance. Arms and legs jostle around the fire, and I cringe away from someone who starts to screech out the lyrics. After months locked away in my bedroom, a countryside flash mob is suddenly feeling like an over-commitment for my social stamina. I'm starting to think I should go find the others when Gideon glances back and seems to notice me leaning away from the scuff of shoes and dust.

'Hey, do you wanna go for a walk?' he says. 'It's kinda loud here.'

I hesitate, since he really just got here and surely has other friends to say hello to—but he's looking at me so earnestly, like he really doesn't mind, and it's so *loud*. 'So long as it's not to the lake.'

He places a hand over his heart. 'I would never presume to besmirch your dignity.'

'Besmirch?'

'I got one of those word-of-the-day calendars for Christmas,' he says, rising to his feet and offering me a hand to help me stand. 'So far my favourite is "snollygoster".'

I laugh, glancing over my shoulder to check where Ava and Miles are, but there's no sign of them. I follow Gideon away from the crowd, careful to watch my steps in the dark. 'Snollygoster?'

'An unprincipled but shrewd person,' he explains. 'For instance, I suspect Miles is a secret snollygoster.'

'Hey, he has principles.'

'Barely. You should see him when there's free snacks around.'

We walk until the party fades away—until the stars blink brighter and the music is a soft thrum in the distance. My breath comes out in white puffs and I shiver, wishing I'd thought to bring a coat.

'So Theo mentioned you used to swim at your old school. There's a place on the team if you're interested.' Gideon's tone is casual, but I can tell he's been waiting to bring it up. Theo is such a little traitor.

'Major pass,' I say, focusing on my feet so I don't accidentally step into a muddy puddle.

'He reckons you were pretty good.'

'Actually, I was excellent, but that's beside the point.'

He laughs and I look up to catch his smile. 'So modest,' he says.

I shrug. 'I always won. It's the only thing I was ever good at right away.'

'So why'd you stop?'

'I...didn't really have time, back home.' The truth is, *technically*, I did have time. I just spent all of it avoiding my real life after The Terrible Thing That Happened. And, eventually, it didn't matter how good I used to be, because our coach kicked me off the team. Too many missed practices. Then there was the time I suddenly felt like the water was flooding my lungs and I crawled out of the pool, panicking that I couldn't breathe, until someone ran and got the nurse and she told me, kindly, that I should really *go see someone* about everything.

Anyway. That was then.

'Turn around,' Gideon says, and I realise we've reached the top of a hill. The town is spread out below us: tiny yellow lights and little-box buildings, like a miniature play set. The party looks so far away, and I wonder how long it took us to climb up here. I can see the fire, and a few people gathered around it, and the lake Miles mentioned, and the cattle sleeping soundly in the next paddock.

'Oh. It's so pretty,' I say. From up here it all looks so neat: toy-sized cars winding through toy-sized streets, the ocean one great blue expanse of sea, no waves or churning white water. It's all very…peaceful.

'I like it up here,' he says. 'It's quiet. It's never quiet down there.' He looks like he might say something else, but then he shakes his head and wanders a little further, finding a cut-off tree trunk that works as a good make-shift seat, and jumps up so his legs are dangling off the edge. I watch him for a few seconds, until he smiles and pats the space beside him. 'Need a hand? Or a stepladder? Cherry picker, maybe?'

I clamber up the trunk, with considerably more effort than it took him, and sigh. 'Very funny,' I say, kicking my heels. 'Getting down again is going to be the real problem.'

He laughs, lying back. The tree trunk is massive—he doesn't even hang off the end of it. 'We can always roll down,' he says.

'I'm sure I'd make so many new friends that way,' I reply, bringing my knees up to my chest. I don't think I'm game enough to lie down beside him. For a minute I think about him lying in my bed and it makes me flush. He was just napping. Without me. It was all very innocent.

'Did you meet anyone nice?' he says, jolting me out of the memory.

'I actually really like Connie,' I say with a grin. 'I'm sure Miles will love that.'

Gideon crosses his arms behind his head. He looks tired again, I realise. And softer, somehow. Lifeguard Gideon is all hard edges and shrewd lines. Party Gideon is a little looser, his smile a little wider. I hesitate before I settle down beside him at last, gazing up at the mottled sky. We didn't have stars like this in the city—the only thing that glowed in the sky were satellites and aeroplanes passing overhead. I tell him that, and he laughs again.

'So you're having fun?' he says. 'I don't think I've ever heard you say so many words all at once. I was starting to think you didn't *want* any friends.'

I can tell he's looking at me, but I keep my eyes fixed above. It's easier to talk to him when I can't see him. I guess that says a lot about my mental state, but that's a problem for another day.

'I didn't really want to move here,' I say slowly, considering each word before I say it. 'My parents kinda decided for us. And I thought, maybe, if they knew I was miserable they'd let me go home again. And then I realised they weren't going to change their minds, and by then it was too late. Everyone already thought I was the weird girl who didn't talk. People were nice to me at first, but I guess I wasn't really nice back.'

'I thought you were nice.'

'You didn't even know my name,' I scoff.

'I still thought you were nice. You probably don't remember, but you smiled at me once, and I was so surprised I didn't get to smile back until you turned away.'

Oh, I remembered. It was one of those awkward moments that haunted me for weeks—every time I was about to fall asleep, or when I was lulled into a false state of relaxation watching *Ghost Hunters*, the thought would pop up: *Hey, remember that time you worked up the courage to smile at the cute boy in class and he totally ignored you?* Not that he needed to know that.

'I saw you in English class,' I admit. 'I knew who you were when we met on the pier.' I think he's going to tease me, but he doesn't. I roll over until we're facing each other, and realise the tree trunk isn't as big as I thought because we're suddenly very close.

'I wish you'd said hello,' he said.

'*You* could have said hello.'

'Don't take this the wrong way, but you're kind of scary.'

'Me? Scary? I'm a whole head shorter than you and I have no friends.'

'Yeah, and I once watched you tell Tanner and his friends

to go fuck themselves because they teased Theo for wearing pink bathers.'

'It was Pride Week. It was just *rude*.'

'My point stands,' he says, and his breath smells sweet and minty.

He looks at me for a long moment, a funny look on his face that reminds me too much of the beach, and eventually I have to look away. 'Do you want to go back?' he says, voice slightly husky. 'Miles will be wondering where we went.'

'Five more minutes?' I ask, and he nods. He's right; it's quiet up here.

He sees me shiver and reaches out to rub my arms, finger-tips trailing across goosebumps that have rushed across my whole body. 'Are you cold?'

'Not anymore,' I say, and then cringe. Why did I say that? Why am I like this? But he just laughs quietly and shuffles a little closer. 'So do you still think I'm scary?' I ask.

'It's about fifty-fifty,' he says with a smirk.

'Hey.'

'See? Tiny but feisty.'

I roll my eyes. 'You know, I thought you'd be different.'

'Different how?'

'I don't know. Like you'd be the popular jock guy, failing his classes and leaving a trail of broken hearts in his wake.'

'Gee, thanks.'

'I thought you'd tell everyone—about the pier. And then you didn't. And I guess I'm trying to say sorry...if I was sort of prickly when you came over the other day. I was just surprised.'

'I figured you'd had enough of a crap day already,' he says. So he did know. I always wondered if Theo told him about the funeral. 'I wouldn't tell a secret if you didn't want me to. And just for the record, my mum would kill me if I failed all my classes for a girl.'

I laugh, reaching out for a second before I realise I was about to touch his shoulder, and we're not really the kind of friends who can do that. I snatch my hand away, hoping he didn't notice. A muscle in his cheek twitches and he looks down at the hand I've shoved in my pants pocket. He seems like he's about to say something, but then changes his mind and shakes his head, and only says, 'We better head back now.'

He jumps off first, then holds up his arms to help me clamber down. His hands slip around my waist and I place my hands carefully on his shoulders. Then suddenly I'm in the air, jumping without thinking and he catches me before I wind up face-first in the grass. He lowers me down, but he doesn't let go even when my feet are safely on the ground. His hands are so *warm*; my shirt rode up when he lifted me, and one of his fingers is touching the bare skin of my back.

My heart starts to tick a little faster. One of us should move. And it should probably be me, but my hands are still on his shoulders, and I desperately want to slip my fingertips under his collar and find out if the skin there is as warm as I think it will be. And it doesn't seem like he wants to let go either, because he steps a little closer and his fingers are playing with the fabric of my top, right at the spot where the shirt meets my jeans.

Maybe he can read my mind, because his eyes seem to cloud over, roaming my face. My heart skips a few beats in my chest. Maybe I should call it now: draw my walls back up and scurry away while I still can. But then his hands pull me a little closer, wandering up my back, and I let him draw me in until I'm flush up against his body. He ducks his head low and waits for a moment, but I can't find any words and all I can do is look up, thinking that maybe this is a bad idea but I don't care because *god* I want to kiss him.

He leans down and kisses me, right on the mouth, so softly that I think maybe I'm mistaken, but no, those are his lips against mine, waiting for me to kiss him back. My hands come up to lie on his chest, and for a second I tilt my head back and let his tongue flicker out to touch mine.

Then I push him away, embarrassed and angry and confused. 'I have to go,' I say, even as he reaches for me again and I think I want to let him. 'I have to go,' I repeat, even though I know he heard me and I'm trying to convince myself more than him.

And I run again, not daring to look back. All the way down the hill and back to the party, out to the main road, while Gideon calls out for me to wait.

But this is what I do. And I don't deserve anything else.

6

HEYA IT'S WILL, leave a message.

'I really need you to answer. I kissed a boy. Except I didn't kiss him, because I'm an idiot, and I was sad and we were talking about Nan but then we weren't anymore and I was like, *Hey Reece you psycho you're meant to be grieving not getting all starry-eyed* and—' I flop back on the bed. 'I need Nina. But she won't answer. She never answers.' I duck my head between my legs, because I read it was good for nausea and I feel like I might be sick. 'Sorry. I'm rambling. I just miss you. I'm sorry. Bye, Will.'

I have three missed calls and a string of worried texts on my phone. I click on the latest one, surprised that it's from Ava. *Are you okay? Did something happen? I love Gideon but I'll still punch him in his dumb face if he did something.*

The phone pings again in my hand and a new message shows under it. *At least say you're home and not murdered by a hitchhiking crazy person.*

I'm both surprised and touched by her concern. It's been a

long time since anyone noticed—or cared—what I did, and I feel bad that I left Miles and Ava behind to worry about me.

Sorry for leaving early, I felt a bit sick, I text.

She replies with a string of emojis and love hearts, and then Miles also texts to say he saw Connie at the bathrooms and almost said hello. I feel the prick of tears in my eyes and throw my phone across the room. Just when I was making friends, I'm going to lose them again.

7

NANA BLACKWELL DID not believe in storage. Her house is a squat little cottage that leans to one side, and inside it's full of dusty furniture and old books. Books in impossible numbers, their pages yellowed and frayed, the text sometimes hardly legible. Drawings rim-marked by errant cups of tea, diagrams with pencilled scribbles in the margins, pages dog-eared mid-chapter and forgotten about. Books in the kitchen, stacked in piles in the hall, shoved between couch cushions and scattered across the floor. Some aren't even books, really—just sheaves of paper bound together with twine, precariously balanced on shelves or between jars of peanut butter in the pantry.

Mum raises a hand to her mouth, covering a gasp and a hiccupped sob. 'I can't believe she lived like this...'

And suddenly, the room takes on a new life and I see what she sees. Not just books, but also notepads with shaky handwriting, boxes of frozen meals in the bin, coffee cups half-full and curdling in the sun. Newspapers with curling corners, cat fur and dust swept to the skirting boards, water stains on the roof and cracks in the walls. It's not horrible, exactly, nothing like a *Hoarders* special where they find flattened cats under VHS tapes. It smells a little of dust and mildew, but there's no towering piles of rubbish or food rotting in the fridge, and she hadn't buried herself in layers of adult diapers and expired coupon codes. It just wasn't somewhere someone should have lived, alone, and it certainly wasn't a place to die. We used to come down all the time, but I guess after The Terrible Thing That Happened we kind of dropped the ball a bit, until Nan got sick and had to move anyway.

I wrap my arms around Mum's shoulders, not knowing what to say. We didn't know it was this bad—just that Nan was a bit forgetful. She used to have a nurse come once a week, and even that was a hard-won victory. 'I'm not an invalid, Olivia,' she would tell Mum, full of haughty indignity. 'I'm old, not incompetent.'

But I suppose she'd got worse, and none of us had been here to notice. I squeeze my eyes shut, swallowing back the bitter regret of time—time that always seemed to slip away, full of half-realised choices.

Mum pulls away, giving her red eyes a perfunctory wipe with the back of her hand, then straightens her shoulders. 'Well, this will take longer than expected,' she sighs.

'What do you mean?'

'I thought we could do it in a few days, but it will take weeks. And that's if the roof doesn't cave in first. I'll call the hardware store, maybe they can deliver more boxes.'

I blink. Surely she's had a mental break. 'Mum, this is a

lot—it'll take months to get through. Maybe we should hire someone to do it—just to pack it all up and donate most of it?'

I wave my arm at a pile of books resting on top of a crystal vase. 'And the books, I was thinking—I found a museum that might want them. They have a special-collections exhibit every year, maybe they could display Nan's stuff. The Museum of Medical Oddities? It's attached—'

'To the university, I know the one.' Mum looks at me, face aghast. 'She left it to you, Clarissa. I know things have... changed lately, but if you don't want the books then we should at least put them into storage.'

I take a breath, trying to be reasonable. When I'd googled places to donate medical texts, the museum seemed like a good option. Sure, the name sounds a bit crackpot, but it's mostly to entice the public and generate ticket sales. The actual exhibits are world class, and they let medical students use the book collection for their studies. It seemed like a better option than setting them all on fire, which is currently my second choice. I don't want these books haunting me, reminding me of the life I could have had. But I don't say that, because Mum already looks so sad. 'Okay. I guess we should just...start.'

I pick up the nearest book, *A Practical System of Surgery*, about to toss it into one of the cardboard boxes. I can tell from the flaked leather on the spine that it's not just old, it's antique old. For a moment, that flare of curiosity kicks in, my eyes scanning pages of tumours and lesions and old-timey medical devices that look better suited to sawing wood than bone. Then I slam the cover shut, pushing the curiosity away.

'What happened to the summer program?' Mum asks gently. 'I thought you might still apply.'

'I missed the deadline,' I lie, determined not to cry.

'Well, what about another internship? Doctors Without Borders isn't the only—'

'I don't really want to talk about it.' I'm about to say something else to soften the words when two pages fall out of *A Practical System of Surgery*, followed by a black-and-white photo that lands face-up on the floor. Nana smiles out from the frame, holding a child in her arms. I read the inscription on the back: *Olivia and Mary Blackwell, 1962.*

Nan was nearly forty when she had Mum. Said she refused to decorate the nursery or even give Mum a name until the day they both came home from the hospital—she knew too well what could go wrong, and had long since given up on the dream of having her own family. Mum was her miracle baby; you can see it in Nan's eyes, the sparkle of joy, pure contentedness.

Mutely, I pass the picture to Mum. She looks at both sides and her mouth hardens. And suddenly, I don't want to be here at all: I don't want to be in Hamilton, or in Nana's house, and I don't want to look at all the medical books that should have been mine to inherit—except that now I don't want that future, either.

'She must have these everywhere,' I say. I flick through the remaining pages, just in case, and only when I find them empty do I carefully lay the tome inside the box, which has already been labelled *Donate*.

Mum sighs, resting on a moth-eaten footstool. 'Reece,

honey, are you sure about this? You don't want to have a look first, before we start packing it all?' She takes the marker from my hand, scribbling over *Donate* and writing *Storage* instead.

I hesitate. I guess there's no harm in looking. Maybe even keeping a few. I open my mouth to say as much, but all of Mum's attention is on the photo. She's cradling it in her palms, her toothless childhood smile grinning up at me. There's a familiar look of regret on her face.

'It's okay, Mum,' I whisper. 'You don't have to help. I can do all this stuff—maybe Theo will help too. We can go through it all and save the important stuff for you.'

She closes her eyes for a minute. 'No, it's okay. You shouldn't have to. But maybe we should leave it a little longer…I suppose it's waited this long, and it's not going anywhere. I think maybe it's all a bit much right now.'

I know she hates the thought of packing away the last of Nan's things. But maybe it's better if she doesn't help—I can pack a few things quickly, and maybe head out later to a new swimming hole I wanted to try, somewhere to wash away this horrible weekend. I cringe, pushing away thoughts of Gideon and the non-kiss.

Focus.

I collect a few more books, as if to demonstrate I can manage alone. 'Mum, I can pack the books at least. But are you *sure* we can't donate them? The museum could probably send someone up to pick out the ones they want. And I'm sure they'll let you know if they find any more photos and stuff. It seems like a waste to just have everything sitting in our garage.'

I think she's about to relent, but instead she lunges across the coffee table and grabs a copy of a glossy Mills & Boon. 'Is this what you want people to think of your grandmother, Clarissa?!' she says, waving its yellowed pages at me.

I snatch the book out of her hand, flicking to the middle. '*The Baron summons me with a flick of his milky-white wrist, and my core tightens in*—oh god, my eyes. I can't believe she read this. And why does it just fall open to this page?' I hold the book gingerly, realising that not only did my grandmother have erotica, but I seem to be holding one of her favourites.

'Clarissa,' my mother warns, taking the book and throwing it into the fireplace. But I can see a smile tugging at her mouth and, before she relinquished the book, her eyes seemed to glance over the pages for a few seconds longer than necessary.

'See? Easy,' she says. 'Velvet member: trash; surgery books: storage. We'll be done in no time.' Her phone buzzes in her pocket and she twists around, waving at me to be quiet. 'Hi, hi, yes—no but I can. Now? I'm fifteen minutes away.' She murmurs a few more questions and I turn away, running my fingertips over the green leather cover of *The Hand and Its Mechanisms*.

I glance over my shoulder: Mum's standing at the window, looking out at the street as though she can't wait to get out of here. The spine of the book is bloated and cracked, the cover flaking ever so slightly in the corner. The pages are stiff and warped, crackling when I thumb through the illustrations—grotesque anatomy, strange faces, little notes in pencil. The book falls open to the cursive script on the cover page: *First published 1854.* I don't think. I just take the book and tuck it under my jacket. Just the one.

'Ready?'

I jump and turn back to Mum. She looks tired, hair frizzing around her ears. 'Sure,' I say, too brightly.

'Sorry, I have to head to the clinic. Client had a fall.' She pulls a worried face, itching to get on the road.

I follow her out but pause in the doorway. On a hunch, I race back into the house, yelling to Mum over my shoulder.

'Just a minute! I forgot something!' I run into Nan's room, searching the cluttered countertops for something—*there*. Sitting on her vanity, covered in dust, is a tiny jewelled box I'd once made her for Christmas. It's messy and ugly and I never understood why she kept it.

I prise the lid off, heart thundering in my chest.

Inside, there's one small key: barely the size of my thumbnail, rusted and dark.

And I know what it opens.

Theo is sprawled across the couch when I get home, tipping chip crumbs from the packet directly into his mouth.

'You're disgusting,' I say, rushing past with the book inside my jacket and the key crushed in my palm.

'Your face is disgusting,' he says, but it's a little half-hearted, and he doesn't even bother looking up. My heart thumps like I've stolen something. I guess I have, sort of.

When I'm safe in my room, I shove the book deep in a box of clean underwear (sorry, Nan) and tape it shut. I don't know why I took it. I just...wanted to have something. And there was something about the illustrations, so wiry and strange, almost otherworldly. I used to find it so fascinating, all the ways we were wrong before we got it right. I'd trace over the pictures while Nan told me what was wrong with them. Sometimes it was funny ('No, Clarissa, I can't say I would recommend heroin for a mild cough') and sometimes they were sad ('One should generally not lock their daughter outdoors for receiving her first period'). I liked the sound of her voice, the slightly stern lilt of her knowledge. Like she knew everything.

I flick the lock on my door and kneel beside my mattress. The book Mr Scott handed me is still there, one corner hidden by an old T-shirt. I pull it towards me, anticipation lighting my veins. I think back to all my conversations with Nan in her final days but, as hard as I try, I can't find a single clue buried in her words—nothing that might tell me why she left this strange book to me, or why it's locked.

My hands are trembling so badly it takes me two attempts to undo the lock. It's old and rusted and the key gets stuck, but at last I hear the metal click, and the bindings pop open.

I flip it open, curiosity flaring. And then I almost drop it.

The book has been hollowed out—it's a trick cover, like on those quaint wooden boxes sold at craft markets. Except this book isn't empty.

On the inside cover, there's an intricate sketch of a skeleton, its mouth gaping into an open grimace. On the other side, where the pages should be, there are twelve tiny drawers with browning labels stuck above their handles, and a glass bottle that looks like an old-fashioned hurricane jar—it has a fat bottom with a thin spout, and a cork seal.

I nudge one of the drawers: maybe there's something inside that would make more sense. Then I squint at the lettering and snatch my hand away—beside each label, there's a tiny symbol painted in black, so small I almost can't see it. A skull and crossbones.

'Poison,' I whisper. Then I yelp, dropping the book, and it lands with a heavy thud, the drawers and glass jangling. I wipe my hands on my pants, as though they've been contaminated.

It must be a joke. Something I've forgotten, some reference I don't understand. Or maybe it's highly valuable and Nan wanted me to sell it. Yes, that must be it. The will said it was a rare and *valuable* collection. She must have kept this one separate, just in case. A rare collector's item, maybe. Not to be left in the home, where anybody might have stumbled across it.

Except…

Why didn't she just tell me about it? Why didn't I get a clue, a letter, *something* that might help me understand?

I close the cover, buckling it shut and locking it. Then I hide the key inside the lid of an old candle and lie in bed, mind reeling.

I need to get outside. I can't just stay here thinking about the strange book under my bed.

I look around my room and realise that it's Sunday afternoon and I have nothing to do. The books on my shelf have all been read. My phone is quiet. I could go downstairs with Theo and watch a bad movie, but I'm too restless to sit still. I used to fill my weekend with activities: brunch and shopping trips, even if I didn't want to buy anything, circling boutiques with Nina and Willow, looking at clothes we couldn't afford, swatching makeup patches all over our arms. Sometimes I'd go to the library, browsing the new releases, borrowing as many books as my tired old card would let me. I'd swim. Hang out with Mum. Go for drives with Dad.

The house is silent. All of that seems so far away. Untouchable. Like a dream, instead of a memory.

So I grab my bathers and running shoes, and pound down the stairs. I need to clear my head, that's all. Get all the nervous energy out.

'I'm going for a run,' I tell Theo. He doesn't react.

I head towards the pier, but the lifeguard tower seems to taunt me, so I jog to the main street instead. I think of Gideon, the surprise on his face as I pushed him away. God, what is *wrong* with me. I spent the last week fantasising about his lips, and then it actually happened and I couldn't even say anything. I just ran. Like a complete freak. Like a very not-sane person. Like someone who shouldn't expect to keep the new friends she made.

When I finally hit the main road, I'm in a full sprint and my lungs ache, but my muscles are singing with the thrill of the pace. Nothing's open, because it's Sunday and the world seems to stop moving here on Sundays. But I don't want to be in town anyway. I run until I hit the back beach and keep going, further still. It'll take me forever to get home, but I wanted to see it myself.

I run past it at first; it's nothing more than a gap between the shrubs, barely a path at all. I pull my headphones out and step out of my runners, dangling them from my fingertips. And suddenly I'm on the beach, waves crashing, not another soul. There are a few rockpools, and I dip my feet into one, careful not to disturb the little creatures that lurk in the corners. The sun is starting to set. I close my eyes, listening to the sound of the ocean, the leaves of brush rustling in the wind. And I think I understand why this was Nan's favourite spot.

What am I missing, Nan? The wind doesn't answer.

'Didn't expect to see you here.'

I jolt, almost slipping from the ledge. *'Jesus.'*

'Nope, just me,' says Ava, parking her board in the sand.

I place a hand over my heart, waiting for the wild beat to still. 'I didn't even hear you coming.'

'Eh, seemed like you were having a moment. I was gonna give you some space until I realised there's only one way out of here,' she says, tilting her chin towards the narrow path just in front of us. Locals feel very passionately about not stepping on the sand dunes, so I've effectively blocked her in.

'Oh,' I say, moving aside. 'Sorry.'

'Soooo,' she says, drawing the word out several syllables. But she doesn't step around me like I thought she would; she takes her surfboard and digs it tail-first into the sand, lounging against it. 'Wanna talk about last night?'

'I really, really don't. I've had a weird day.'

Ava cocks an eyebrow at me. She looks, somehow, even tinier in a head-to-toe wetsuit. The surfboard is easily twice her height. 'Okay. I won't ask. But you're okay?'

'I'm fine. Confused. But fine. And about last night...it's my fault, don't blame Gideon.'

'Interesting.'

'Interesting how?'

She's grinning at me. 'I thought you didn't wanna talk about it. But if you did want to talk about it, I'd say that *some* people should try and talk to *other* people. I'm not saying that I know anything, but maybe I know some things I shouldn't know. You know?'

I frown, trying to string together everything she just said into some semblance of meaning. 'I really, really don't.'

'Never mind.' She sighs, and nods at the ocean. 'So. You surf?'

'Nope. Tried once. Fell off a lot.'

She fluffs damp hair out of her suit, rising to her feet. 'Well, it's cold as balls in there, but come on.'

'Wait, what? Oh no. No thank you.'

'Come on, you're all mopey. You know where you can't mope? On a surfboard.'

'You know, this really doesn't fit with your whole vintage-goth-music-genius-vibe.'

She rolls her eyes. 'Urgh, I know, it's so off-brand. Why do you think I come all the way out here? Now come on, let's catch a few waves before the sun's down.'

And by the time I trudge home, jogging in the dark, sea-salt hair slicked back against my neck, I feel like maybe, *maybe*, not all hope is lost.

8

I GET TO school early on Monday, parking my bike in the last empty stall and rushing straight to my first class. Although Ava continued to niggle me for details while I repeatedly fell off her surfboard, I couldn't quite bring myself to admit what happened and, in the end, she gave up on both the gossip and the surfing, declaring me to be terrible at both.

The rooms are open already, so I sit at the back of the class and work through some of the homework I didn't do until the bell rings. A few students have already filed in by the time Miles drops into the seat beside me and holds his hand in front of my face.

'Reece, my lady. This hand. Is. Magic.'

I raise an eyebrow at him, both surprised and pleased we're still talking. He doesn't wait for a reply before he continues, 'This hand has touched Connie Davies.'

'Ew, Miles. Too much info.'

'On the *arm*, you little perv. She slipped in mud. I helped her up. We exchanged actual real words. It was magic.'

'I'm very proud of you,' I say, smiling at my bio books. Poor Miles. That girl is gonna break his heart before they ever get together. If they get together. Miles might spontaneously combust before that happens.

'Thank you. Are you feeling better? Ava said you had *lady problems.*'

I hate her. 'Yeah. Sorry. I just…needed to get home.'

'Fair fair, just seriously grab one of us next time. Those kangaroos are feral, they can take you out. Also the whole murdery thing, you know. Small town. No lights. No reception. Et cetera et cetera.'

His genuine concern leaves me feeling remorseful. 'I'm really sorry,' I say.

He looks surprised by the tone of my voice. 'Hey, don't worry, it's cool, we were just worried. Are you sure you're good? Is it the lady stuff or…?'

'I'm fine. I just…' *Kissed Gideon. Ran away. Didn't explain.* 'I went to my nan's house yesterday,' I say, deflecting with another half-truth. 'It was kind of weird.' *Book-full-of-poisons weird.*

'Well, I have something that will make you feel better.' He unzips his bag and presents me with a Tupperware container. It smells like heaven when I take the lid off: sweet honey and warm pastry.

'I love you,' I say, shoving a piece of cake into my mouth.

'Yeah, you're cute but I'd rather be friends.'

'Shut up.'

'Also, you have crumbs in your hair.'

'Never mind, I hate you again.'

He grins, kicking back in his chair. 'Now come on. Osmosis something something mitosis?'

I groan. 'That's not even close.' We end up bickering about the project while Ms Atwood flicks through slides we already covered at my old school, and eventually he relinquishes more cake so long as I promise to do fifty-five per cent of the work, which seems like a good deal at the time.

And somehow, the day doesn't suck.

I end up getting pretty good at avoiding Gideon, so long as I'm early to all my classes and sit at the back in English. He's always late, so he usually ends up having to sit at the front, but maybe he's avoiding me too because he doesn't show up for class on Monday. By Tuesday I've only glimpsed him from across the yard, and at one point I wait in the library for half an hour while he stands by my bike chatting to Theo. I swear Theo's in on it, but I don't say anything because I hate the thought of them talking about it at swim practice. I can just picture the conversation now:

So I kissed your sister and she ran away.

Did you know she looks like a swamp monster in the mornings and she doesn't even floss every day?

Urgh. By Wednesday night I'm exhausted from the sneaking around and I'm too wired to ride straight home after school, so I end up pedalling to Nan's old house. Mum had a key cut for me, so now I can get in whenever I need to. I've brought the hollowed-out book with me, because the thought of having it under my bed creeped me out.

The house is dark and cold, even though the sun is still

out. The trees outside are so overgrown they cover most of the windows, and I shiver in my T-shirt and shorts. Without Mum, the mess seems even more overwhelming. She had more boxes delivered, and bought some extra tape guns and cleaning supplies. Now the space looks more cluttered, everything too squished-together. It makes me sad to think we could have done this while Nan was still here. How many times did I visit her in the nursing home? I never thought to ask if she wanted to come back here. I don't really believe in ghosts or an afterlife, but everything in here reminds me so much of her that I half-expect to turn my head and find her getting comfy on the recliner or putting the kettle to boil. Under the odour of mildew and acrid rust, I smell rose petals and vanilla, the scent of her perfume. There's also something earthy and warm, like her old sweaters that she used to knit from scratch. The tang of Dettol, which she stocked at post-apocalyptic levels.

'Hi, Nan,' I whisper, just in case. 'I'm really sorry—I'm really sorry I wasn't there. And I miss you a lot.' I blink back tears, feeling stupid. There's nothing here. It's just an empty house, like a body without a soul.

I sniff and shake myself out, trying to push back a wave of fresh emotion—grief that threatens to spill over the dam walls and flood everything in sight. There's nothing left to do but start again. So I grab some gloves and a rubbish bag, and start filtering through the mess. I toss a cup with half-drunk tea, empty the bins, rummage through the bathroom cupboards and the pantry. Anything that can't be used again goes in the trash: old frozen bread, her toothbrush, a dried tub of nail polish. With every item I manage to toss, I shed a new tear. By the time I've cleared a proper space in the lounge room, I've succumbed to chest-shattering sobs. It's her hairbrush that breaks me. She used to have beautiful hair, and I'd watch her braid it carefully. But I don't know what to do with the brush. She can't use it again, but someone else could—after all, it's just a brush. I could take it home and shove it in the bathroom drawer. But it seems wrong, because it's not just a brush, it's *her* brush, with little grey hairs and the smell of her shampoo clinging to the bristles. I hold it in my hands, unable to decide whether it should be thrown away forever or saved.

I jump as the back door bangs open, left unlocked from my multiple trips to the bins outside. I try to control my sobs, half-rising to my feet. 'Hello? Mum?'

The figure that steps around the corner isn't Mum at all. My brain can't put the pieces together, and under the confusion there's the thought that Gideon looks unfairly good in his lifeguard uniform and I'm quite certain I have snot on my face. I sniff and try to covertly wipe my eyes on the edge of my shirt.

'What are you doing here?' I say, panic in my voice.

He seems to be making an effort to look anywhere but at me. 'Don't worry, I didn't stalk you. I live in the bungalow at the back, I saw you come in. I thought we should talk—'

I scuff my feet on the carpet, desperate for him to leave before he realises what a mess I am, scrubbing at my tear-stained face. 'We really don't have to talk about it.'

'I just wanted to say sorry, I thought—'

'*Please* can we not talk about it.' My cheeks are burning and I feel like I'm going to cry again, which is stupid, because he's being perfectly nice about it—if a bit tortured and awkward—but somehow that makes me feel worse.

'Okay,' he says hesitantly. 'We won't talk about it ever again.'

I nod.

He takes a breath. 'But I'm really sorry I upset you and I swear I wouldn't have kissed you if I thought you didn't want to,' he says in a rush. Then he smiles, but it's half-strength, no dimples. 'Okay, *now* we never have to talk about it.'

'Thanks,' I say, blushing furiously.

'So, guess you have to clean this place up now, huh? I haven't been in here for a while.'

I blink a few times. 'Wait, you've been in here before?' Also, sorry, backtrack: *he* lives in the bungalow out the back? His family are the tenants in Nan's will?

'Yeah. Maggie was cool. Helped me study a few times for chem. I really liked her,' he says quietly. He runs his hands over the fireplace, now layered in months of dust, then picks up one of her crossword books and smiles. He seems to be mulling over his next words and I wait, arms crossed over my waist, unsure how I feel about this revelation: Gideon knew my grandmother. He calls her Maggie.

'I didn't know she was your grandmother when we met,' he says. 'I didn't mean to…you know, I wasn't hiding it. But there never seemed to be a good time to bring it up, once I realised. But I just wanted to say sorry, because I know you guys were close. She talked about you all the time.'

Something has lodged in my throat. 'She talked about me?'

'Yeah. I used to come over and help out when she needed it. You know, leaky ceiling, big spiders, that kind of thing.' He seems embarrassed, but I can't tell if it's because he admitted to hanging out with my nan or because he kept it from me.

And now I really am crying, tears falling down my cheeks, and I sniff into my sleeve.

'Hey, hey, I'm sorry. Oh fuck, I thought—' He runs a hand through his hair, his forehead furrowed into deep lines.

'S'okay,' I mumble. 'I'm not mad. I'm glad she had someone.'

It's quiet for a while. Gideon has lost the ability to control his hands. They flap uselessly at his side, and the crossword book is now hopelessly crumpled. He waits until my tears have stopped before he speaks again. 'Want me to tell you more?'

I nod, looking around the room and seeing the life of a stranger. How odd to think he knew this part of her when I didn't.

'Okay. She used to make me watch *Downtown Abbey* with her, mostly because it was saved on her DVR and she never figured out how to work it. Then I got kinda into it. I was so bummed when Matthew died.'

I laugh, but it turns into another sob. He hesitates, then crosses the space between us in a few long strides and wraps his arms around me.

'I promise not to kiss you again,' he says. 'You just look really pathetic right now.'

'Thanks,' I say, snotting a little on his T-shirt.

'You're very welcome,' he answers, and another laugh bubbles out of my chest. His chin comes to rest on top of my head, and his arms stay secure around my body. When he talks, I can feel his chest rumble against my cheek.

'Did you know she used to boil eggs in the kettle?'

I grimace. 'We were wondering what the smell was.'

'Mmm. She used to offer me egg sandwiches so much I pretended I was allergic.'

'That's terrible karma,' I say, but I'm smiling.

'I know. Plus, then she started buying Spam for me, and I felt so bad she was wasting her money that I ate it. Do you know what's in Spam?'

'No.'

'Me neither, but it's definitely not meat,' he says and shudders. That gets a proper laugh, and he pulls away in time to see me smile. 'You okay now?'

I'm still clutching the hairbrush. 'Yeah. I just...I don't know what to do with this. It felt wrong to throw it away, but I don't want to look at my dead grandmother's hairbrush every day. And then I started thinking about everything else she left behind, and it sort of snowballed.'

He carefully pries the brush from my fingertips. 'I don't think she'll miss this,' he says gently. 'Maybe you should go grab one thing you want from her room—something better than a brush. I can drop you home after, if you like.'

I shake my head. 'I can't pick. There's so much, it's everywhere and I just...' I can feel the tears welling again, and I wish Gideon would simultaneously disappear and hug me again. He seems to settle on a middle ground, placing an arm around my shoulders and leading me away from the chaos I've created in the lounge room.

'She left me something,' I whisper. 'I mean, she left me a lot, but there's one thing she *really* wanted me to have, and I don't know what to do with it.'

'What was it?'

I bite my lip, weaving for a moment. I don't really know Gideon, not really. But there are too many secrets clamouring for attention, and I need to let one of them slip.

'Maybe I should just show you.' I haul the book out from my backpack, lay it flat on the table, and unlock it with the key stuffed inside my pocket. I open it and, from the inside cover, the skeleton taunts me with its crooked grin. 'I don't know what it is,' I confess. 'The lawyer said she had it locked in their office. She never mentioned it to me—or at least, I don't think she did. I keep going over and over every conversation, and I just don't know what to think.'

Gideon leans close, giving a low whistle. 'This is kind of cool. Do you know what's in the drawers?'

I shake my head, crossing my arms over my torso. I was warm a moment ago, but the chill has crept back in. 'I kinda freaked out and shoved it under my bed.'

He nods and starts tapping on his phone, double-checking the labels stuck to the drawers as he types. Wordlessly, he tips the screen towards me. '*Aconitum*. Wolf's bane?' He starts to read from the search box. 'Extremely poisonous, can be used as a paralytic...' He trails off, looking alarmed.

'What about this one?' I point to a label that says *Atropa belladonna.* I watch him type the words over his shoulder—it comes up with a result for deadly nightshade.

'One of the most toxic naturally occurring plants… causes respiratory problems, hallucinations, delirium and convulsions.' Gideon's face is almost apologetic. 'Reece, maybe you should call it a night. Whatever this is, there must be a good reason. You said she gave it to someone to look after—maybe it's just old and expensive. Or a family heirloom she forgot to mention.'

'Right. I guess so.' Then I frown, noticing the light glinting off something white, something I didn't see before. The glass in the centre has turned sideways—it must have moved when I shoved it in my backpack. And behind it, there's a little semi-circle carved into the wood. Without thinking, I hook my finger into the groove, and pull. The drawers come away from the back cover, like a secret book-shelf revealing the entrance to another room.

'What the hell—'

I stare down at the book. Between the cabinets and the back cover, someone has jammed a series of pages, all hand-written in blue ink.

I know that writing.

I pry it loose, the papers stiff and brittle.

'What does it say?' Gideon asks, his voice close in my ear.

I read aloud, feeling the colour draining from my face. 'They're just names. They're…girls' names.' It looks like the pages have been ripped out of a larger section—the edges are jagged, and the writing on the final page stops mid-sentence. For a moment, I'm sure that there's been some kind of mistake. But then I stop, because Nan's initials are penned in the top corner.

It makes no sense—why would she have this chest? These notes? I flick through, but they're mostly names, and some meaningless dates. I flick to the very last page, the paper barely marked.

Emilia Marco: April '43–

Michelle Nichols: November 1945–July '46

Alba Thornton. February 1946–August '46

Then the list stops abruptly. In a hurried scrawl, Nan has written: *It's all over. Miss Thornton the last. I must leave at once, before they discover the others.*

I shove the paper inside my backpack before Gideon can glimpse it properly. I don't know what to think—everything is coming undone. Maybe yesterday I could have convinced myself this strange chest had nothing to do with my sweet old grandmother. But now…here are her handwritten notes stuffed inside, hidden from everyone except *me*.

'Come on,' Gideon says. 'It will all be here tomorrow— maybe you can ask your parents. Let's just go. I'll even watch *Ghost Hunters* with you.'

But I know I can't ask Mum about this. It seems like *my* secret, for one. Also, she's already too sad.

I decide to leave the book at Nan's house—I end up wrapping it in a towel and hiding it in her old washing machine. I figure no one will be looking there for a while, plus it's fireproof.

Then I sit on Gideon's car bonnet while he locks up; he

knows where everything goes, right down to the spare key under the gnome by the door. I wonder how many times he's done this: closing the curtains, drawing the storm shutters, stopping to double check the hose isn't dripping. I try to think back to whether Nan ever mentioned the boy who cared so much he ate terrible Spam sandwiches and watched TV dramas with her at night. All I remember is the occasional mention of a neighbour who took her bins out and chased the cat in at night. I wonder if that was Gideon, too. I glance at the bungalow, wondering if his mum also helped out. That would make more sense.

'You don't have to drive me home,' I say, when he's done at last. 'I'm sorry, I feel much better now. I can ride.'

He answers by hoisting my bike into the boot. 'Clarissa Blackwell, get your butt into the car.'

I bite my lip to stop myself from smiling, then crawl into the passenger seat. 'Are you really going to watch *Ghost Hunters* with me?' I ask when he slips into the driver's side— he's so tall he doesn't have to do the embarrassing half-jump I needed to get into the seat.

'What's the alternative?'

'How do you feel about zombie movies?'

He makes a face. '*Ghost Hunters* it is.'

'Hey, Gideon?'

'Yeah?'

'Thanks for being so nice about everything.'

'Reece—'

'Really. And I know we're not supposed to talk about it ever again but the other night...' I feel sick as I try to get the words out, stumbling for a moment. 'It wasn't your fault. That's all.'

'Okay. But I'm still sorry. So now we're both sorry and we're both not talking about it, right?'

'Perfect.'

Heya it's Will, leave a message.

'It's me. I should stop calling, I know. But I just wanted to say sorry, in case you're listening. The whole Gideon thing is weird, but now it's nice weird, I guess. I still miss you guys so much, but it's starting to feel...like I can breathe again. Anyway, this is silly. I'm sorry. Bye, Will.'

I end the call, but I don't put the phone down. I think about what I'm about to do for all of three seconds before I type out the text.

Gideon Hawthorn sat on my couch all night and it was not weird at all. So thanks, I guess. Also, please never tell your brother about the thing that you definitely don't know but kinda seems like you know. You know?

I smile as I read it over, and click send. And then I drop the phone so quickly it smacks against the floorboards and the screen shatters.

Because I didn't send the text to Ava, like I meant to.

I sent it to Nina.

9

MILES IS IN a funk on Monday, muttering endlessly about an upcoming piano exam and drumming his fingers across the table in silent scales. This suits me just fine, since I'm not especially focused on Ms Atwood's lecture about immune responses to mutating pathogens. Or something.

I texted Nina. I couldn't sleep last night—I stared at the blank screen in my hand, waiting for something to happen, half-expecting the walls to crumble around me as I fell into an emotional black hole. Trying not to think about The Terrible Thing That Happened. Trying not to think of Nan's cluttered house and the strange book now hidden in her washing machine. Trying not to think, full stop.

In the end I gave up on the notion of sleep, and spent the night staring at the ceiling fan spin until the sun rose and golden-yellow light began to flood the room. I tossed off the blankets and biked to school before anyone else woke up, hiding in the library until first bell.

I glance down at the broken screen, hidden in the pocket

of my jumper. There are no new messages. No nothing.

'Something interesting to share, Reece?'

I jolt in my seat as twenty heads turn towards me simultaneously.

'No. Sorry, Ms Atwood,' I say, tucking the phone away. She eyes me for a moment, and I think maybe she'll confiscate it, but instead she just shakes her head and turns back to the board.

'Dude, you're weird today,' Miles says, nudging my ribs. 'What's up?'

I ignore him, making a show of taking notes from the board, even though I'm hardly concentrating and I'm not sure what the words I'm writing actually say. 'I'm not weird, you're weird.'

'I'm stressed. You're like…*bugging*.'

'I'm just tired.'

'Sure,' he says, sceptically. 'Is this like…about Gideon or something?'

I close my eyes for a second. 'No, Miles. This is not a Gideon thing.'

'But it is a *thing*?'

'I didn't say that.'

'You didn't *not* say that.'

'I just—I'm having a bad day, okay? And I don't want to talk about it.'

He's quiet for a few minutes then lowers his voice, all trace of amusement gone. 'You want some pasteli?'

I hiccup a little half-laugh, half-sob, and he passes me a plastic container under the table. 'Thanks,' I say, grateful for the sugar rush, for the comfort.

'Come on,' he says when the bell finally chimes. He leads me down the corridor, winding effortlessly through the tide of bodies until we get to our next class.

He lets me be quiet, and at lunch he does most of the talking so I don't have to pretend to have something clever to say. Ava gives me a shoulder-nudge and a thin smile, and I think she probably wants to know if I ever followed through on her advice, but that day at the beach feels like a million years ago. So they bicker and I watch, orbiting their little world but never quite touching it. But every time I think I'm lost, one of them grabs my hand or pinches my arm, offers me food or laughs just the right kind of way. I rest my head on Ava's shoulder and she braids my hair without asking, winding it around the crown of my head and down my back. It's strange how easily I slotted into their lives, I think.

Just as I'm starting to wonder if he's skipped another day of school, Gideon arrives and wolfs down a sandwich, dripping wet and smelling of chlorine. 'This season will be the death of me,' he groans, lying along the seat to dry out.

Miles pokes him in the stomach. 'You're such a jock sometimes. Look at these rock-hard abs. Nerd.'

Gideon swats him away. 'Swimming equals scholarship,' he says, his voice tired and flat.

'So does music.'

'My hands aren't that coordinated.'

Miles sniggers and makes a filthy joke that earns him a proper swat on the head, and soon they're leaping over tables and chasing each other with frozen-yoghurt toppings.

Ava sighs. 'They're such children.'

'Yeah, but doesn't it look fun?' I toss a blueberry at her head.

'Oh, it's *on*.'

It's not hard to slip out of the house after dinner—I tell Mum I'm going for a run and she nods, only half-listening as she helps Dad clear the table. Theo seems suspicious when I grab my bike helmet, but he's too tired to rat me out. I guess the swim coach is running the whole team down.

It's dark by the time I get to Nan's house, and my heart sinks a little as I pull into her overgrown driveway. Her windows were never dim like this; they were always filled with bright yellow light and the flickering shadows of her TV. It's stranger still to be greeted by silence inside; I still expect her to be there, calling out my name, kettle on the stove, radio playing all day whether she was listening to it or not.

With the lights on low, I settle into the patch of clear space on the carpet. I pull out my laptop, feeling slightly criminal. This is the reason I didn't tell Mum where I was going.

Dear Reece, we would be delighted to exhibit your grandmother's collection. Mary Blackwell was an immensely respected figure in the medical world, and we expect the exhibition to attract a great deal of attention.

It goes on to include various details, and they've sent me a checklist of items to look for. Even though Mum said no, I think she'll come around to the idea. The truth is, ever since The Terrible Thing That Happened, she can be a little...suffocating. I love her so much, but she also makes me want to jump off the pier again, Bruce be damned. So if I get everything sorted myself, maybe Mum'll realise that it was a good idea after all.

Plus, Nana was kind of amazing. And maybe it's a bit selfish, a convenient way to escape my inheritance, but there's also part of me that wants to share her with the world.

I click back to the main page. The Museum of Medical Oddities is attached to one of the best medical universities back in the city. They have a rotating display of exhibits that's open to the public, but they also use some of the artefacts for teaching. They have everything from an artificial kidney (ineffective) to heroin-laced cough medicine (ineffective *and* addictive), and even slices of someone's brain in one-milli-metre frames (surprisingly useful, apparently).

Most importantly, they have an archive of medical texts, available for everyone to browse in their public library. They can all be borrowed, though some of the rarer editions require a special permission slip, and you can only look at them under a glass dome while wearing latex gloves. Once a year they put on an exhibition of the weirdest and wackiest books, and they want to dedicate this year's event to Nan.

Everything is perfectly laid out. I just have to figure out how to tell my parents.

I glance at the email one more time, but I don't reply. They want me to confirm whether the books will be a bequest or a loan, and although the thought of inheriting all these books makes me want to cry again, I can admit in the quiet comfort of Nan's lounge room that there's a reason I always wanted them. To help people like she did, to have that power lying in my own hands. But it seems like everyone who ever needed my saving couldn't be helped, and now I don't know what I want.

I set the laptop to one side and run through the list they've provided—an antiques-for-dummies, essentially. I flick to the title page of the nearest book. According to the museum, I'm looking for first editions, rare items, spines intact and dust jackets on.

The book I'm holding is called *Accessory Organs*, and apparently some dude once thought you didn't really need *both* lungs. Bummer for his patients. It's not worth anything, because the inside cover says tenth edition and a quick Google search shows a bunch of brand-new listings for more just like it. I toss it on the coffee table, declaring that the start of the 'worthless' pile.

The next one has yellowed pages and a red leather cover, and the inside font is such an elegant cursive that I can hardly make it out. That one comes up for a price worth more than my laptop.

Over the next hour, I sort through a whole stack of books, placing them on the couch (valuable), on the coffee table (worthless) or in the fireplace (Nan's bodice rippers).

If anyone were to go through my search history, they would find something to the effect of:

A Text Book of Practical Histology, cheap reprint.

Modern Trends in Anaesthesia, not old enough to be funny yet.

The Dissector's Guide, gross...possibly interesting?

The Scoundrel Prince and the Midnight Bride, a highly erotic novel that I spend too much time flicking through, trying to find bad sex scenes.

I sigh, disappointed that the scoundrel prince was such a bore in the end, and check my phone for the time. How far do my parents feasibly think I can run in one night?

I set aside the Mills & Boon, and stretch my arms over my head to ease my aching back. My T-shirt is sticking to me, covered in sweat from hefting books around the house, and my fingertips are covered in black filth. I'm about to call it a night when there's a sharp rap at the back door and I shriek, almost toppling over the computer cord. Gideon grins at me through the sliding door.

I roll my eyes so far back I see stars. 'You can come in,' I yell.

He nudges the door open using the spare key, and lets out a low whistle. 'Any particular vendetta against books, or just cleaning in general?'

'Very funny. Here, be useful, carry these for me.' I lug a few hardbacks into his arms, and direct him to the packing boxes on the kitchen bench.

'What *are* these?' he asks, grunting as he sets the books inside and closes the cardboard lid.

'These are books that don't exist on the internet, and I think I might have to go to an *actual* store and speak with an *actual* human to find out if they're worth anything.'

He frowns but tries to smooth it away. 'You're selling everything?'

'No, some museum might want them, back in the city. I can figure out most by myself but it takes ages and these are the ones I gave up on.' I pat the box, then realise too late that my secret visit was meant to be, well, a secret. 'Uh, don't tell Theo. Or my parents. I'll tell them eventually, but it's not really a good...time.'

I look up and realise Gideon is in his lifeguard uniform, salt drying around his hair and ears. Jeez, I think, he never stops. I wave a hand at him and his little bungalow out the back, light warm and beckoning in the dark. 'Sorry, you're probably starving. Never mind, it's stupid.'

'I'm always starving,' he says, 'and I don't think it's stupid. For what it's worth.'

'Thanks,' I murmur. I have the urge to shove my hands inside his shirt, now that I know how glorious that feels, but the memory of him kissing me still makes me cringe. Although, technically, it's the memory of running away that makes me cringe. The kiss was pretty great.

'I know the owner at that old second-hand bookstore you hate so much,' he says. 'He's a family friend. I could introduce you if you like. He might be able to help you get some of this stuff valued.'

'Really?'

'Sure. Plus, all this stuff is never gonna fit on your bike. I can drive you over.'

I narrow my eyes at him. 'And all this out of the kind-ness of your heart?'

He grins, and I sense a major *but* coming. 'Now that you mention it, we are short a girl on the swim team.

Monica broke her arm last week. She's out for the rest of the season.'

'Why do you even need me?' I groan. 'There are other girls who can swim. It's not that hard. Arm-kick-arm-kick-don't-drown.'

'Because we don't need someone who can swim, we need someone who can *win*.'

I throw up my arms. 'Will it really be the end of the world if you don't make the state race?'

'It's the only way to get a sports scholarship,' he says quietly, turning away to flick through one of the books tossed on the table. It's the second time he's mentioned it, I realise.

'Wait, you want to be a professional swimmer?'

He looks genuinely pained by the idea. 'I really, really don't. It's just a means to an end—easier to board in the city, with a scholarship.'

'I'll...think about it,' I say.

'Thanks.' He says it as though that was more than he expected. 'Any update on the *you-know-what*?'

I cringe. 'I have decided to ignore it until it goes away.'

'Good plan,' he says. 'Come on. I gotta run inside quickly, then I'll drop you back.'

I nod and wait for him to jog up to the house. I don't have the heart to tell him what else I discovered: while I was sifting through the piles of junk, I found an old newspaper wedged between the TV guides and old magazines. I didn't think it was strange until I noticed the headline:

Vanished: search continues for local girl Emilia Marco. And the year, stamped in the corner: 1943.

She's one of Nan's mystery girls.

And she's nowhere to be found.

10

IN THE END, it's Theo who wears me down. He mopes around the house for the next week, mood turning sour. 'It's bullshit,' he raves over breakfast one morning. 'They can't cancel the whole team just because we're *one* girl short.'

So I trudge into the pool that Friday, in the pre-dawn quiet, and ask the coach if I can try out for the spot. No one else bothers to show up—it's the last day of training before the state board forces the team to forfeit.

I stand on the diving board, praying my muscles still work the way they used to because my little jerk brother deserves to have something decent in his life since it's sort of my fault we got uprooted and ended up living here.

And maybe looking at my old swimsuit made me a little nostalgic.

So that's how I end up on the swimming team, as I explain to Miles and Ava on Saturday night, my body aching and my arms like jelly. My muscles still work, it turns out, but I've paid a price for all those months out of the water.

'I can't believe you joined the team,' Miles says in disgust, for the millionth time. 'You're like, twenty per cent less cool now. Who even does organised sports? Voluntarily?' He tosses popcorn at my head.

I shrug, trying to stretch my cramping feet. *Everything* hurts. Especially after I spent the morning training at the local rec centre, trying to make up for lost time. One ear was still clogged with water. 'I needed a hobby,' I say, only half-convincing myself.

'You could have taken up an instrument,' says Ava, who is similarly disgusted. She's wearing about one solid inch of eyeliner and a T-shirt that says *Witch Please*, so her glare is particularly effective.

'I can't play an instrument.'

'You could play percussion,' says Miles. 'Any idiot can whack a tambourine.'

'Miles, don't be *rude*.'

'Yeah, yeah, your precious Sally, I know.' They bicker about whether Miles could actually play the drums if he set his mind to it, while I wait for a lapse in conversation to ask the question I've been hanging on to all night.

'So where is Gideon, by the way?' I ask, trying to be subtle, but Ava rolls her eyes at me behind her cushion. I texted him to invite him over, and all he replied with was *wish I could* and a sad-face emoji.

'He had stuff on,' says Miles.

'Stuff?'

'Yeah. Stuff. Responsibilities and whatnot.'

I glance at Ava but she doesn't shed any light either. 'This movie is creepy as hell,' she says, ducking behind her pillow at a zombie jump-scare.

'Chickenshit!' calls Theo from somewhere above us. He's been suspiciously quiet till now, in his room with Billy Martin and a video game that involves shooting everything in sight.

'Listen here, you little dweeb!' Miles thunders up the stairs, armed with his box of popcorn and another pillow.

I pause the movie as Theo screeches something about his hair, which is followed by the unmistakable sound of some kind of wrestling.

'So. Gideon.' Ava wriggles her eyebrows suggestively.

'I feel like all your sentences start like this.'

She gives me a serene smile. 'Well, if you would *tell* me things, I wouldn't have to *ask*.'

'There's nothing to tell. We've barely talked all week, I don't know what's going on. He's late to class, he didn't show up at swim practice on Friday—I mean, not that anyone else did either. I don't know, should I be worried?'

'Maybe he's just busy? Although…now you mention it, he did seem kinda off the other night. He came over to see Miles and they just left for, like, two hours.'

'Weird,' I say. 'Maybe he has a secret girlfriend.'

She nudges me in the ribs. 'Jealous?'

'No. Gideon can date whoever he wants. As previously established, I do not care. At all.'

'Uh huh. Well, this is only my advice, but you could try *talking* to him. You do know where he lives. Seems like it wouldn't be hard to find a reason to go over there. Ask for a cup of sugar. Get help killing a spider. A towering muscle-man to ogle for your viewing pleasure—'

She stops there because I whack her in the face with one of Mum's ornamental pillows. 'I hate you,' I say. 'You're too rational.'

'It is my greatest flaw.'

'Your greatest flaw is hating horror movies.'

She groans, sinking further into the couch as I press play. I'm relieved I've managed to change the topic. 'I hate it,' Ava moans. 'Why isn't she wearing shoes? Why don't they just text each on their phones? And why is she running outside? That's where the zombies are.'

'Because the zombie alligator is *inside* the house.'

'Of course it is.'

'And she has to get to the underground safe haven.'

'Oh my god.'

I give her a mock punch in the arm. 'It's a classic!'

She dumps more popcorn on my head. 'This is why you don't know how to talk to boys.'

'*You* don't know how to talk to boys.'

'I don't *want* to talk to boys. I only talk to Gideon because he's...well, actually, because he's always with Miles, but still. I like Gid. He's not a complete moron.'

'Yes he is,' says Miles, leaping over the back of the couch. 'Why are we talking about Gideon? I swear, Ava, if you have a crush on him, I will vomit in my mouth, right here.'

She pretends to gag in response. 'Gross, no thank you.'

He looks dubious, but settles back into the couch. 'Yo, Reece's Pieces, you good lately?'

I smile, eyes on the zombie apocalypse as Ava rewinds the bit he just missed. 'Yeah, Miles. I'm good.'

I see him nod from the corner of my eye, and give him a friendly kick.

Mum and Dad get home from date night just as the movie ends, and they make more noise than strictly necessary before unlocking the door.

'Offspring! We are home!' calls Dad. He pokes his head in the door, easing it open while Mum tries to peer around him. When he catches sight of us all sprawled on the couch he flings the door wide, letting Mum through.

'It's okay, I don't know enough people to throw a rave,' I say from my chocolate-popcorn-induced coma on the couch.

'I don't *like* enough people to throw a rave,' says Ava, scrolling through the Netflix grid.

Mum gives Dad a smile, seemingly content that I have made at least two very normal friends. 'Well, you're welcome anytime,' she says, smoothing down her hair. 'It was very nice to meet you both.' Dad waves goodnight, calling out to Theo and Billy as my parents thump their way upstairs.

'Come on, dweeb. Mum's nearly here.' Miles disentangles himself from a mountain of cushions and throw rugs, shaking out his lanky frame. He gives me a bone-crushing hug, and Ava squeezes me tight too. Miles is halfway to the front door when he turns around. 'Hey, by the way, I saw that picture of your friends back home. They look really cool, you should invite them down sometime.'

I stumble back a step, mouth dropping open in shock.

'Um, yeah, maybe. It's…it's a really long drive though. I don't know.'

Ava frowns, looking between me and Miles. I shake my head just a little and she tugs on Miles's sleeve. 'Hey, Mum's here, let's go.'

He waves at me as she pulls him towards the car. 'Yeah, yeah, I'm coming,' he grumbles, swatting at her hands.

I wait until they're down the driveway before I close the door, wondering how long I can keep track of all my lies.

In theory, talking to Gideon should be simple. His door is about five metres away. And I know he's home, because his car is in the driveway.

I tell myself I had to pass by anyway. I was going to the Beach Bean. Maybe he'd want to come? We could sunbake on the foreshore. Right. That's all. A friendly house call. Plus, he doesn't know I've joined the swim team. That's exciting news, right?

I pivot away from the door, marching back to Nan's house and dropping my head between my legs. The heat isn't helping. It's been hot and muggy all week, and I'm sweating from the short bike ride here, even though I'm only wearing a singlet and shorts. My hair has frizzed to impossible new heights, and seems permanently stuck to the back of my neck. I run my fingers through the tangled curls, combing them down into a semi-presentable nest.

I take another deep breath and make my way back up to his front door, weaving through the overgrown palms and stepping carefully on the splintered wooden deck. The bungalow used to be Nan's office, before I was born. She built it when she first moved down here—she would always tell people she was semi-retired, though I never remember her *actually* resting.

I've been inside a few times, but it must have been updated for people to live in full-time. In my childhood it was small but neat, a long stretched-out rectangle with each room in a row. Nan installed a handrail on the porch for her elderly patients and a ramp on one side for wheelchairs.

My watch says 9.30 a.m., which I guess is a little early for house calls, but I was too nervous to sleep or stay in bed. Maybe I should come back…but no, if I leave, I'll never get up the courage to return. I thump my fist on the door more heavily than I mean to.

It's quiet: maybe no one is home after all. But then I hear a woman's voice call out and some mumbling, and Gideon opens the door.

'What are you doing here?' He seems more alarmed than pleased to see me. He's wearing boxer shorts and his hair is sticking up on one side. I try to keep my eyes from bugging out of my head, because he's also not wearing a shirt and the view is quite delightful.

'I'm sorry,' I stammer, trying to remember why I'm on Gideon's front step. 'I just came to make sure everything was okay. But I should have texted first. Because you were sleeping. Because it's Sunday. And probably your only day off. Um. I'll go. Sorry. Again.' I spin on one heel, mortified, and start marching down the driveway.

'Wait! Wait—ow, damn.'

I turn and find him hopping in my direction. 'Reece, hang on. I need shoes. I need coffee. Oh god, what time is it?' He looks around hopelessly, his eyes only half open and his cheeks marked with pillow creases.

'Nine-thirty. Sorry, it's too early, I should have waited.'

He looks physically pained by this news. 'It's fine, just... give me a sec.'

'Do you want me to wait inside?' I take a step towards him but he throws up his hands.

'No! I mean, no, it's messy right now. Just...I'll meet you at Mary's. Give me five minutes.'

He closes the door before I can say anything, and I wish I'd thought to sneak a peek behind him while I had the chance. With nothing else to do, I make my way back to Nan's, opening all the windows and pumping her tiny air conditioner to max speed. I thumb through ten-year-old magazines on the dining-room table, which is the only clean surface—I had to wipe it down last week in order to eat my two bags of takeaway.

When he returns, his hair is curling with specks of water around his eyes, and he's wearing shorts and an old band T-shirt. 'So. What's up? At nine-thirty. On a Sunday.'

'Oh. I just...wanted to check on you, actually. You haven't been around much this week, and you missed swim practice, plus I know the whole book thing was weird—I mean, I'm about ninety per cent sure my sweet old grandmother never murdered anyone with a secret poison chest, but still—and you didn't come to movie night, so I thought maybe something was wrong, and Ava said, um, nothing, she didn't say anything, but if you're avoiding me for some reason—'

His rueful, lopsided smile shows off one of his dimples. 'I wasn't avoiding you, Reece. I just had some family stuff on.'

'Oh. So you were just…'

'Late and tired.'

'Oh.'

'How'd you know I missed swim practice?'

I feel my cheeks turning red. 'I sort of…joined the team.'

His smile broadens into a tired grin. 'Damn, sorry I missed it. Thanks, Reece, that's pretty cool of you.'

'I didn't do it for you,' I say in a rush. 'Theo was being extra-annoying about it, so…'

'I know. I'm still really glad you did.' It's then I realise how dull his blue eyes seem, how his shoulders are sagging. He's not bouncing on his feet like usual, desperate to be moving all the time. I reach out a hand then stop myself. 'Hey, Gid, are you really okay?'

He draws himself up, and it's like watching a puppet being brought to life—as though someone's tugged on strings to yank his cheeks wide and his spine straight. 'Yeah. It's just been a long week.'

'Do you wanna do something today?' The words fall out of my mouth unbidden. I meant to say *Let's go to the Beach Bean to see Miles and Ava.*

He looks surprised for a second, then genuinely pleased. 'Yeah. Yeah, sure. Actually, I have an idea. Wait right here.'

He bounds out of the house, leaving me with enough time to send Ava a frantic *SOS hanging out with Gideon what does he like???* text message, to which she unhelpfully replies with a series of suggestive emojis and *I don't know, Miles, chicken, swimming?* I stuff my phone into my pocket just as Gideon's car slides down the driveway.

I lock eyes with a picture of my nan shaking hands with a former prime minister. 'Help me out here,' I whisper. 'I need some guidance.' She just stares cheerily out of the frame, and I end up getting into Gideon's car with absolutely no divine intervention.

'Are you wearing bathers under that?' he asks from the driver's seat.

I groan and rest my head on the dashboard. 'Yes, but no more laps, I beg you. Everything hurts.'

He laughs, donning a pair of sunglasses and pulling out into the street. 'No laps, promise.'

At first I think he's just going to take me to the back beach for some lazy paddling, but he heads out of town and we blow right past the *Welcome to sunny Hamilton!* sign.

'Uhhh, where are you taking me? Should I be concerned?'

'If I was going to kidnap you and leave your body in a ditch, I wouldn't have told my mum I'd be home for dinner.'

'I think a whole day is plenty of time to dispose of a body, but I suppose that's comforting.'

I like how Gideon drives. He keeps his eyes on the road and both hands on the wheel. His fingertips are smudged with black again, curled around the steering grip at perfect ten-and-two positions. I squint, trying to focus on the blotches instead of giving in to the urge to admire the sun on his face and the wind whipping through his hair.

'Take my phone,' he says, and tilts his chin towards the AUX cord. 'You can pick the music.'

I scroll through his playlist and pick a song called 'Bury Me with Dead Roses'.

'Real morbid,' he says, a touch of a sardonic smile on his lips.

I give him an angelic flutter of my eyelashes, then sink into the seat to prop my feet on the open window—I'm short enough that I don't knee myself in the chin.

Gideon's playlist is not what I expected; it's Brit bands and vintage rock and folk music. I picked him for a generic techno-pop kinda person, and when I tell him this he screws up his nose.

'No, thank you. Also, I feel judged.'

'It's the whole...thing,' I say, waving a hand over his general presence.

'*Thing*?'

'You know. Tall. Blonde. Sports star. You've got to have some flaws, and I figured that flaw was Skrillex or something.'

He complains some more but when I pick a song I recognise from my own collection he starts singing along. My eyebrows shoot up—Gideon can actually, quite decently, sing. His voice is throaty and rich, and I want to tell him this but I'm worried he'll get self-conscious and stop.

He glances over when I've been silent for a while and his cheeks turn pink. 'Uh, don't tell anyone.'

'Men,' I say, with an eye-roll. I pick a new song I think will suit his voice and poke him in the ribs. 'Go on. I know you want to.'

'Only if you join in.'

'Oh no. I'm tone deaf. Please no.'

'Everyone can sing,' he insists.

'Not *well*.'

'Come on. One chorus. Or I'll leave you out here.'

'You wouldn't!'

He slows the car down until we're crawling along the shoulder, and I begrudgingly screech out a couple of bars.

'Oh my god,' he says. 'Get out. That was terrible.'

'I told you!'

He tries to look stern, but he bites his lip to keep from smiling. 'Clarissa, please get out of the car.'

I'm sure he's joking. Wherever we are, there's no one around and we're surrounded by sweeping gum trees that blot out the sky. 'You're not serious.' The car has completely stopped now.

'Deadly,' he says, leaning over me to open the passenger-side door.

'Gideon!'

He laughs. 'We're getting out because we're here,' he says, then turns the car off and grabs a few towels from the boot.

I'm slightly concerned that maybe he is a psychopathic killer after all, but I have full reception so we can't be that far out of town—we drove for only thirty minutes or so. He calls out my name and starts walking into the tree line, and I'm glad I wore tennis shoes because the ground is full of spiky underbrush and uneven bark.

'Are you going to tell me where we're going?' I ask, my breath ragged after about five minutes of uphill trekking.

'Nope.'

'Are we worried about snakes at all?'

'Eh, they're more scared of us.'

'That's really not helpful.'

After a while we hit a proper trail, and there's an old wooden sign that points towards something called the Cave Gardens. There's not a single other person out here.

'How did you find this place?' I ask. He must've known the trail was here—he wouldn't have been able to find it from where we parked, since it wasn't visible from the road or marked in any way. In fact, it seems like nobody has used the trail lately—it's overgrown with weeds, and the signs are half-broken and mostly illegible.

He's quiet for so long that I think he won't answer. 'My parents used to hike. They brought me here when I was little. It used to be a popular trail, but the rangers opened a newer path a few years ago that leads up the mountain. There's a viewing platform people seem pretty obsessed with, but I like this one still.'

'When you say your parents...' I ask, desperate to pry without seeming like I'm snooping. 'I don't think I've heard you mention your dad before.'

'He took off a few years ago. It's just me and Mum now.'

He doesn't offer any further explanation and I don't ask.

We reach a fallen tree, its roots spiralling into the air, and he waits for me to clamber up, then gets ready to catch me on the way down. It reminds me a lot of the paddock, when I stood up on the stump with his hands around my waist. But now he seems careful to let me go as soon as my feet touch the ground, and his eyes seem to skim over my lips for only the barest second.

And then I'm staring at the bluest water I've seen in my life, and the opening of a cave that glitters with dripping wax spirals.

'Oh my god,' I whisper. 'What is this?'

Gideon is smiling down at me, pleased I'm enjoying his surprise.

'This is the old mining cave,' he says. 'They filled in the trenches with water when there was nothing left to find. Don't try diving to the bottom, you'll run out of air.'

I walk to the edge and dip my feet into the water. It's warm on the surface but I have no doubt the centre of the lake will be ice-cold. 'Can we swim in it?'

He's already shrugging his shirt off. 'Such a city girl,' he jokes. 'Of course you can.'

He starts wading in, but I don't know if I'm game yet. 'Are you sure? What about alligators?'

'Alligators are American,' he says, easing back until he's floating.

'What about zombie alligators?'

'Huh?'

'Never mind,' I mutter. Why did I make Ava and Miles watch that movie? 'Crocodiles?'

'The nearest river is five kilometres away. The mine doesn't connect to anything else.'

'So...'

'So that is a very long way for a crocodile to walk.'

'Okay,' I say, eyeing the water suspiciously.

He's standing waist-deep, arms crossed over his chest. 'Want me to come get you?'

I start backing away. 'No, thank you.'

He laughs again and dive-bombs a little further out. He turns to me, treading water. 'Come on, Reece! We drove all this way.'

'Okay,' I say, mostly to myself. 'Okay.' I start getting undressed, then realise he's still watching me. It shouldn't be weird, because I've spent half my life swimming laps with strangers and friends, but now my bikini suddenly feels very much like underwear and I hesitate for an awkwardly long moment, shorts half-off one leg. As if on cue, Gideon dunks himself under the surface, giving me time to finish taking off my clothes and edge into the water. It's warmer than at the beach, but I can also feel a cool pull at my feet. I've seen photos of filled-in mines, but I've never swum in one. They usually have a series of shelves, getting drastically deeper at each step, and the centre of the lake can be hundreds of metres deep, depending on how old the land is. Gideon seems to be skirting the edges, never drifting more than a few metres from me. I take a breath and dive out, and the rush hits me all at once. I've flung myself out so far my feet dangle over the edge, and it's thrilling and terrifying to see nothing below my toes.

'This is…magic,' I say, slicking my hair back.

He floats towards me, eyes on the sky. 'This week kinda sucked,' he says, after a while, and blows out a long sigh. 'I'm glad you knocked on my door this morning.'

I paddle closer, wanting to run my hands through his

hair. It's drifting in a golden halo around his head, his curls stretched out in wild tendrils. Instead I just brush his shoulder. 'Hey. Is everything really okay?'

He shakes his head, and I don't know if that means he's not okay or he doesn't want to talk about it. 'I just don't want to think about it today. Is that all right?'

'Of course,' I say. I want to tell him all the things I try not to think about. The list of lies I keep. But instead I reach out and hold his hand, tugging him through the water, which he lets me do for a while, until I sprinkle water on his face and a proper splash-off ensues. We paddle together to the cave mouth after Gideon swears a thousand times that there are no water snakes and promises to save me if I get sucked into a whirlpool. We skirt the long way round, and Gideon says he's only swum through the centre a few times—once when he was young and stupid, and again when there were enough friends here to notice if someone disappeared.

By the time we reach the cave mouth my arms are tired and I end up drifting as slowly as possible. But it's beautiful inside: stalactites drip from the ceiling, shimmering like pearl and moonstone, bouncing soft, waxy light onto the lake's surface. The water glitters with white and purple and turquoise, like a kaleidoscope.

When we're both shaking with cold, we swim back to shore and wrap ourselves in sun-warmed towels. Gideon is jumping up and down and my teeth are chattering. The water was freezing under the shade of the cave, and even the blistering heat can't seem to banish the bone-deep chill we've caught.

He laughs as I shudder, and wraps his arms around my body. My face is pressed into his towel, and I close my eyes as I accept I'm perfectly happy to stay here, even if it blurs the boundaries of our friendship.

'Thank you,' I hear him say, chest rumbling under my ear.

'For what?'

'Joining the team.'

'You said that already.'

'I know. I just want you to know I really mean it. I don't even think you realise...'

'You don't have to tell me. It's fine. And I wanted to.'

He sighs, pulling me closer and letting his chin rest on top of my head. 'I can't afford to leave,' he says. 'Unless I have a scholarship, I'll be stuck here. Even then.' He scrubs a hand over his face. 'Maybe I should just get a job, after school. Save some money. I don't know anymore. I don't know what I'm doing.'

'Me neither,' I tell him. 'I wanted to be a doctor. I wanted to be just like my nan. And it feels like it's all gone now. That was kind of my life plan—I never thought I'd need a back-up.'

'At least you *had* a life plan. Mine was just getting the hell out of here.'

'Was?'

He sighs again. 'Things are getting complicated.'

He's still holding me close, and I let him because I think it's easier for him to talk to me like this. 'What would you do if you could do anything you wanted?' I ask.

He's quiet for too long, and I pull back to find him blushing. 'It's stupid,' he says.

'I'm positive that nothing you want is stupid.'

'Even Miles doesn't know.'

'I cross my heart, I'll never tell. Besides, I owe you a secret. You kept mine,' I say, reminding him of the day on the pier.

He steps away and lays out his towel so he can sit. 'So, sometimes I draw...' he says, eyes flicking up to watch my reaction. I'm already beaming. 'And I made this comic, and I posted it online, and now people follow it...'

I squeal and start clapping my hands. 'Which one, which one!'

His shock is palpable. 'You don't—I didn't think—'

'If you're about to say you didn't think I read comics because I'm a girl, I will summon the nearest crocodile from five kilometres away to nibble your toes off.'

'No, I just...didn't think you'd be excited.' He starts to smile, and then lies back. 'I've never told anyone. I was just hoping I could squeeze in some art credits without anyone noticing too much.'

'Gideon, you should! Can I read it? Please? *Please*?'

'Absolutely not.'

'You say that now, but I'll wear you down. My womanly wiles are very persuasive.'

He raises an eyebrow. 'You're very welcome to try your wiles on me,' he says, and then I throw a gumnut at him. We lie in the sun for a while, both quiet for different reasons, but the nice kind of quiet. He seems happier than this morning, even when he drags himself to his feet and says we should start heading back.

I'm so tired I fall asleep in the passenger seat halfway home. I wake up to Gideon whispering my name and touching my shoulder, which I mistake for a dream and nearly say *Why is your shirt on.*

'Thanks,' I mumble instead.

'You snore,' he says cheerfully.

'I do not,' I say. 'You can ask Mr Snuggles.'

He just smiles. 'Bye, Reece.'

'Bye, Gideon. Gonna go stalk you online.' I jump out of the car before he can say anything else.

I spend the rest of the night surfing DeviantArt and Tumblr, and texting him cool comics that I think he could have drawn. He doesn't answer for ages, and when he does it's just one message: a drawing of me, hair out, mouth wide and laughing, holding his phone in my hand with my feet on the dash. A series of broken music notes surround my head. And although it's incredible how he's captured this moment so perfectly, I'm also feeling a bit sick.

The non-crush has developed to full-blown infatuation. And I think I'm in trouble.

11

MUM IS BECOMING increasingly suspicious of my absences, although I think she's kind of *hoping* I'm having a salacious affair with a boy. Anything would be better than the previous months, which I've spent cooped up in my room with nothing to do but read and surf the internet.

Still, she reminds me to be home at a decent hour whenever I make up an excuse to get out of the house for a few hours—going for a run, studying with Miles, surfing with Ava, chemistry club (I panicked. Our school doesn't technically have a chemistry club, but now we meet every Wednesday night). Plus, I actually would hang out with Miles and Ava, but they're both preparing for their piano exams with a ferocity approaching fanaticism. They've barely spoken to anyone all week, except to invite me to their concert next Saturday.

Either way, when I remind her it's Wednesday and slip out the back door, all she does is scoff and remind me to pack some snacks.

I run down the block and around the street corner. Gideon has the car idling, and I jump into the passenger seat.

'You know, it would have made a lot more sense to just tell your mum we were working on a group project together. This all feels very cloak and dagger, considering there is zero delinquent behaviour going on.'

'Shut up and drive the getaway car.'

'Yes, ma'am.'

Being with him gives me a familiar flutter. Ever since the day at the lake, something's changed and we seem to be edging our way around a strange new friendship. Sometimes I think I catch him staring at me, but then he's suddenly occupied by his English book or frozen yoghurt. And other times I think I need a cold shower to deflate my enormous ego. Either way, we've been spending most evenings together, sifting through the books and marking new piles to be checked, googled or appraised. He even took some for me to the second-hand bookshop and came back with handwritten notes on the titles I couldn't find online. One of them makes me choke— it's worth twice as much as my laptop.

Some nights he doesn't stay long, and some nights he waits until I'm almost falling asleep and drives me home. It's nice to have the company, and it makes the process quicker.

'Oh look at this one,' he says, both delighted and disgusted by a book called *The Human Corpse*. 'There are...so many pictures.' I glance up and wince as he proudly shows off a flayed human chest.

'Gross. Also, it's translated. The original is French.' I point to the coffee table, and he sighs and places the book amid the other worthless copies. The museum has been emailing me regularly to confirm which books they'll take, and I'm starting to get a sense of what's interesting, old or weird enough for them to select for an exhibit.

'You spend too much time here.'

'I was short on hobbies.'

'How about *The Encyclopedia of Witchcraft and Demonology*?' he asks. '"The witches gathered by the sound of a cornucopia, blown by the devil himself, and took to dancing, mayhem and other liberties." Oh, look, here's a potion that makes a child not look like their true father. It's indexed under "Adultery".'

I screw up my nose. 'I really hope Nan wasn't running around a field taking "other liberties".'

He holds up a particularly obscene sketch. 'What about anointing oneself with kittens, toads and sage oil to summon Beelzebub?'

'Sounds like a good Saturday night. Put it in the maybe pile.'

He ignores me and thumbs through some more pages. 'Do we know any "lustful rank girls and young widows"? I wanna see if they'll cure me of life-threatening melancholia and save my hairline.'

'Your hair is fine. That would be a waste of a lustful rank girl.'

'True,' he says, fluffing out his curls. He reaches across my legs to place the book on the couch, then steals the laptop to make note of the title. 'My brain hurts. I feel like I should be doing homework, but this is weirdly fun.'

I shuffle some of the loose papers I was sorting through—receipts, a ten-year-old prescription for medicated eye drops, and an old birthday card from Mum. I add the card to the stash inside my bag. I still haven't told Gideon about the missing girl, Emilia, though I've been checking the house for more clues. Maybe it's a coincidence? Maybe they were friends? It's like an equation that doesn't balance: poison books + missing girls ≠ Nana Blackwell.

I turn my attention back to Gideon. 'What did you ever do for fun before I came to town?' It's a rhetorical question, but he thinks about it for a minute.

'Well, there was cow-tipping, of course,' he jokes. 'Listening to Miles play piano. Swimming. Hanging out with my mum—don't laugh, she's cool. And I guess the odd date. Did you know Connie Davies once vomited on my nicest shoes?'

'I did not,' I reply, studiously refusing to look up at the word *date* and choosing something else to focus on. 'So do I ever get to meet your mum?'

Gideon fumbles with a book, swearing as it slips out of his grasp and lands on his shoe. 'Um, maybe.'

I peek over the edge of my book, and find him looking everywhere but at me. Huh. I hadn't really meant anything by it, but he's definitely avoiding the question.

'She's just—I mean—uh, strict,' he continues. 'About girls. Inside.'

'Oh. Right.'

'Yeah. Sorry.'

'So what does she do?' I ask, aiming for casual, but my

voice squeaks a little.

'She's...sort of retired, I guess. It's complicated. After my dad left...'

Now I feel like a jerk. 'No, I'm sorry I asked. Forget I mentioned it.'

'Don't worry about it. Hey, actually, I'm really tired. Do you mind if I drop you home now?'

'Sure.' I brush the dust off my knees and shorts as I stand, and Gideon grabs one of the archive boxes and hauls it out to the car.

'I thought maybe we could swing by the second-hand bookshop together this weekend,' he says. His voice sounds strange but I can't quite pick why. 'Before Miles and Ava's concert? We could stop for dinner on the way.'

I cock my head to one side.

'It's not a date,' he clarifies. 'Just some platonic meal-sharing in formalwear.'

A smile spreads across my face before I can stop it. 'That sounds great.'

He puts the box in the boot then doubles back to the mailbox. 'Oh hey, wait, I almost forgot. This came for you today—it was in Maggie's letterbox.' He passes me a thick embossed envelope with my name on the front. There's only a generic PO Box address on the return label.

'I wasn't sure if it was important or something,' he adds.

I shove the letter in my pocket. 'It's probably just junk mail.'

He opens the passenger door and gives me a hand into the cab, and he sings me a fairly decent cover of a Patti Smith song on the way home. It's not until I'm getting into the shower later that night I remember the letter, ripping it open as the bathroom fills with steam.

Dear Clarissa Blackwell, We are delighted to invite you to the opening night of The Museum of Medical Oddities' summer exhibition debut, Marvels and Malaise: The Private Collection of Mary Blackwell. Please confirm your attendance at the address below.

I flick the card over, colour draining from my face. There must have been some mistake. I only said I'd donate the books. I never said when, or thought they'd start to invite people to the exhibition.

'Shit.'

Theo bangs on the door. 'What's taking so long? Grown a demon tail yet?'

'I wish,' I whisper. The date is exactly four months from today. I have four months to tell my parents I'm giving away the only thing my grandmother left to me.

12

I AM WILDLY unprepared for the following week. I forget my English assessment, bungle a biology proposal and nearly singe Connie's hair off in chemistry. On Monday I forget my goggles, on Tuesday I forget my swimming cap, and this morning I somehow managed to leave the house without any pants, and found myself immensely grateful that we live in a seaside town where it's somewhat acceptable to frantically pedal home in my dripping wet bathers.

In retrospect, joining the swim team in my final year of high school—in the final months, no less—was perhaps a little ambitious.

By Friday afternoon I'm tired and grumpy and can barely follow Miles as he continues to be outraged at my lack of classical-music knowledge.

'How do you not know it? You know it, trust me.'

'Miles, please stop humming Beethoven's *Moonlight Sonata*,' I mumble, sure that I'll be able to fall asleep if only everyone would be quiet for just one minute. Gideon let me steal his usual spot, and I'm curled up on the bench with my feet in his lap.

'You know? It's like—ow!'

I swat him on the shoulder, cutting off another attempt to hum the entire piece. 'Miles. I believe you.'

'Yeesh. Gideon. Come on. You know it.'

Gideon barely looks up from his book. 'I know it because I've heard you play it seven hundred times.'

I sigh, resigning myself to the fact that I won't be napping anytime soon. 'Don't you have any other interests?'

'Sure,' Miles answers, bouncing on his feet. 'Eating. Superhero movies. Video games. *Swamp People*—underrated television gold. But I'm not about to be assessed on any of these things, and thus they are momentarily banned from occupying precious space in my brain.'

'Who says "and thus"?' Ava has her head on the table, and until now I thought she might have actually managed to fall asleep.

'Shut up, dweeber.'

'Miles. Please stop talking. For. One. Goddamn. Minute.'

They've been feral all week. Ava tried explaining something about them being in the same category even though she's younger, but I'm still not entirely sure why it matters.

I reach out and grab her hand, giving it a quick squeeze. 'You guys are gonna do great tomorrow,' I say. 'Right, Gideon?'

'You guys are gonna do great,' he mimics. 'Because otherwise Miles will have an aneurysm. And also, he's a musical prodigy.'

'Thanks, man.'

'You're welcome, bud.' They perform a complicated fist bump that results in a back-slapping man hug, though I think they both hold on to each other longer than usual.

Miles peels himself away from the tables just before the bell. 'I gotta go beg Mr Carrol for an extension,' he groans.

Gideon follows suit. 'Me too, hang on, I'll come.'

They disappear down the corridor, Miles continuing to hum his piece until Gideon physically blocks his ears.

I frown and look over at Ava, who has deep circles under her eyes. Her olive skin is paler than usual and her eyeliner is reasonably subdued, which I've come to realise is an impending sign of doom.

'Hey,' I say, tapping her palm. 'Are you really okay? You and Miles seem…more lethal than usual.'

She slumps against my shoulder. 'I don't know. I'm not even stressed about the exams. But Miles is so competitive. And I feel like he'll be upset if I get a better mark, even though it doesn't even matter because I'm not asking for a scholarship, and it sucks because I wish he could just be happy for me, you know?'

'Why does he care so much?' I ask.

'It's sort of—urgh, it's dumb. Don't worry.'

'It's not dumb. You can tell me.'

She sits up and her eyes are glassy. 'Dad was the one who wanted us to learn,' she murmurs. 'He's the one who played, the one who bought the piano. He was teaching Miles, and it was always their special thing—Mum always said I was too young to mess around with it. And when Dad died, I guess Miles sort of wanted it to stay his thing. Like, that was the way he remembered Dad. He was so angry when Mum let me learn. I think that's why it bothers him—that it came more naturally to me. Because he plays for Dad, and I play for me.'

I blink back tears, even though it's not my loss to mourn. Mrs Kostakis had told me about being widowed a while ago, when I complimented her ring one day. She still wears it, every day. Said she'd found her one person and wasn't interested in finding another. 'Ava, I'm so sorry. You must miss him so much.'

'It's fine. I don't even remember him very well. Miles does, though.'

'It doesn't matter. He was still your dad.'

'Yeah. Well.' She sniffs, wiping her nose. 'Life sucks, you know?'

I drag her into a hug, and after a surprised minute she hugs me back.

'I just wish we could both be happy,' she whispers into my hair. 'Can you talk to him? Maybe tomorrow? He won't listen to me.'

'Of course I will. But Ava?'

'Yeah?'

'It's okay to play just for you. It's okay that you're good.'

She emits a single sob, and I feel the last year rushing back all at once. The Terrible Thing That Happened. Everything that's taken place since. She draws herself back, and glares at a few junior kids who are glancing our way.

'I gotta go,' she says. 'Thanks, Reece. For everything.

Sorry I'm such a mess today, I'm just tired.'

'Anytime. Hey, Ava...' I know it's the wrong time to ask, but Ava waits. 'I was just wondering...what do you know about Gideon's parents? I'm not being nosy, I just feel like I'm constantly saying the wrong thing.'

She hesitates before answering. 'I don't know what he's told you, exactly. But Miles has always just said his dad is a colossal fuck-brain...And, um, his mum doesn't really come to any of the school stuff. She gets sick, sort of. You should ask him though.'

I force a smile, waving her off to her next class and ignoring the final bell.

My hand finds the museum envelope in my pocket, and I draw it out again, reading and re-reading the words as though they might change if I concentrate hard enough. But even though my eyes are tracing the gold-foiled letters, my mind is elsewhere.

She's sort of retired.

Looks like Gideon and I are both keeping secrets.

At midnight I lie awake, too hot to fall asleep. I toss and turn until finally I pull out my phone and scroll through old photos before I give up and dial the number.

Heya it's Will, leave a message.

But I don't know how to say all the things I'm feeling, and I hang up.

Gideon picks me up at three o'clock, and somehow I'm still only half-dressed, stumbling into my denim shorts and trying to pull my hair back and button my shirt all at the same time. At least I've already shoved everything I need into my overnight bag, and I manage to trip down the stairs before Mum can ask him to stay for another coffee. I didn't lie, exactly, about staying at Ava's. I just omitted the finer details, like that Gideon and Miles would be there also. I mean, *obviously* Miles was going to be there, but I think Mum prefers not to think about it and one extra male body might have pushed her over the edge. And I don't want Gideon to spill the beans just because I can't find a single one of the seven thousand bobby pins I own.

'Coming, I'm coming!' I call out.

'Nobody cares,' mutters Theo from his bedroom.

Gideon is perched on one of the counter seats, hair properly brushed for possibly the first time since we've met. He's also wearing a shirt that appears to have been ironed. He looks ridiculous—like a thirty-year-old actor playing a high-school student in a cheesy teen movie.

'Um, should we get going?' I suggest.

'Sure,' he says, standing and washing his mug. Mum's eyes are moon-wide, and she gives me a secret little smirk.

I push Gideon out the front door before she can say something embarrassing. 'Bye, Mum, love you!'

'Thanks for having me!' Gideon yells over my shoulder. He tilts his chin down over his shoulder, bemused by the force with which I'm shoving him down the driveway. 'You know, you're freakishly strong for a tiny person.'

'I'm not tiny,' I grumble.

'That's what a tiny person would *say*. Want a boost into

the car?'

'Shut up.' But still, he takes my bag and hurls it into the boot, then gives me a hand into the passenger seat with only a small amount of teasing.

He jumps into the driver's seat but hesitates before starting the engine. 'Um, you have...' he starts to say, then reaches across and fiddles with my collar, his fingers brushing my throat. 'Sorry, you did up the wrong button.'

He turns away before I can respond with something witty or, actually, anything at all, and we drive in silence to the town centre while my heart beats a wild rhythm that pounds against my ribs.

I've been to the second-hand bookshop exactly once: sometime in the first month of living here, when Nan was in the nursing home and had nothing to do but read all day. The sign painted on the window reads *Twice Loved Pages*, and although the books are mostly second-hand, you can get a book ordered in if you catch the owner in a good mood. On that day, however, I did not.

'I've been thinking,' Gideon says. 'About the book. You know—*the* book. Your nan was a good person. There's no way she hurt anyone.'

I nod, my stomach churning. 'It must have been a gift, right? Some kind of weird joke? And the pages don't mean anything, or she could have been investigating...something. I don't know. But Nan always said helping women to be safe and healthy was what gave her job meaning, so there's obviously something we're missing. Right?'

'Right.'

I almost tell him about Emilia Marco. But people go missing all the time. And maybe Nan was interested because it was connected to her work somehow. I've tried and tried to google Emilia, but nothing ever comes up. I've wanted to search for the other women, too, but I've been too scared of what I'll find.

Gideon grabs the archive box from the back seat and wrangles it into the shop, ducking low under the stooped doorway.

The store is how I remember it—musty and dark, with dust clouds dancing in the beams of sunlight that find their way through dark curtains and tall cupboards. Piles of books sit everywhere in no discernible order. There are pink calligraphic romance covers next to stacks of crime novels, and a pile of Penguin classics threatening to topple over. There are rows and rows of dark oak bookshelves, but all the books are double-stacked, and if you're looking for something alphabetically you'd have to snake through the whole store to find the next letter. Stuck on the end of the shelves are posters, some peeling and almost illegible with age. The nearest one advertises a concert for a band whose lead singer died last year. The one next to it is a home-made sign for a missing cat named Mr Pickles. Something catches my eye, a photo buried under everything, but a voice wrenches my gaze away.

'If you're selling something, I don't bloody want it.'

Gideon laughs and sets the box down on the counter, waiting. 'You know, the customer service in here is atrocious.'

A pile of books collapses somewhere. 'The damn nerve!

I'll have you—oh, Gideon, it's only you.' An elderly man hobbles out of the back room and jabs Gideon in the chest. 'Been a while since you came by.'

'Sorry, Francis. Been busy lately,' Gideon replies, tilting his head towards me.

The old man pushes a pair of glasses up his nose, and seems to notice me for the first time.

'Well hello there,' he says, hoisting himself onto a stool behind the counter. His face is weathered and brown from a lifetime of sun, though his eyes are sharp and focused. His jumper is pockmarked by moth-eaten threads, but he still straightens his tie as we appraise each other.

'Francis, this is Reece. She's the owner of those books you love so much,' Gideon says.

Francis leans across the counter to shake my hand; his fingers are cold and papery, but he has a firm grip. 'Pleasure, my dear. Now, what have you brought me today?'

My mouth goes dry, and I have to clear my throat twice before actual words come out. This is an entirely different experience from the last time I was here, when Francis told me the shop was closed and, if I wanted the latest Liane Moriarty for my grandmother, I should take myself to Big W. I'm also shocked that Gideon, sports star extraordinaire, part-time lifeguard and general heartthrob, seems to have a thing for befriending old people. I graze a hand self-consciously over the box, dusting away some dirt that's settled on its lid. 'I guess Gideon's told you already? They're some of my grandmother's books.'

'Ah yes, you're Mary's girl.' Though Francis's tone is

perpetually cranky, I realise he has a friendly face; his skin has wrinkled where he would smile, if he ever chose to. 'I believe I once told you to get out of my store.'

'Oh, well...yes.' I don't add that I *was* Mary's girl. Past tense. I don't know who I am anymore.

'Bygones?' he says, holding up his coffee.

'Sure,' I reply, tapping the paper cup in mock salute, not willing to risk being ejected again.

Gideon opens the box and presents three of our latest conundrums. He lays the books on the counter, and Francis pulls out a pair of white cloth gloves and a magnifying glass from behind the till.

'Mmm. Yes, yes,' he mutters, cracking the spine on a book called *Fever and Febrile Diseases*. 'Published 1805, first run...mmm. You're missing the first volume?'

'I didn't realise there was one,' I reply, trying to recall any similar covers in the house.

'Doesn't matter so much unless you're selling. Front board is original, though the spine's been re-bound at some stage. Now the author, interesting man, first to devise the use of a thermometer—though he also suggested a cold bath might cure yellow fever. I'd have to make a few calls, but I suppose the historical value could be reasonable.'

I feel the shock written across my face. 'How do you know all that?'

'Oh, used to be a doctor. Didn't particularly enjoy retirement, so now I come in when I get bored.'

Gideon adds, 'Frank has also been a university lecturer, a flying doctor, a music therapist and, briefly, a dog groomer.'

'Got bored a lot,' Francis concedes. 'The old noodle got too slack watching those daytime shows.' He thumps his forehead more vigorously than seems healthy, and Gideon passes him another book. Francis stares at it. '*Treatise on Surgery.* Good gods, this can't be real. What time is it? I need a drink.'

'Still coffee hours,' says Gideon.

Francis grumbles something unintelligible, then peels one of the pages to the side. I don't dare mention how carelessly I flung that book into the box, thinking its frayed cover and dislodged pages would surely be worthless.

'Ambroise Paré. Strange man. Quite genius, I suppose, for his time. You know him?'

Gideon and I shake our heads.

'Well then. He was a doctor—a surgeon, I suppose we say now, though he didn't know it yet. The first to seal amputated ligaments instead of cauterising them with boiling-hot oil. Made an egg-yolk-and-turpentine mixture to treat infections. Not that the egg was any good, but you can't fault the outcome. Used to lance gums—cut them open, I mean—on children, thinking if their teeth didn't come through they might die. That one wasn't true,' Francis explains. 'He also convinced his cook to agree to be poisoned to death, to test the effectiveness of brimstone as an antidote.'

'Did it work?'

Francis mimes being hanged, which I take as a strong *no*. 'Don't worry, the cook was already convicted,' he adds. 'Stole the silverware, apparently. Well, anyway, this is—this is priceless. I'm not sure you should even have it. This belongs in a museum.'

'That's the idea,' I say, with false cheer. I still haven't found the right time to tell my parents about the exhibition.

'Oh no, not that old wackadoodle. The Louvre. The Museum of Natural History. The Metropolitan. Uffizi, even.' He wipes his brow. 'I'm afraid I'm not qualified. It looks real—certainly old enough. You'll have to take it to the city.' He scribbles an address on a piece of paper, awe and excitement on his face. 'Are you sure you don't have a nip on you?'

'Surprisingly, Frank,' says Gideon, 'I don't tend to carry a flask of whiskey around with me.'

'Well, you should. Anything else? I think I need a lie-down.'

Gideon and I glance at each other, nervous. I pick up the last of the three books, this time ensuring I have a firm grasp.

'I was wondering,' I say slowly, 'if I could ask you about this.'

Now that I know its pages are false, they do look slightly wooden. Francis seems to catch on quickly, running a finger along the cover. He flips it open and his face is overcome with glee.

'Ah! I haven't seen one of these in quite some time.'

I wonder again about the little drawers, the glass bottle nestled safely in its place. 'What is it, exactly?'

Francis twists the book around so the skeleton faces us. 'My dear, this is an assassin's cabinet.'

He looks between the twin expressions of horror on our faces and laughs, slapping his hand against the counter. 'No, no, I'm only joking. Well, a little. Also called an apothecary's curio, a travelling medicine cabinet, and so on. Quite popular in the sixteenth century.'

'I—I'm sorry, I don't think I follow?'

Francis removes one of the drawers and sets it on the counter. I don't know whether I should be relieved that it's empty. 'One might have two purposes for carrying this,' he says. 'One, as an assassin. Obvious implications. Bella-donna has killed a lot of royal husbands, I can tell you that much. Two, more commonly, it was just a fancy travelling kit. These herbs are poisonous, yes, but they have practical uses too. This one—here—could choke you to death, but it was also used as a mild paralytic before modern anaesthesia was invented. Even nightshade can be used safely—it's quite helpful as a muscle relaxant, anti-inflammatory, and what-have-you. Not that you'd use it now, but in times gone by it was perfectly suitable.'

Francis proceeds to poke through the drawers, and his casual ease puts some of my wilder fantasies to rest.

'It was my grandmother's,' I say, since he'd likely work it out anyway. 'I don't know what to do with it. Is it worth anything? Should I donate it?'

'Quite valuable as a curiosity, yes. Financially, who knows. The original cases would be worth eight, nine, maybe even ten thousand dollars. But they're also quite popular as reproductions, and there's almost no way to tell. It could be worthless.' He pauses, wiping his glasses on his shirt. 'Just be careful before you give it away—they often hold secret compartments. Lover's notes, deathbed confessions, that kind of thing.'

Gideon has been quiet through all this, but his hand reaches out to touch mine under the table. 'Maybe we should leave the rest for today,' he suggests.

'Yes. Yes. Quite enough excitement.' Francis pats Gideon on the shoulder. 'How's your mum doing? That new stuff working?'

Gideon's face changes: just slightly enough that most people wouldn't notice. His smile strains, too bright. 'Yeah. All good, Frank, don't worry about it.'

'What about—'

'Another day,' Gideon says quickly, and they both glance at me for a split second.

'Quite right,' says Francis, before giving me a trembling wave. 'You seem to be a good lass. Keep the kid out of trouble for me, eh?'

I nod stiffly. 'Of course.'

'You should come back, another time. I knew your Mags quite well. Wouldn't mind remembering some of the better things.'

'That would be nice,' I lie. Talking about Nana only ever makes me want to cry.

Gideon threads an arm through mine, sensing my need to get out. 'We better get going,' he says. 'Don't want to be late.'

I thank Francis on the way out, but he's already turned away. 'Be a dear and flick the *closed* sign, won't you.'

Gideon strides ahead with the archive box, and woodenly places it on the back seat of his car. He's rattled, and I'm at a loss at what to say. A quick glance at my watch reveals we're hardly going to be late, but without any other options

I jump into the front seat and clip my seatbelt.

It's too quiet. When I can't stand the strange silence anymore I blurt out the first thing that comes to mind: 'He seems—'

'Don't say nice, I'll know you're lying.'

'I was going to say "well informed".'

He takes his eyes off the road long enough to give me a baleful glare. 'Well, mystery solved at least,' he says, pulling onto the highway. 'The book must have been a gift, some-one's old-timey treasure chest. You said people would give your nan weird presents all the time, right?'

I sigh, secretly relieved. 'It must have been. I wish I knew where it came from, though.' I don't say anything about the papers shoved inside. I definitely don't say anything about Emilia or the other girls. *That* is still a mystery.

Gideon doesn't sing today. In fact he's quiet most of the way until I pull out my makeup bag and start precariously applying foundation while the road is smooth.

'Uh, what are you doing?'

'The invitation said formal, I want to look nice.'

'I see. Do I need to warn you of oncoming potholes?'

'Please.'

As he drives, I can sense his interest in the process of me becoming what I call Peak Reece: glowy and refined, eyes gleaming with shimmer powder and long lashes, pink blushing cheeks and a perfectly lined cupid's bow. I brush out my hair, using Mum's expensive comb, and run product through the ends so that it sits in glossy blonde waves.

'You, ah, you look really nice.' His voice catches and he

coughs, covering the squeak.

I lean towards the minuscule dashboard mirror, pleased with my handiwork. 'Thank you,' I say, managing to refrain from any self-sabotaging word vomit. I used to do this every weekend with Nina and Willow. The lipstick is an expensive one we all saved for. We all bought it in the same shade called Riot Club, which Nina duly renamed our group chat. Whenever we were invited somewhere, she would say, 'I'll only go if I can bring the Riot Club.' Which is deeply ironic, considering we rarely performed any kind of rioting, and mostly stayed indoors binge-watching TV.

'Pothole,' Gideon says, and when I glance up, he's still looking at me.

We arrive at the hall just in time, trickling inside and taking our seats as the lights dim. Mrs Kostakis waves from a few rows ahead, her eyes wide and proud. We stopped for dinner along the way, and I changed into my dress in the bathroom there. It's a silver beaded mini-dress with a tie-waist, long sleeves and a plunging neckline. When he saw me, Gideon's eyes almost popped out of his head, and he could only stammer a few words at a time.

I smile at the memory as the first musician takes the stage and tunes their instrument. The students play one by one and, had I not known otherwise, I would have mistaken them as professionals. Each one seems more talented than the last, ripping through powerful ballads and lingering on melancholy requiems.

At last, they announce Miles's name, and Mrs Kostakis

yells louder than anyone else has all night. She clutches her hands to her chest and crosses herself as he takes a seat at the piano. I feel nervous for him—heart beating faster, hands ice-cold.

He looks so unlike the Miles I know: face stern and focused, hair smoothed down, walk confident and purposeful. He unbuttons his blazer and pauses, fingers hovering over the keys. He glances at the audience, just for a moment, and then he plays.

And he's magic.

Miles plays like a person possessed. At first I think it's just a pretty tune: sad and languid, but lovely. Then it shifts, like water, and the sadness becomes something visceral. Listening to Miles play feels like drowning—like being dragged down in murky water and not minding as long as the music keeps going. The melody is soft but urgent, beckoning to the listener: *nearer, closer.* It's music that bleeds loss, that sounds like something broken.

Then it changes. A solitary note echoes across the silent hall, and my skin crawls. And then the quiet gives way to a deafening roar, and Miles's hands become a blur as they fly across the keys. The music is manic, a building crescendo that's fearsome and terrible and dark. I am certain, in that moment, that nothing else I hear will ever compare to this. If sound could be captured I'd have a library full of notes, and they'd all belong to Miles.

When the last note is played, every single person is frozen, leaning forward in their seats. The applause that follows is thunderous. People lurch to their feet, and no one cheers louder than Gideon, who whoops and jumps with his fist pumping the air. He grins at me, and his whole face glows with pride. I see Mrs Kostakis sniffle into a tissue, and when I lift a hand to my cheek I'm surprised that it comes away wet. Miles beams from the stage, and I know the flush in his cheeks isn't just from the lights.

He throws out a peace sign and bows, hurrying off the stage all too quickly.

Then Ava takes his place. She has none of her usual confidence; her gait is too stiff and wary. She shakes her hands out twice before she settles on the keys. But then she begins, and I slump back in my seat. She's outrageous. If Miles was manic, Ava's something divine. Otherworldly. I look at Gideon and he's enraptured. She plays for ten minutes, an hour, an eternity. The world could be burning outside and not a soul in this theatre would move to stop it. People start clapping before the final note is done, but she doesn't hear it. Her face is devastated, and she turns and rushes to the wings without looking back.

'She's—' I struggle for words. *Gifted*.

Gideon gives me a kind smile. He knows. He must have heard them play a thousand times. 'Don't tell Miles,' he says.

'Okay,' I whisper. Now I know why Ava was so upset. Miles is genius, but she's something different altogether. I can't imagine what they'd sound like if they ever played together.

The lights come on a little while later, and my heart is still pounding. 'I loved it,' I blurt, to no one in particular. Gideon laughs, throwing an arm around my shoulder.

Mrs Kostakis finds us in the crowd and plants a kiss

on my cheek. 'I'm going to find them backstage and head home,' she says. 'You kids have fun tonight. I'll see you in the morning.' She scuttles away, deliriously happy.

'Let's wait outside,' Gideon says, and we make our way through the crowd.

The sky has fallen dark and stars are blinking above. Gideon helps me up onto the bonnet of his car, and we sit there, waiting for Miles and Ava to come out.

'I didn't know music could sound like that,' I say. 'I mean, I knew, I'd heard it. But it's different, watching it actually happen.'

Gideon lies back against the windshield. 'The first time I heard them play, I thought it was a prank. I swore they'd hidden a speaker somewhere.'

I snicker at that, tugging the edge of my dress down. 'What a talented group of friends you all are.' He looks confused. 'You didn't think I'd forget about the whole web-comic thing, did you?'

He groans, folding his arms over his face. 'I regret telling you that.'

I poke him in the stomach. 'No, you don't. I bet you've been dying to tell someone.'

'Truly. I rue the day. I'll never have peace again.'

'Shut up,' I say happily, kicking my legs in the air. Then I spot two familiar faces and squeal, jumping off the car. 'They're here!'

Miles rushes over, crushing my ribs as he lifts me into a hug. 'Reece! Go on, tell me I'm a genius. Tell me there's no one better.' I catch Ava's eye over his shoulder and she gives a tired shrug.

'You're a genius, Miles. You both are.' I wriggle free and pull Ava into a hug, and she holds on tight. If Miles is nervous about the evening, he no longer shows it. Maybe he's come around after all—for all their competitive bitching, they seem to have reached a temporary truce. Miles rubs his hands together, a wicked gleam in his eyes.

'And now, my friend, my lady, my one true dweeber,' he addresses us in turn. 'Are you ready to party? Because I have twelve years' worth of pent-up anxiety and sensible dancing shoes.'

Miles calls shotgun and races to the front seat, leaving me and Ava in the back. She looks exhausted, but she smiles and jokes with the rest of us, and as we get closer to town she seems revived.

'So here's the thing,' she says, applying ox-blood red to her lips. 'Beat Repeat is the only club within twenty kilometres of Hamilton, so don't do anything you don't want anyone to see because, trust me, they'll see it.'

Gideon's eyes flicker to me in the rearview mirror, and I lower my gaze to my lap. Suddenly, a shadow-filled room with loud music seems incredibly appealing. 'Also, the DJ is super hot,' says Ava, interrupting that particular train of thought. 'Unless you're taken, of course.' She smirks, and I'm thankful that Miles is busy curating his latest playlist.

'I hate you,' I hiss.

'You wish.'

Beat Repeat is exactly how I pictured it: weary neon lights, a glowing dance floor dulled by spilt drinks, and cracked leather couches shoved into dark corners. The girls wear glittering dresses, and the guys wear collared shirts and too much cologne. The music thrums so loudly Ava has to scream twice in my ear before giving an exasperated eye-roll and pointing towards the bar. The menu consists of poorly thought-out puns: Mai Tide, Beach Bellini, Hamilton Highball. I don't recognise anything so I just point to something, and the bartender delivers a bubble-gum pink cocktail that burns the back of my throat when I take a sip. Miles orders the same, and Gideon and Ava order lemonades.

We dance together, writhing in the crowd, and make fun of Miles as he lets loose some truly horrid moves. I finish my drink and Ava hands me another. She's lithe and gorgeous, twisting more elegantly than the rest of us. People make room for her and she settles in the beat while Miles starts the chicken dance beside her. Gideon does that awkward shuffle guys do when they don't know how to dance, so I grab his hands and sway with him, laughing into his suit jacket.

It's so easy here, squished between Ava and Gideon, Miles dancing circles around us. We stay on the light-up floor, and I can feel the music vibrating through my bones. My feet start to ache and my hair is sweaty, but it doesn't matter. Someone fetches me another drink and it makes my head spin in a pleasant sort of way.

Miles eventually yells that he has to pee and Ava gets a mischievous glint in her eye. She slips away between two girls in pink jumpsuits before I can snatch at her wrist and make her stay. With Gideon beside me, all I can think is that I want to stay here forever, happy and aimless for the first time in a long time.

The drink makes me bold enough to grab Gideon's hands again. 'Hi,' he says, with a lopsided smile.

'Hi.'

He steps on my feet but I just laugh, tipping my head back until he has to catch me and the lights throw strange shadows across the room.

'How are you doing down there?'

'Perfect,' I answer, swaying out of time with him to the music. 'Except you're not really dancing.'

'I can't really dance,' he says, hands slowly running over my shoulders.

'Everyone can dance,' I tease, leaning in a little closer than necessary, desperate to catch the scent of ocean again on his skin. Sometimes my sheets still smell like it, and it drives me crazy, wondering if I'm imagining it or not.

'Did you just sniff my shirt?'

I realise that somehow my fingers are clawed around the soft fabric of his shirt, and I may have had my head buried in it but I can't quite remember. He doesn't seem to mind. He looks lovely under these lights, and boys aren't supposed to look lovely but he does.

He wraps his arms around my waist. *He's too tall*, I think. I'm always stretching back to look up at him like he's the sky and it could go on forever. *You're drunk*, is the second thing I think.

But I don't care, because Gideon bought me dinner and took me to the bookshop, and he's smiling at me even though I'm standing on his feet. We're so close that his knees knock into mine. *I keep waiting for you to kiss me again.*

He's surprised.

He's surprised because I said it out loud. *Oh god.* Mistake, mistake. Stupid pink drinks and stupid lights and—

But then, as requested, he kisses me. He holds me very carefully, like he's prepared for me to run away again, or throw myself off the nearest pier. His hands skim the fabric of my dress. It's not even a real kiss, just a brush of lips.

Then the song changes, and he lets me go.

I blink up at him, unsteady. My head feels strange. I hold my hand up, meaning to catch him, but I miss, and the only reason I don't slip on the floor is because he catches my wrist at the last second. 'Come on,' he says, hoisting me up. 'Let's get you some water. I think you're a bit drunk.'

'Hey, Party Gideon is supposed to be having fun.'

'I *am* having fun,' he says, smiling.

'You should kiss me again,' I say, emboldened.

'Maybe when you're sober.'

I cackle as he leads me to the bar, leaving me on a stool with a glass of water and a promise to be back in a minute. I nod, but my head spins, and I lay my forehead on the cold steel countertop, nausea roiling in my stomach. I flick open my phone, scrolling through the names. I really don't want Gideon to see me vomit. I don't even feel that tipsy, it's just all the sugar churning around in my stomach. Yes, it's just the sugar.

'Heya it's Will, leave a message.'

'I need you,' I groan. 'Please pick up. Please answer. Just this once. I don't know what to do. I need help. I—' *I want to kiss this boy all over his glorious face and also I think I might be sick*, is what I want to say. *And I don't know how to dry-clean this dress and it has nuclear-pink splashes on it.* But then there's another glass of water in front of me so I hang up and I drink the water gratefully.

'How you feeling, Blackwell?' Gideon says.

'Stupendous,' I answer, before slipping sideways off my chair.

Miles appears as if out of nowhere and sets me right. 'Oh, Reece, you tiny lightweight. You good?'

I grin at him, feeling fuzzy at the edges. 'Miles! Miles, you're a genius. A piano genius. Beethoven with good ears. Mozart without the untimely death. Wagner without the whole…racist thing.'

He pats my head affectionately. 'Reece, babe, I love the flattery, but also you seem super drunk.'

I narrow my eyes until there's only one Miles staring down at me. 'Not super. Just…slightly buzzed.' Gideon flags down another glass of water.

'You wanna bounce?' asks Miles.

'No,' I say, even though my stomach is churning. 'You and Ava are having fun. Gideon's here, I'm fine. Go dance.'

'Nah, I'm tired anyway. C'mon, there's a kebab place across the street. You want some chips?'

'I want…chocolate cake. And a cheese toastie.'

Gideon passes me the fresh glass. 'How about water and chips tonight, and I'll buy you a whole cake tomorrow?'

'That is…' I pause, distracted by the lights. 'Oh. Yes. That's nice. Potatoes. I want potatoes.'

They manage to wrangle Ava out of the crowd and soon we're stumbling into the lamp-lit street. Somehow my blood is running warm, and I don't feel the chill until we've ordered and found a spot huddled on a park seat, eating our food. Gideon shrugs off his jacket and places it around my shoulders. Ava lays her head in my lap, complaining that her toes hurt, and Miles has gone really quiet—he's staring up at the sky, and every so often he just says 'whoa', and tells Gideon that the universe is probably an illusion and we're all living in the video game of a benevolent teenage god. It's a lot for my brain to follow, and I find myself pressing my cheek into Gideon's shoulder.

'S'nice,' I murmur, exhausted.

'What is?'

'You.'

'Me, Gideon?'

'Mmm. And Ava. And Miles. And potatoes. I love it. I love this. I think I'm…happy.'

Someone kisses my head. 'Go to sleep, Reece. I'll wake you up when we're home.'

I wake up feeling like something has died in my mouth. My head spins when I sit up, but it doesn't throb like I expect it to—like I probably deserve. Somewhere in the dark, Ava is snoring. Her foot dangles over the edge of her bed, above my trundle on the floor. There's an enormous bottle of water beside me, which I unscrew and drain right down to the final drop.

I flop back down into the twisted sheets, swamped by

an oversized band T-shirt that Ava dug out for me. The ride home was a blur—I just remember gratefully crashing into bed and the boys whispering goodnight as they hurried into Miles's room.

The boys.

Gideon.

I rocket up in bed, cracking my knee on something sharp in the dark. I swear under my breath. Gideon. Who I kissed. *Oh. My. God.* I really need to make better kissing decisions.

Not that I didn't want to kiss him. Because I did. Quite a lot. It's just, maybe I should have done it sober? And not drooled potato into his lap afterwards.

I run my fingers through clammy strands of hair, certain I won't be getting back to sleep for a while. The clock by Ava's head says 4.02 a.m. I kick off the sheets and tiptoe out into the hall, using my phone to light the way.

Their bathroom is small but well stocked. I find a spare toothbrush to brush my teeth, and a face washer to scrub off the remnants of glitter eyeshadow that trails down my cheeks and across my nose. The cold water on my skin makes me feel much fresher. There's a bristle brush by the sink, but I worry that it's not Ava's and end up teasing out my tangled hair with my fingers.

When I'm done, the girl in the mirror looks bright and wild. I smile, and my cheeks are shiny and full. Then I roll my eyes at myself for good measure.

I open the door just a crack, making sure no one else has woken up. But the house is silent and still, so I creep into the kitchen, fill a glass as quietly as I can, and shove a whole mini-muffin in my mouth.

I'm still not tired, so I settle on the couch, watching the tide wash in under the sweeping lighthouse beam. My phone buzzes with a forgotten notification—a missed call—before dying in my hand. I worry it might have been Mum, but she would have called Ava or Mrs Kostakis if she really needed me. Probably just Theo whingeing about the Netflix password (I changed it after he spoiled the ending to *Twin Peaks* last week. I can't believe I went eighteen years avoiding spoilers and that little jerk ruined it for me because he read a freaking *BuzzFeed* article).

There's a creak in the hallway and I pull my shirt down with a jolt, conscious I'm not wearing pants.

'Ava?' I hiss.

Gideon stumbles into the lounge room, rubbing his eyes. He freezes when he sees me on the couch. 'Sorry,' he whispers. 'I thought—I heard something.'

He looks out of focus, like a watercolour painting smudged at the edges. His hair is sticking up in curling tufts, his cheeks are flushed, and his lips are swollen and pink.

I fold my legs under my body, tugging the shirt until it covers my knees. 'Sorry,' I say, my heart spluttering to life. 'Couldn't sleep. I didn't mean to wake you.'

'S'okay. I'm a light sleeper. And Miles would sleep through the apocalypse.'

I laugh, quietly. It's strange, here, in the small hours of the morning, alone with Gideon. My throat goes dry. All my words are gone, and my hands are trembling.

'Can I…' he asks, and takes a step towards the couch.

I nod and slide over, leaving a whole cushion of space between us.

He's wearing a big white shirt and striped shorts. As much as I enjoyed shirtless Gideon the day that I surprised him, I'm glad he's wearing clothes right now. I think my heart would combust otherwise.

'Um,' I manage to squeak. 'About the…'

'Chocolate cake I owe you? Calm down, Blackwell, I'll get you one in the morning.' It's a joke, but his lips don't smile the right way.

I bite my lip. 'The kiss, actually.'

'It's okay,' he says, closing his eyes and sinking back into the couch. 'I know the rules.'

'The rules?'

'No talking about the kiss. Kisses. Plural.'

'Oh…' I shake my head, disappointed. I thought maybe he wanted…but maybe not.

He opens one eye. *'Oh?'*

'No, it's fine. It's silly.'

'Reece…'

'I was just going to say, I'm, uh, sorry for drunk-kissing you.'

He sighs. 'I was going to say *I* was sorry for drunk-kissing *you*. I'm sorry, I didn't realise you'd drunk so much until after. Anyway, don't worry about it, I know you didn't mean it.'

My fingernails are digging into my palms. Everything feels electric. I am a bolt of lightning and I'm about to blow up my own life. 'I meant it,' I say in a rush. Then I say it again, just to make sure he heard me, because he's gone very, very still. 'I meant it. I'm sorry for standing on your feet a lot, but I'm not sorry I kissed you.'

'Oh.' He's blinking at the wall, a lot. But he's not really saying anything. Maybe I've misread everything.

Well, it's nice to know you can't actually die of mortification, but it would be sort of nice if the universe could give it a go just this once.

'I'm just...I'll go back to bed. You can stay.' I get up to rush back to Ava's room, but Gideon snags the back of my shirt and suddenly I'm in his lap, and his hands are on my face. His thumb runs across my lips, his eyes searching mine for something. He must find it, because then he's kissing me, finally, properly, at last. Not a quick brush of skin against skin, not a drunken mistake. My lips are crushed against his, and he's so gentle and so careful. We knock teeth and laugh, but then his lips are on mine again and I don't have the air left in my lungs to do anything but *this*.

Somehow I end up straddled across his legs. His hands find their way up the back of my shirt, and I feel a flush of goosebumps across my skin. I'm very, very aware that I'm not wearing a bra, but his hands seem content to wander the peaks of my spine and the curve of my waist. My fingers are greedily running across his shoulders and down his shirt. I pull my mouth away long enough to dot a trail of kisses down his neck, and I'm delirious with the thought that he really does smell like the ocean—like sea salt and sunscreen. I fall back on the couch, and Gideon's hovering above me, arms braced either side of my head. I tug at the bottom of his shirt and it's gone, my hands on his warm skin with nothing in the way. We kiss until my lips ache and my chest heaves, until I'm tangled so thoroughly around his body I'm not sure how I'll ever come undone.

His hands skim my waistband and I wrench myself away, my palms coming to a rest on his chest. 'Wait—'

He lets go at once, cold air rushing in where his hands had been seconds before.

'Well, you didn't have to stop *that* much.'

'I'm sorry...did I...are you okay?' He looks horrified, blinking wildly.

I shift back closer to him. My body is humming, magnetised to Gideon. 'I'm fine, it's just, you know, we're on Miles's couch.'

The fog in his eyes lifts. '*God*. Right. Yes.' He blows out a long, slow breath, then rests his forehead against mine. 'Um, I'm guessing we don't want to tell people about this right away?'

'I would really rather the whole Kostakis household *not* wake up to us defiling their living room.'

Gideon laughs. 'I didn't defile anything, for the record.'

I'm glad it's dark because I'm sure my cheeks are burning red. We stay kissing and giggling for a while, but with less fervour, both listening for the sound of a door cracking open or curious footsteps.

'Do you want to go back to bed?' he whispers.

'I really, really don't.'

He kisses my forehead. 'What if I promise we can do

this again tomorrow?'

'Really?'

He gives me a quizzical look. 'Did you…I mean…is this a one-time thing?'

'No! I mean…no? I don't want it to be. Unless you want it to be. I don't—oh god.' I cover my face to physically stop the torrent of words falling from my mouth.

He peels one of my hands away, kissing my cheek when he finds it. 'Hey, Reece?'

'Mmm.'

'I'd really like to do this again tomorrow.'

'Okay,' I say, my lips against his. 'I'd like that too.'

He drags me back to Ava's door when the sky turns pink, and gives me a sweet, soft kiss goodnight. I collapse into the trundle bed, and fall asleep to the smell of the ocean.

Gideon and I sit through a very awkward breakfast, both of us smiling far too much and trying to avoid eye contact. We've hardly finished eating when he invents a reason for us to leave, and the second his car door slams shut he leans over to kiss me again.

'Good morning,' he says, with a lopsided grin.

'You said that already.'

'Mmm. Words are overrated.'

I laugh and wind my hands around his neck. I could stay like this for hours, but we're both worried that someone might see.

'Is there anything you have to do today?' I ask. 'Because, you know, I think I have a whole season of *Ghost Hunters* saved up. It's on my laptop. In my room.'

His face falls. 'Oh *shit*—I'm working today. What time is it?'

I check my phone but the screen is still dead. 'Are you gonna be late?'

'I don't think so. Sorry—I can come over after, though? Dinner, maybe?'

'Sure. I'd like that. A lot.' I don't even bother to hide the goofy grin that takes over my face.

He drives me home, singing to a Brit band I've never heard of, making up sounds to match the instrumental riffs. When we pull into the driveway, he starts to lean over for a kiss, but his eyes slide past my shoulder.

'Hey, Reece, who's that?'

I turn, wishing that whoever it is would go away.

And then my heart stops. My blood turns cold. The girl sitting on my front steps is glaring at me, her eyes steady and strong. It's the face of a ghost, a memory I've thought about so much that the edges seem worn through like old paper. I half-expect her to disappear, but she doesn't move.

I throw open the door, stumbling out of the car, getting stuck in my seatbelt. She stays so silent. So still. And I don't understand. This shouldn't be happening.

'Nina?'

She stands up sharply, and for the first time in my life I don't know what she's thinking. But I don't care. Tears spring to my eyes and I'm a half-second away from crushing her into a hug when her mouth drops open. 'What. The. *Fuck*. Reece.'

'Nina, what are you—'

But she just spins on her heel, marches through my own front door and slams it shut.

'Reece?' Gideon says, a hand on my shoulder. 'Is everything okay? Who is that?'

I choke down something bitter before I answer. 'That's Nina Reyes,' I say, voice broken. 'My best friend.'

13

NINA REYES IS a hurricane, dark and wild and uncontained. I've spent most of my life trying to get close enough to feel the static thrill of something electric and magic without getting sucked into the vortex. Most of the time, she's happy to have me there, pulling her back down to earth before she crash-lands. Most of the time, we make a great team.

Right now, she's looking at me like she wishes a storm would come and sweep us both away.

My kitchen has never felt so alien, a hostile place occupied by a teenage girl wearing denim shorts and a wicked glare. The rest of the house is silent. My parents are out, I remember. Theo must be swimming. The door clicks shut and sounds like a landmine. Gideon—I think I told him to leave. I can't remember. I'm trying not to remember. Because I can't think about Nina without thinking about Willow, and thinking about Willow carves my soul in half.

'Nina...' I speak first because I know she won't. Her mouth is set in a thin line. 'What are you doing here?'

I think she'll implode. Uncontained damage. But even though she's trembling, her voice comes out even and flat. 'Are you okay?'

Her eyes flick over me. Converse shoes and a shirt that's not mine. I wonder if I look different—if she'll notice the sun has bleached my hair and freckled my skin in the way I always lamented but secretly loved. I wonder if she'll notice two sets of goggles on the counter, new pictures on the wall with a sacrilegious smile splitting my face. She looks the same, I think. Dark skin and shiny hair and a pinched expression that usually means she's tired or annoyed. But she's different, I realise: a washed-out version of Nina. She seems sallow, her cheeks a little too grey and thin. Her eyes are rimmed red. I've only seen her cry once. Just that once...

'Nina, I'm fine. I don't understand...How did you get here? You should have called—' I bite off the words. We've never been friends who had to call. We've always trampled in uninvited, raiding each other's fridges, climbing through windows until we finally gave in and got spare keys cut to each other's houses. Her mum used to buy the brand of yoghurt I liked. Nina had her own bed at my house, the sheets washed fresh every week just in case.

'I did call. And then I called Theo. I drove all night,' she says, like that explains things.

'You called Theo?'

Her nod is curt, perfunctory, like she can't stand the thought of wasting unnecessary energy on this conversation. 'He didn't know where you were.'

'Why did you—I was with friends—' God, I can't stop

saying the wrong thing. It's never been this hard. Nina used to know my thoughts before I did. We once got a phone bill for a five-hour conversation that our parents made us split and pay out of our pocket money.

She takes a breath, very much resembling a person trying not to lose their shit.

'Nina.' I reach for her even when she jerks away. 'Why are you here?'

And then she hits, Hurricane Nina. Her arms fling wide as she rockets away from the island bench. 'Because I thought you needed me! Jesus. I got your message, okay? I thought you knew.'

'Knew *what*?'

She pulls a phone from her pocket, and plays a message. '*I need you. Please pick up. Please answer. Just this once. I don't know what to do. I need help. I—*'

'Her parents gave me her phone,' she mutters. 'I thought you knew. I thought you needed help. Sorry for giving a shit.'

'I didn't—Nina, I swear, I didn't know. I would never have left all those messages...'

'You didn't find it strange the number kept ringing? That the message box was never full?'

I shake my head. 'Nina, I'm so sorry.'

'You know what the worst part is?' I think there are tears in her eyes, but she's too furious for me to be sure. 'I listened to you say all those things, all those messages on her phone, and they were never for me. You never called *me*, not once.'

'You told me never to speak to you again!'

'Because I was mad at you! Not because I meant it!'

'Why didn't you call me then? Why didn't you ever text me back?'

'What, come crawling back into your life when you had so clearly made yourself a new one? No *thank you*. You know what, I'm sorry I fucking bothered. Just carry on—enjoy your nice new life, and your nice new friends.' She starts to leave, and it's like losing her all over again.

'It's not—'

She waves an arm to cut me off. 'I officially do not care anymore.' She turns in the doorway, chin tipped defiantly. 'And *stop calling her.*'

After she slams the door shut, I sink to the floor, hands around my chest to keep it from breaking. I stay there, sobbing, until Theo comes home and carries me upstairs, waiting until I fall asleep and dream of all the things I've lost.

I wake up when Mum taps on my door. I rub my sleep-crusted eyes and bury myself further under the sheets. It got dark outside, somehow. I've slept most of the day.

'Mum, I'm fine, but I don't feel like talking to anyone right now.' My throat is thick and clogged from crying. She comes in anyway.

'Sweetie, someone's here to see you.'

'Mum, I can't…I didn't know she'd be here.'

'It's not Nina. It's that boy. Gideon?'

I twist into my pillow, and heave a brand-new sob. Mum rubs a soothing circle on my back. 'Can you tell him—can you tell him I'm not feeling well?'

She doesn't say anything, but tucks the blankets up under

my chin and slips away. I hear murmured voices downstairs and squeeze my eyes shut. My phone dings a second later— it's Gideon, because of course it is, asking if everything is okay. *No*, I think. *My universe is falling apart and I'm a black hole in the middle.* But there are no emojis for that and so I ignore him, tossing the phone to my feet.

The sound of footsteps hovers at my door. 'Mum, I'm *fine.*'

'It's me,' says Theo. 'Can I come in?'

I think of him picking me off the floor, frantic because he thought I was physically hurt, then terrified because I wasn't. 'Sure.'

He perches at the end of my bed as though I really am sick and deathly contagious. 'I, um, I'm really sorry. She called me and said you'd left a weird message and it sounded like you were at a bar and there was some dude in the background. She was, like, fully freaked out. I thought you were at Ava's so...'

'It's fine. Did you tell Mum?'

'Nah, I called Ava first. She said it was just Gideon and you were all leaving anyway. I would have called Nina back but her number's private and she blocked me on Facebook. *Man* that chick's petty.'

Despite everything, I laugh. Not a proper laugh—a snotty huff. 'Yeah, I know.'

Theo goes quiet. He's never quiet. He pulls down a square of my blanket, just enough so he can look at me properly. 'Hey, Reece...is it gonna be bad again? Like before?'

I want to go back to sleep. But instead I shake my head.

'I don't think so. I was just...it was worse that I wasn't expecting it.'

'I'm sorry,' he says again. 'I tried to warn you. Your phone kept going to message bank. Then I figured, you know, you guys would want some privacy. And Nina still scares me a little.'

'Nina scares *me* a little.'

'What are you gonna do?'

'I don't know. I never thought she'd talk to me again.'

'Maybe you should talk to someone about it.'

I aggressively roll my eyes. I endured months of my parents trying to usher me off to see a shrink, and I relented just so they'd stop asking. 'I did, and I hated it. Never again.'

'I meant...Gideon. Or Miles. Or Ava. Or me...'

Oh. I sit up, clutching Mr Snuggles to my chest. 'I don't know...I made Mum send Gideon away.'

'I heard.'

'Was he mad?'

Theo scoffs. 'The dude's a freakin' saint. Of course he wasn't mad. He was *worried* about you.' He nudges my feet. 'Maybe you should get out for a bit. Go down to the beach?'

'Mmm.'

'If you wanna crawl out the window I'll tell Mum you're sleeping again.' He grabs a pair of shoes and leaves them by the bed. 'Text me if you need an SOS.'

Then he shuts the door, and whisper-shouts 'goodnight' loud enough for my parents to hear. I eye my sneakers.

Maybe it's irony or fate, but I end up running to the pier. I sprint right to the end before I pull up short, my toes nudging over the edge of the boardwalk. I look around, but it's dark and cold and no one's around.

I wish Gideon was here.

I'm glad he's not.

I walk back to the beach, dragging my feet in the sand. The moon is bright enough to light the way—that's the thing out here, without the city lights drowning everything out. Without meaning to, I find myself wandering up to the lifeguard shack.

There's a single light on, and the low hum of music spills out the open door. I almost knock, but then I see Gideon curled over the viewing deck, pens sprawled across the table and sketches laid out to dry.

I lean against the doorframe, watching him draw. His fingers are long and sure, striking out in short, quick strokes. Some of the scenes I recognise: Miles playing a piano, Ava leaning over our lunch table, Theo diving off a board. Elsewhere, there's a superhero cape, a wheelchair, a swamp monster. And there's me, a sketch that seems brand new: a dark outline, the page almost entirely black except for a shard of light cast from a disco ball. I'm smiling. Dancing. The nuclear-pink drink is in my hand, the only splash of colour on the page. Was that just yesterday? It feels like a year, a decade, a lifetime. I wish I could smile like that, I think.

He looks up at last, and finds me hovering in the doorway. He stands and wraps his arms around me. 'Reece...'

I want to wrench myself away—this was a mistake. I can already feel the tears resurfacing.

'You don't have to tell me,' he says. 'If you don't want.'

And then I'm crying so hard I couldn't say anything even if I wanted to. He doesn't seem to mind that I'm sweaty and windswept. He pulls us both to the floor and lets me snot into his shirt. He's patting my hair and whispering so many lies: it'll be okay, he says. Everything will be okay. It's my favourite lie. I wish he'd tell me more.

When the tears have calmed to small hiccups, he finds me a glass of water and passes me a thermos of terrible coffee.

'Sorry,' he says. 'It's the instant stuff.'

It tastes metallic and sweet, but I have a headache and the sugar helps. 'It's fine. Thank you.'

He's sitting cross-legged, hair tipped over his forehead as he gazes at his lap. 'Reece...' he begins again, scrubbing a hand over tired eyes. 'No. Sorry. I said we don't have to talk about it, and I meant it, but can you at least tell me if you're all right? I've never seen you like that.'

'Not really,' I say, my voice so quiet I don't know if he's heard.

'Can you...do you want to call one of your other friends? What about the other girl? Willow?'

Her name makes me feel sick. *It's all my fault.*

I shake my head, clawing at my hair. 'I'm cursed,' I say. 'I'm cursed. I did it.'

He pulls my hands away. 'Reece, stop...'

'It's all my fault.'

'I'm sure—'

'She *died*, Gideon. She's dead,' I whisper, not able to look at him. 'Willow died and it's my fault, and Nina hates me and that's my fault too.' The words choke me, a confession I

186

never thought I'd make. I thought I'd left it all behind, not daring to look back long enough to let it hurt again.

He lurches back like I've hit him. And I want to swallow the words down, but all the secrets are suffocating me.

I think he will hate me. That he'll be disgusted. It's my fault, after all. Instead, he wraps his hand around mine and asks: 'What happened?'

So this is what I tell him:

Willow was the best of us. Kind and sweet and patient. The oldest.

We snuck out to see a band. Well, Nina and I snuck out, because we were only seventeen, and Willow told her parents she'd be home late. The band was playing on the other side of the city, so Willow drove us, and we sang along to their album on her crappy car stereo. We danced in a smoke-filled dive bar, lip synced as they performed, kissed the bathroom mirrors with our Riot Club lipstick. We took dumb photos with filters over our faces. And when we were finally danced out, we stumbled back to Willow's car and took turns messing with the radio.

She dropped me home last. She hugged me as we pulled into the driveway, squishing me until I laughed, and said she'd see me in the morning. Then she stuck a big red kiss on my cheek and drove away.

She never made it home.

Then I tell him about Queen Mab, that I was running late. That I cursed us all with bad luck. And then after, I couldn't eat, or sleep, or go to school. I was hardly living at all, except to shuffle to the shower when Mum pulled me out of bed. It was so bad I had spent my birthday with Nan's stethoscope pressed to my chest, listening to the beat, the only way to be sure I wasn't dying too. The stubborn, too-quick *tick-tick-tick*, the heart that kept beating and breathing and living, even when I didn't bother to open my eyes long enough to know or care if the world kept going.

It all tumbles out in a nonsensical burst, and when I'm done I can't stand the look of pity on his face.

'Reece,' Gideon says, his eyes wide and wild. 'You didn't curse anyone. It's not your fault. You don't really believe that, do you?'

'Please don't. Please don't try to make me feel better. She's gone, forever.' The worst thing is, I still can't tell him all of it, what really happened. I've never told anyone, not even my parents. *It was my fault...*

'Reece. I'm so, so sorry that you lost your friend. I'm sorry you hurt this much. I'm sorry you never felt like you could tell us. But you don't know what happened in that car. And I know that's worse, but maybe it would have happened no matter what. Either way, it's not your fault.'

I can't tell him, I think. *I can't tell him because he'll hate me. Everyone should hate me.*

Suddenly I'm on my feet. I'm hysterical. *I'm having a panic attack*, I think. But knowing you're having a panic attack doesn't stop it from happening, and so I end up clutching my chest, wondering why my lungs won't work properly.

'Reece! Breathe, breathe.' He holds my hands and makes me count the seconds as I inhale and exhale. His fingers are over my wrist—trying to be subtle about checking my pulse.

But the tension in his eyes relaxes after a few minutes, and I start to feel like I have enough air again.

'That's better,' he murmurs. 'You're doing really good. A few more.'

He's still and calm, just holding me, counting, telling me to keep going for a few minutes more. I don't feel the moment it passes. I just realise at some point that it's gone, and it's been gone for a while.

'Sorry,' I say, my hands still in his. 'I didn't—That hasn't happened for a while.'

'It's okay,' he says. 'You want some laughing gas? Now seems like a pretty good time to abuse my drug-cabinet privileges.' He doesn't wait for me to answer, just pulls me in again. And I know the world isn't better because I kissed Gideon Hawthorn, but I think it might be better because he's *here*, and he doesn't seem to mind how many tears pour out of me, and he listens while I tell him some better things.

Like Willow's epic cookie obsession. Once I went over and there were three hundred choc-mint cookies spread around her kitchen. She never did tell me why.

She was friends with Nina first. They saw me getting teased one day in primary school, and Willow went to find a teacher while Nina just socked the kid in the nose (his name was Seth Simmons, and he told me years later that the crooked tilt was a real hit *with the ladies*).

She made us watch Christmas movies every year, marathon hours of Santas and star-crossed lovers, and Nina would have us all at her house on Christmas Eve to sing carols with her family. We exchanged gifts and made fake snow for the windows.

We started a terrible Easter tradition, and no one remembers who first came up with the game, but it involved a stealthy mission to be the first person to egg the other two by the end of the school break. Willow only ever won the year she got me on a diving board—right as the race horn blew, she cracked it on my cap. I wasn't even mad because it took some pretty genius planning.

I never believed in curses, but Willow did. She believed in curses and destiny and ghosts and crystals. Even when she made me run under Queen Mab, that very first day when I forgot, I didn't really believe. It was a joke, and I was laughing as they watched.

Joke's on me, I guess.

There's a bolt of lightning outside. Another storm—not close, but close enough that the waves start to sound more vicious. I realise that I'm tired and cried out. At some stage, I've ended up against Gideon's chest, and feeling his steady breaths through my shoulders is oddly comforting.

'Do you wanna go home?' he murmurs.

I check my phone. There's only one message from Theo. *Rents asleep. All clear.* Actually, there's a second message that says, *Is now a bad time to ask for the Netflix password?*

'I can stay for a while,' I say.

Gideon pulls me to my feet. 'I gotta go home quickly, but I have an idea. Come with me?'

Nan's house is almost unrecognisable: the floors have been cleared and the books neatly stacked. The piles of wrinkled magazines are gone, the untouched dishes washed, all the dust swept away and the cobwebs banished. I almost cry again because it looks the way I remember it—a cosy sanctuary with yellow-tinged wallpaper and pictures smiling down at me from the wall.

'It's so...clean,' I manage to say. 'Did you do this?'

Gideon shakes his head. 'I saw your dad come in the other day.'

'I didn't even know.'

'He stopped to say hello. Said your mum couldn't bring herself to come back for a while.'

I'm a terrible child because all I can think is *Thank god*— Dad wouldn't know if a few things were missing. All mess looks the same to him, but Mum notices everything.

Gideon unravels the bundle in his arms, unfurling a fluffy blanket and two pillows, plus a throw rug for good measure. Then he retrieves a basket from the kitchen and sets it down: there's a fresh thermos of warm tea, some scones still in a store-bought packet, a few half-crumbled biscuits and little wrapped chocolates. 'Sorry,' he says with a sheepish smile. 'It's all I could manage for a last-minute picnic.'

I pick up a scone and shove it whole in my mouth. 'This is perfect. Thank you.'

He flicks crumbs off my shirt and fiddles with the TV remote. 'I'm very excited by this.'

'If this is porn, I'm going to be so mad.'

He screws up his nose. 'Please don't say that in your grandmother's house.'

'You don't even believe in ghosts.'

'Um, one, *hell yes* I do. I'm not messing with the other side, you don't know what's there. And two, it's just wrong. And three, Mags, if you're listening, I'm very sorry about your granddaughter's terrible manners, and I hope they've got those digestive biscuits you like so much up there.'

'So the reason you won't watch *Ghost Hunters*...'

'Because it's creepy!'

'You know, I'm really reconsidering this friendship.'

'Shush, you,' he says, taking a seat beside me. 'Welcome to British cinematic genius.' He presses play and a semi-familiar theme song begins.

I groan, covering my eyes. 'Is this—'

Gideon looks immensely pleased with himself. 'I can't believe you've never seen *Downton Abbey*. I mean, we have to get through the whole Richard period but then it gets really good. We are obviously Team Matthew, by the way.'

'Hey. Spoilers.'

'It's been out ten years, Blackwell.'

'Yeah, but *still*.' I cannot believe Gideon has watched this. I cannot believe Gideon has watched this with my grandmother.

We watch in companionable silence, and I slip under Gideon's arm, though that's about as salacious as things get. I guess snotting all over him earlier kind of put him off getting near my face. But eventually I stop wondering what he's thinking or whether Nina got home safely or if my parents are still asleep, and I feel like I can breathe again. Deep, full lungfuls of sea-salt air.

By the time Gideon shakes me gently awake, the credits are rolling.

'C'mon, Clarissa. Let's get you home.'

'Don't call me Clarissa,' I mumble, half asleep.

'C'mon, sleepy Smurf. Let's get you home.'

'Urgh, I'm awake.'

He's grinning at me, hair sticking up on one side where he must have lain down. 'You're cute when you're sleepy.'

'You're just cute,' I mutter. 'It's very annoying.'

'So I've been told.'

'I knew something was going on between you and Miles,' I say, and he laughs. 'I'm not tired,' I protest.

'Really?'

I hesitate. 'I just…I don't want to go home yet.' *I have nightmares,* I think. *Where I'm in the passenger seat and she disappears and I can't reach the wheel.*

Gideon holds up the remote. 'Another episode? And before you ask, no, this thing does not have internet. Pretty sure the TV still only has four channels.'

'Barbaric.'

'It's rustic.'

'Show me your comic,' I blurt out.

He blinks. 'What?'

I sit up, shaking the blanket from my shoulders, wide awake now. 'Go get it. I know you have it, you draw in ink.' I grab his hands, the tips coated in black. I always thought he must have been fiddling with his car or perpetually fixing bike chains—I didn't realise until tonight that the stains were ink bled from the tip of a felt pen.

'Um,' he says, his eyes fixed somewhere above my head.

'Please.'

'Uh.'

'I'll trade you.'

'Trade me what?'

'A stick drawing?'

He laughs, ears red. 'It's stupid,' he says.

'Oh my god, it's fan-fiction, isn't it? Please tell me it's some sordid Harry–Draco comic.'

'Is that…a thing?'

'We're circling back to Drarry later. Come on, I promise I won't tell anyone. Cross my heart. You can throw me to Bruce if I ever break it.'

He scruffs the back of his hair, and for a glorious moment I'm treated to a sliver of sun-browned skin. I think he has hip muscles. Is that a thing?

'Fine,' he says. 'But only a little bit, not all of it.'

I squeak something nonverbal, clapping my hands. 'Thank you, *thank you!*'

He disappears into the dark, and in the time he's gone I text Theo to say *I'm gonna be late* and *The password is TheoIsABooger123.*

Theo: ???

Me: TheoPayForYourOwnAccountYouCheapo was too long.

Theo: I was gonna stuff pillows in your bed but now I'm just gonna let you get caught

Me: Sneaking out was your idea!

Theo: For some air, not snogging Gideon for three hours

Me: How do you know i'm snogging Gideon???

Me: Who even says snogging?

Me: Wait did someone see us?
Me: Because it's sort of a secret…
Me: THEO????

The back door clangs open, and I stare up at Gideon, my heart pounding, mind running through all the possibilities. I mean, maybe him dropping me home was kinda obvious. And it's not a *secret* secret, it's just a *we haven't had time to tell Miles and Ava yet because it literally just happened last night* secret. Right?

'What happened?' he asks cautiously, settling on the floor next to me.

'Nothing.' I shove my phone under my butt.

'You look kinda wired.'

'Nope. All good. I—'

I forget whatever I was about to say. Silently, gently, I pry the pages from Gideon's hands. They're so beautiful, so lifelike I think for a moment I'm staring at photographs. Faces that I don't quite recognise: cheekbones and smiles and scars, all so carefully etched they seem to breathe real air. I spread them out in front of me, shuffling them to a semblance of order. The most realistic pictures were stacked on top. Beneath, there are panels and drawings like the ones I saw earlier tonight. There's a story running through each pane; I don't know what it is exactly, but there's a boy who looks a lot like Gideon wearing a cape and a lightning-bolt vest. There are a few hapless swimmers, a pretty girl with red hair, a boy who looks like Miles if Miles were taller and darker and wore a top hat.

'They're the Bad Luck Buddies. Don't laugh, I came up with the name when I was eleven.'

I struggle to control my features, smoothing out a smile. He leafs through the pages, settling on one that looks most like him.

'This is Captain Curse. He can save everyone around him by absorbing their bad luck. He's very handsome and tortured because I was going through an Alan Moore phase.' I snort, and he keeps going. 'He's technically invincible, but the bad luck still hurts. So if he gets hit by a car, it still feels like he got hit by a car.'

'Poor Captain.'

He pulls out another frame, a boy and girl side by side. 'This is Leap. He can time travel, but only ten seconds forward or back. And that's Nightshade—she's invisible but only in the dark. During the day she's a barista named Melanie.'

I lift the pages to follow the snippets of their story. They're funny and sad, tragic and silly. Leap can't save his dad because it takes more than ten seconds to stop a train. Nightshade tries to be invisible an hour earlier in daylight savings. Captain Curse saves a girl and then drowns three times. A man who looks an awful lot like Francis sends them on missions, but mostly they seem to be struggling through a high school for superheroes where everyone else has better powers.

I giggle at one pane, in which Captain Curse adopts a black cat named Jinx, only to find out she's good luck. She keeps bringing him four-leaf clovers and he keeps losing them.

'Gideon, these are really good.'

His eyes are fixed on the floor. 'You have to say that, I'm sitting right here.'

'No! I mean it, I love them. Oh, poor Leap—' I get distracted by a series of panes where the trio tries to find dates to their formal dance. Leap gets stuck in a time loop, jumping forward and back, testing one-liners on a girl. She's not impressed by any of them and ends up going to the dance with Melanie.

'Who's this?' I hold up a page, so life-like I almost mistake it for a photo. There's a blonde woman smiling, a laugh half-caught on her lips. Her hands rest on the edges of a wheelchair, though the picture has been abandoned halfway through. Her knees fade out of the frame.

'Oh,' Gideon says, taking the picture and considering it for a moment. 'Just a character I thought about adding.' He sets it to one side, face down.

He lets me flick through the stories, mumbling comments whenever I laugh or gasp, drawn into the world he's created.

'I know it's kind of stupid,' he repeats.

'Gideon.'

'It's just for fun, really. I don't—'

He shuts up when I lean over and kiss him. 'Thank you,' I say.

His hands wrap around my neck, one thumb caressing my jawline. 'For what?'

'Making me laugh.'

And we don't talk for a while, because his lips are on my lips, and my heart is beating too fast. Then his hands are under my shirt, tracing a line across my ribs. We kiss until my lips are sore and Gideon's breath is ragged. And when he drops me home, the moon is far too high in the sky and I know I'll barely fall asleep before my alarm wakes me up again. But it doesn't matter, because now there are no more secrets. And if there are no more secrets, maybe I can start laying the foundations of a new life, one that feels a little sturdier beneath my feet.

Maybe I can live.

Maybe I can breathe again.

14

MONDAY COMES FAR too soon, my body raw and aching from too many late nights and swimming sessions, the skin permanently pruned on my fingertips. My hair is matted into a chlorinated mess, the curls heaped on one side, dried in a haphazard tangle where my head hit the pillow.

Gideon picks me up so early that the sun hasn't even risen yet. He waits leaning against his car, smiling as I thrust my overloaded gym bag at him.

'I hate mornings. I hate swimming. I hate you.'

He drops a kiss on my head and tosses the bag into his trunk. 'Good morning to you too. How about coffee first?'

I grunt at him and buckle myself in as he starts the car. We texted until I fell asleep with my phone propped in my hand, and I jolted awake to the sound of an alarm I dearly wanted to throw against a stack of bricks.

A car pulls up behind us, idling on the kerb. I spin around, clutching the headrest. It's too dark to see the driver, but that ridiculous red doorless Jeep is instantly recognisable.

'Is that *Billy Martin*?'

Gideon shrugs. 'Yeah, guess so.'

'Is he even old enough to drive?'

Theo comes bounding out of the house and throws himself into the car, far more awake than I am. My mouth gapes open and I wave my arms frantically through the rear window—he does an excellent job of pretending not to see me.

'Kid's been driving since he was twelve,' Gideon says. 'Sorry, city girl, things are kinda different round here. He probably shouldn't be driving himself into town, though I doubt anyone would ticket him.'

'I didn't realise he and Theo were such *buds*. I can't believe him. Is he sneaking around? I swear to god, if that moron corrupts my baby brother into sneaking out and drinking—'

'Like we did—'

'That's different.'

He smirks, so I stick my finger in one of his dimples.

'You're vicious before caffeine,' he says.

'Just drive the car, Hawthorn.'

I narrow my eyes at the rearview mirror, catching a glimpse of a red plaid shirt. I'm pretty sure I've seen that shirt before, and it was on Theo's floor. But no, that's ridiculous. Billy is aggressively heteronormative—he wears Bintang singlets, his favourite movie is the fifth *Fast and the Furious* movie and half his meals are protein shakes. There's *no way*.

We pull up at the Beach Bean and find that Mrs Kostakis already has our coffees made. I run in and out, pausing long enough to yell thank you over my shoulder, conscious that we're probably late.

Sure enough, when we arrive, everyone else is already in the water. The coach makes us swim in separate lanes, which devolves into me and Gideon trying to race each other without properly racing. Then we're set to drills, dives and a final relay set.

Just as I think my arms might actually turn to rubber, the coach blows the blessed whistle to signal the end of practice and calls out, 'States next week! Don't forget your permission slips!'

I don't get the chance to talk to Theo until he slinks out of the showers, hair dripping onto his collar. I nab him by the sleeve, waiting until most of the boys have passed. 'Hey. What the hell, Theo. You can't get into a car with underage drivers.'

He rolls his eyes at me. 'Chill out, the dude's a better driver than—'

Than you. I glance around out of habit, but nobody's heard and nobody would care even if they had. Theo looks ashamed anyway, and brushes a hand nervously over the back of his neck. 'Yeah. Whatever. Sorry. He was going this way anyway.'

'If you don't wanna ride your bike, you can drive with me and Gideon.'

He gags. 'Pass. You guys are so gross.'

'Theo—'

'Yeah, yeah. Gotta go.'

He shoulders his way out of the gym, the doors banging

shut behind him. I frown, realising that we've missed too many zombie-movie nights and that I don't really know what's going on with Theo lately. Is he happy here? Does he really like guys like Billy, who seem so unlike the Theo I know? Billy Martin is just so…macho. He's all red plaid shirts and rough sports and pictures of half-naked girls stuck inside the doors of his locker. He laughs at period jokes. Theo's still an idiot, but at least he's moderately aware for a teenage boy. He doesn't need to be reminded to buy birthday cards for Mum, and he lets our neighbour's kids paint his nails pink whenever they want.

Gideon appears behind me, his hand barely grazing mine. 'Hey.'

'Hey.'

'Can you be late?'

I lean forward on my toes and kiss him quickly. 'No, but I *can* meet you for a picnic dinner tonight. But only if there's actual homework involved,' I warn.

'Deal.'

I spread out what meagre rations I could scramble together: bread rolls, a few greens, half a roast chicken from last night, and the remains of a chocolate gift box with only the reject flavours left. I set everything on Nan's old table, then drift back to the unsorted books. I should be focusing on my English essay, but there are so few titles left to sort through. Somehow, through late nights and stolen moments, Gideon and I have managed to archive almost every book in Nana's house. Despite my surreptitious snooping, however, I couldn't find any more information on the girls whose names were on the pages inside the apothecary curio. I eventually built up the courage to google them, but these women lived long before the internet news cycle was a thing. I shake my head, trying to push the thought away.

In the corner of Nan's spare room, there's a special crate labelled *Museum*. My entire plan depends on my mother not stepping foot in this part of the house for another two weeks. I prise the lid off, inspecting the collection so far. The apothecary curio isn't there. It's still stashed in the washing machine, hidden from the world.

If the pang in my chest is regret, I've become very good at ignoring it.

The curation card sits atop the pile, as yet unmarked: *Loan or bequest*.

The prompt remains uncircled, unsigned. I don't know. Where am I going to put one hundred priceless books? It's not like I can shove them in my wardrobe, next to my shoes and winter coats. And where am I going to put the hundreds more that are worthless, or worth so little they can be bought on eBay for twenty bucks?

I sigh, lying back and covering my face with a crooked elbow. I'm so *tired*. Gideon will be here any minute. He texted me ten minutes earlier: *Driving home now, there soon*.

He disappeared before last period, but I never asked why. Family stuff? He never did say anything more after that day at the swimming hole, and I've been too self-absorbed to ask. I resolve to talk to him tonight. Whenever he gets here.

My eyelids feel so heavy.

Just for a minute, I tell myself.

Gideon will wake me up. I should set a timer. Just in case.

Just...

I jolt awake, mouth dry and head dizzy. The house is pitch-black, the sun well and truly set. I know, with a sick feeling in my stomach, that too much time has passed, and I scramble to fling myself upright. My head throbs and my neck aches, and my shoulders are sore where they've dug into the hard floor. My phone screen is lit up with messages.

Dad: *missed call*

Theo: *Dad wants to know if you're coming home soon?*

Dad: *Dad left a message. Dial 321 to listen.*

I scroll through the notifications, fingers trembling, but there's nothing else. Icy dread rushes through my veins. *No no no.* Not again. The time on my screen says it's ten o'clock. Gideon is five hours late. He hasn't called. And maybe he just forgot, but he's not that stupid. He knew. He was on his way. He was in the car—

I sprint from the house, wrenching the back door open and flying up the garden path. His car isn't in the driveway. I rush to the front door of the bungalow, hand hesitating. He's fine, he must be fine. Maybe his car broke down and his phone died. Maybe he's with Miles and forgot. I'm just overreacting.

Maybe he crashed his car.

My fist slams against the door. 'Gideon? Are you okay? Gideon!'

There's a tumbling noise, and someone speaking softly. It seems like an age before the door cracks open, and when it does my stomach drops.

'Hello,' says a shaky voice.

The woman who stares up at me is pretty, blonde hair frizzed around her ears. She's in her pyjamas, feet clad in fuzzy slippers. She looks so much like Gideon that she couldn't possibly be anyone but his mother. She's sitting in a wheelchair, her shoulders stooped forward and hands shaking with tremors she seems unable to control.

'I'm—I'm sorry,' I stammer. 'I was—I…My name is Reece. I was meant to meet Gideon to study, and he never came, and I got so worried. I'm sorry. I shouldn't have—'

She raises a hand slowly, and the cuff of her sleeve quivers. 'Oh, h-hello, darling.' She smiles kindly, though it only seems to light half her face. 'He's not home yet. Come in, come in.' She navigates her wheelchair back a few inches, making room, even though she struggles to make her hands obey. 'Gideon's talked about you so much.'

I feel, stupidly, like I'm going to cry. This is why Gideon doesn't want to leave Hamilton. I think of all the times I pushed him, without understanding. I smile back, as warmly as I can, and step across the threshold.

'Do you—um, I'm sorry, would you like some help?'

She laughs, a rattling sound that echoes with some of Gideon's huskiness. 'This damn chair, the wheels are useless. If you can steer me to the couch, I'll get myself up.'

I do as she asks. 'Not supposed to be walking today,' she says, wincing as she eases herself onto the threadbare couch. 'I had a bit of a fall. Gideon's gone to see if the doctor will come, I'm sorry he's missed your study session. It's silly, really. The tiles were wet…' There's a walker parked in the corner of the room, and from the worn leather seat it seems well used.

'Where are my manners? I'm Grace, and it's very lovely to meet you, Reece.'

'It's really nice to meet you too. Can I—maybe I could make you some tea? While you wait?' I cringe, because it's her house, and I shouldn't be offering to poke around, but she seems a little grey and her eyes are pinched in the corner like she's in pain.

'I suppose I should be the one offering,' she says wryly, as though she's seen the thought written on my face. 'But so long as you don't mind, I'd love a peppermint. Tea bags are on the counter, help yourself to whatever you can find.' She pauses to take a breath. 'It's not much. A few bad days lately.'

I nod, like I understand, and rifle through the cabinets. They're too empty. I try to remember the last time Gideon ate lunch, and think of the half-empty packets of biscuits he'd brought to Nan's the other night. I wonder if the crumbled scones and wrapped chocolates cost him more than I knew, then push the thought away. Maybe we have more secrets than I thought.

I find the cups and kettle, careful not to overfill Grace's cup, then bring everything back. 'You're a sweet girl,' she says, taking a slow sip and ignoring the few splotches of tea that end up on her shirt. 'Mary's granddaughter, if I'm not mistaken?'

I nod again.

'Well, that woman was a godsend. I miss her very, very much.'

'You knew my grandmother too?'

'I did. I started helping her when she first moved in, and then, well, she ended up helping me.' She smiles, sadly, and I glance down at my own half-filled cup.

'Will Gideon be long? I can wait with you, if you like.'

'You're very kind, Reece, but I expect you should be getting home. I'm sure he'll be back soon—the on-call doctor can get pretty booked up.'

I try to remember the name I'm sure Mum's mentioned before. 'Mr Gregory? He has the twenty-four-hour practice?' That's not exactly how Mum described him. I'm pretty sure she called him *an obsolete crackpot who can barely take a piss unassisted.* Or something like that. I also know he's the only free doctor in Hamilton—the rest are private clinics with fees to match.

'That's him.'

A set of lights flare through the curtains. As Grace tries to stand, I wonder if she's made too light of the fall she mentioned. 'I'll get the door,' I offer, waiting until she waves me forward.

Gideon's face is ashen, and it falls further when he sees me. 'Reece...'

I shake my head, barely. 'I shouldn't have invited myself

in. I'll go.' But he doesn't move, and I can't slip through the crack between him and the flyscreen door. He's still standing on the porch, eyes red like he's been crying.

'Gideon,' I whisper. 'What's wrong?'

He's quiet for a long time before answering, his throat bobbing wildly. 'The doctor won't come. I don't know what to do. I have to—she won't go to the hospital, but last time—'

His hands are flying everywhere and I take hold of them. 'What happened?'

'She was getting in the shower, and she wasn't using her walker. It was a good day, she said. And then she fell, and her hip is black and I think maybe it's broken, but she won't go to the hospital because they won't let her come home, and I can't—I can't think, I don't know...'

I pull him to the front steps, guiding him to sit. Then I dig my phone out of my pocket and dial.

'Mum? I need your help.'

'Ms Hawthorn, I should have known.' Mum arrives in her pyjamas, emergency gumboots pulled over her penguin-patterned leggings plastered with the words *I'm a cool mum*.

Her face is lit up, all bright cheer and friendly chatter. She sets her things on Gideon's dining-room table and goes about her medical assessment, kneading Grace's hip and clucking in mock disapproval and making Grace laugh. All the while, Gideon sits beside me, silent and stiff, refusing to look at me but never letting go of my hand.

When Mum has finished, she sits next to Gideon. 'You took very good care of her, Gideon. I know a fall can be scary, but it looks like all she's done is some soft tissue damage. I'm going to take her into the clinic now, to do some scans and make sure nothing's broken, and her neurologist should check on her medications. Now, are you awake enough to drive Reece home? You kids should get some sleep, you've got school tomorrow.'

He nods, stiffly, and Mum rises, clapping her hands. 'Right. Let's get moving, Grace. If we get there before midnight we won't have to deal with that dreadful intern.'

Gideon stands too. He seems dazed for a moment, then manages to find the words. 'Thank you, Mrs Blackwell. For coming.'

Mum never lets her work face slip. But for a split second, she looks impossibly sad. Then she pats him on the cheek and smiles. 'It's Olivia, darling. And you're welcome anytime. Now help me get your mum into the car and we'll get her comfy.'

They wheel Grace to the car and lift her inside. Gideon watches them pull out of the driveway, wandering a few steps forward like he might follow the car all the way to the hospital. I wait a minute; two, five, ten.

Finally, I clear my throat and gently touch his shoulder, 'Gideon? It's cold, you should come inside.'

He turns, as if surprised I'm still here. 'What are you doing?'

'What do you mean?'

'Why were you here?'

'Oh. You never showed up. I got worried when your car was gone...'

He remains rooted to his spot on the driveway, so I venture out. 'I was going to tell you,' he says.

'Gideon...'

He shakes his head. 'I just wanted to feel normal. For once, I wanted to not have to think about frozen dinners and medicine and doctors' appointments and what the hell we're supposed to do next year. But I should have told you sooner.' He looks around, like the world we're standing in is suddenly foreign to him. 'I'm not ashamed of my mum,' he says, his voice deepening with seriousness. 'I *want* to be here. I *want* to help. But I don't tell many people because it's none of their business, and they ask shit questions, and then they tell her to try fucking yoga.'

'It's okay, I understand.'

His legs seem to fold out as he sits on the porch steps, like he's got no more energy, nothing left to give to the world. 'It's Parkinson's. Stage three.'

I don't know what to say. Mum's treated Parkinson's patients before, but I don't remember how rapidly the stages can change or what they mean.

'She got it early,' he continues. 'Just really shitty, shitty luck.' He leans back, until his head is resting against the porch, and closes his eyes. 'I'm so tired.'

I hold out my hands. 'Come on.'

He sighs, opening his eyes too slowly. 'Yeah. Yeah, come on. Where's your bike?'

'No, I mean. Come on. To bed.' He stares at me blankly. 'I'm not leaving you here, Gideon. I'll stay until they come back.'

'No, you don't have to—'

'I'll sleep on the couch. Come on. We're both tired, and you shouldn't be driving. You can stress as much as you want tomorrow, but right now there's nothing else you can do. And you look like you're going to crash and I can't carry you inside.' I poke his shoulder, solid and unyielding under my fingertip, to make my point.

He gives a breathy half-laugh, wiping a hand over his face. 'Okay. I guess that would be okay.'

He makes me wait in the lounge room while he tidies his room and bathroom. I text Dad and tell him I'm sleeping at Nan's house and that Mum said it was okay—which is sort of a lie, but not one I think I'll get in trouble for.

I realise there's so much I didn't notice when Grace first opened the door. The bungalow is small but sweet; someone has taken the time to add loving touches. The walls have been painted a periwinkle blue, which seems quite soothing the longer I look at it. The floors are mostly worn carpet, except in the kitchen, which has only one hotplate and the smallest sink I've ever seen. The table in the corner is set with a vase and fresh flowers in the centre. It has three seats, and a spare spot where I suppose the wheelchair must fit when his mum needs it. The walls are loaded with picture frames, all white wood but different shapes, laid out in a perfectly curated grid. I smile at tiny versions of Gideon, and laugh at one of him naked in a paddling pool. I'm surprised to see Nan in another, a pot of tea in one hand, the other wrapped around Grace's shoulders. Grace is so striking: tall and slim, with straight teeth and a wild grin. She's holding a baby in her arms, blissfully happy. No hint of illness. No hesitation in the way she stands. There's another of her and Gideon, the picture folded in half like someone's been cut out. Gideon looks around ten years old, awkward long limbs and red spots on his cheeks. But they're smiling together at the edge of the waterhole, their hiking boots covered in mud.

There's a gadget on the coffee table, labelled MediAlert. We tried to give Nan one, right before she moved into the nursing home—it's basically a fancy panic button with a GPS inside. I pick it up, wondering if Nan gave it to Gideon after we told her the shop wouldn't let us return it. She hated it so much, and they're pretty expensive.

I don't hear Gideon return. He must have been standing behind me for a while, because he seems to scuff his feet purposefully. 'Um, there's a spare toothbrush in the bath-room. And you can wear these, if you want. I don't think they'll fit but...'

'Sorry,' I say, setting the device back down.

He just shrugs, falling back against the couch.

I brush my teeth and change as quickly as I can. He's given me a T-shirt that comes down to my knees, and old Spider-Man bottoms that barely hit my ankle. I wonder where I dug these out from, because they definitely haven't fit him for a while.

From the corridor I can see inside one of the bedrooms. It looks like a hospital, too cold and clinical to be lived in properly. The adjustable bed is set to a half-rise, and there are pill bottles on the nightstand. There's nothing on the floor, no other furniture—no sharp edges, if I had to guess.

It feels too invasive to look any closer, so I walk past the other closed door and emerge in the lounge room. Gideon is holding the MediAlert in his hands, flipping it over and over.

'I thought she was dead,' he whispers. 'I got the alert when I was halfway home. I've never driven so fast. She was just lying there, so still, and I thought, I'm too late, she hit her head or she stopped breathing or…I don't know. Then she sat up, and she was all black on one side. Mum freezes, sometimes. Everything can be fine, and then she just…stops. She said the floor was wet and she couldn't reach the handrail.'

'I'm so sorry. That's awful, you shouldn't have to deal with all this alone.'

'The doctor wouldn't even come, because he said she should be in assisted living. Said it wasn't covered by general practice and to call the ambulance. He was just being a dick. I wanted to punch him in the face but I needed my hand to drive home again.'

'I'm sorry,' I say again, which feels so useless, but I don't know what else to say. 'You should get some sleep. I'll wait up for a bit, in case they call.'

He shakes his head. 'I'll take the couch. I won't sleep anyway.'

I sigh, walking to the light switch and flicking it off. I grab a cushion and toss it at him, then carefully stretch out on the sofa and drag him down beside me.

'What are you doing?' he asks, his breath ruffling my hair.

'If you're going to be stubborn and stay out here, then at least lie down. And move over, you're hogging all the room.'

'Reece—'

'Look, I'm pretty sure Mum will be *more* mad if she comes back and finds me in your bed. So we're going to lie here awake together, being stubborn, and tomorrow we'll deal with whatever we need to. Deal?'

He's quiet for a while. Then his hand wraps around my waist and he pulls me a little closer. 'Deal,' he whispers.

'Hey, Gideon?'

'Yeah?'

'How old were you the last time you wore these pants?'

He laughs, leaning his head against my spine. 'Go to sleep, Reece.'

And without meaning to, I do.

15

THIS IS THE deal we establish: Mum agrees not to ground me forever on compassionate grounds, and Grace reaches the same conclusion with the additional clause that she would really prefer we keep any future hypothetical doors open, and also do we know how condoms work? I've never seen Gideon turn so red, and I only manage to keep from laughing by slamming a hand over my mouth.

I suspected it the night Mum raced to Gideon's in her beaten-up station-wagon chariot: she'd already been treating Grace at the clinic. Grace was okay, in the end—bruised but nothing broken. But that's all Mum'll tell me, because they have doctor–patient confidentiality, and it's none of my business anyway.

Actually, that's not quite true. A few days later, when Dad and Theo are out, she comes to sit beside me on the bed, and wraps me in a hug.

'I'm really proud of you, honey.'

I hug her back, surprised. 'For what?'

'For being smart enough to call me, even if you thought you'd get in trouble.'

'I'm really glad you came, Mum. Thank you.' And it's true. Watching her work with Grace, I felt the sick feeling in my stomach ease immediately. I knew Grace would be okay with Mum. No other possibility crossed my mind.

'I do need to speak to you about something,' Mum says, haltingly. 'And it might be unprofessional of me to do so, and you can't ever tell anyone that we had this conversation.'

I nod, holding Mr Snuggles tight to my chest.

'The lines are a little blurred here. But I think Gideon might listen to you more than a nameless doctor shoving them around a hospital ward. Honey, his mum really needs to start thinking about assisted living. Falls like that are only going to keep happening, and I know Gideon means well, but one day he won't be able to help. Parkinson's is a shit of a disease, and it's cruel and unfair. And it only ever gets worse. That's a terrible guarantee.'

She pauses, and I can tell she's wondering how much to tell me. It's okay to talk about Gideon; *he's* not her patient. But it's also not his life, and I can feel Mum reaching for the words to find the right balance. 'Grace is…worried he takes on too much already, but he keeps insisting they'll manage. You don't have to push him, but if it comes up, he might feel better if you could be…supportive of the idea.'

I fidget, taking care not to agree. I doubt I could ever tell Gideon he should send his mum away, no matter the circumstances. 'I don't think they can afford it…' I say, in an attempt at an answer. I don't know how much else I can tell her, without betraying Gideon's secrets.

Mum sits back, a little surprised. 'Ah. That makes more sense. I did wonder.' She leans against my headboard and changes the subject. 'So. Tell your old mum some gossip. Are you two dating? Boyfriend-girlfriend?'

'Oh my god,' I groan, shoving my face behind a pillow.

She reaches over to tickle me on the ribs. 'Going steady? Did he pin you?'

'Gross, what does that even *mean*?'

Mum laughs, settling in beside me. 'Want to go watch some *Ghost Hunters* and I promise to stop asking about your sex life?'

I turn beet-red. 'Would it make you feel better if I said I don't *have* a sex life?'

'You know, it makes me a bad feminist, but yes it does. Do we need to go over "the talk", just in case?'

'*Way* too late, Mum. Nan gave me *Where Did I Come From?* when I was, like, seven. Then regular refreshers over the years.'

Mum screws up her nose. 'She made me watch a childbirth video when I got my first boyfriend. Nothing kills the mood quite like the memory of a good crowning.'

I try to block the image from my mind, but end up laughing too. 'I miss her,' I say, for the first time since she died.

'Me too, honey. Me too. But it's nice, hearing good memories. Like she's sticking around, just a little longer.'

I sit up, head tilted to one side. Mum's happy. Relaxed. I should tell her. Just spit the words out. *Mum, I gave away my inheritance. It's on display soon. Strangers will pick apart the books Nan treasured and I'll let them.*

'Mum?'

'Yes, honey?'

I bite down on my lip. Say it. Just tell her now. 'Um, can you help me with my biology homework?'

She blinks, and I wonder if she can hear the lie in my voice. 'Oh. Sure. Come on, let's go see if Theo left anything in the pantry.'

I'll tell her. I just want one good night.

I'll tell her, I will.

Soon.

I don't tell her. The state swimming competition arrives too quickly, and I'm too nervous to tackle any conversations that require any more than a few begrudging 'yes' or 'no' answers.

I hate competing. I love swimming, but I hate the crowds watching. I don't even look at the heat list—Gideon has to write down my races on a separate piece of paper. Relay and freestyle. That's all I want to know until I need to be in the water.

'I'm gonna vomit.'

Ava holds out a Beach Bean paper bag. 'Aim for that.'

Miles turns around in the front seat of the car. He somehow still called shotgun, despite the fact that I'm the one on my way to compete. 'When I get stage fright I just imagine—'

'Everyone naked?' I scowl at him, a fresh wave of nausea gripping my stomach.

'No, I was gonna say I imagine I'm a pre-programmed

robot and that I can't make a mistake because it's not physically possible.'

I groan, leaning forward into Ava's bag. 'Not helpful.'

Ava pats my shoulder. 'It's okay, Reece, what's the worst that could happen?'

'I could have a panic attack, sink in the deep end, inhale water and drown.'

Gideon's eyes find me in the rearview mirror. 'Trained lifeguard in the front seat,' he reminds me. He's even wearing his yellow lifeguard jacket.

'Oh. That actually *is* helpful.' I am fairly certain Gideon won't let me drown. Plus, he looks cute in yellow.

Ava mutters something obscene about other ways Gideon can help me de-stress. I look up at her with wild-eyed panic, but Miles is too occupied by the AUX cord to have heard anything.

We'll tell Miles. But the last week has been a bit weird. Gideon and I haven't really seen each other outside school, because (a) swimming practice for states has taken up every spare moment and (b) Gideon rushes home straight after to take care of his mum, and seems reluctant to invite me along. Which I guess I understand. Maybe he's just trying to keep everything in his life separate for now. Or maybe he's going to break up with me. Even though we're not really dating. Can you break up with a non-boyfriend? But he's been so nice, and he still picks me up in the morning, so maybe we're fine. But he hasn't kissed me since the Sunday when Nina showed up, so maybe we're not. Maybe—

I curl up sideways, the straps of my swimsuit digging into

my shoulders. Ava wriggles over to give me some space. I can't differentiate between real-life stress and swim stress, so I keep my eyes shut, picturing an empty swimming pool with empty stands.

'We're here,' Gideon says. 'Do you guys wanna go get seats? Reece and I have to head to the changerooms.'

Miles peeks at me from the front seat. 'Rooting for you, Reece. Kick his butt.'

'Please go away, I'm trying to forget people are here.'

Two doors slam shut. I close my eyes again. The door beside my head opens.

'Move over.'

I open one eye. Gideon's standing in the door, the light on his hair making it glow like he's some kind of patron saint of nauseated teenage girls. 'What are you doing?' I ask suspiciously, ready to cause him bodily harm if he tries to drag me out of the car by force.

But he squeezes into the back seat and closes the door. 'Just checking on you,' he says. He seems amused by my panic.

'I hate races,' I mumble, tipping forward into his chest. I don't care if he's going to break up with me, I just want to have as much access to his stupid perfect torso as possible before that happens.

'And yet, you are very, very good at them,' he answers, an arm coming to rest across my shoulders.

'Are you okay?' I ask, because now seems as good a time as any. We've texted, but he always manages to evade the question.

He takes a big breath. His muscles move under my cheek, and his heartbeat thrums against my ears. 'I think so,' he says. 'I don't really want to talk about it though. I get stressed, and I think only one of us can freak out right now.'

'You can have a turn if you want.'

He laughs. 'It's okay. You do your thing.'

'*Urgh.*'

'Come on,' he says. 'You're tough as hell, Reece. Let's go win some shit.'

We win *a lot* of shit. Theo is good. Gideon is great. I'm better. The girls' relay team wins by ten whole seconds. I couldn't even see the other swimmers when my hand slapped onto the concrete and my teammates pulled me out of the water, screaming a victory chant. I hear Miles and Ava hollering my name in the stands. Gideon throws me over his shoulder after the final whistle, then tosses me in the dive pool. Soon the whole team is in with us, flipping off the high boards and creating such a scene that the coach comes and yells at us to stop acting like *goddamn waterlogged miscreants*. It doesn't matter. It's a good day, and all the nerves are gone. Gideon has two gold medals around his neck, and he's bouncing on his feet when we finally drag ourselves out of the water and onto dry land. He bounds into the change-rooms, promising to hurry.

I cast my eye back at the stands, searching for Mum and Dad. I could hear them when I stepped onto the starting block, but I couldn't pick them out of the crowd. Miles and Ava made a sign covered in glitter that they're still waving, and Billy Martin is here too, for some reason. I finally catch sight of my parents, right in the middle section, and only because Theo is with them, wearing his neon-yellow cap. I wave at them, signal to the changeroom, then pause.

There's a familiar swish of hair in the very back row. A face I think I recognise trying to sneak out the rear doors. But it can't be.

My feet are moving anyway. Then I'm running, even though the lifeguard calls after me to slow down. Past the stands, out the door, into the car park.

'Nina!'

She goes still. Turns around. 'You're still fucking magic in the water, you know that?'

Then she gets in her car and drives away.

Miles and Ava have run after me. They're staring after Nina's car, which is already turning out of the lot. They have matching looks of bewilderment on their faces.

'Who was *that*?'

I smile. 'Someone who might not hate me anymore.'

16

I JOLT AWAKE in my bed to the sound of voices yelling. This is particularly unpleasant because Gideon drove us all home very late and my eyelids feel like they've been glued shut.

'You can't tell me what to do!' says Theo, his voice haughtier than usual.

I can tell this is going to be a big fight, because Mum's least favourite thing to be told is how she can and can't raise her children—especially *by* her children. I groan, rolling over and pulling a pillow over my head.

'The hell I can't!' Mum fires back. 'My house, my rules.'

'Would you have cared if it was a girl?'

Dad interjects, his voice low and calm, and I almost can't make out his words through the wall. 'Of course we would have cared, son. And it's not about that, it's—'

'What's "that", Dad? That I'm gay? Is that inconvenient? A bit too much to handle before coffee? Should we just keep ignoring it for a little while longer?'

'What? Where is this coming from?'

I throw off the covers, and I'm already running to the kitchen before I hear anything else. Theo is standing on the staircase, wearing only boxer shorts.

'We all know you don't want a big gay son,' Theo yells, waving towards his room, 'and that's why we never talk about—'

'Theo,' I say, putting my hand on his shoulder. He whirls around, his chest heaving. 'It's okay, you don't have to do this if you don't want to.'

'Well, now I want to,' he says. 'I'm sick of not talking about it. I'm gay, Dad. Surprise!'

Dad takes off his glasses and pinches the bridge of his nose. 'Not that surprised, actually,' he mutters.

Mum and I frown at each other. 'Wait, what?'

'I realise,' Dad goes on, in a measured voice, 'that my upbringing was conservative, and that my family has some old-fashioned views. But that does not mean that they are *my* views, and that certainly doesn't mean that I don't love my son and accept him exactly as he is. And I was not ignoring you, Theo. I was giving you space to tell me in your own time, because I thought you'd tell me when you were ready.'

'Oh,' Theo says. 'Oh. So…'

'All I want is for you to feel happy and safe. And I love you very much.'

'Oh.' Theo's hand finds mine. 'Wait, so…this really is because there's a person in my bed, and not because it's a dude?'

My eyebrows arch into my hairline. 'There's a person in your bed?'

'Precisely,' Mum says. She rolls her eyes skyward. 'I'm going to need to find some literature on this.'

'Jesus, Mum, we're not banging.'

'Theo, don't say "banging",' Dad chastises.

I laugh. I don't mean to. It's a little hysterical. 'Sorry,' I say. I lean my forehead on Theo's shoulder. 'You okay?' I ask.

'Yeah, I guess,' he replies. 'This is kinda anticlimactic. I had a whole speech thing I was gonna say.'

Dad walks over to Theo and wraps him in a hug. 'You are still very much in trouble for hosting an unapproved sleepover.'

'Whatever,' Theo says, but he hugs Dad back.

'I would like us to talk about this properly,' Dad says. 'When you're ready, and somewhere you feel safe.'

Theo nods, and holds on to Dad a little tighter.

Then my parents step away, and Mum starts whispering frantically about setting boundaries and trying to decide on an appropriate method of discipline that conveys that they love and support him but *also* that he can't have house guests without asking.

I sit on the stairs. What a way to wake up. I always thought Dad *suspected*. But way back when Theo first came out, he told us he wanted more time before telling Dad. They were always so close, and I think we were all a little afraid that Dad's fire-and-brimstone upbringing might have…well, lingered. But I also thought it was strange that we stopped spending Christmas with Dad's side of the family a few years ago, and now I wonder if there was a reason behind it.

I nudge Theo's shoulder. 'So. Who's the dude in your

bed?' I almost ask if it really *is* Billy Martin, but I don't think I want to know the answer.

He grunts. 'This is so bullshit, he wasn't even *in* my bed. He was, like, bed adjacent. We were just studying late.'

'Studying late shirtless?'

He gives me a look. 'How's Gideon lately? Enjoying chemistry club?'

'Point taken.'

'Whatever, he's probably crawled down the drainpipe by now.'

'You're not gonna tell me, are you?'

He grins at me. 'Not a chance.' Then he stands up. 'So, ah, given the whole kinda-coming-out thing, I'm gonna go take a shower and chill out,' he announces to the room. 'You can yell at me later. That cool?'

Mum waves an exasperated hand at him. 'So long as you're being safe—'

'Oh my god,' Theo says, then sprints back up the stairs.

I clear my throat. Dad seems a little dazed. Mum is googling something on her phone.

'So. Coffee?'

Dad and Theo disappear for a long time. They used to do this all the time—they'd just drive around, and sometimes when they'd come back they'd be soaking wet or covered in dirt. Mum would ask where they'd been, and Dad would smile and say, *why, we've been on an adventure.* Once they went to a stadium concert on a whim. They came back covered in glitter and grinning like maniacs.

I peeked in Theo's room when they left, but I couldn't find any clues about the mystery boy. Whoever he is, he really must have crawled down the drainpipe because he definitely didn't go out the front door. I didn't hear a car start though—another point against Billy, since he drives that obnoxious four-wheel-drive everywhere.

I resign myself to a day of study and I'm halfway through our chemistry assessment when the phone rings. It's a blocked number, so I ignore it until it rings out. Then they ring back.

'Hello?' I answer.

'Hello, I'm looking for Ms Blackwell. My name is Gloria Akehurst. I'm the curator of the Museum of Medical Oddities. We're hosting the exhibition in memory of your grandmother?'

'Oh. Um. Well, that's me.'

'I'm pleased to have caught you. We've been waiting on some final paperwork for the exhibition, and a guest list with any family or friends who might want to attend. It's getting quite urgent so I wanted to call and make sure everything was all right?'

My stomach clenches. I think of the form I'm yet to fill in. *Loan or bequest?* Share my grandmother's legacy, or give it away forever?

'I'm sorry,' I hear myself say. 'We're still, um, arranging a few things. When do you need an answer by?'

The line is quiet while she thinks. 'Perhaps we can give you a little more time. I understand it can be a very difficult process. Shall we say next month?'

'Okay. Next month. I can do that.'

'And will you be needing a courier?'

'A what?'

'For a collection of this value, we usually send a specialised courier to collect the items. But if you'd prefer, you're welcome—'

'I can do it,' I say in a rush. I imagine some stranger picking their way through Nan's things, throwing them in the back of a van, ferrying them away. Taking the apothecary chest and poking through it, making assumptions. No, I'd rather do it myself.

'All right,' she says. 'Thank you very much, Clarissa. We'll talk soon, yes?'

'Yes,' I say. 'Soon.'

I hang up and look at the calendar. One month.

I'm running out of time.

All the symbols on my page blur together. It looks like a foreign language, a pattern I almost recognise but fail to understand.

I can't stay inside anymore. And in fact, there's somewhere else I realise I need to be. I thumb through the numbers on my phone and dial.

'Ava? I'm mopey again. Wanna surf?'

She squeals down the phone, delighted by the idea of dunking me in the swells. I bike down to the back beach, and she's already there, waxing her board.

'Come on,' she calls out. 'Ocean therapy.'

I tell her between waves. It helps to have surfing to focus on, so the words don't sting as much. Everything comes out in fragments. The collection. My mum's determination to hold on to everything. My old dream of joining Doctors Without Borders.

'I don't get it,' she says, frowning. 'What changed? You just woke up one day and didn't wanna do it anymore?'

I climb up on the board, sitting on the edge. She pulls herself up beside me, facing the sunset. It's getting quiet now. There hasn't been a decent wave in a while. The water laps at the board.

'Our friend died,' I whisper. 'It was a car crash. And after that…I don't know, I realised that doctors can't fix everyone.' I think of Willow lying in her casket. Her body whole and perfect from the outside. I didn't understand why they couldn't just put her back, the part of her that had come loose. *Wake up*, I screamed. *Just wake up.*

'I'm sorry,' Ava says, leaning against my shoulder. 'I had no idea.'

'It's not that I didn't want to tell you. It was more that, I don't know…it was nice not to be the sad girl with the dead friend.'

'So that girl from yesterday…'

'Nina.' I sigh. 'We were all so close. The three of us were best friends. And after everything happened, Nina wanted to talk about Willow all the time. It was like she was scared of forgetting. She started a journal, writing down all the things she could remember. Just little moments, or funny things she said. But I just…I kind of checked out. I couldn't talk about Willow without crying, so I just stopped talking about her altogether. I thought about her all the time, but I couldn't say it. Then Mum and Dad got worried, because I wasn't doing so well in school and I dropped out of swimming. I sort of became a hermit. They decided we needed a sea change, away from everything, and I just…left.'

I can't look at Ava, so I wrap my hands around my legs, tucking them close to my chest. The board rocks beneath us.

'I didn't tell Nina. I was leaving her all alone, and I didn't even say goodbye. I just couldn't do it—I couldn't say I missed Willow so much I had stopped functioning without her. Couldn't say that moving would feel like losing another friend. So we left, and she stopped answering my messages. And until yesterday, I thought she'd never speak to me again.'

'Jesus Christ,' Ava whispers. 'That's some heavy shit, Reece.'

'Sorry.'

'Don't be sorry. When we lost Dad, it was the same. I was little, so I didn't really understand, but I knew that if I talked about Dad, Mum would cry. So I learned to say nothing.'

I squeeze her hand. 'Sorry. I can't imagine losing my dad.'

'It hurts less now,' she says. 'It's always there, in the back of my mind. But it feels…healed. Like a scar. You'll never forget, but you'll live. Does that make sense?'

I nod, tears dripping down my cheeks.

'Okay, now, two things,' she says. 'Firstly, it sounds like you have to work out what you want from the world. Just because you can't save everyone, it doesn't mean you shouldn't try.'

I hiccup and she smiles. 'And the second thing?'

'Call her.'

'Call who?'

'Nina! Dude, she must have driven hours to watch you race. That's not a girl who hates you. That's a girl who *cares*.'

And as Ava tips me off the board and laughs maniacally, I think about Nina and the things we lost—and that I don't want this to be another piece that's taken away. Not when there's a chance: the smallest, peskiest glimmer of hope. Not when I can picture her in that car park, the way I'm sure she smiled before she turned away.

I think, maybe, I am finally tired of losing things.

17

AFTER AVA'S PEP talk, I decide to act on at least one piece of advice. I return to Frank's bookshop and ask him where I can get the curio valued. I may not know what I want, but it's worth finding out my options, at least. He gives me a white and gold card with an address listed in the city.

It turns out we don't have to wait long before Gideon finds a reason to drive us up. His mum needs special medication that's stocked at only a few locations. I haven't seen Grace again since that first night, and whenever I ask how she's doing he just says, 'She's okay,' and changes the topic.

So we pack ourselves into his car, start a playlist and drive through four hours of bush and farmland before arriving in the glorious, shiny city. I grin as we pass through the tunnel, emerging in one of my favourite spots—where the city meets the water's edge, and a cafe plays live music all night, and the boardwalk is always warm from the sun. Willow, Nina and I spent a lot of time there.

Gideon squints up at the signs. 'I have no idea where I'm

going,' he says cheerfully.

I check the card again. It's embossed and foiled in delicate gold. 'Head to the expensive part of town,' I say, punching the address into my phone.

We arrive ten minutes later. This place is nothing like the second-hand shop in Hamilton. There's a golden crest affixed to the doorway, beneath an etched sign that reads *Auctioneers of Antiques and Fine Arts*. Gideon and I share a nervous glance, then push forward through the heavy wooden doors—and just like that, we're swallowed whole, slipping out of the blistering summer heat and into a polished interior that hums with air conditioning and whispering voices. A white-gloved receptionist hurries to greet us, checking our names against a leather-bound appointment book, then ushers us into the showroom.

The scuff of my cheap tennis shoes seems absurd amid so much wealth: antique wooden dressers and golden ornaments, plain-looking vases bearing tags with too many zeroes. There's so much art on the wall it could pass for a gallery.

And books. So many books. Each stored lying flat, barely brushing against each other on the shelves. I hardly have time to gape at it all before we're shown to a private room with a table, a velvet tray, and two chairs that might be for sitting or for display—they're covered in old velvet and supported by ornate carved legs, and seem like they might splinter apart with any considerable weight. I decide to stand, just in case, and try to telepathically project my thoughts to Gideon: *Don't you dare sit in that chair, Hawthorn, or the million-dollar bill is going straight to your house.*

The receptionist coughs politely. 'Just a moment, Ms Blackwell. The auditor will be with you shortly.'

The door clicks shut, and we're alone. I have the wild thought that I should shove as much of this pageantry in my bag and spend the rest of my days living on a beach, surviving on the spoils of my theft, but then I think that (a) Mum would probably drag me home and (b) there are at least seven cameras in this room.

'Maybe this was a mistake,' I hiss at Gideon, my hands sweating. This feels absurd. It's just an old book. They have plenty of those already. 'What if they laugh at us? What if they just take it from us? How did Nan even get this thing anyway—oh my god, what if she stole it?'

'Yes, your grandmother broke into a heavily guarded museum and stole an antique book. Retirement wasn't thrilling enough, so she turned to a life of international crime.'

I hate him. 'Please shut up.'

He shoves his hands into his pockets and obliges. He's dressed up for the occasion, and he actually looks quite adorable in chinos and a button-down shirt that's a little wrinkly in the arms but nevertheless well intentioned.

I try to discreetly wipe my sweaty palms against my dress. It's mint green and linen, and I haven't worn it since Mum bought it for me to wear last Christmas, because it requires an excessive amount of ironing to be wearable. It's a nice dress, but my shoes are grey at the toes and one of the laces is frayed. Should I have bought a new pair? I'm still fretting when a woman in a tailored suit walks in, the heels of her shoes clicking on the marble floors.

'Clarissa?'

I nod, not trusting my own voice. Now I'm sure I should have bought new shoes.

The woman smiles. Her teeth are very straight and very white. 'I'm Bronwyn. I believe Frank referred you?'

I nod again. Gideon has his palms collapsed in front of him like a choir girl. I squint at him, trying to tell him: *Stop being weird.*

Bronwyn winks at me. 'Don't be nervous, we're not as fancy as we seem. And you can sit in those chairs.'

'Thank you for seeing us,' I manage to squeak out. 'I feel a bit silly, actually, now I'm here. Maybe we should—'

Gideon pulls a chair out and gently sits me down in it. I will kill him if it breaks under my butt, though it feels surprisingly steady.

'Don't feel silly,' Bronwyn says. 'A man came in last week to have an artefact appraised —he swore it was Meiji era, hundreds of years old. Turned out to be his kid's old school project, poor dear.'

Gideon muffles a laugh, and I feel my shoulders relax. 'Okay. Well, I don't think this is a school project, but...'

I place the book on the velvet tray. The buckles are already undone, and I flip open the cover. Bronwyn goes very still.

'Oh my god,' she whispers. 'Is that...' She hurries to pull on a pair of white gloves, and retrieves something that looks like a pair of tweezers from her desk drawer. She eases a few drawers open and leans in close to inspect the bindings. She casts her eye over the inscription page—words I'd never really noticed below the skeleton—then picks the book up and squints at the back cover. I wonder if she can tell it's a false seal, ideal for hiding secrets. 'Never re-bound. Remarkable,' Bronwyn mutters. 'Original casing. Iron gall ink, almost certainly. Some erosion, but not bad, considering. I'd suggest it's pre-1860s. This is shellac coating, and the dovetail work looks rustic—and these grooves here, likely made with a spokeshave, or a drawknife.'

'You sound a lot like Frank,' Gideon jokes.

Bronwyn looks up, one eyebrow arched. 'Well, I probably should, he's my uncle. *No* respect for quality material if you ask me.'

She shucks off her gloves. 'Well. I don't know what to say. If it's real, and I think it is, this is…I don't know what to say, Ms Blackwell. Something like this, for the right buyer? Ten thousand, maybe more if there's some history behind it?'

'Fuck *me*,' says Gideon, before slapping a hand over his mouth. I feel my heart stop. I'm sure of it: one moment it's beating there, in my chest, and then it's not. A long, empty pause, in which I cannot comprehend what Bronwyn has just said. I thought Frank was *joking.*

'I don't…*what*?'

There's a bit of mischief in Bronwyn's eyes now. 'We could get more if we auctioned in Europe. Sotheby's could probably sell it for twenty if you let them do a private appraisal. Commission is steep but…'

'Ten *thousand*? That's ridiculous,' I blurt out. 'It's a *book.*'

'It's a relic. Part of history. People are alive—or, well, possibly dead—today because of what this contains,' Brownyn says, holding the velvet tray aloft. 'It's not pages and words; it's lives lost and saved. Faith tested. It's theories that were dreamed up before there was any hope of proving them. This is a part of the world, Clarissa, and people pay nicely for the honour.'

'But I put it in my nan's *washing machine.*'

Bronwyn cringes. 'I'm going to pretend I didn't hear you say that.'

'What do we do?' says Gideon. 'We can't just put this in the trunk and take it home again. Can we?'

'We'll provide you with a written appraisal,' Bronwyn answers, scribbling details on letterhead paper. 'And given its value, we'll send you away with a ventilated case for storage. Please *don't* put it back in the washing machine when you get home. A cool, dark room, please, and the case will start beeping if it becomes too humid or too dry. And for god's sake, don't eat or drink near it.'

'But what do we *do?*' I ask, failing to verbalise all the ways in which I am deeply confused by this new information.

'Well, if you want to proceed with auction, we'll make all the arrangements. It may take up to six months, so don't go buying a superyacht just yet. Otherwise you keep it, as part of a private collection. You can rent it out, if you'd like, to public exhibitions. Let people examine it safely and return it.'

I look down at the tray, the book nestled within. 'What would you do?'

'Me?'

'Yeah.'

Bronwyn considers this, and I like her better for it. Anyone self-serving would have said *sell it* without a moment's hesitation, and got a decent cut of the commission. 'Well,' she says, 'I would ask myself if I loved it—if it was precious not because of the monetary value attached to it but because of memories. You won't get this back if you sell it, so make sure that's what you want. And it was your grandmother's, I understand? I'd like to know how she came to possess it: is there a story there? Was it a gift? What would she have wanted? I'm afraid I can't tell you what to do, Clarissa, but I would recommend you spend a while thinking about it. I find people rarely regret taking that time.'

I nod, and I'm still nodding when she hands me a certificate of authenticity, the obscene value scribbled discreetly at the bottom of the page, and I keep nodding as she packs the book up in its special box.

Finally, we're back in the car and Gideon asks me: 'Do you know what you want to do?'

'I have no idea.'

We end up at my favourite place. It's the only cafe I remember, the only cafe in the whole world, as far as I'm currently concerned. The barista gives an excited wave when we tumble in. She's worked here forever, and she used to put extra marshmallows in our hot chocolates. We used to chat. Now I can't remember her name.

I duck into our old booth—the one Willow and Nina and I used to sit in. I run my fingers under the table, the wood grain bumpy and uneven where we carved our names.

'This is nice,' Gideon says. The booths are cosy blue velvet, the ceilings are high and peaked, and the counter is packed with freshly baked cookies and muffins. At night, the windows collapse away, and a band sets up on the pier. When it's really quiet, you can hear water under the floorboards. We spent hours here. Homework, gossiping, family dinners.

The barista floats over to our table. 'Well hello, darling, haven't seen your face round here in a long time!' She grins, tipping her head so her dreadlocks fall to one side. 'You visiting? We miss you. Not the same without…well, you know. Sorry. None of my business. What would you like, love?'

'Hot chocolate, please,' I say, eyes on my menu.

I feel Gideon scrutinising me from across the table. 'It's forty degrees outside.'

'Trust me,' I say. *Zoey*: the barista's name comes back to me suddenly. 'He'll have one too,' I tell her.

'And, uh, cold water?' Gideon adds.

Zoey winks. 'Sure thing, doll.'

I drum my fingers on the tabletop. I can't tell if I'm nervous because there are too many memories here, or because a *ten-thousand-dollar* book is sitting in Gideon's truck. I considered bringing it inside, but decided the likelihood of me spilling food on it was higher than the chance of someone stealing Gideon's car.

'So,' Gideon says. 'How are you feeling?'

I cross my arms and rest my head in the crook of my elbow. 'I feel sick. I don't think I can talk about it.'

'You know, a lot of people would be happy about this,' he says, and I realise his voice has gone tight.

'I'm not...ungrateful,' I say. 'Just surprised. And it feels like it's not mine to sell.'

'You could do pretty much anything. Get out of Hamilton. Travel the world.'

'You sick of me already?' I joke.

He gives me half a smile. 'Not what I meant.'

But he doesn't tell me what he meant, and then Zoey brings our hot chocolates and a bowl heaped with marshmallows. 'Making up for lost time,' she says. I wonder if I should tell her I can never make up for all the things I lost.

Maybe that's why the situation with the book feels so wrong. It feels like blood money: I had to lose my nan to get it. I hear Bronwyn's voice in my mind: *I'd want to know if there's a story there.*

Gideon gulps down his hot chocolate. 'That's delicious,' he says. 'You weren't lying.'

I stir my own cup, dropping in three marshmallows. 'What would you do?'

He sighs. 'That much money? God, what wouldn't I do. Get my mum proper care. Go to uni. Mail my dad a bunch of exploding glitter to piss him off.'

'You can do those things, you know,' I say, hesitantly.

'Well, glitter is pretty cheap. University, however...'

'You could still get a scholarship. Definitely for swimming, but also, your art is really good, Gideon. You should submit.'

'I don't think...any of that is happening anymore.' He

fiddles with a sugar packet. 'I can't leave Mum. Not now.'

'She could get live-in care.'

'Yeah? You know how much that costs? More than we have. More than we'll *ever* have, all combined. Look, it's fine, I just don't want to talk about it.'

'So what are you going to do next year?'

'I don't know. Get a job. Go to the shitty local TAFE and do evening classes. Get a degree in something boring and well paid. Write angry letters to our local minister about the lack of disability care and caregiver subsidies.'

'But that's not the life you want,' I whisper. 'You'd be throwing everything else away.'

'I don't have a choice.'

'There's always a choice.'

He looks at me, his eyes sad. 'That's what people say when they've never known anything else. It's not that easy.'

'But you could—'

'Drop it, Reece. Please.' His throat bobs. 'I know. Okay. I don't like to think about it. All the things I'll never do because I have shit luck and a crap dad.'

I reach out a hand. 'I'm sorry. I didn't mean it like that.'

He pulls away and stands. 'I have to go pick up Mum's medication. You good here for a while?'

'You don't want me to come?'

'I just...need a minute.'

'Okay,' I say. 'Sure. I'll hang here. Gideon, I'm really—'

He shakes his head. Then he leans down and kisses my cheek. 'Don't be sorry. I'm being a jerk. We'll do something fun later, I just gotta do this first.'

He slips out the front door, paying for our drinks on the way. Zoey comes over to collect our cups. 'You want me to let your friend know you're here?'

'Gideon? He's coming back later.'

She tilts her chin towards the back of the cafe. 'No, honey. Her.'

I turn in my seat. Nina is perched in the last booth, staring daggers in my general direction.

'Thank you,' I mumble to Zoey. Then I'm moving without thinking about it.

Nina crosses her arms as I approach. 'What are you doing here,' she says.

'Just visiting,' I say, gingerly sliding into the seat opposite hers. She raises an eyebrow, but doesn't say anything.

'You should have stayed. The other day, at the pool. We could have talked—'

Nina rolls her eyes. 'Sure, Reece, let's chat. How's your year been? Mine's been *super duper*. I mean, one of my best friends died in a horrific car crash, and the other one left town without saying goodbye. Not to mention, I hauled ass down to the country because I thought my idiot friend needed me, only to find she's *completely fine* and has a nice new life. How are you?'

'I'm not,' I whisper.

'Not what?'

'Not fine.'

Nina looks at me. Swallows. 'Move over.' She shuffles over to my side and hands me a napkin. 'Don't cry. I'll feel sorry for you, and I'm not done being mad yet.'

'I'm not crying,' I say, wiping tears away until the napkin is soaked. 'I'm so sorry. I shouldn't have left like that. But I didn't know how to tell you. I couldn't say goodbye to another friend, but I couldn't *stay*. My locker was next to hers…' I have to stop because my voice is all choked up. The hot chocolate turns sour in my stomach. 'Every day, people would come up to her locker and stick pictures on it, and they'd say how sad it was like they actually cared, even when they didn't know her and they only came to the funeral so they could talk about it later. And all I could think was that they buried her in her least favourite dress and she looked so cold.'

Nina is picking at the hem of her shorts, a thread fraying in her fingertips.

'Nina, I'm so sorry. I should have called you before I left—you're right, and I'm so sorry. I miss you so much. I always catch myself thinking about all the things I want to tell you, and it kills me that I can't.'

'You're such an idiot, Reece,' she mutters.

'I know. I'm sorry.'

Her face crumples. 'I needed you,' she says, her voice cracking. 'You just left me here, and I had *no one*.'

I fling my arms around her shoulders, crushing her into me while she cries and my hair gets sticky with tears. Then she stops as soon as she started, swiping a hand across her cheeks. 'God, that's disgusting. Why do people do that?'

'Not usually voluntarily.'

'Still gross.' She flips out a mirror, carefully erasing all signs of sadness. She digs around in her bag and reapplies her lipstick. I recognise it at once: Riot Club. I thought they'd stopped making it. A guilty expression comes over Nina's face. 'It's hers. I found it in her car…after…'

I nod, because I've never been able to talk about After.

After, when her parents called us to help clear her room.

After, when I sat on her bed and had my first panic attack.

After, when Willow's mum thought I was dying too, and called an ambulance.

'I'm sorry,' I say again.

Nina shakes her head. 'The worst part is that I understand. I would have left too, if Mum had let me. School's just…I don't know, it's hard to concentrate on Chekhov when you've had to pick out songs to play at your best friend's funeral.'

'I think I'm failing,' I confess. I try not to think about it too much, because I'm pretty sure I've ruined the rest of my life, but there's no dancing around it. It's not just Hamilton: even before we got here, I knew I was in trouble. Everything *after* just seemed impossible. Getting out of bed, getting dressed, going to school. Homework was the last thing on my mind—if I bothered to turn in assignments at all, they were usually late, and my grades tanked. It's been better lately, but there's no way to salvage it: my final marks are going to be skewed towards 'abysmal'.

'No shit, Blackwell.' She leans back into the seat. 'It's not like "thriving academically" is one of the stages of grief.' She pulls a face, and I realise she's probably struggling too. Nina never used to care about school, but there's a tiny line of concern between her brows that makes me wonder if things changed after I left.

'So,' she says, changing the subject before I can ask. 'Who's the *Baywatch* babe?'

'Who?'

'Blondie outside. You know. Six foot, tanned, human embodiment of a golden retriever. Practically drooling on your feet?'

'Oh.' I have no idea where to look. She must have been watching when we arrived. 'That's my...Gideon.'

'That's your Gideon?' she echoes, one eyebrow arched.

I cover my face with my hands. 'I don't know. How's Luca?'

'We broke up. He was sick of me being sad.'

I cringe. 'Sorry.'

'It's fine. I'm sorry about your nan, by the way.'

'Thanks. She really liked you.'

Nina almost cracks a smile. 'Nana B was a badass.' It goes quiet. 'I'm still mad at you,' she whispers.

'I know.'

'We can't just magically fix everything.'

'I know.'

She sighs. 'I really want to, though.'

'I know,' I say, and grab her hand.

She looks like a hurricane burnt out from the inside. Dark and unwound, collapsing inwards. 'I can't stay long,' she says after a while. 'I have a psych appointment. *Don't* look at me like that—just because you hate therapy, it doesn't mean the rest of us do.'

I know she's right. 'Does it help?'

'Sometimes it's nice. Sometimes I just scream for an hour. You ever go back?'

I shake my head.

She bumps my shoulder with hers. 'You know, she loved it here.'

'Yeah. Remember when they hired that cute chef?'

Nina laughs. 'Poor Will. Shame he had a husband already.'

'I missed you,' I say.

'Yeah, well. I missed you too, I guess.' She rolls her eyes. 'All those annoying texts. Made it hard to forget you.'

'You came to watch me race,' I tease.

She tilts her nose up. 'I just wanted to make sure you were still alive, for your information.'

'Oh?'

'Yeah. I mean, Theo said you weren't doing so good after I left.'

'You talked to Theo?'

'The little idiot kept friending me on Facebook. I caved.'

'He had a boy in his bed the other week.'

'Shut. Up. Who? Kids these days. I didn't sneak a boy inside until I was at *least* seventeen.'

'He won't tell me!'

'What a little sneak.' She leans her head on my shoulder, and grumbles, 'You're too easy to love. Why aren't you annoying and awful and covered in boils?'

'Sorry.'

'I gotta get going but…maybe I could come down and visit? Or you could come stay? I'm tired of being angry all the time. I miss my best friend.'

I smile at her. 'I'd really like that.'

She hugs me again, all sun-warmed skin and strawberry

perfume. 'And you can tell me more about your Gideon person.'

I feel my cheeks turning pink. 'Well, this was nice. Bye-bye now.'

She flicks my shoulder. 'Nope. Not gonna forget. Want all the details.' She slides out of the booth, then turns. 'Love you, Reece.'

'Love you too, Nina.'

Her smile gets a little watery, then she struts off. Same old Nina. But she hesitates at the door, turning around as though to make sure I'm still here, still real. The old Nina never needed to check if I was following. Her footsteps were never uncertain.

Then she grins at me and blows a kiss.

I guess the old Nina is still in there after all.

Gideon and I drive home in the dark, giggling at the radio and scraping the bottom of our ice-cream cups. We stopped at a beachside fair on the way home, playing rigged games for stuffed toys and riding an old Ferris wheel until it got too cold to be outside. I tell him about Nina, and he talks a bit more about his mum. Grace used to be a wildlife carer, and she doesn't have any family but has a lot of friends. She was still pretty independent until last year. Now she needs the walker more often, and can't really make her own meals or dress herself easily. Some days are better than others. Her friends help out as much as possible, but most of them have little kids and it's been getting harder and harder to lean on them lately. His neighbour comes over in the evenings when Gideon is going to be home late, to check on Grace and watch bad television soaps together.

I also spend a good amount of time needling him about his comics, and eventually he relents and gives me *one* clue. When we arrive home, he gives me a very chaste kiss on the cheek and promises to hide the book and its archive box safely at his place.

The clue he gave me is a good one: he told me which website he posts to. And sure, there's about a million contributors and there's no way of sifting through them by anything useful like, say, highly specific coastal locations. But still. I've seen his sketches. I know what I'm looking for now.

It takes me a few hours. I almost miss it. It's a tiny frame, a chin stuck out just so. Miles.

I click on it, and suck in a breath. Here it is: his whole fictional universe, from beginning to end. I click on the timeline, bringing up each story in order.

He's been uploading his work for years. At first the lines are sloppier and the faces aren't quite right. But about a year ago he posted a thread of reboots—he went right back to the start and edited the story, created new art. Hundreds of people have commented; thousands of people have read it. His stories all feature a bad-luck charm: there's a Broken Mirror series, Friday the 13th specials, and a whole alternate-universe story about what happens when Leap forgets to forward a chain letter.

It's funny and sad, and there's so much of Gideon's real life here that it feels like reading his diary. Captain Curse breaks seven mirrors as a child and blames himself for making his mother sick. Grace is never fully in the frame, but sometimes there's a walking frame or a wheelchair in the corner of his pictures. In these pages, he reveals all the things he never says out loud.

Leap loses his dad, again and again. Nightshade seems sad, distant. It's as if Gideon sees all the things Ava hides from the world. I wonder how long he's spent watching people. Catching all the things that make them smile. Cry. Laugh. The things that should mean nothing and somehow mean everything.

Halfway through a story, I click something by accident, and suddenly I see myself on screen. Her name is Lucky Penny. This girl has my curling hair and dark eyes. She smiles the way I wish I could: wide and silly. She's cleverer than I am, and funnier too. She's me and not. So much the same, but too beautiful, too perfect. But I recognise my freckles and the frown that's never really gone. There's the scar on my shoulder, the chip in my tooth. I click to the start of the strip, smiling when I see the cramped font scribbled in the corner.

We got a box of lucky charms.

She drops rabbit feet and lucky coins, tosses salt over her shoulder. She walks on a bed of four-leaf clovers and stumbles into the end of a rainbow.

Then she gives all her luck to Captain Curse. She bottles it up in a nuclear-pink drink and tricks him into drinking it.

And the story is unfinished.

My mouth drops open. This must be his latest story, because it doesn't have an ending. The last pane is a picture of Captain Curse, blindfolded, floating, his lips stained pink.

He looks like Fortuna, the Roman god of luck. It's so striking I save the picture and print it out. I hold it in my hands for a moment, then fold it carefully and shove it in my diary, unsure what I meant to do with it in the first place.

I stretch out on my bed. I dangle my hands over my head and think about the world Gideon's created, so beautiful and intricate that it seems almost a shame to call them comics because they're much, much more than that. I lie in the dark, thinking about the ocean surrounding Captain Curse.

Nightshade, half lost to the dark.

Leap, grinning in seven different places all at once.

Lucky Penny with the nuclear-pink drink.

He drew so much of Hamilton too. The swimming hole. The pier. Frank's bookshop.

I reach for my phone, a thought unfurling in the back of my mind. Gideon's work basically amounts to a portfolio. Portraits and landscapes. Fine line work and digital etchings. Rough sketches and progress shots and final works. I type in the name of the city's best art school, and click the section marked *Future Students*.

I read for another hour. All the criteria. All the details. Everything a potential applicant would need to submit.

Luck be damned. Gideon can make his own future.

I'm just going to help him get there.

18

I FAILED MY chemistry assessment. This is not exactly an unexpected turn of events, but it's nevertheless disappointing, and I have to battle tears as my teacher explains that it's not enough to *simply show a passing interest in the materials*, I must also *apply myself meaningfully* and perhaps I am *stretched a little thin with my extracurricular activities*. I want to tell him I am actually just *very fucking tired* but I don't think he'll appreciate that.

He says I can re-sit the test, but only for a pass/fail grade. Which means my overall class average will tank, no matter what I do.

With clenched teeth, I manage to thank him and take the paper, willing myself not to cry in the hallway. The weekend with Gideon left little time for study, and I stayed up too late looking at his artwork. I tried to cram this morning but then we had swim practice for nationals, and I was barely on time for class, stumbling in and leaving puddles on the linoleum.

I snap a photo of the angry red mark and press *send*. Nina

replies almost straight away. She's sent a picture of an English essay with a red comment in the top-right corner: *Nina—this is not even the prescribed text??? See me after class.*

My phone buzzes, and she doesn't wait for me to say hello. 'Okay, but since when is Harry Potter not on the curriculum?'

'Since…always?' I answer, checking over my shoulder, but the hallway is empty.

'Urgh. *Confringo* syllabus.'

'Arson is never the answer.'

'*Sometimes* arson is the answer.'

'Like when?'

'*Fahrenheit 451*?'

'I think you seriously misunderstood that book.'

'No shit. I—' Static rushes through the phone. 'Yes, Mr Reynolds, I *would* like to share with the class—' The phone disconnects with a beep and I snort, glancing up just in time to avoid colliding with Miles.

'My lady!' he cries, swooping me into his arms. 'How fare thee?'

I glare at him, kicking my legs until he sets me down. 'You're in a weirdly good mood.'

He gasps. 'I'm always in a good mood.'

'Lies. But go on. What's the news?'

'Who says I *have* news?'

'Miles!'

He grins, bouncing on his feet with enough energy to lift off into orbit. 'Fine. You're such a spoilsport. Guess who got early admission into the National Academy of Music?'

'Ava?'

He fake-punches me on the arm, and I let out a high-pitched squeal as I hug him. 'I'm so proud of you, Miles. You worked really hard for this.'

His shoulders cave as I hold him, as though a weight has lifted. 'I can't believe it,' he says. 'I mean, technically I still have to pass my exams, but I'm in. I'm in. I'm actually going.' He pulls back, eyes wild with joy. 'I gotta tell Mum. They delivered the letter this morning, but she was already gone. And hey, I'll be with you in the city next year!'

I think of the failed test crumpled in my hand, balling it up so it's hidden. 'We should celebrate,' I say. 'Let's have a movie night this weekend. Have you told the others yet?'

'No, I'm gonna go find them now. I've just been telling everyone I see.'

'Go,' I urge. 'I'll find you later. I just gotta do something first.'

I haven't been in Principal Pearson's office since I started. She looks up in surprise as I tap on her door, half a muesli bar shoved in her mouth.

'Oh, Clarissa! Hello, come in. You know you're really meant to make an appointment.'

I take a seat, grateful she's allowing me to stay. 'I know, sorry. There's just something I've been meaning to talk to you about...'

Mum is sitting on the couch when I get home from school, which is weird because it's a weekday, and it's four p.m. She doesn't usually roll in until the evening news is done, at least.

I drop my bag on the counter and grab an apple.

'Hey, Mum, what's up? You're home early.'

I expect her to be playing on her iPad or reading a book, but it seems she's truly just…sitting there. Her face is tense, lines pressed into her lips and eyebrows.

'A very nice lady rang me today,' she says, and my blood runs cold at her clipped tone. 'The Museum of Medical Oddities. The strangest thing: she wanted my RSVP for my mother's collection.'

She waits. My mouth has gone very dry, and I set the apple back down.

'The thing is,' she continues, 'I told her my mother hadn't *left* a bequest in her will. But she was very insistent, and in the end, she suggested I speak to Clarissa. So, Clarissa. Is there anything you'd like to share?'

'Mum,' I stammer. 'I can explain—'

She stands up sharply, an empty coffee cup in her hand. There are three more on the table, and a wine glass on the bench. I wonder how long she's been sitting here, seething. The worst part is I deserve it. I deserve it all. How many times did I promise myself I'd tell her?

'Yes, please explain, Reece. Your grandmother left you her prized possessions, collected over fifty years, and you've sent them all away without thinking to tell the rest of us. What else? Have you hawked her jewellery? Sold her car? Should I check Airbnb to see if her house is listed?'

I almost roll my eyes because she always gets carried away in an argument, but this time the words have hit home. 'Mum, that's not the same thing—'

'And what about the book Mr Scott gave you? I can't find it anywhere. Did you give that away too? What about her journals and notes? Her clinical papers?'

'Did you go through my room?' She's *never* disrespected my privacy.

She waves a hand dismissively, and I can't tell if she's conceding the point or not. 'The thing is, Reece, you could have just told me. What am I supposed to make of this lie instead? She was my mother, and I—' Her voice chokes.

When she speaks again, she's much quieter. 'I have so little of her left. And you've decided to give another piece away.'

'It's just a loan, Mum.'

'Is it? I wouldn't know, because you never thought to tell me.'

'I'm so sorry. I was going to tell you.'

'Did you ever think,' Mum says, 'that she never donated those books for a reason? She knew what they were worth, Reece, she wasn't stupid. And she kept them anyway. You got so wrapped up in thinking that you could, you didn't stop to wonder if you *should*.'

That stops me. My mouth is open, ready for rebuttal. But then I think again of Bronwyn's words at the auction house. *I'd wonder where she got it...*

'I didn't...I don't...'

'I didn't get to say goodbye. That's the worst part. And now you've made this decision without me too, and I missed another goodbye. Maybe you think they're just books, Reece, but they're my mother's thoughts, her words, her work. There's nothing more precious than that. Nothing else that keeps her so alive.'

'But you never wanted to go to the house,' I whisper. 'You couldn't even look at photos.'

Her face is a mix of anger and sadness and disappointment. But she still reaches out a hand, placing it on my shoulder. 'And when Willow died, honey, did you want to go to her house? Look at her things?' Her voice isn't cruel. All the bitterness is burnt out, and she's almost gentle, because even now she knows how much it hurts to hear Willow's name. Even now, she's protecting me when she's furious at me.

Tears drip from my eyes as I shake my head.

'Did that mean you didn't care?'

'No.'

She wipes my tears with her sleeve, her own eyes red and glassy. 'We all need time, Reece. I thought you'd know that better than anyone. I wasn't ready, but that doesn't mean I didn't care.'

'I'm really sorry, Mum. I didn't think…I didn't mean to hide it, but I didn't want to upset you, and then it got to be this big secret and I didn't want to make you mad.'

She pauses, one foot on the stairs. I hate that she looks like this—like she curled into a ball and stayed that way for a long time. I should know. I've been there. 'I have a headache,' she says eventually. 'I need to lie down and think things through.'

'Okay,' I say. 'Mum, I—'

'And you're grounded, you know that, right?'

I nod. 'Okay. Can I do anything?'

She doesn't respond, and instead turns to disappear up the stairs. I hear her sob when the door clicks shut.

I'm out of time. Out of luck. And I don't know what to do, so I sit there, on the bottom stair, waiting in case she calls out, in case she changes her mind. I sit there until Dad comes home. He scruffs my hair as he makes his way to their room.

That night I lie in bed, Nan's stethoscope pressed to my chest. *I never wanted this to happen,* I think. *I didn't know anyone would get hurt.*

But my heart beats in my ears, and it whispers: *Liar, liar, liar.*

Hamilton becomes something strange in the following days: unseasonably cold, for one, and lonely, for another.

Mum speaks to me only in single-word questions and answers. Things like 'Dinner?' and 'Homework?' and 'Salt.' Theo natters almost incessantly, trying to fill the frosty void, and Dad seems dazed, weaving between loyalty to Mum and pity for me.

We've never really argued. I know every cheesy movie makes it seem like parents and teenagers are meant to fight, but Mum and I hardly do. The last time, it was about a month after Willow died and Mum wanted me to leave my room at least once a day. In retrospect, it was a fairly reasonable request—except that I responded with a flood of tears and banshee-like screams before cursing her out of my room. I wonder if we're destined to disagree about death, forever. But that's a morbid thought, so I just shove the salt and pepper shakers at Mum, then excuse myself from the table.

Miles and Ava have bombarded the group chat, trying to fill in the gaps from the last few months. They've pieced together enough of the backstory that their questions make me prickle. *So you didn't tell your mum you'd decided to give away all that stuff and then she found out on her own? How long had you been sneaking around for? What do you mean she had a book of poisons? Like, poison poison, or 1800s Coca-Cola that had a bit of crack in it?* I still haven't told Mum about that one. Nan left that book to me and, even if I don't know why, I'm sure there was a reason.

Gideon has been steadfastly refusing to contribute to the chat, letting me decide how much I want to tell Miles and Ava about my newly imposed curfew (home by five, no after-school activities except swimming).

I type another vague response, then toss my phone on the nightstand. I'm restless, too cooped up in here. Mum and Dad won't even let me go for a bike ride, since they're convinced I'll ride to Gideon's house. Which, I mean, I guess I would. But right now I'd kill just to be able to run.

The cool change rolled in on Monday night and has stuck around. The skies are overcast and the gum trees rattle in the breeze. I've been sleeping with the doona tugged up to my chin, and yet I still wake up with goosebumps covering my arms—I had to dig out my box of winter clothes to find a jumper this morning. It sits abandoned by my desk, spewing its woollen contents. It's basically half-unpacked now. I should just shove the rest of it in a drawer somewhere and get rid of at least one box.

I'm struck by the idea, and soon I'm sweating and huffing, lugging the boxes into one corner and methodically unpacking them. Boots and snow jackets and thick socks all get shoved into a corner of my cupboard, almost certainly never to be used in Hamilton. Shorts and bathers get packed into my chest of drawers. Another box jangles when I pick it up and, when I prise open the taped-down lid, I discover bubble-wrapped frames and artwork I'd forgotten about. It takes forever to unwrap it all, but it's worth it. There's a photo of me and Willow, dressed up for a party in primary school. She's smiling with crooked teeth, teetering on her toes, trying to look taller than me. She was always so annoyed that she was the oldest but shortest. The glass is cracked, and I trace a fingertip over the fragments. I remember yanking the photo off my bedroom wall on the night I realised she'd never have another birthday—that I'd always be older than her. Now, I laugh at her wild hair, her ruddy cheeks, the way she's balancing on my shoulder. I set it beside me, and unpack another: Nina and me at a boyband concert, the two of us slightly blurred from the bright stage lights. Willow's behind the camera, and I remember singing along that night, feeling very adult and cool, even though my dad was sitting in the row behind us. There's more: first day of high school, Nina's quinceañera, Willow's sixteenth birthday. The three of us in the school band, which I've never told Miles about because I'm sure he'll mock me for my choice of instrument (trumpet and, no, I wasn't very good at it). There are Nina's own sketches too, which I had framed and proudly displayed in my old room. My favourite is a warrior girl poised with her sword held high to strike. And even though she seems flawless and vicious, there's a bandage wrapped around her hand. 'No one gets out unscathed,' Nina had said.

My eyes drift to the sea of photos resting on my knees. Maybe it's time they went back up.

I text Theo and tell him to check the pantry for spare hooks. He thumps up the stairs a few minutes later, barging in without knocking.

'Did you get robbed?' he says, tossing the packet at my head. 'Where's all your stuff?'

'I unpacked,' I answer, snatching the hooks out of the air.

He whistles in response. 'Shit. I can see your floor. How bored *are* you?'

'No comment.'

He bounces on my bed, setting the glass frames jangling. 'Wanna watch a zombie movie downstairs?'

Yes, but not with the arctic freeze between me and Mum. 'Nah, it's okay.'

'Mum and Dad went out.'

'Oh. Then yeah, sure. Where'd they go?'

'Dunno. Some work friend had a kid. Or a dog. Whatever, they said they'd be home late.'

'Okay. Help me hang these first?'

He grunts, but agrees (and barters for fresh popcorn in return for his service). It doesn't take long to set everything up; there's a nook by the window that I've wanted to decorate since we first moved in, but I guess I've been resisting as part of my silent protest. The afternoon sun catches it, and I like to sit there and read. Now the wall is crowded with frames and Washi-Taped pictures. Theo admires his handi-work. 'You should add new ones, too.'

'New ones?'

'Yeah. Miles and Ava. And *Giiiideeoon.*' He makes smoochy noises until I whack him in the head, but he's right. The floors of my room are bare; the walls are bright. Maybe I didn't get out of my old life unscathed, but I'm starting to think I can live with those scars.

I follow Theo downstairs and discover he has a gory horror movie all lined up. He flops on the couch pillows, waiting while I melt butter in a saucepan and pop the corn kernels. (It's old-fashioned, but it's the only way. Don't even mention microwave popcorn in this house.)

Theo rams fistfuls of it into his mouth while we watch, cackling at the jump scares and cheering on the zombie army.

'You might be deranged,' I say, flicking an unpopped kernel at his head.

'Eh, the humans had a good run.'

'You wouldn't save *any* of the humans?'

He thinks about this for a minute. 'Maybe, like, one or two. Hugh Jackman, cause he's Wolverine. Stephen King, so he can write about the zombie apocalypse. A Hemsworth brother, cause, you know.'

'What about secret sleepover boy?' I tease.

Theo turns bright red and piffs a pillow at me. 'Shut up.'

'Ohh, is it someone I know?'

'There's, like, thirty people in this whole town. Yes, you know him.'

'Have I *met* him?'

He groans. 'I'm not going to tell you. And how am I supposed to know who you've met?'

I tap a finger on my chin. 'Interesting. So I know him, but I'm not friends with him.'

'You have literally two friends and a Gideon.'

'Hey!'

He curls up in the corner of the couch, squinting at me. 'What *are* you guys anyway?'

'I don't—he's not—we haven't—Stop changing the subject!'

'Does he *luurve* you?'

'Oh my god,' I moan, hiding behind my hands.

From the way Theo laughs, I can tell he's happy. Actually happy, not just taking pleasure in a few quick quips and a tired smirk. I poke his hip with my foot. 'Hey, Theo?'

'Yeah?'

'You're good, right? Things with Dad are okay?'

His smile softens. I don't get to see that smile a lot. It makes him look young and sweet, like when he was a little kid. 'Yeah. I'm good. I'm really good.' He nudges me back.

'Your feet stink,' I observe.

He attempts to shove his feet under my nose. 'These are my lucky socks. Haven't washed these babies since the great race of 2013.'

I shriek, twisting away from him, and he leaps over the back of the sofa, tossing pillows and popcorn at me. He hops on one foot, tugging a sock off and taunting me with it.

'*Oh my god*, why is it crusty, you little pervert?' I gag, ducking under the kitchen counter.

'It's chalk from the gym!' He throws one at me and it catches me on the shoulder.

'You haven't done gymnastics for three years!'

'They're lucky socks,' he says indignantly. 'You can't wash the luck out them!'

I gag again, whipping a pair of tongs out of the drawer to pick up the sock. 'Don't come any closer,' I warn. 'I *will* wash this sock.' I dangle it over the sink, and flick the tap on for emphasis.

'Reece, come on!'

I laugh, finally having the upper hand. 'I'll give it back on one condition.'

'What?'

'Tell me who sleepover boy is.'

'Reece!' He lunges, swiping for the sock.

'Don't come any closer! Oh look, detergent...'

'You wouldn't dare!'

'I *would* dare!' I nudge closer to the water.

'Stop! Oh my god, get your own life. It's Billy, okay? Are you happy now?'

'Billy Martin? Chicken-farm Billy? Underage-driver Billy?' So I *was* right about that red shirt.

'Hey, he's a good driver.'

'I have so many questions...' Seriously, so many questions. Starting with: how? And *why*?

He snatches the sock, which releases putrid fumes as it swings through the air. 'That's all you get,' he says. 'And if you tell Mum or Dad, you'll wake up with sock on your face.'

'Okay, okay. Truce.'

He holds out a hand. 'Truce.'

I take his hand and he farts on cue. 'You're disgusting,' I say, wheeling back towards the couch to escape the inevitable stench.

He grins at me, sliding his sock back onto his foot. 'You took my lucky sock.'

'Urgh, come on, let's finish this movie. And you can tell me more about Billy.'

He tells me nothing about Billy. Not how they met, or what the deal is with all the girls Billy has very publicly groped in front of the bike shed, and definitely not why he was sleeping on Theo's floor. In the end, the movie credits roll, and I know nothing more than I did an hour ago.

'Put another one on,' I say, wriggling to get comfy. 'I'm too tired to move.'

Theo plays one we've seen a million times. My eyes droop, occasionally opening long enough to catch a glimpse of Theo snoring, until the familiarity lulls me to sleep.

When I wake up, the house is dark and the television has switched itself off. My mouth feels dry and my neck aches, plus Theo is sprawled across the couch and I'm tucked into one tiny corner. The clock says it's just after eleven. I sit up, confused. Something woke me up, I just can't…

The phone in my pocket vibrates. I fumble with the zipper, half asleep and still groggy. Where are Mum and Dad? Why didn't they wake us up?

I frown as I pick up. 'Gideon? Is everything—'

'Reece,' he says. Just my name. But suddenly I'm wide awake, jolted to my feet, because I know something has gone terribly wrong. 'Reece, it's Mum...I need...' His voice is broken, and I can't understand what he's trying to say.

'It's okay,' I tell him, shoving my feet into the first pair of shoes I can see. I nudge Theo awake—he starts to complain until he sees the look on my face, then sits up silently. 'Gideon, where are you?'

'At home, we're home, I need—Is Olivia there? I don't know what to do, she fell, she fell and she's not...I called the ambulance, but they're too far away, and I don't—What do I do, Reece?'

I point at the staircase and Theo thunders up, while I search for the spare car keys. I tip over the stupid ceramic bowl we shove all our useless shit into, upending receipts and loose coins and old keychains. The car keys clatter onto the countertop just as Theo returns, shaking his head.

'She's not here,' I tell Gideon. 'Call the hospital again, find out where the ambulance is. I'm on my way.' I hang up, already striding towards the front door.

'I'm pretty sure you're still grounded,' Theo says, eyeing the keys in my hand.

'Tell Mum I'm sorry.'

I haven't driven since Willow died. I fumble with the keys and stall the engine. My hands are so slippery on the wheel that I almost steer into a tree.

But none of it matters.

I fly down the road, high beams lighting the way. I barely notice the drive: my heart, stuttering in my chest, begs my ruined, panicked mind to hold on for five more minutes.

This is how she died, I think, tears welling.

'But someone needs you now,' I say out loud, pushing the thought away. 'He needs you,' I repeat, quietly. 'Grace needs you.'

I don't dare touch my phone in the car, but the second I park outside Gideon's I yank it out and dial Mum's number. It goes to message bank. 'Mum, I need you. I know you're mad at me, but if you get this, please come to the hospital.' Then I hang up, because Gideon is standing over a stretcher as a paramedic lifts it into the ambulance. I sprint up the driveway.

'Gideon!'

He turns, face white, hands shaking. I'm too scared to look down at Grace. I'm scared her face will be blank, the way Willow's was at her funeral. But I take Gideon's hand, and follow the stretcher. She's awake, though her face is locked in a grimace. She's trying to say something, but all that's coming out is a long moan, and soon they're hooking her up to needles and machines and forcing me out of the ambulance.

'Do you want to go with them?' I ask, but he's standing there in his pyjamas, watching as they close the doors, and I don't think he can hear me. I tug on his sleeve. 'Gideon? Do you want to go in the ambulance?'

He jerks his head, signalling no. 'She needs...she needs her things. She won't have anything. To wear. They didn't take her bag,' he whispers. 'She always has a hospital bag, and they didn't take it. I have to go...go get it.' He sways, and I awkwardly try to catch him and steer him towards the

266

car. 'It's okay,' I tell him, leading him to the passenger seat. 'Tell me what you need, I'll go get it.'

He mumbles a few words and I race into the house. The bag is beside Grace's bed, and I quickly check that everything is there, then snag her toothbrush from the ensuite and extra underwear from her drawers, not even bothered about the total invasion of privacy. I notice a bag full of medication sitting on her dresser and grab it as well. I'm sure they have it all at the hospital, but I've heard too many horror stories from Nan over the years about family not knowing what a patient should take or when. It tends to end badly when you don't take your life-saving medication on time.

Gideon is shaking by the time I get back to the car and I desperately want to hold his hand, but I'm too nervous to relinquish my white-knuckled grip on the steering wheel as I speed towards the hospital, praying that the Hamilton police force is already in bed.

'You're d-driving,' he stutters. Street lights are whipping by us at an alarming pace, and I ease up on the pedal as we pass open farmland—the last thing we need is a kangaroo flying through the windshield.

'It's okay,' I say, eyes locked on the road. I'm terrified of wildlife. I'm terrified of trees. I'm terrified of hitting a pothole the wrong way and flipping us into certain death.

'I can drive, if you w-want.'

'It's okay, Gideon, just breathe. We're almost there. Are you cold?' I hesitate, wondering if I'm brave enough to let go long enough to turn the heater on. *This is how she died.*

'No. I don't know what's…'

I risk a glance away from the road, and see his forehead is covered in sweat and his lips are blue. 'Gideon, I think you might be in, um, shock.'

'Shock,' he repeats. 'That's what they said.'

'Who said?'

'The paramedic.'

'Did they give you anything?' I don't actually know what to do for a person in shock. Give them a blanket? Sugar? Lie them down or keep them awake?

'N-no. Told them to look after Mum.'

'Okay. Okay. Just hold on. We're nearly there.'

I've sped so quickly that we catch up to the ambulance just as it pulls up to the emergency entrance at the hospital. Gideon falls out the door before I've even come to a stop, racing towards his mum. I grab her bag and chase after him, mostly worried that he's going to run out of adrenaline and collapse.

The paramedics let us follow them to the ER doors, but then they turn down a corridor marked *Intensive Care* and a nurse stops us from going any further.

'Are you family?'

'Yes,' I say. 'He is. What's going on? What's happening?'

The nurse looks between me and Gideon, and her face softens. 'Let's get some forms filled out. You might be in for a long wait. Is there anyone you can call?' She directs that question at Gideon, who's still trembling. I wrap a hand around his arm, steadying him.

'It's just me,' he says, on the verge of tears.

The nurse nods, then takes us to a quiet section of the

emergency room, away from a mum holding her green-tinged daughter and a man with a bloody bandage around his arm.

She brings Gideon some papers, a cup of hot chocolate and a silver blanket. 'You're not looking so good there, son. You just wait until you're ready, those papers aren't urgent. It's Grace Hawthorn, isn't it?' She rattles off an emergency contact, too, which must be correct because Gideon nods. The hot chocolate ripples in his hands.

The nurse taps a quick message on her pager. 'Okay, we have all her allergies and history on file,' she says, sounding relieved. She turns to me. 'You sure there's no one else to call?'

I shake my head, and she kneels down to speak to Gideon. 'All right. Well, I'm sorry to say it's going to be a long night, and your mum isn't doing too good right now, but they're going to take real good care of her. And you don't look so great either, so I'm going to ask your friend here to make sure you stay warm and drink all that hot chocolate. My name is Sophia—if you need anything else, you can come see me at the nurses' station.'

I thank her as she goes to help a teenager who comes in puking into a bucket. I slide the forms out of Gideon's hands, and tug the blanket a little tighter around his shoulders.

'Gideon?' I murmur. 'Are you all right? You're scaring me a bit. Maybe they should look at you again?'

He obediently takes a sip of his drink. 'I'm f-fine. Just... She was doing so good lately. I don't know what...'

I find his hand and hold on tight. 'What happened, exactly?'

'She just...she just kind of froze? Like she couldn't breathe, and she couldn't swallow, and I was only a few steps away, but I didn't—didn't get there in time, and she fell, and the sound, and the blood...She's fallen before, but this was worse, so much worse, and I'm scared...'

And then he really is crying, quietly, like he doesn't want to disturb anyone but he can't help it, so I pull him into my lap and hold him. We stay like that for a while, until his breathing evens out and he falls asleep. I wait, watching people with their injuries and their illnesses streaming in and out, wondering how many of them can be fixed, put back together just the right way. I watch Sophia, ever calm, hold together two pieces of bone that are sticking horrifically out of a firefighter's arm, and I watch her force air into the lungs of a girl having an asthma attack. Inevitably, they all disappear behind the white folding doors, and I don't see any of them come back out, so I'll never know how their stories end.

In a quiet stretch, I make Gideon a pillow of my jumper, slip out from under his golden curls, and approach the station. I apologise to Sophia for bothering her, then explain, 'I was just wondering if there's any news.'

'Family only, honey,' she says kindly, as another nurse walks past. Then we're alone again and she adds, 'But if you *were* family, I'd say there's no news. She's in surgery now.'

'Surgery?'

She hears the panic in my voice. 'She's not in a good way right now, but they're doing everything they can.'

'I don't understand, Gideon said she fell...'

Her smile is tinged with pity. 'I'm sorry, that's all I know.

How's your friend?'

'He's…okay. Less blue.'

'That's good. Keep him close, he'll need someone to lean on.'

I wander back to Gideon, stopping at the vending machine for a chocolate bar. I check my phone, but there's nothing new, even though it's now one o'clock in the morning. I try Mum's mobile again and it rings out. I text Theo to tell him what's happening. I think about calling Miles and Ava, getting them to wake their mum up so we have at least one proper adult here, but if Gideon wanted them to know he would have called them already. So I sit. And I wait.

A woman bursts through the doors of the ER, and for a moment I think she's about to start yelling, like the woman who came in half an hour ago screaming she needed a doctor before her baby was born on the footpath. But this woman is calm and efficient, marching straight to the nurses' station.

'Mum?' I'm out of my seat and running to her, and I crash into her open arms. 'I didn't think you were going to come, I don't know what to do.'

She's shushing me, a hand on my hair, rocking me back and forth. 'I came as soon as I got your message,' she says. 'I'm so sorry, honey, I'm so sorry.'

Gideon wakes up at the sound of our voices and, when he sees us hugging, his eyes go glassy again. 'Hey, Mrs B,' he croaks out.

Then Mum's hugging him too, and even though he's taller and wider, she's holding him so tightly he somehow looks very small. He blushes when he steps away. 'Is there any news?' he says.

I shake my head. 'They won't tell us anything but... Gideon, did you know she would be in surgery?'

A tiny jerk of his chin. No, he didn't know either.

'Mum? Can you do anything?' I whisper. Technically, she works in the outpatient part of the hospital. Still, she must have some kind of clearance, because she flashes her badge at Sophia and disappears behind the doors.

We wait.

And we wait.

It's two o'clock in the morning. Gideon fills out the paperwork, managing to scribble with halting, awkward letters. He sighs every time his hand shakes, and doesn't protest when I pull the blanket over his shoulders again.

Finally, Mum emerges, her face taut and grim. She sits beside Gideon and holds her hands over his own. 'All right, Gideon, the most important thing is that your mum is okay. She has a good doctor, and she's out of surgery.' Mum pauses. 'She had a bad fracture in her ribs, and a nasty head wound. Has she seemed worse recently? Mentioned anything to you?' Her voice is so gentle, and she's trying so hard not to break him, but I can see him shattering to pieces. I think of our trip to the city, the medication he mentioned he couldn't get in town.

'She, um, she had her neuro appointment last month,' he whispers. 'They increased her meds. Started some new ones, too. Said it might be...progressing. But she seemed okay. It seemed like it was working. I thought—' He looks at me helplessly. Mum nods, patting his hand.

'I'll tell the doctor,' she says. 'You can see her now, if you want. She's sleeping, but you can sit with her.'

The relief that washes over his face makes my heart ache. He picks up the overnight bag, discarded at my feet, and stands. I start to take a step towards him, but Mum holds me back.

'Family only,' she says softly, 'and one person in the room at a time.'

'I'll wait,' I tell Gideon. 'I'll wait as long as you need.'

He hesitates, and I don't want to make him go alone, but even Sophia is keeping an eye on us, and I don't think anyone is going to bend the rules for us this time.

'Thank you,' he says. 'For everything.' Then Sophia guides him away, her sure hand on the square of his shoulders.

I collapse into the plastic chair once more. Mum threads a hand through my hair. 'So,' she says. 'You have a pretty loose definition of being grounded.'

'I'm so sorry.'

'And you stole a car.' But she's wearing a half-smile.

'Sorry,' I mutter again. 'I promise to be properly grounded in the morning.'

Mum squeezes my hand. 'Maybe we can let this one slide.'

I nod, rubbing a hand over my tired eyes.

'You drove,' Mum says, casually, like she doesn't need a response.

'I hated it.'

'But you did it.'

'Yeah. Yeah I did.'

'You wanna talk about it?'

'Nah.' Then I ask the question I was too scared to ask in front of Gideon. 'Mum, is Grace really going to be okay?'

Mum eases back, thinking about the answer. 'She's young, she's stronger than a lot of people in her condition. But it's getting worse, and if she hits the next stage, she really won't be able to stay with Gideon much longer. It's a turning point, Reece. Their family might not be the same again.'

'Gideon doesn't want to leave her. And I don't think they can afford care.'

'I know it's tough, but soon he won't be able to manage on his own. Will he help her shower? Help her toilet? Will he make her meals and help her eat? He'll never be able to leave her alone, not really, not without proper monitoring equipment. And what about Grace—is that what *she* really wants: for herself, for her son? She deserves dignity too, and company. Will Gideon be that for her?' Mum hesitates, erring into uncertain territory. I wonder how much Grace has confided.

Mum takes a breath, refocusing the conversation. 'And what if Gideon gets hurt? He'll have to lift her out of bed every day, turn her to prevent bedsores. That's okay now, he's young, but what about five years from now? Ten?'

I notice Mum cuts herself off after that, and I feel sick at the thought of Gideon on his own in the world. I feel my eyes brimming with tears, and I shouldn't cry because it's not my life to mourn, but it's so cruel and unfair.

'Oh, sweetie, I'm sorry, I didn't mean to upset you. It's just that Gideon and Grace are going to have to make some choices soon, and they're not going to be easy ones.'

'I don't know what to do,' I whisper. 'I don't know how to help.'

Mum squeezes my hand again. 'You're here. Sometimes that's help enough.'

19

GIDEON MISSES A lot of school. Not enough to fail, but enough that people start to whisper that he finally got himself kicked out for doing something stupid. I remember when I started here, thinking the same thing: that he was just a blonde jock who didn't care enough to come to class on time. But I don't say anything. If Gideon wanted help, he'd ask.

His mum stays in the hospital for a few days. When Grace is finally let out, the doctors recommend a home-care nurse to keep an eye on her for a while. Mum brings them food and bandages and medicine. Grace's friends do the same, and soon there's hardly any room left in their freezer. But Mum's right. Gideon can't do this alone. He doesn't say as much, but I see the sadness in his eyes when I visit one night, and in the end he asks if I'd mind leaving early so he can catch up on some sleep. I stood in the doorway, watching as he turned away, deep purple bags carved beneath his eyes.

I think he lost a bit too much that night. Grace came home, but the pieces didn't quite fit right.

We text, but not much. I'm always left with a string of unanswered messages, and he's always apologising because he had to help his mum change her clothes, or get into the bath, or make her breakfast, or get more of her medication from the pharmacy.

Miles goes over a few times, and just shakes his head when I ask how Gideon's doing. If he knows anything, he's not going to say. I get restless. The days are too long, and I find myself pacing my room at night, googling everything I can about Parkinson's and carers' support, which usually ends in an emotional black hole and my phone being flung across the room in frustration. Usually I'd vent my frustrations on the nearest person, but Ava's sleeping at Sally's house, and Theo spends all his spare time with Billy.

I find myself cycling into town one afternoon, desperate for a cup of Mrs Kostakis's terrible coffee and Miles's company. I consider cycling all the way to Gideon's, but the last unanswered message glares up at me from my phone screen.

Hamilton is sleepy today. An icy breeze has cleared the beachfront, and a smattering of rain has kept the locals inside. Not even the surfers are out; the waves break on empty crests, washing into shore alone. Some of the stores have closed early, not bothering with the few tourists who've found themselves in this unseasonable chill. But Frank's bookshop is open, the door clattering in the wind. A cat is perched in the window, hissing as I park my bike.

'Hello?' I call out. 'It's me. I was just getting coffee, I thought you might like—'

'*I don't want yer bloody StarWhatsIt or —*'

I smirk as Francis rounds the corner, a Dan Brown novel raised above his head like a weapon. 'Hey, Frank.'

He grunts, lowering *The Da Vinci Code* to non-threatening levels. 'You shouldn't sneak up on people like that, you know,' he grumbles.

'I said hello, that's hardly sneaky,' I protest. I tilt my head towards the window. 'New cat?'

'Old cat. Not even mine. Just wandered in one day. Keeps the mice away though.' The cat wanders towards the counter, as though summoned by our conversation. 'Eh? Know we're talking about you, old bastard?'

I kneel, intending to scratch his ears, but he hisses again and arches his back.

Franks guffaws, shooing the cat away. 'Wouldn't pat him if you're particularly attached to your fingers. Hates everyone, that cat. You miserable git, go on. There's cream in the saucer. Go on, Lucifer, shoo.' The cat disappears between two shelves. 'No Gideon today?'

I shake my head, hesitating. 'His mum isn't doing too well. He's looking after her.'

Frank's mouth twists down as he hops on the chair behind the counter. 'That kid,' he mutters, rapping his knuckles on the counter. 'That kid has a heart of gold.'

I kick at the dust on the floor. 'I don't know what else he can do...what *I* can do. I feel so useless, just hanging around.'

Frank is gazing down at me. His weathered old face has crinkled around the eyes, a lifetime of smiles etched in broken lines. 'He's lucky he has you. Never seen the kid smile so bloody much in his life.'

I pick up a book so I have something to do with my hands, then set it down again when I realise it's an erotic novel. 'Well,' I say, feeling the intense need to sanitise my hands, 'if you don't want any coffee, I think I should get going.'

'No books for me today?'

I cough, trying to hide my discomfort. 'Ah, no. My mum sort of…she has some *reservations* about the museum. The books are on hold. Temporarily.'

Frank curses under his breath. 'Please tell me you didn't steal the bleeding things. That's all I need. Accessory to theft. I'm too old to go to prison.'

'What? No! No, they were mine. I just sort of—uh— forgot to mention it…'

He isn't assuaged. '*Just be nice, Frank*, I said. *Don't be such an old geezer. Seems a good lass*, I said. Look where it gets me.'

'I didn't steal them! I would never.' My voice jumps a few octaves, which only seems more incriminating.

'Ay, semantics. I need to have a liedown. Get out of my store, you pesky thing.'

I collect my bag and weave my way towards the door, stepping around old paperbacks and splintered shelves. The shop cat winds through my ankles, slowing my progress. It meows petulantly, so I pause, waiting as it nuzzles my socks. I know better than to pat it now, so I wait, gazing around me. Frank shuffles away, his footsteps fading until a door slams shut and the store goes quiet. I'm stuck between rows and rows of Austen and Brontë and Vonnegut; some of them are beautiful editions, with cloth-bound spines and hand-painted covers. I wonder if I could write Frank a note and pay him—

My eyes snag on something. The picture I noticed last week. The face I thought I recognised. I peer closer. There's a band poster covering half of it, so I step forward to brush it aside.

The cat hisses and takes a swipe at my ankle.

'Ow! You little—'

I tumble forward, colliding with the shelf and unsettling the crumbling papers stuck to it. But when I look up, the photo remains. It's been pinned carefully to the shelf—whoever stuck it here was proud of it. I pry away one corner and find the wood below is a shade darker than the rest of the shelf: a perfectly preserved shadow. There's no writing on the back, but when I turn it over again my heart stops.

I know that statue.

It's hard to forget the thing that cursed you.

Queen Mab.

'It's her,' I tell Nina, riding furiously to the Beach Bean, one hand on my handlebar, the other pressing the phone to my ear.

'Are you sure?'

'Yes I'm sure!'

'Well, did you ask the old dude who it was?'

I half-groan, half-scream into the mouthpiece in frustration. 'No! I couldn't find him. He just disappeared.' I searched the shop up and down. Frank wasn't there. My back had only turned for a minute but, *poof,* he'd vanished. Part of me thought it might be a magic trick. The more logical part thought he'd probably nipped down to the basement for some whiskey and locked the door behind him. I'd taken the photo anyway, tucking it inside my jumper.

'Send me a picture,' Nina says. 'Maybe someone will recognise it. I can ask the school librarian, they're good at sleuthing and shit, right?'

'That's...actually not a bad idea,' I concede. For all the rumours of where the school statue came from, no one ever cared enough to ask. In any case, the possibilities always seemed better than the truth—until it followed me all the way to Hamilton. 'This can't be a coincidence,' I mutter.

'All right, Nancy Drew, calm down. The statue isn't haunting you. It's just an old piece of junk.'

'I guess.'

'Are you okay? You sound...funky.'

'Yeah.' I sigh. 'Yeah, sorry. It's been a weird week. I gotta go, but I'll call you later.'

She blows me a kiss down the line, then hangs up as I pull into the Bean. I throw down my bike and rush into the store. There's no one I need more right now than the town gossip herself, Mrs Kostakis.

'Miles!' I call out. 'Is your mum here?'

He crinkles his nose. 'Uh well hello, Reece. Yeah I'm good, kinda slow in here today. But nice to have the place to myself without Ava here.'

I take a deep, steadying breath. 'Hello, Miles. How are you? That's nice. Is your mum here?'

He hollers down the hallway. 'Ma! Reece wants you.'

'Also a coffee, please,' I add, smiling sweetly.

'Some people,' he mutters, jabbing the till. It pings open and he slams it shut without charging me, then lumbers over to the coffee machine and flicks the steam nozzle on.

Mrs Kostakis comes bustling over, wiping her hands on her apron. 'Clarissa! So nice to see you. What can I do for you?'

I pull out the photo from my pocket and lay it on the countertop.

'Do you know what this is?' I ask, a little too breathlessly, feeling my palms turn sweaty as she leans over it. Miles peers over the coffee machine with renewed interest.

'Hmm,' she says, sliding it closer. 'I'm sorry, honey, this looks pretty old, and I haven't been around town that long. What is it?'

My heart sinks as I remember what Ava told me: her parents moved here just before Miles was born. Of course Mrs Kostakis wouldn't know anything before that.

I rotate the photo to examine it better. It's an old photo—sepia, preserved in hues of muted browns and warm yellows. The statue stands proudly, a glint of sunlight beaming from its hat, while a man stands beside it, beaming at the camera. Huh. Maybe Queen Mab was King Mab. 'It's nothing,' I mumble. 'It's going to sound silly.'

'Spill,' Miles says, rounding the counter and setting a coffee cup at my elbow.

I take a sip, wondering where to start. 'At my old school, we had this statue. As in, *this exact* statue. And nobody knows who it is, or where it came from, but every year the entire senior class has to run under her arm or be cursed with bad luck.'

They wait, blinking at me.

'It's *cursed*.'

Miles glances sideways at his mum.

'I'm not crazy,' I huff.

'No. No, no, you're right. This is definitely sense-making Reece. Normal Reece. Clear and scientifically minded Reece.'

I groan, wishing I'd never bothered to show them. But they seem to be waiting for the rest of the story, so I close my eyes and forge ahead. 'I got cursed. I was running late for the first day of school and I didn't run under her arm. And…bad things happened.'

'O-kaaaay,' Miles says.

But Mrs Kostakis nods emphatically. '*Mati*,' she says. 'Evil eye.'

'Mum, she didn't get evil-eyed from a statue.'

Mrs Kostakis mumbles under her breath and throws salt over her shoulder for good measure. 'Well, I'm sorry I don't recognise it, Reece. But see that hall in the background?' She taps the photograph, indicating a sign behind the statue.

'Hamilton Historical Society,' I whisper, squinting at the words.

'They might know, honey. It seems like they might have organised it.'

'Thanks,' I say, folding the photo back inside my jacket. I hurl my backpack over one shoulder and down the rest of my coffee. There's still plenty of daylight: I can make it if I hurry.

'Hang on,' Mrs Kostakis says, a hand stilling my elbow. 'The Historical Society is only open Wednesday to Friday. You'll have to wait a few days.'

I resist the urge to scream, inwardly cursing this stupid backwards town and its bizarre opening hours. Maybe tomorrow I can go back to the bookshop and track down Frank. He has to know who it is if he stuck it up.

'More coffee?' Miles says.

'Much more,' I agree.

The sky is dark by the time I pedal home again. I call out a miserable hello as I stomp inside, cranky and over-caffeinated. Just to satiate my curiosity, I rode by the Hamilton Historical Society on my way home. It was closed, just like Mrs Kostakis said it would be.

No one answers, but the television is on so I assume at least one person is home. I make my way to the fridge, pausing to stick the photo to the door with a magnet—I've sent a copy to Nina, but I don't want to lose it while I rummage for snacks.

'Honey?' Mum calls out.

'It's me, Mum!' I yell out, quickly chugging juice straight from the bottle. I twist the cap back on right as she hits the landing. We've called a truce. Well, not officially. It's more that we're putting off the inevitable. I haven't mentioned the museum, and Mum hasn't either. The past week sucked enough without us arguing about it.

'Dad and Theo?' I ask, peering into the fridge for something more substantial.

She leans against the counter, a quirk in her smile. 'On an adventure,' she says.

The world has righted itself. I beam back at her. 'That's good.'

'Mmm. But your brother ate all the dinner so if you're hungry it's a cheese toastie or whatever's still in the freezer.'

'Urgh. Little heathen.'

Mum chuckles, smoothing my hair. 'You were the same at sixteen.'

'You know, I've watched him tip a whole bag of dry cereal in his mouth.' I slam the fridge door closed before it starts to beep.

Mum opens her mouth to say something, then stops. 'Oh my...' She reaches out a hand.

I touch my face, worried I've dribbled juice everywhere. But she's looking behind me and, when I turn around, her fingertips graze the photograph.

'Oh yeah. Guess you've never seen it. It's the statue from high school. Well, my old high school.' Queen Mab faced the teachers' car park at the back of the school grounds: it was less of a car park and more a pile of mud and gravel assembled in the vague *shape* of a car park. Anyway, the area is pretty much next to the year twelve lockers, so most of us would cut through in the mornings, rather than walking all the way to the front gates on the opposite side of the school.

Mum slips the photo out from underneath the magnet. 'I *have* seen this,' she murmurs. 'I thought I'd lost it forever. Where did you find it?'

'At the second-hand bookshop. What do you mean you've

seen it? Do you know who that is?' My heart is racing so fast I think I'll be sick. It can't be this easy. It *can't*.

Mum looks up, puzzled. 'Of course I know who it is,' she says. She taps the man in the photo. 'That's Mayor Thornton,' she says, then taps the statue. 'And that's your grandmother.'

My blood runs cold.

MAB.

Mary Anne Blackwell.

'Nana?' I croak. 'That's Nana?'

Tears threaten to spill. My eyes are stinging and I reach up to swipe them with the cuff of my jumper.

'Reece, honey, are you…upset? What's wrong?'

I back away from her. 'No, no, it can't be her. It's cursed. That's not Nan.' Everything's coming out in a jumble. Nothing makes sense. Mum gnaws at her lip, torn between letting me speak and shushing me like she used to when I was little.

'Honey, what do you mean it's cursed?'

'That statue!' I put my hands over my ears. They're ringing, echoing, and I don't know where the noise is coming from.

Mum holds up the photo. 'This statue?'

'Yes!'

She reaches out and takes my hands. 'Baby, shh, it's all right. It's not cursed, look—it's just a statue. Just bronze. They made it when she became the first female surgeon at the hospital, before I was even born. I've only seen it once, in this photo. Mum used to have it on the wall. Then the hospital found someone new to celebrate, and they donated the statue somewhere, but she said she never cared enough to find out where. I guess it makes sense they gave it to her old school…'

Tears are streaming down my cheeks in earnest now. I knew Nan went to my school, but back then it was a private ladies' college. I'd never even thought about the fact that we'd stomped upon the very same ground. 'That can't be Nan,' I croak. 'It can't.'

'Why not?' Mum asks, pulling me in. 'Tell me what's going on, I don't understand.' She wraps her arms around me, rubbing a soothing circle on my back.

I cling to her, chest heaving. 'Because it was my fault,' I whisper. 'It was *my* fault Willow died. Because the statue cursed me. But if it's not cursed, if it's just Nan…then Will died for nothing. There was no reason.' My voice is thick and broken. I don't know if Mum can even understand me, but it all comes tumbling out and I can't seem to stop. 'It has to be cursed. It *has* to be. Otherwise there was no reason. And it's not fair, I can't—I can't live in a world where she died for nothing. For no *reason*. Because she was tired? Because she checked her phone? That's so stupid, she shouldn't be dead, she should be here. It's not fair,' I sob. 'She should *be here*. It was just one second. One stupid second, and she's not here, and she's not graduating, and she'll never be older and she'll never laugh and—and *god* I think about her in the ground and I have nightmares because I wonder what she looks like now and I hate it, I hate it, I can't—I can't—'

Mum catches me before I hit the ground. I tip forward into her lap, a high, keening sound ripping from my lungs.

'It was all for nothing,' I sob. 'She was better than nothing.'

'Reece, honey, do you really think it was your fault?'

And I suddenly know I can't keep it a secret anymore. I have to tell Mum, because it's been eating me alive, and I didn't even notice it happening. The secret that's been festering and eating away at everything that matters. 'I messaged her,' I whisper. 'The night she died. She dropped me home when she wasn't meant to, and then I texted her.'

This is how it happened: the night of the concert, Willow drove Nina home first. I was supposed to sleep over, but I had swim practice early in the morning and changed my mind at the last second.

Willow didn't care. 'So long as I can pick the music,' she said. And when she dropped me home, she blew me a kiss and drove away.

The police said she didn't even swerve. They said she was either distracted or asleep. It happens all the time, they said, as though we'd feel better knowing about all the dead girls who slipped away just because they drove home too late or looked away at the wrong second.

I never told anyone I texted her. Willow never checked her phone when she drove. She always kept it in the door, and only once did I see her glance at it at a red light. But she must have: she wasn't tired. She was singing along to the radio. She was laughing.

And if I'd just stayed at Nina's, if Willow hadn't driven me home, if I hadn't messaged her, if I hadn't been late that first day of school and forgotten Queen Mab…I cursed us all, and Willow died because of it.

Except Mum's right. It's just a statue. It's always been just a statue. But it's easier to blame superstition than to admit it was all my fault.

'Maybe she still would have crashed,' I whisper. 'But maybe if *one* thing had been different—if I hadn't decided to come home, if she hadn't driven that exact road at that exact time—maybe she would have made it. Maybe she wouldn't have hit that rail. Maybe she would have just been hurt but still *here*. I could have lived with her hating me forever but I can't live with her being *gone*.'

Mum hesitates. 'Reece?'

'It's my fault either way. The police said—' I hiccup on a sob, and Mum shushes me. She knows what the police said. She sat on the couch and held my hand while they told me. Snippets that still haunt me. *An accident. Distracted. Maybe tired. Happens all the time. Sorry for your loss.*

Mum cups my cheeks in her hands. 'Clarissa, honey, listen to me. It's not your fault. Nothing is your fault. Willow got in that car. Willow drove. And I love her, I love her so much, sweetheart. It's not her fault either—she was young and she was clever and she never would have gotten in that car if she thought it wasn't safe. But it was a mistake. An accident. And she *did* deserve better, she deserved the whole world. All you girls do. But the world doesn't make sense, Reece. It doesn't always go the way we want it to. Sometimes people die for no good reason, and it's awful and cruel and unfair. But you loved her, and she had a good life. That's not nothing, honey. That's everything. That's all we can ask for.' She pulls me to her again, kissing my forehead as

I sob. She holds me until I'm done, until there's no more tears, and when I sit back my eyes are tired and dry, and I feel the weight of my secret lifting. Mum doesn't hate me. The world didn't end.

'Is this why you didn't want to go back to school?' Mum asks gently. 'Why things got so hard with Nina?'

I nod, sniffing.

'Oh, baby. I wish you'd told me earlier. I'm so sorry you've been going through this alone.' She pauses, considering her next words. 'Have you...have you told her? I know you two have just started talking again, but...'

'No,' I murmur, picking at a thread on my jeans. 'I never told anyone.'

'I think you should talk to her,' Mum says. 'You've got a good heart, Reece. Give her a chance. Stop carrying this alone.'

I see a flash of Willow in my mind, blowing a kiss through the open window of her car. *I miss you so much.* The memory of her laughs, pulling away exactly like she did on that final night. I wish I'd stopped her. I wish I'd known. If I'd known that was all we got, I would have hugged her longer. Told her I loved her. Made sure I remembered the sound of her voice. Memorised her words. Asked her about all the things she wanted to do.

I would have made her stay.

Mum tugs me to my feet. I follow, letting her tuck me into the couch. We sit watching a home-renovation show while she pats my hair and yet more tears spill onto the cushions.

'You can have the books,' Mum says after a while. I sit up, thinking I've misheard. She's looking at the photo of Nan's statue, stroking it fondly. 'Keeping them won't bring her back. They should be shared. And she left them to you for a reason. I'm sorry, Reece. I shouldn't have gotten so angry.'

'I shouldn't have kept it from you.'

She shakes her head. 'No more secrets.'

I hold out a pinkie and she takes it, chuckling. 'No more secrets,' I echo. 'But Mum? If there's no more secrets, I have to tell you something else.'

I go to my room and fish out the papers. The curio is at Gideon's house, but I took photos on my phone so I show her those first. I lay the list of names in her lap, and she sifts through them, confused. 'I only ever found one clue,' I explain. 'Emilia. She went missing, they never found her.'

I tell her about Frank and Bronwyn, and that the chest is probably harmless. She flinches when I say *probably*.

'Your grandmother loved her secrets,' Mum says. 'I suspect we'll never uncover all of them. Let me make some calls, she still has some old friends.'

I nod, glad to share this burden at last with a real adult.

'I was thinking...' she starts.

'You can tell me.'

Her eyes are bright, a spark of something there. 'It's up to you. But I was thinking, if you wanted to sell some of the books, we could use the money to open a proper clinic down here, in her old house,' Mum says. 'It's yours, of course. You could use the money to travel, or to pay off university. Whatever you want. But even with a little, we could start something. That hospital is a bloody shitshow. No wonder Mum kept working as long as she did.' She sighs at the thought. 'Anyway. I know you wanted to be a doctor. Or used to.' She waits for me to respond. I nod, slowly. Another secret unleashed. 'Well, if you still want that, it could be yours one day.'

'Mine?'

'Sure. You could do whatever you wanted. Specialise in something and bring it down here. Or sell it when your dad and I retire to the Italian countryside one day and get fat on wine and pasta,' she jokes. I give her a watery smile.

'Mum...' I clear my throat.

She's listening.

'I think maybe...I think maybe I want to keep the books. Or at least some. Would that be okay?'

'Of course it is. It's okay. Whatever you choose, Reece, it's going to be okay. I promise.'

20

I STAND ON Gideon's doorstep, nervous and jittery. There's no good reason for it. Maybe because I haven't seen him in a few days. Or maybe because he sounded happy on the phone this morning, and I'm scared something terrible will have happened in the time it took me to cycle here.

When I tap on the door, Grace is the one who opens it, smiling broadly at me from her walker.

'Well, good morning, Reece. I wondered why my son was spending so much time combing his hair this morning.'

She ushers me in, and I'm pleased to see that she's looking better. She still has a painful-looking row of stitches above her ear, but there's colour in her face and she seems stronger.

'So, a celebration for Miles?' she says, gesturing for me to sit. 'Tell him I say congratulations.'

I promise her I will. After everything that happened last week, Miles's good news about getting into the academy got overshadowed, so Mum and Dad agreed to let me have a small party in his honour while they're away for the weekend at a wedding. Their only conditions were no booze, and that the house had better be spotless when they return.

'How are you feeling?' I ask.

'Sore and stiff. More of the same,' she jokes, but the smile on her face slips away too quickly 'The doctors recommended more advanced care.'

I don't know what to say. *I'm sorry* feels wrong. Feigning surprise would be a lie.

'Gideon told me,' I say instead.

'I thought he might.'

'What do—' I break off, shaking my head. 'I'm sorry, it's none of my business.'

Grace winks. 'Go on, you've seen my underwear drawer now. Not much else is secret, might as well.'

'What do *you* want to do?'

We both glance at the corridor, but there's no sign of Gideon yet.

'It's selfish,' she says, 'but part of me wants to stay here a while longer. I don't feel old. I'm *not* old, really. My body might not cooperate sometimes, but my brain still works. And there's not a lot of care facilities for people like me, so I might well end up where your nan was.' She looks around, at the blue walls and the memories framed there. 'This is our home. Gideon's home—the only one he really knows. I thought I'd live here forever. Be the nutty neighbour that feeds the magpies and stops wearing shoes to the supermarket.'

'But?'

'But,' she says, then pauses, choosing her words carefully.

'What good is home if it's not happy? It's getting harder, I think. For both of us.'

I nod, as though I could possibly understand what she's going through, the choices she has to make.

'Would you talk to him?' she says, reaching out a hand. The tremors are worse now, but she can still grip my fingers in her own. 'I want him to start thinking about next year. And I think he might listen to you.'

'He—he loves you,' I say, though it's not enough to capture everything I mean. *He doesn't want to leave. He wants to help.*

'I know. But living his life won't mean he loves me any less. It will just be different.' She leans back again and forces a laugh. 'Plus, sometimes I'd love to chat to someone born before the nineties. God I miss your nan, she was great for a laugh.'

As if on cue, Gideon comes out of his bedroom, holding the archive box with the curio. After I told Mum the story of what was inside, she asked to see it before we lent it to the museum. 'Let's go,' he says. 'Balloons are ready to pick up. Mum, Delilah will be here in five, will you be okay?'

'Yes, son, I will survive by myself for five whole minutes, in my own home, as I have for nearly fifty years. Get out, go be kids. Have fun!'

We pile everything into the boot, then race around town collecting everything we need: bunting, streamers, sparkly top hats, gold stars, and a bunch of food brimming with artificial colouring and flavours.

Gideon and I arrive back home just as Billy pulls up,

Theo hopping out the passenger side.

'What did I say about riding in cars with boys?' I mutter as he saunters over.

'Don't get pregnant? No, wait...'

'Smartass. Help us unload, people will be here soon.'

Nina's car splutters to the kerb just as I wrangle a bag of helium balloons from Gideon's boot, her engine shuddering to a stop amid a plume of smoke.

I wave at her as Billy ambles past, red-checked plaid shirt pushed to his elbows. 'That chick needs to get her radiator checked,' he says, lugging a crate of soft drink inside.

'Says the underage driver,' I mutter.

'Barely underage,' he protests. 'I got held back a year. Cause of, like, English and shit.'

I lock eyes with Gideon, suppressing an eye-roll so strong I may actually see the back of my skull if I give in to it.

Nina piles out of her car, hesitating for a moment. 'Thanks for coming,' I say, and lean in to give her a hug. It's only slightly awkward. I'm still happy she drove down— part of me wasn't sure if she would. But I guess Ava was right after all.

'Did you know I had to stop on the highway for cows?' she says, her cheeks dotted in gold and pink.

'Oh. The McPhearson farm. They cross over because— never mind.'

She grins at me, then peers around the bag of balloons. 'Hello, Gideon,' she says sweetly. 'I have lots of invasive personal questions to ask you. I'm Nina, by the way.'

I glance over my shoulder. He's giving her the full-dimple

smile. 'I'll tell you whatever you want to know,' he says. He holds out a hand in greeting and she bats it away.

'People are so polite down here, it's weird,' she says, pecking his cheek instead. 'All right, who's gonna help me carry my shit? I panic-packed and brought two suitcases.'

We ferry things back and forth from the car, and I'm careful to hide the curio in my room, where it won't get damaged.

Ava invited a few of their cousins and some kids Miles is close to so it felt like a proper party. Connie Davies was also invited and arrives with her girlfriend, Tess, which she seems shy about until Theo gives her a high five and whispers something that makes her laugh. By the time Miles arrives, an episode of *Ghost Hunters* is playing loudly, drowning out any chatter that might give us away. Ava comes in first, a palm slapped over his eyes, and guides him to the centre of the room.

'I swear, dweeber, if you put something weird on my face—'

'SURPRISE!'

She lifts her hand just as everyone leaps out from their hiding places, cheering for Miles. I race over to squish a sparkly hat on his head, squeezing him in a hug. 'Congratulations, Miles,' I say, then set him free into the sea of waiting people.

He bounces into outstretched arms and high-fives. He weaves between the bodies, saying hello to our little crowd, laughing as he's presented with gifts: a music box that only plays 'Greensleeves' (which he threatens to throw off the pier), a keyring from Sally in the shape of drums (also threatened with a watery death), and a backpack that zips up in a line of piano keys. He even hugs Connie's girlfriend when she presents him with homemade cupcakes.

I grin up at Gideon, laughing when he laughs. Then Miles lifts me by the waist and tosses me over one shoulder. 'You're the best, you know that?' he says.

'Hey,' Ava says, frowning.

'Second *hey*,' Gideon adds, but he tweaks my nose before Miles sets me down again.

'Seriously, guys, thanks,' says Miles, his voice lowered so only our circle can hear. 'I know you've had a shit week, and this is...this is more than the Coles mudcake I expected.'

Nina chooses that moment to emerge from the bathroom, having arranged her hair into a series of elaborate braids. 'I missed it!' Then her eyes land on Miles. 'Oh. Hello.'

Miles looks like he's been struck by lightning. 'Hi. Hello. Um.' He sticks out a hand. 'Miles. I'm Miles.'

'So you're the piano genius,' Nina says, sizing him up. 'Huh. Kind of expected more of a nerd, to be honest.'

Ava snorts. 'Keep expecting. Ow!' she says as Miles swats her in the ribs, silencing any more retorts, before he gets dragged away by one of their cousins.

Nina delights in telling stories about embarrassing tween-age Reece—especially the one where Scott Folley and I kissed for the first time and our braces got so stuck together the fire brigade had to come and separate us. Gideon tries and fails to smother a laugh.

When Miles returns from his latest lap of the room, there's a big red kiss mark on his cheek. I wipe it away with my thumb. 'What happened here?'

'Finally got a kiss from Connie.' He sighs. 'She and Tess are going on a trip together for gap year. Surfing in Fiji. Or Hawaii. Somewhere hot and almost exactly like Hamilton.'

Gideon's dimples disappear, but Miles continues, oblivious. 'Man, I can't believe school is done in like, what, a month?'

I give him a weak smile. It's all I can manage. I can't tell them. Not yet.

Nina tilts her head towards the back door, and I jump off my bench stool, patting Miles on the head. 'Be right back.'

I grab a shawl from the coat stand, my toes sinking into grass as I follow Nina into the yard. She heads for the hanging love seat and curls inside it.

'Come sit,' she says. 'That was an SOS look if I've ever seen one.'

'SOS?'

'You looked like you were drowning. What's up? And don't lie, I'll know if you do.'

I sigh, settling against the rattan seat. I have to tell someone. 'Next year,' I start. 'Next year...I'm not sure if I'm staying in Hamilton.'

Nina throws up her arms. 'Well, that's not exactly a secret. What were you going to do here? Start baking, raise some sheep? You're not a small-town girl, Reece. There's gotta be more to it than that.'

Why is Nina never surprised when I expect her to be? Sometimes I forget how well she knows me. But confessing is easier when someone already knows your sins, so I keep going. 'But…I don't think I'm going to uni, either.' Actually, I know I'm not. But it's not a lie and, after a long, stern look, Nina seems to accept it. She kicks her legs so that the seat starts to rock.

'So what's the plan? Get a job in the city? Save some money?' She pauses, and drops her gaze. 'Take that gap year Willow planned for us?'

She bites her lip. A moment of shared sadness washes over us, and she finds my hand in the dark. Willow was obsessed with Paris. She wanted us to go together: rent an apartment by the Seine, and spend the summer trawling through antique stores and vintage markets, living off croissants and croques-monsieur.

Nina's head comes to rest on my shoulder. 'It's okay if you want to go,' she says.

I shake my head. 'Maybe someday. But not without her… not without you.'

She laughs, poking me in the stomach. 'You big softie.'

I swallow, blinking back tears. 'Nina, I have to tell you something.' *You can't carry this alone.* 'About Willow,' I continue, as her face darkens. 'The night she died.'

'Reece—'

'Just let me get this out, because if you're going to hate me again, I'd rather know now.'

'I never hated you.'

'You might,' I say, miserably. 'Remember how I was supposed to sleep at your house? That night? And I had a swim meet in the morning so I—'

'I remember.' Nina's face is blank. I can't tell what she's thinking.

Just do it, I tell myself. *All at once, no turning back. You lost Nina once, you can do it again. But you can't be friends again with this secret festering between us.* 'I texted her. And the police said maybe she was tired, or maybe she looked down for a second too long, and I think—I think—' The words are stuck in my throat.

Nina's eyes are shining and I realise she's gripping my hands so tightly that my knuckles have gone white.

'You're such an idiot,' she says. 'You're so stupid, Reece.'

'I know. I'm so sorry, I didn't know—'

'*No*, I meant, it's not your fault, Reece. I texted her too. Do you know what I sent? What was so important that I couldn't wait until she got home? I told her, *I want Kylo Ren to squish me with his big dumb body.*'

I stare at her. And then I laugh. It's a little hysterical. There are tears on my face. And Nina smiles. She doesn't hate me.

'I wish you'd told me,' Nina says. 'Because I felt the same. I thought it was my fault, and I clung to you so much because I needed to feel like the universe didn't hate me. I ended up in *therapy*, Reece. Which was actually a good idea, but that's not the point. But remember I told you her parents gave me her phone?'

I freeze, realising what she's about to say. I'd never thought about it before.

'She never opened them, Reece. Maybe she tried to. Maybe she glanced down. But you know Willow, and I don't think she did. I think she was tired, or something went wrong. And we'll never know—maybe her shoe got stuck on the pedal, or she dropped something, or she was trying to find a good song on the radio. But I know we didn't make her crash that car. And I know she wouldn't be mad at us. I know she loves us, wherever she is. And *that* cost me a good amount of money and a lot of tears to figure out.'

'But if I had just stayed at your house—'

'She still might have crashed. And maybe she would have hit someone else. You can't know, Reece. And you can't punish yourself forever, wondering about the possibilities.'

I can't help it: I've thrown my arms around Nina, and I'm trying not to cry. Somehow, her words are like a balm on my broken heart. *I know she loves us.* And for the first time in ages, I've found something that means more to me than Willow's death does. Losing her took such a huge part of me. And Nina just put something back.

'I love her so much,' I say, fairly certain I'm ruining Nina's silk shirt by crushing my face into it.

'Me too, Reece. I love her so much that sometimes I don't know how to live without her. But she wouldn't want us to be stuck. She was too stubborn for that.'

'When did you get so smart?'

'When I had nothing to do but read and get zen for about six months? And there's this group I go to. I think you should come sometime. You can just listen. I know you think it sounds stupid, but it helps. All these people who know how it feels.'

'Maybe,' I say, sitting up, brushing a hand over my cheek.

'That actually sounds…not dumb.'

She smiles at me. 'I love you, Reece. And your big stupid face and your terrible secret-keeping.'

'I love you too, Nina.' I think we'll always be like this, now. Not wasting a moment. Saying it, just in case.

'We should get tattoos,' she declares.

'Tattoos?'

'Mm-hmm. I think I want a bee.'

She starts explaining a very elaborate metaphor when Gideon and Miles emerge, arms loaded with snacks. 'We come bearing gifts,' Miles says, taking a seat on the grass. He looks sheepishly at Nina. 'I didn't know what you liked so I got one of everything.'

'Are there sour gummies?'

'Yes, ma'am.' He tosses her the packet. She opens it and rips off a snake head with her teeth.

'Acceftaffle,' she says, the word garbled.

Gideon sprawls on his back, resting his head in the crook of his elbow. 'So, Miles. Tell us your grand plan.'

'Well,' Miles says, more abashed than I've ever seen him, 'it's not—I mean—It's the best music program in the country, so I guess I'll go and play every day, and try to keep up.'

'And then…?'

'I've heard it's, like, mega-competitive. These kids think it's Juilliard or something. So don't go making new friends, because I'm not sure I'll have any,' Miles jokes. 'And then, I don't know. Find whatever work I can. They'll probably make me play one of those lame Harry Potter concerts—'

'Hey,' Nina protests. 'I like Harry Potter.'

'Oh, me too. Love Harry Potter. Love the...pottering. And um, the Hogwarts. Great. Love it.' Miles wrings his hands, and even from my place in the loveseat I can tell they're sweating. 'So, Nina,' he continues, overly casual. 'Do you play? Piano? Violin? Harp—'

Nina tosses her braids over one shoulder. 'I play the flute, actually.' She smirks. 'And cello. A little keyboard, just for fun.'

Miles puts a hand over his heart. 'Marry me.'

She can also play guitar, but she never tells anyone because, and I quote: *It's not like it's hard, any idiot can read tabs.* (I cannot read tabs. Neither could Willow.)

She giggles, tilting her head just so, *and oh my god Nina Reyes is flirting with Miles.* She's going to eat him alive. I discreetly shove her with my foot, and she takes the opportunity to leap out of the seat. 'Come on, piano man. Let's give the lovers some space, and you can give me all the good gossip.' She grabs Miles by the hand and leads him back inside the house.

I call after them, protesting. 'We're not—'

Gideon laughs, dropping into Nina's vacated spot. 'They're gone,' he says. 'And I think Miles is in love.'

'How quickly he forgot Connie.'

'Connie doesn't play three instruments.'

'Alas.'

He pushes his foot on the ground, rocking the seat with more grace than Nina did. The cuffs of his jeans are rolled up and his shoes have come off at some point. I hitch my dress up to my knees and wriggle until my head is in his lap.

'Tired?' he asks, hand covering mine. We really need to figure out what we're doing before we run out of time. We never quite seem to get past the kissing to an actual conversation.

'Mm. Happy-tired,' I murmur, pressing myself into the warmth of his shirt. I mean, I guess we don't need to figure it out right *now*.

'Nina's nice.'

I snort. 'No, she's not.'

'Fine, she's funny. I can picture you two together. You sort of…match.'

'She's not as scary as she pretends to be.'

'Oh, just to be very clear, she still scares me.'

I laugh and twist a little, so I'm looking up at the stars. 'I think she's lonely, more than anything else,' I say.

'I can imagine. She lost Willow. And then you. Couldn't have been easy, on her own…'

'I'm still here,' I insist.

His smile is sad. 'You know what I mean. I guess I should get used to it. No Miles, no you. I might start drinking with Frank just to have something to do next year.'

There's a familiar pang in my chest. 'We don't have to talk about next year…'

'I know. Just tonight…Never mind.'

I squeeze his hand. 'Tell me. You can tell me anything.'

He tips his head back, curls spilling over his collar. 'I think I'm jealous,' he whispers. 'It always seemed okay, you know? I'd stay with Mum as long as I could. Get a job. Maybe it wasn't what I had planned, but it was okay. But now everyone here is going somewhere, and I'm just…stuck. And then I feel guilty for thinking that at all, because she needs me, and it's not her fault she got sick. And I should be grateful, because she's still Mum, and a lot of people don't get the time that we've had.'

Someone opens a door and closes it, music and laughter spilling out of the house.

'Sorry,' Gideon says. 'I didn't mean to…Anyway. It's fine.'

'It's not fine if you're not happy,' I say. I think of Grace, how she said almost the same thing only a few hours ago.

His fingers twist in a lock of my hair. 'Will you come visit me? Bring me some good city coffee?'

'Gideon—'

I stop myself when I see the half-smile stuck on his face. It's almost a grimace. Then he pulls a letter out of his pocket. 'I got this in the mail today,' he says. 'An art school in the city. They want me to come for an interview. Bring some portfolio pieces. Weird, since I never actually applied.'

His eyes lock on mine. I am desperately, hopelessly, drowning.

'I'm sorry,' I blurt. 'I should have asked.'

'How did you even…It doesn't matter. I'm staying, Reece. I can't afford to go.' He slips out the pamphlet, and I can't help but notice the edges are frayed, like he's thumbed through it a million times already. I take it from him, and the pages fall open to a section marked *Fees and Board*. There are too many zeroes on the pages, and I think it must be a mistake. Gideon's face has turned desperately sad: it's the mask of someone looking at a future they fiercely want but can't have.

'No more,' he says, gently taking the booklet from my clenched fists.

'But—'

He leans over and kisses my temple. 'No more,' he repeats. 'There's already not enough money for rent, for Mum's medication. The hospital sank us even more. I owe the school money just to graduate. This—this can't happen.'

'There must be—'

'There isn't. Just—I'm tired, I think I might go home. Tell Miles I'm sorry.' He stands and starts to leave.

I scramble to my feet, calling after him. 'Gideon, we could make it work. You wouldn't have to board, you could drive and sort your classes so they're all on a few days. You could—'

He turns and holds up a hand. 'I'm sorry, Reece. That things aren't different. I'm just…I'm so tired of fighting it. I'm tired of wanting more and never having it. So just stop, because I don't think I can stand losing another thing I can't have.' His voice breaks, and he holds up the pamphlet in his hand. 'I really, really wanted this. Being so close has just made everything worse. I can't keep hoping things will change. I need to let it go. *You* need to let it go.'

Then he walks back inside, closing the door behind him.

And I don't follow.

21

THE HOUSE IS quiet when I wake up. Miles is snoring on our sofa, and Nina is sprawled nearby. I hesitate in the kitchen, noticing his hoodie draped across her shoulders. *That's* an interesting development. The rest of the lounge room is empty—Ava crawled into bed beside me last night, moaning that the air bed was too uncomfortable to sleep on. I woke up this morning when she kicked me in the back—she went back to sleep, but I was wide awake. I squeezed my eyes shut, trying not to think of Gideon's hurt look last night when he showed me the art-school brochure, but I couldn't put it out of my mind. I kicked off the doona covers as the magpies started their morning warble, and crept downstairs. Maybe in the daylight, it'll be easier to forgive. I'll visit him this afternoon and apologise for interfering.

I glance at the clock on the kitchen wall. No one will be up for at least another hour. I start tidying as quietly as I can—there's not much mess anyway, everyone was pretty chill. I take down the streamers, pick up stray cups, toss rubbish in the bin.

Ava stumbles downstairs at some point, stretching. 'G'mornin,' she mumbles. She grabs a rubbish bag and starts to help, until Miles wakes up too and groans.

'Dweeb. What time is it?'

'Ten.'

'Urgh. Come on, we gotta hurry. Yiayia and Papou are coming today—we promised we'd go to church for once.'

Ava looks pained by this news, and hugs me. 'Come to the Bean later, I'll make you a decent coffee.'

Miles ambles over and squishes me, too. 'Thanks for everything. Hey, was everything okay with Gid? He left so early.'

I shrug. 'Just tired, I think.'

'Fair. See you crazy kids later.' He makes finger guns and a *pew pew* noise, then cringes when Nina sits up. She waits until the front door closes behind them to pad into the kitchen.

'I'm thinking…pancakes,' she says. 'I had fun, by the way. Thanks for inviting me.'

'I'm glad.'

'Your friends are nice.'

'You mean *Miles* is nice,' I say. 'Gee, I wonder why she wants pancakes…Maybe at a particular cafe?'

She sits on the kitchen bench, huffing. 'I don't know what you mean.'

'Let me have a shower and get changed. We can hang around the Bean. Their grandparents never stay long.'

I wander back upstairs, ignoring Theo's closed door.

Now that I think about it, I never saw Billy leave last night…

I pause in my bedroom doorway, eyes on the archive box. Huh. Weird. The lid is open. It's no longer pushed to the corner of my room, and I definitely triple-checked the lid was closed when Gideon brought it up here. Maybe Ava accidentally tripped on it? Or she could have been looking for something in the dark.

I take a few steps forward. 'No. No, no, no.' The box is empty. I tip it upside down, as though the book could possibly be hidden, and search the floor, hands running over bare floorboards. I look under the bed, tear open cupboards, toss clothes out of drawers. It doesn't make sense.

I text Ava and ask if she remembers seeing it. She replies almost immediately.

Book? Sorry Reece, I just faceplanted in your bed, didn't really notice. Everything good?

I don't reply, because everything is *not* good. And everything is so much worse, because I put Nan's papers back in one of the tiny drawers. If anyone were to find them, to make assumptions, it wouldn't look good for her. I start methodically pulling apart everything that's upstairs.

Nina finally comes to find me when I knock over an old candlestick from the linen cupboard, and it clatters on the floor. 'Reece, what are you *doing*?'

'I can't find it,' I answer. 'It's gone.'

I race downstairs and Nina follows. She watches me rummage through the cupboards, chests and drawers. I fling every saucepan out of the kitchen, search under the sofa, check every room.

'Are you gonna tell me what you're looking for?' she says, leaning against the stairwell.

I screech in frustration, because I can't keep it in anymore. Nina comes to kneel beside me on the floor, the contents of our crockery cupboard strewn around my feet.

'What's going on?'

'I lost Nan's book,' I mutter, miserable.

'All this for a book?'

'No, it's—it's hard to explain.'

But I try, in fits and bursts, as she helps me search for it. How the lawyer gave it to me, and the secret pages, the missing girl, Gideon's help through it all.

'Wait. Why don't you ask him?'

'Gideon?'

'Yeah. Maybe he accidentally left it, or took it for...I don't know, something. Whatever weird hobby it is you two have developed.'

I scrunch up my nose. 'We kinda had a fight.'

'Reece, it's a ten-thousand-dollar book. Just call him.'

I make her wait downstairs so I can have this conversation in private. The phone rings three, four, five times, until the line goes dead and his voicemail message kicks in.

'Hey,' I say. 'It's me. Sorry. I know you're—we're—whatever. Have you seen Nan's book? It's missing, and I'm worried someone took it. Not that I think *you* took it, but the box is open, and I don't where else—' I take a breath, slapping one hand over my face in a silent groan. 'Just...just text me, if you can. Uh, bye.'

I hang up before I can dig myself any further into this grave.

Nina appears in the doorway. 'That was not quite what I meant when I said you should ask him.' She must have heard everything.

'He didn't even answer. He'll never talk to me again.'

'Stop being dramatic,' she says, her serious-Nina face firmly in place. 'He's probably just busy. Anyway, we're going to find it. Are you sure we looked everywhere? Let's double-check.'

I spy Theo's closed door. 'There's one place I haven't looked,' I say. I march down the corridor and pound on the door. 'Wake up, and don't be naked.'

Nina tugs on my shoulder. 'Reece, calm down—'

Theo blinks up at the sudden light. 'Did you take it?' I ask, standing over him.

'What the *fuck*, Reece?'

'Did you take Nan's book?'

'What? What book?'

'The book! With the poisons and the glass!'

He pulls the sheet over his head. 'That sounds *so* boring, and I don't even read. Get out, you're being a total bitch queen.'

'What about Billy?'

The sheet comes back down. 'What *about* Billy?'

'Maybe he took it. It's worth a lot of money, Theo. Guys like Billy—'

His gaze turns lethal, and I realise I've crossed a line. 'Guys like Billy *what*, Reece? Just because you're in a fucking mood and you're pissed off at Gideon, don't take it out on me.'

'I just meant that Billy isn't always...' I'm flailing. I have nothing. Nina is hissing at me to get out but I can't seem to stop. 'He got held back! I mean, Theo, why are you even with him? I wouldn't be surprised if he took it just to be funny.'

Theo rushes out of bed, looming above me. 'I know you've been through some stuff this year, but that does not give you the right to storm into my room and be a total douche. Deal with your shit, Reece, you're starting to lose it.' He storms down the corridor and slams the bathroom door, before throwing it open again. 'And just for the record, he's not dumb, he's dyslexic. That's why I help him study so much, because this *shitty* school in this *shitty* town that we had to move to because of *you* doesn't have a special studies program.' Then he slams the door again, and this time I know it's final.

Nina ushers me out of the house, still wearing her fuzzy bunny slippers. She drags me down the driveway and points at the passenger-side door of her car. 'Sit,' she commands.

She sits in the driver's seat and grabs my frantic hands, forcing me to be still. 'You know you have a self-destruct button, right? I don't know if this is about Gideon, or Willow, or your nan, or even me. But you need to *figure it out*, before you obliterate everything else. Because that? That was not okay. That was full nuclear.'

I dip my head. 'It's everything. It's so many layers of everything I don't know where to start.'

'You need to apologise to him.'

'I know. Oh god, I know.' I cup my face in my hands, humiliated. I can't believe I accused Billy of stealing from me for no good reason. And yelled at Theo. I mean, we yell all the time, but that felt different.

'Okay. Now we're going to give him the house for a minute, and sit here to talk this through. Think, Reece. Where else could the book be?'

'It could be at Nan's...'

'Great, let's start there.'

'Everyone is going to hate me,' I moan.

'*Oh my god,* could you stop being dramatic for five seconds?'

'I'm not being dramatic,' I retort, fully aware that I am, in fact, being dramatic.

'Calm. Down. Just breathe for a minute. Urgh, I need coffee, I can't deal with this on an empty stomach.' She shoves her key into the ignition and the car rumbles to life. She's seriously going to wear her fuzzy bunny slippers to breakfast.

'I don't know if I feel like going to the Bean,' I mumble.

Nina gives me a flat glare. 'Tough shit. You moved to a town with one coffee shop and crappy mobile reception. This one's on you.'

After we stop at the Beach Bean for breakfast, we search through Nan's house—everywhere. We unpack boxes and repack them again. I look in the washing machine, her DVD cabinet, her pantry.

'It's gone. It's just gone.' I throw my hands up in frustration. 'How did this even happen?'

Even Nina is starting to look concerned. Her cool veneer is wearing thin and she's rummaging with increasing vigour. 'I don't understand...there must be an explanation. We're missing *something*.'

There's a tap at the back door, and I sigh. 'It's probably Gideon. I should go talk to him.'

She nods, slipping further into the house to give us privacy.

I pull the curtains back and find Gideon waiting, as expected. He looks haggard and pale, a wretched look on his face. And then I glance down, and see what he's holding.

'I'm sorry,' he starts. 'I can explain.'

I stare at him in disbelief. 'You had it?'

'I didn't mean—I didn't plan to take it. And last night, everyone was talking about their futures, and then the uni—I messed up, Reece. I'm so sorry.'

I snatch the curio out of his hands, too hurt to even be angry. 'You knew what this meant to me. You knew I'd be looking for it.'

'I know, I feel terrible. I wanted to give it straight back, I thought maybe I could return it before you noticed. It was one stupid moment. I was so angry and frustrated, and you were going to give it away anyway—'

'That was *my* choice.'

He hangs his head, defeated. 'I know. I'm so sorry, Reece. I'm so, so sorry. I would never have gone through with it. I cared about Maggie too, I wouldn't have —'

'Don't call her that.'

'Reece, can I just—'

'*No.* Just go, Gideon. I don't want to talk to you right now.'

'Please—'

Nina appears behind me. 'She said she's done, loverboy.'

He looks torn, his expression sad and lost. This isn't the Gideon I know. I can't meet his gaze. 'I'm sorry,' he whispers. 'I'll go.'

We watch him retreat up the path, and Nina's hand finds mine. 'Come on,' she says. 'Let's go home.'

We drive back in silence. In the lounge room, Theo is brooding on the sofa, and resolutely ignores us when we pass. In the mirror, I notice his eyes flicker to the book clutched in my arms. I hesitate at the bottom of the stairs, looking to Nina for guidance. She shrugs and slips upstairs.

'Theo—' I start.

'I know.'

'I just wanted to say I'm so sorry.'

'I can't hear my show.'

'I didn't mean it. And I shouldn't have said anything about Billy, that was mean. All of it was wrong. I'm so, so sorry.'

He turns, the barest hint of acknowledgment. 'You owe me a lot of lasagne.'

I lean over the couch and kiss his cheek. He wipes it away. 'I'm glad you found your stupid book or whatever,' he mumbles.

I nod, and head upstairs too. Nina's already lying on my

bed, waiting for me. 'That was a lot,' she says, oddly calm. 'Are you mad at him?'

'Gideon?'

She nods.

I try to think, but everything is murky. 'Yes. But also just sad. Mostly…hurt.'

She sits up, fiddling with her hair, then lets out a sigh. 'Look, I'll just say this and then I'll shut up. But from everything you told me, that dude is a freaking *saint*. He drove you around, kept your secrets, helped you *clean out your nan's house*, looks after his sick mum, works double time to pay the bills, cooks, cleans, and never complains. He shouldn't have taken the book: that was a really, really shitty thing to do. But, I guess what I'm saying is, maybe he deserves a break. Not right now. Let him sweat it out for a while. But he'd just had this whole future dangled in front of him and then snatched away.'

She looks down, and I realise she has a photo of Willow in her hands. She must have taken it from my wall. 'You know what that feels like,' Nina says, handing me the picture. 'Wouldn't you have done anything to have that future back?'

'I wouldn't have hurt anyone,' I say, then I flinch, because I know that's not true.

Nina smiles. 'Yeah, you would. I would too. Just…think about it for a bit.'

I nod, holding the picture close. *Hey, Will*, I think. *What would you do?*

But she doesn't answer.

22

'SO, WHAT'S THE deal with this book—treasure-chest thing—anyway?'

We're sitting in Nan's house, which is now mostly clean and restored the way I remember it: cluttered but orderly, the furniture a bit dated but comforting. We left her crystals in the windows, her hand-stitched placemats on the table. Soon, we'll have to take those out too, but for now I can almost convince myself that she's just in the other room, just out of reach.

Nina has her legs propped up on the overstuffed green recliner, hair spread in a glossy sheet across the carpet, balancing the book on her lap. It's turned into a long and lazy day, the kind of humid-hot that makes your limbs feel heavy and sticks your hair to the back of your neck. Nan's ancient little air conditioner splutters uncertainly, threatening to give up at any moment.

'Curio,' I correct, slapping her hands off the cover. 'And put gloves on when you touch it. That thing is worth more than your car.'

'Most things are worth more than my car,' she replies, snapping a rubber glove over one hand. She opens the cover again, cringing when the spine makes an audible crack. 'Anyway, what is this *actually*? You don't seriously think it's a—what did you call it—assassin's cabinet?' Nina squints at the ominous marks beneath each vial, pressing her nose close. 'Nana B was cool, but she wasn't *assassin* cool.'

A bead of sweat drips down my spine. 'Okay, firstly, no assassins are cool.'

'I mean, that's just not true. What about—'

'And secondly...I mean, no? I guess not? The valuer said it could just be used as a medicine cabinet.' But I can tell when my voice trails off that I sound unconvinced. I shake the thought away. I don't think my nan would hurt anyone—I *know* she wouldn't. I feel that truth right down to my bones. But I do think she had a lot of secrets, and maybe she kept a few the day she died.

Nina cranes her neck, looking sceptical. 'But it was locked?'

I press my lips together. 'Yes.'

'And she hid the key?'

'Also yes.'

She holds up the papers in her free hand. 'And this is a list of names? That she hid?'

'Uh-huh.' I regret showing her those now.

'Babe—'

'Don't say it,' I warn, walking over to snatch the list back.

'Okay. Fine,' she says, and tumbles off the chair to sit upright. 'Have you looked for any of these women? Maybe they were her friends or, like, an underground group of suffragettes?'

'She wasn't *that* old.'

'It's suffragettes or bodies in the basements, Reece. Work with me here.'

I glare at her. She glares back. The air conditioner coughs out a dusty stream of cool air.

I blink first. 'Honestly, I never looked that hard,' I admit. 'I was worried about what I'd find. I looked online but this stuff seems pretty old, and the digital archives I found don't go back far enough. But…' I hesitate, on the verge of telling Nina. A secret I can't take back. I sigh, realising I'm too tired to keep this from her—and it's too late, anyway. I already told her the rest. 'I found one of them, in an old newspaper that Nan had kept. Emilia. She was sort of…missing.'

'Right.' Nina screws up her face, as if trying to ignore the sour part of that sentence. 'So you and Gideon spent a whole bunch of time "investigating" and you basically found…nothing? Hmm,' she says, drumming her fingers on her chin. 'What were you two doing in here all that time?'

I feel my cheeks burning red and turn away, reshuffling the pages. I haven't spoken to Gideon since he returned the curio. Even being here, so close to the bungalow, makes me nervous, and I get a tingle up my spine every time a shadow crosses the window. I'm not ready, not yet, and Nina has been a welcome distraction. Well, mostly.

She snorts, sticking her finger in my red cheeks. 'Did you microfiche?'

'Did we *what*?'

She taps on her phone and holds up a picture: what seems to be a clear plastic sheet with a series of tiny negatives lined up in a row, projected onto a clunky computer screen. 'This town is a billion years old—I bet they've kept all their old newspapers at the library or something. You can basically look up any dates and they're all preserved on these little slides. You just have to know when to look.'

I look down at the notes in my hand. They're all dated—we know what year we're looking in, even the month for some of them. Sure, it might take a while to trawl through each individual day, but at least we'd know roughly where to start.

And I *do* need to know: Nan left the curio and her notes to me for a reason. It will *haunt* me if I never find out why. Not so long ago I would have shoved everything under my bed and tried to forget about it, but now...now I have Nina. And I have a fragment of myself back, something that was chipped and displaced, glued together again. Weaker than before, but not shattered.

'Hey, Nina?'

'Yeah?'

'When did you become such a nerd?'

I grin as she swats me. The Nina I knew would hardly open a book.

'Be honest,' I say. 'Is this why Luca broke up with you?'

'*Hey!*'

'Do you watch documentaries now? Tell me about a podcast—any podcast.'

'If you tell anyone about this,' she threatens, 'I will post that picture from last summer with the fish tank.'

'You *wouldn't*.'

'I *would*.'

I pretend to scoff in indignation and she laughs. 'Come on, let's go to the library.' She leans over to whisper faux-seductively in my ear. 'I'll recite the Dewey decimal system to you on the way.'

The library is musty and cold, a welcome reprieve from Nina's too-hot car. The original stone building has been updated with a few study carrels and a narrow bank of computers, and the sun drifts in through skylights overhead.

The librarian seemed, frankly, thrilled with our request, and spent the better part of an hour setting us up in a private room with a stack of negatives and a clunky screen to scan them on. We'd told her we were working on a school project, and she enthusiastically gave us a bunch of tips to speed up the process before leaving us alone.

I eye the pile with trepidation. 'Maybe we should have started with just the *one* name...'

Nina is all business—she sets Nan's papers between us, so we can see each of the names lined up—and pulls out a pair of glasses I've never seen before. 'If we started with only one name, we might miss the others, and we'd have to start over every single time.'

I grudgingly admit this is a good point. If the chances are already slim that we'll find our answers in these pages, at least we're not limiting ourselves any further.

We settle into a steady routine: I select a sheet of negatives and slide it into the machine, and Nina operates the knobs and dials that let us zoom in on the page. From time to time, one of us will return to the list and recite the names; we do this so often over the next two hours that the list seems to develop a rhythm.

We look for Emilia and Alba and Michelle. For Alice and Ruth and Dorothea. For June and Rosemary and Esther.

Occasionally, Nina will exclaim in a small, hopeful voice, then slump in disappointment. For the first hour, we scan each word on every page, searching for even the smallest mention. But after a while, we find ourselves speeding through the articles, settling into a system where Nina scans the left and I scan the right, muttering 'done' when we reach the end of each page, like we did in school when we had to share the one science textbook because Nina sold hers to buy hair dye.

Nina's eyes race across the page, darting so quickly I think she can't possibly be taking it all in. But then she'll complain about how often a racehorse by the name of Fat Tom is mentioned, or that one of the jelly-prawn recipes looks particularly revolting, and I'll peer over her shoulder and laugh with her.

I have no idea how much time has passed—hours, I'd guess—when Nina finally stands up, cracks her wrists and fingers, and stretches with arms overhead. 'Man, television made this look way more glamorous.'

'They also have those handy time-jumps. Where's our amusing supercut with snacks and shenanigans?'

Nina presses her nose to the glass door. 'I think there's a

vending machine. I need sugar. Do you need sugar?'

'I need *coffee*.'

'They have one of those percolators where the coffee sits all day stewing in its own juices.' She pretends to gag. 'Will that do?'

'Hard pass.' I throw her my phone. 'Text Miles. Ask if he'll bring us something,'

Her smile turns ferocious. 'With pleasure.'

'Nina, be nice.'

'I'm always nice.'

'You're always…never mind. Ask if they have baklava.'

She taps out a message on my phone, then sits back down and props her legs on the desk, sneakered feet tapping together.

'So,' she says, drawing the word out into at least three syllables. 'What's going on with you and Gideon? Any news?'

My hand clenches on the plastic controller. 'Nothing. Nothing is going on.'

'Nothing?'

'Nothing,' I repeat, focusing pointedly on the screen— an article about a fruit crop that was, apparently, yielding poorly. I pretend not to see Nina glaring at me, keeping my eyes on the article, suddenly enthralled by the mechanics of irrigation systems and moon cycles.

'Reece?' She nudges my shoulder with her shoe. I swat her away, and she does it again.

'*What?*'

'I mean, are you talking or are you not? Don't think I didn't notice how you made me circle the block twice before we could park outside your nan's place.'

'Wanted a good spot is all.'

'You tried to make me crawl through the cat flap.'

'What? I couldn't find my keys.'

'Uh-huh. So that would be a no to the talking, then?'

I let my head thunk on the desk. 'No, we're not talking. He's still mad at me. I'm still mad at him.'

I open my mouth to elaborate: to say that I miss him and sometimes I find myself looking at my phone, thumb hovering over his number. I think about how he did this one stupid thing, and I don't know how to stack it against all the good things that came before it. But then I picture him standing in the doorway, holding the curio, and I feel that flash of anger all over again. And fine, maybe, there's a twinge of shame there too. For invading his privacy, for the part I played in everything that went wrong.

I start sorting through more negatives, glad for the distraction. Nina just sighs, then slumps in her chair to scroll through her phone for a while.

Then something hits the glass door, followed by a deep voice that groans and says, 'Please tell me nobody saw that.'

Miles rubs his head as he gingerly steps around the partially opened door. 'Man, they really should dirty these things up. That door is way too clean.' He holds out a tray in one hand. He's dressed in a short-sleeved shirt and jeans, even though it's a million degrees outside, and I know for a *fact* he usually works his shifts at the Bean in a ratty coffee-stained T-shirt and boardshorts. And he's combed his hair, which he smooths as he grins at me. 'Don't worry, protected your coffee.'

'Thanks,' I say, taking the cup scribbled with my name. 'Uh, there's only the two of us here, who else are these for?' There are five coffees left in the tray.

'Oh.' He blushes all the way up to his hairline as he turns to face Nina. 'I, uh, I didn't know what kind of coffee you liked, so I...made them all. There's regular, skinny, soy, almond and black,' he says, pointing to each.

Nina smirks at him and takes one of the cups. 'Thank you, Miles,' she says, her voice silky and strange. I shove her chair with my foot and roll my eyes.

'That looks like it hurt,' she says to Miles, undeterred. 'Want me to kiss it better?'

I snort, and coffee comes out my nose, which saves him from having to answer as he shoves a handful of napkins at me.

'So,' he says, his voice cracking, leading to his own coughing fit. 'So,' he repeats. 'What are you guys doing in here anyway?'

Nina explains the process again, waving to the stacks we've worked through and the notes Nan left behind.

'Oh cool,' he says, peering at the pile of negatives beside me, then wanders over to the next table where a discarded stack has been tossed aside from the librarian's initial filtering. 'What are these ones?'

'Births, deaths, marriages,' Nina answers. 'All the boring stuff.'

Miles and I look at her with an identical expression of disbelief. I clear my throat. 'And that didn't seem important, in this context?'

She frowns. 'Well, no, unless you were looking for someone who...oh.'

'Nina!' I screech. 'We've been here for two hours!'

She has the fucking nerve to *giggle*. 'My bad?'

'*Your bad?* Oh my god.' I count to three. Then five. Then ten. Start over.

'Well,' Miles says, backing away from the scene. 'Glad you're not cursed, Reece. Imma let you two...deal with all this.'

'Well, thanks for the coffee, Miles,' Nina says. 'We'll swing by later, okay?'

'Sure,' he says, bouncing on his heels and grinning at her. 'See you later?'

She winks at him and waves goodbye. Then she glances over her shoulder and pouts. 'Hey, you can't be mad. You wouldn't have gotten this far without me.'

I mumble something uncharitable, then hold out a hand so she can pass me a sheet from the newly discovered stack.

It takes ten minutes.

One name.

Esther Wilson.

My breath hitches in my throat, the sound so sudden and strange that Nina bolts upright. 'Did you find one? What does it—' She hovers over my shoulder, reading along silently.

Services are being arranged for Miss Esther Wilson—beloved daughter and sister—who passed suddenly on Tuesday night at the Hamilton Hospital. She is survived by her parents, Joan and Michael Wilson.

'Passed suddenly,' I stammer. 'What does that mean?'

'I don't know,' Nina says. 'An accident, maybe?'

'Maybe.' Maybe the list is simply women who Nan couldn't save—she wrote their names down, consumed by guilt, or…something. I can't think anything else. I won't.

Then we find the next girl.

Seventeen-year-old Rosemary Porter died in Hamilton Hospital after suffering convulsions on the evening of 15 June. She is survived—

'Convulsions?' Nina asks, confused.

A dull throb begins in my temple. I try to think back to the first-aid training Mum let me take years ago, indulging my medical curiosity. 'Could be anything. Epilepsy, brain tumour. Rabies. Low blood pressure.'

We stare at the screen. 'Pass me the next one,' I whisper.

Jennifer Omar. Sepsis.

Ruth Matthews. Haemorrhage.

Dorothea Gomez. Abruption.

Dead. Every single one of them.

My heart breaks, and it breaks, and it breaks.

'Reece,' Nina says gently. 'Stop. That's enough.' She peels my hand away from the keyboard and spins my chair so that we're facing each other. 'You don't know what this means, okay? All of this—all those girls—none of them are suspicious, okay? You don't know what happened.'

'That's not true. I know they died.'

Nina picks up Nan's papers again. We've found at least half of the girls now. 'What about this one?' she says. 'Alba Thornton? *The last one*—what does that mean?'

I don't know what any of it means. I rise from the chair, crossing my arms over my chest, shivering. Nina is in hurricane mode behind me, shuffling papers and negatives, swearing quietly, not caring about the sheets that tumble to the floor—and exclaiming when she finds the one she's looking for. She loads it into the machine, muttering, 'Come on, come on...'

Silence.

Then.

'Oh, shit.'

Curious, I creep back to the computer. I force myself to look.

Alba Thornton—

That's it. That's all it says. Her name is listed in the obituaries, but the rest is blurry and illegible. There are jagged little scratches right where her tribute is listed. I pull it out of the machine and flip it over twice, unbelieving.

'It's—it's damaged. I can't read it.' I frown, bringing the negative close. The scratches are neat, orderly. 'I think...I think someone did this on purpose.'

'That sounds extreme. This stuff is pretty delicate, it might have just been...'

I hold up the negative, showing her the neat gouges.

'Fine,' she admits. 'That is...mildly suspicious.'

'Mildly?'

'Part way between "might be nothing" and "might be murder".'

'*Nina!*'

She holds both hands up in surrender. 'Hey, that's not

what I meant. Sorry, poor choice of words. Breathe, okay? Breathe.' Ridiculously, she inhales and waits for me to follow, then exhales slowly. She does it again, and I copy her, making a face. She used to do this for me when I got panic attacks. I would pretend it didn't help, but it's annoyingly effective.

'Okay,' she says. 'This is all...a little bit strange. But Reece, maybe that's why your nan kept their names. She was a smart woman, and she had more power than most back then. She wasn't, like, an evil scientist, okay? She helped people. She *listened*.'

I nod, miserably.

'We're gonna figure this out. Okay?'

'Okay,' I whisper, clutching Alba's name, her incomplete obituary. A life cut short then stolen away. It seems unfair that she died and left no legacy: only a name, and what was a name without a story? *What happened to you, Alba? What did Nan know?*

'Maybe your mum knows something?' says Nina.

'She's asked around, discreetly. No one knows anything— at least no one who's still, you know...' *Alive.*

I stare down at the pages in my hand, wondering if the grandmother I knew was really the woman she seemed. I wish I had her stethoscope now, but instead I place a hand on my heart, willing it to calm. *Tick tick tick*, like the hands of a too-quick clock, time rushing by.

I picture her smile, kind and patient. I remember the way she fixed my fractured arm, putting the broken pieces back together. I remember the cards and letters and photographs, the patients who would write just to say thank you.

I remember the bungalow she built. The people she *helped*.

'We're missing something,' I whisper. 'This can't be it. There has to be more.'

I stare down at Alba's name, scribbled in Nan's cramped writing, and the scratched-out negative beside it. There has to be more: but right now, I don't know how to separate the secrets she kept from the truth we've uncovered.

23

NINA STICKS AROUND for a few more days. She spends a suspicious amount of time at the Beach Bean, while I spend my time avoiding Gideon. Avoiding my problems. Easier, since school has officially wrapped before exams.

Nina flicks the back of my head. 'Earth to Reece.'

I shake my head. 'What?'

She links her arm through mine, dragging me up the boardwalk. She's been wanting to do all the touristy things: beach, boardwalk, pier. Not like there's much else to do.

She licks a stream of strawberry sorbet off her hand. 'I sfaid, whephes thfe boophshop?' I hand her a swath of napkins, sponging up pink goo as it drips hopelessly onto the footpath. 'And why is it *so freaking hot* all the time?' she adds, viciously pulling her sunglasses down to shield her eyes. They land a little crooked on her nose, but she doesn't seem to mind.

I smirk, tilting my face to the sun, enjoying the final rays of the day. Nina stares at me expectantly, and I wave a hand over my shoulder. 'That way. There's only the one. Look, you can see it from here?'

'Oh good. I need a book for the beach.'

'Frank's not really your friendly neighbourhood bookseller.'

'Does he have air conditioning?'

'Uh, I think so?'

'Great! Let's go!'

She pivots on the spot, powering her way to Frank's shop. She practically skips through the front door, toppling a stack of romance novels. 'Ohh, spicy,' she observes, picking one up. 'Mitch the sheep farmer. Look at his shearing rod. Kinky.'

'Nina,' I hiss, 'put that down.'

The store is silent. I call out and hear a faint kerfuffle from somewhere, but Frank doesn't emerge right away, and I lose Nina to a row of crime novels.

'Look, Reece, there's a cat!'

Out the corner of my eye, I see her reach down, her arms spread wide. I jerk forward in horror. 'Nina, no—!'

She scoops the cat into her arms, nuzzling her cheek into its fur. 'Who's a good little kit-kit? What's your name? Aren't you the cutest little fluffball.'

'That cat hates everyone,' I warn, expecting it to turn on her at any moment.

The tiny traitor mews in her arms, stretching its back. She cackles, tickling its scruffy ears and fat belly until the cat begins to purr. 'Who's a tiny little demon?' she coos. 'You are! Oh, Reece, he's going to lick me to death,' she says sarcastically.

I stare at Lucifer. Of course he loves her.

Just as I'm about to reply, there's another noise from somewhere in the shop.

'Frank?' I call. 'You alive?'

'Clarissa? I'm buried in a stack of rural romance!'

I hurry through the aisles, turning corners until I find Frank sprawled on the floor. I rush to his side, easing him up. A book flops to the ground, and I pick it up dubiously. '*Hammer and Tongs: A Blacksmith Novel*. Now I know where Nana got her Mills & Boons from.'

Frank waves a dismissive hand at me and whacks one hip with frustration. 'Damn metal contraption. Bloody thing jams half the bloody time.'

Nina appears in the doorway, Lucifer perched on her shoulder like a witch's familiar. 'Good lord, this is a raunchy room,' she says, eyeing a shelf full of bodice-rippers.

'Who are you?' Frank grouches. Then his eyes lock on her shoulder. 'And what did you do to my cat?' He shoves an accusatory finger at the beast and it hisses at him, swiping a paw.

Nina grins. 'He likes me. Can I keep him?'

'No.'

'I'll call him Crookshanks.'

'No.'

'And I'll get him a little kitty run and a yarn ball.'

'*No*. And who are you? We're all out of books, get out.'

Nina laughs, twirling a piece of her hair for the cat to play with. Frank squints at her, perplexed. 'She's not leaving,' he says to me.

'She's not,' I agree.

'Well, *why not*.'

'Frank, this is Nina. She's my best friend from back home,' I say, then worry that things haven't thawed enough between us for me to say that. But I glance up at her and she's smiling. 'She, um, she wanted to do all the touristy things before she goes home…so we thought we'd come say hello.'

Nina steps towards Frank and sticks her hand out. 'Hi. Nice to meet you. *¿Me puedo quedar con su gato?*'

'No!'

'Fine,' she says, pouting. 'And Reece is sort of right, but I also wanted to ask you about *this*.' Then, before I realise what she's about to do, she whips something out of her pocket with a flourish. It's obviously a copy, printed on regular computer paper, but it's still recognisable: Nan's statue.

Frank holds out a shaky hand. 'Come,' he says, chewing on his lip. 'I think we should sit down.'

He leads us to his apartment upstairs: it's surprisingly nice, all dark wood and leather sofas, and framed artwork covering the walls. The art looks like the expensive kind, and I wonder if Bronwyn had anything to do with it. He sits us down at a round dining table, the surface stained with coffee rings and spilled ink, and shuffles into the kitchen, where he sets a kettle to boil over the flame, like Nan used to. Nina tries to catch my eye while we wait, but I'm clutching both hands in my lap, trying to count the ink stains to keep myself from bolting out the front door.

'Let me tell you something about Mary Anne Blackwell,' Frank says when he returns at last. He pulls his chair back, and it screeches across the floorboards. 'That woman was a force to be reckoned with—best thing that ever happened to this place, if you ask me. Damn impressive. Always sharp as a tack. Spoke her mind, didn't care who listened. And I'll tell you something else,' he continues, pushing a cup of tea towards me. 'This town missed a trick when they chased her out.'

I pause with the cup halfway to my lips. 'When they *what*?'

He pours tea for Nina too. 'This was long before your time, back in the forties—before my time, even. Though I think you must know some of it already. Or suspect,' he says, raising a wiry grey eyebrow.

I think of the papers shoved in the curio, the names and dates, the women we found at the library. I push my lips together, eyes trailing across the wooden grain on the table. Truth is, I don't know *what* I suspect.

'See,' Frank continues, 'Mary Anne was something of a…modern woman. First lady doctor. First lady surgeon. First lady head of the hospital. The first and only, for a long while,' he says, reaching out to tap the photo Nina's laid out on the table. 'She was celebrated. A new era. People here were sceptical at first, but she proved herself a damn fine surgeon and no one was going to argue with that. But there were women…women who might have gotten into a little trouble, or been forced into it. Women who, one way or the other, found themselves as a single mother at a time when such a thing wasn't considered quite right. The nurses, the male doctors, they all suggested the babies be taken.

Rehomed somewhere with two parents, as they thought it should be. But Mary had other ideas.'

My heart seizes. Stutters and stops. I don't dare breathe, or hope. Nina is struggling to keep her features blank. Her foot taps mine under the table, a small reassurance.

'See, she was from a big city,' Frank says. 'And she knew if you were given the chance, you could start over. So she took those girls, and she offered them something in the quiet halls at midnight, when no one else was around.'

My fingernails are scratching the brittle wood under the table.

'She would deliver their babies and keep them safe,' Frank says, and my lungs ache with relief as I feel an enormous pressure lift from my chest. *She kept them safe,* I think, blinking away tears. *Safe. They were safe.*

'Mary would tell the nurses the poor young mother and child had died in labour. If anyone wanted to see the body, she had herbs that might slow the heart, give the illusion of death. There were a few who knew, of course. Looked the other way—might have privately agreed with what she did, but wouldn't risk too much to help. And so Mary went on, for as long as she could, helping the women who needed her most.'

I think of Nan's book of poisons. And I feel so stupid. It was Frank himself who told us those herbs had other uses. *Mild paralytic. Muscle relaxants.* She must have given the women just enough that no one would question it.

'Where did the women go?' I ask, voice thick with emotion. Where was Emilia? Alba? And all the other girls, their names preserved on Nan's papers, kept all these years in secret.

Frank just smiles. 'They were holed up in Mary's house, of course, getting ready to start a new life. She even had that bungalow built, eventually. And it was easy, especially after the war—lot of widows going around. Not so hard to believe a young woman might need a fresh start in a new city, near good schools for her poor fatherless child.'

Nina's eyes are wide as saucers. 'Reece, your nan was a total badass.'

I'm still confused. 'Wait,' I say to Frank. 'How do you know this? If it was such a big secret, how do you know?'

Frank shuffles to the hallway stand and scoops up a small bronze frame, the edges scalloped and dainty. He rubs a thumb over the glass. 'This,' he says proudly, 'is my dear old mum. She was only a wee thing herself when she fell in love with a travelling Frenchman who promised her a life of adventure. Left her without so much as a goodbye.'

He quirks an eyebrow. 'And when I turned eighteen, she told me to find Mary Anne Blackwell and thank her for the life we had because of her kindness.'

'You're one of the babies,' I say, thunderstruck.

He spreads his hands wide like a magician who's performed a trick. 'I am indeed. Even became a doctor, knowing what good it could do for the world.'

'Fucking *hell*.' Nina slams her cup down, something delirious and wild on her face. 'Sorry. It's just—what a scandal. Wait, you said she got run out of town. What happened?'

'I never did work that one out,' Frank says. 'She always

said it wasn't her secret to tell, though I assume she offered her services to the wrong family. Seemed to have mightily pissed off a few folks though—traditional lot around here, you know. That statue,' he says, smoothing out the copy Nina brought, 'was taken down shortly after she finished up at the hospital. Personally, I always figured someone worked out what she had done, or someone had told. It was no small thing, back then, to start over—might have been one of the girls who gave her up, in the end. Guess now we'll never know.'

I recall the final, hurried words she wrote. *It's all over. Miss Thornton the last. I must leave at once, before they discover the others.*

'Frank,' I say. 'Did you ever know a Thornton family?'

'Thornton?' he says. 'As in, the old Mayor Thornton? Of course, their family has been here since—'

'Since Nan? Before that, even?'

He sits back in his chair, shoulders hunched. 'Indeed. Mayor Thornton was the one who had her statue removed, actually. Bad blood between them, I understand. Though I heard he was never quite right after...oh.' He squints into the distance. 'After his daughter died. Any reason you ask?'

I open my mouth to tell him—but if Nan never did, maybe there was a reason. Or maybe, as he said, it wasn't her secret to tell. 'I'm not sure,' I hedge, which is a half-truth. 'We were trying to find them. Some of them had obituaries, in the paper. We thought...I don't know what we thought,' I finish, pathetically. I don't want to explain to Frank that we had worried, even for a moment, that Nan had ever been any less than exceptional and good and kind.

He nods. 'You know, I'm not sure they want to be found. Careful where you dig, understand?'

'I just—I just want to know what happened. To Nan, at least.' Why did she leave? Why did she stay away for so long? How did the statue end up at school? I feel like I'm holding half a story in my hands, and someone has ripped out the ending.

Nina taps a rhythm against her teacup. 'I have a theory,' she says, in a strange tone. 'But I don't know that you're going to like it.'

Frank raises a knobbly finger. 'Hold that thought. Thornton. Thornton. Hmm.' He wanders to another room, where the sounds of something heavy being shoved and boxes being ripped open echo down the hall.

'Where is it, bastard of a thing...out the way, Lucy, out!'

Nina and I frown at each other. 'Want some help, Frank?' I say.

'Just a minute! It's in here, it's in here...' There's some indistinguishable muttering, and finally neither of us can bear sitting at the table any longer. We follow his voice into what seems to be another storage room. It's piled high with boxes stacked on top of each other, some of them seeming to be water-damaged or shredded by a tiny paw. Frank has wedged himself between two stacks.

Nina lets out a whistle. 'Wow, this is a lot.'

Frank grunts. 'Bit of a collector.'

'Hoarder,' she mutters, nudging a box marked *1986* with one foot.

'I heard that!' Frank's grey head bobs above the mess. 'Ha! Oh. I'm stuck. Clarissa?'

I wade into the depths, wriggling my shoulders through the narrow passage he's created. I find him tucked into a corner, trying to liberate a box trapped mid-pile—I can only heft the stack up by an inch, but it's enough for him to free the one he's after.

I take the box from him, sneezing at the accumulated dust that rolls off the lid. 'What is this anyway?' I ask, hauling it back to the dining table. Nina clears our cups so I can set it down, and Frank prises off the lid.

'People drop all sorts off here,' he says. 'Books, of course, mostly. Some of it I can't use, but seems wrong to get rid of it. Here.' He flicks through a handwritten journal. 'Meant to donate this stuff to the historical society, but never got round to it.'

He spins the box, so that whatever is written on the outside is now facing us.

Thornton.

'His wife brought it here after he died. Seemed she wasn't overly, ah, bereaved by his passing. Said she didn't want it in her house anymore. She's gone, too, now,' he says sadly. 'Anyway, don't know what good it will be to you, but if you're looking for answers, you might find them in here.'

I place my hands gently on the lid, as though disturbing it too suddenly will unleash its hidden history all at once. 'Thank you, Frank.'

'You remind me of her, you know. Mary.'

I smile. 'How so?'

He removes the stopper from a crystal decanter of whiskey, pouring the amber liquid into his teacup. 'Stubborn as all hell,' he says with a wink, and throws back his head to down the shot. 'Now get out, my show's about to start and I don't know how to record it.'

It's early evening when we end up back at Nan's. After leaving Frank's, we got fish and chips, which Nina doused in so much vinegar that it burned my mouth. Miles lumbered out of the Bean while we were waiting on the bench outside for our order. We could see the ocean from where we sat: the little lifeguard hut and the flags waving in the breeze. Nina looped her long legs over Miles's lap and spilled the story of Nana Blackwell and the missing girls. I didn't mind telling Miles, but it felt wrong to piece it all together without Gideon. I wondered if he was down there on the beach, zipped into his lifeguard hoodie, watching the last surfers paddle into shore. It would have been so easy to walk down there and check. I could feel the suggestion on my lips, the words on my tongue. Instead, we piled into the back of Nina's car and drove back here.

Miles has made himself at home on Nan's favourite recliner. He scoffs every time my greasy fingers leave a mark on the glass-topped coffee table. 'My mum would have a conniption watching you eat,' he says, lips pulled back in disgust. 'She left the plastic covering on our new couches for a full year after we got them.'

I roll my eyes and wipe the finger mark away with some paper towel. 'Happy?'

'You missed a spot.'

I fling a chip at his head. He lets it hit him so it doesn't touch the couch.

'Children,' Nina mutters, deftly tearing her potato cake in half.

We eat until the sky turns purple, and Miles offers to clean up, scrunching all the leftover paper into a ball and tossing it into the bins outside. Nina trails behind me to wash our hands in the bathroom.

She nudges my shoulder. 'You good?'

I nudge her back. 'For now. It's just bothering me, something about Alba—'

I'm interrupted by Miles calling out from the kitchen. 'Reece! Where do these cups go?'

I sigh and wipe my wet hands on my shorts—the hand towels are all gone now. In the kitchen, I help Miles dry the old plastic cups and slot them back into the cupboard. They have seashells on them, and they've been in this house as long as I can remember—edges scratched and grey from a lifetime of cordial on hot days and milk for dunking biscuits in winter. Everything in this house feels like that: memories held in ordinary objects. I remember finding Nan's hairbrush the day Gideon came. This whole house is filled with memories. I realise I don't ever want to see it empty. Maybe that's why Mum never came back. Maybe that's why Dad left the boxes but never packed them. We're still holding on, to the things she left behind.

And I think that's why the names matter. Why Alba is stuck in my mind.

And most of all, I need to know why Nan left the curio to me, when there was so much else left behind in this house; her hairbrush and cups and tea towels. Of everything she had, she left me *this*.

Nina and Miles are whispering on the couch. I hesitate in the kitchen, happy to give them a few more moments. She has to go home soon—exams start next week, and even if she's not expecting to pass, she still has to take them. I wonder what Hamilton will feel like without her now. It was so easy to slip back into the way things were. So easy to feel whole again.

There's a tap at the door, and my stomach drops. The shadow behind the blinds is too tall to be Grace, too broad to be Mum or Dad.

I hold my breath until my lungs ache, and blow it out all at once. I slide the door open a crack.

'Hey,' says Gideon, quietly. He looks tired, pale. His cheeks are grey under the dim porch light. 'I saw the lights on,' he says. 'I thought—'

Nina bounds up behind me. 'Who are you talking to? *Oh*. Loverboy. Hello.'

He forces the smile a little wider. His puppet-string smile, I think. 'Hey, Nina.'

She flings an arm around my shoulders, both a display of easy friendship and an excuse to squeeze me tight, to let me know she's there. 'Does this mean Reece spilled the big mystery?'

His eyes travel behind us. Miles lifts an arm to say hello, the bottle of soft drink still on the coffee table. Gideon shakes his head. 'Just thought I'd stop by. Sorry, I didn't mean to, uh, interrupt.'

I can feel Miles shooting lasers at the back of my head, so I inch the door open wider. 'It's fine. Come in.'

Gideon hesitates, his foot hovering over Nan's dusty old welcome mat. Nina drifts back into the lounge room. 'Are you sure?' he murmurs.

'Just—just come in,' I say, and turn away, so I don't have to watch him decide.

I hear his heavy footsteps follow, so I end up folding myself into Nan's recliner, leaving the couch for Miles and Gideon to sit beside each other. Gideon eyes the curio, set on top of the TV, no longer relegated to the washing mashing or kept in the fancy temperature-controlled box. It's astounding how careless you can be with a priceless antique once you get used to it being around.

'So,' Gideon says, eyeing the box marked *Thornton*. 'What's the big mystery?'

Nina sits on the floor beside me, warm shoulders pushing into my knees. I take a piece of her hair and start pulling strands into a long braid, an old habit preserved from our primary-school days.

A very small, vindictive part of me wants to ignore Gideon, but I already asked him to come in and we've uncovered so much of this together. So I relay everything we've found out: about the women and their babies, Nan getting caught, Frank's history all muddled up in hers. And now, an opportunity to fill in the blanks.

'Huh,' Gideon says when I'm done. 'That's…a lot.'

'Yep.' I laugh nervously and shake out my trembling hands. 'So...I guess...we should open this?'

Nina claps, excited. 'Oh, to desecrate the memories of old white men. I hope there's a journal in here.'

Miles snorts. 'Should we be here for this?' he asks, looking to me. 'Or is this, like, a sacred moment?'

'You already know the rest, might as well stay for the end,' I tell him.

With a nod from me, Nina flips the lid and begins separating the contents into four neat stacks. She flicks through the pages before she assigns them: fiction, journals, notepads and loose bits of paper. She seizes a pile of notepads and paper, and beckons to Miles. 'Come on, let's spread these out in the bedroom.'

He frowns. 'What? Why? I just—'

She hoists him to his feet, and he stumbles along behind her.

Gideon blinks awkwardly. 'Well...this feels like old times.'

I slide off the recliner and sit cross-legged on the floor. I let my hair fall in a frizzy curtain between us, hiding behind the thin veil it provides as I sort through the small stack of journals. I hand Gideon one without looking, the book hovering between us. For a moment I think he won't take it, then I feel the weight lift, and hear him rustling the pages. The seconds stretch between us.

'I'm sorry,' he says at last. 'I still feel terrible.'

I sniff, flicking through the journal on my lap. 'You should.'

The truth is, I feel terrible too. Maybe Nina was right—it was cruel to dangle the university in front of him when I knew he couldn't take it. My eyes stay glued to the page before me, but I can't see anything; the words are jumbled grey and black, nonsense strung together. I blink and realise it's because there are tears brimming on my eyelashes, blurring everything. I surreptitiously wipe them away with the back of my hand, disguising the movement with a cough.

Something warm brushes my elbow, but when I turn, Gideon is shuffling to his feet.

'What was the daughter's name again?' he says, typing something on his phone.

'Alba. Alba Thornton.'

He wanders away a few steps and I look up, hopeless. I don't know how to fix us. I open my mouth to say something, but I don't know what. So I watch him retreat into the yellow light of the kitchen, taking down one of the seashell cups to fill with water while he lounges against the counter.

I sigh and look down at my lap. The diary is small and leather-bound, gold embossed initials stamped on the front. *RT*: Richard Thornton. The leather is worn smooth, almost thin in some places. I leaf through the pages again, not really sure what I'm looking for. Nan's name? Some kind of conveniently incriminating entry about wayward daughters? The cursive font is difficult to read, so I curl towards the lamp and sit hunched directly under the beam. I can hear Miles and Nina hissing at each other in the next room; something loud clatters to the ground, followed by silence.

I roll my eyes, focusing on the journal. It's pretty boring

stuff: town meetings, his wife's casserole, Alba's early achievements. But one particular page near the end catches my attention. The corner is ripped, the words scrawled so angrily the ink has bled through the paper.

Damn that doctor. She has ruined it all.

'Gross,' I mutter, and continue reading his tirade against *the cursed doctor* and several long passages lamenting the pollution of his family lineage and the prestige of the Thornton name. Still, I'm not certain the entries are about Nan until I find an entry that references the statue: it was too expensive to destroy, so he sold it back to her old school for a fraction of the cost. I like that—the perverse sense of stubbornness that Nan would not go quietly, even in bronzed form.

I keep reading, but Alba is never mentioned again, and the diary ends abruptly.

I'm about to voice my despair when Nina calls out, triumphant. 'Found something!' She rushes in with Miles, her lips red and hair mussed, while he seems to have a hickey blooming on his neck.

She ignores my questioning stare and holds up what looks like another journal, though this one is soft and floral, with cheap ring bindings—the kind that can be bought from a newsagent.

'I think this was actually Mrs Thornton's journal.' She pulls out a loose piece of paper from the back—a newspaper clipping. 'And *this* is Alba's obituary.'

Miles sets the journal carefully on the coffee table, then pries the obituary out of Nina's clasped hands. 'It says…Alba Thornton: born 1928, died 1946. Cause of death, drowning by misadventure.' There's a second page behind it—a news story, the headline splashed in large font. Alba's photo is printed beside it; I catch a glimpse of dark curls, a soft smile. 'Wait, this says her body was never found. Her dad was... the only witness. Do you think...?'

I glance down at the diary I was reading, the angry hate-filled scrawl spilling from its pages. 'Dick Thornton,' I mutter. 'I don't know. It doesn't say anything about Alba dying. It just ends.' I say a silent prayer for her, to whichever god might be listening. Maybe she got away. Maybe Nan helped her after all.

The room is quiet.

And then a throat clears.

'She's not dead,' Gideon declares, bringing my melancholia to an abrupt end. 'Alba Thornton: born 1928. Son, Heath Thornton, born 1946.'

Nina stares up at him, incredulous. 'How could you *possibly* know that?'

He holds up his phone, showing us the screen. 'Google.' He grins.

I snort, reaching for the phone. Our fingers brush and I jerk back, almost dropping it. Gideon's found the Thorntons on an ancestry website. Heath seems to be the one who created the profile—there's a little email box to contact him. I wonder if he would really want to know where he came from, since it seems his grandfather hated him before he was even born. It looks like Alba has kept her secrets. I hand the phone back.

'Now what?' Miles asks.

'I guess that's mystery solved then,' Nina says with a shrug, though her voice is tinged with disappointment—that our investigation has fizzled suddenly to an incomplete end. I try to remind myself that Alba got out—all the girls did. And maybe we don't have the full story, but it seems like this is all we're likely to get. 'Reece, did it say anything about the statue at least?'

'Oh. He had it sold. Looks like he basically forced Nan to quit then tried to get rid of any trace she'd ever been there. The dude really seemed to have a problem with women in general.'

'That's…incredibly creepy.' Nina squeezes my hand. 'I'm sorry, Reece.'

I look around the living room. Nan's chair. Her lamp. Seashell cup on the kitchen counter. Kettle on the stovetop like she might have one more cup of tea before bed. I place a hand over my chest, feeling my heart tick. *Just listen*, I hear her say. I listen to the rhythm, *tick, tick, tick*. A calm, persistent sound.

'This is *bullshit*,' I blurt out, and find three shocked faces staring back at me. 'Sorry. But she did all this on her own, helped all those people, and basically nobody knows—*and* they took her statue? It's bullshit,' I repeat.

Miles comes over and puts a comforting hand on my knee, but doesn't say anything—he just lets me process. I look around the room, at the paper strewn across tables and counters and armrests—over the mantle on the fireplace and one piece even stuck to the bottom of Nina's shoe. There's more, though, than just paper. The legacy of Nan's life, contained in this single room, a secret shared between the four of us.

I remember coming to this town and hating it because I was so alone; now I can hardly remember the feeling at all. This house is so full of *us*: me and Gideon and Miles and Nina. And it's also full of *them*: Nan and the women she saved. How many paths crossed through this house? How many women took their first step into a new life here? Maybe that's why Nan couldn't stay away, even all those years later.

I dig my palms into my eyes, suddenly tired and worn out. A half-hysterical laugh bubbles from my throat. 'I'm glad Nan came back here. Shame she waited until old Richard kicked the bucket—he would have had a fit to see her back in the hospital.'

'Man, we really should tell people what Thornton was like,' Miles says, snatching the diary, leafing through the end. 'Egg his grave, or something.'

'You can't,' I warn. 'It's not our secret to tell. Also, I'm pretty sure that's illegal.'

'Yeah, but come on. He got rid of her statue. That's just *petty.*'

The room goes silent for a long, long while. Miles and Gideon share a similar look of defeat.

But Nina has a gleam in her eye.

I know that look. That look makes me nervous. 'What?' I ask her.

She grins. 'I have an idea. But I don't know if you're going to like it.' She wedges herself between the couch and the coffee table, and wiggles her fingers like she's orchestrating a pantomime. 'What if we just…stole it back? The statue?'

'We're not *stealing* anything,' I insist.

'Why not?'

'Because we'll get arrested! Because it's school property! Because it's an eight-hour round trip!'

Nina gives a dismissive flick of her hand. 'It's not even stealing. We're just putting it back. Restoring the statue is, like, restoring the universe to its natural order. Look, don't you think it's total crap that your nan worked her whole life on this huge, enormous secret thing, and instead of being recognised she basically lost everything?'

'Of course I do,' I shoot back, looking to Miles and Gideon for support—though they both seem suddenly fascinated by the sconces on the ceiling. 'I just don't know what we can do about it.'

'We can. Steal. It. Back. Come on, this Thornton dude seems like a total psycho,' she says. 'Do you really want him to be the one that wins?'

I hesitate just long enough for Gideon to look sideways at Nina and say, quietly, 'It's not the worst idea.' He notices me glaring and shrugs. 'What? I liked your nan. Besides…I don't know, she'd think it was funny.'

'Pretty epic prank,' Miles agrees. 'But we have exams,' he adds hastily. 'Still, I'm down if the rest of you are. Cause I'm cool. I'm easy. Easy breezy.'

'So?' Nina turns back to me, pleading. 'Come on, Reece. One last adventure. We'd be there and back in a day. Just tell your parents you want to drop me home—my car hardly runs anyway, it's partly true.'

And as I sit there, thinking that Nina has finally lost her mind, my eyes fall on one of the framed pictures on the wall. Nan is standing proud in front of the hospital, alone, shoulders square, chin tilted. It was the day she made head surgeon. No one else had wanted to stand beside her.

I feel Nan all around me, here in her house. I remember her laughing and holding my tiny hands as she swung me high and caught me before I fell. I think of the women who fled and started over. Is it all doomed to be swept away? History is written by the victors, and all that.

The thing is, I've been getting tired of losing.

'On one condition,' I say. 'We go together, or not at all.'

24

'I SHOULD REALLY be studying,' Miles whines.

Nina kicks her feet up on the passenger-side window, flicking through her road-trip playlist. 'Calm down, genius boy, you already got into uni.'

'I still have to *pass*,' he grumbles. 'And besides, what about the rest of you? Exams start next week. Maybe we should turn around.'

Nina rolls her eyes. 'I'm not even going to university next year.'

'Neither,' says Gideon from the driver's seat. His eyes cut to me in the rearview mirror.

Nina squints at me emphatically and I ignore her, watching the trees whip by outside. She taps a furious message on her phone, then my screen pings a second later.

> *Nina: When are you going to tell them?*
> *Me: I was sort of waiting for Gideon to un-hate me first.*
> *Nina: Chicken.*

I don't respond. Then my phone buzzes again.

Nina: *You have to tell them, Reece. I'd want to know. Trust me, it sucks being the one left behind. And we both know he doesn't hate you.*

I look up, expecting a stern glare, but Nina gives me a sad smile instead.

'What's going on?' says Miles, peering around the headrest.

'Nothing,' we answer in unison, shoving our phones away.

'Y'all are shady, but okay,' he says. 'I'm just saying, I want it noted on the *official* record that I've changed my mind and I think this is a terrible idea.'

'We know!' everyone yells at once, and Miles sinks back into his seat. A hint of a smile is playing on Gideon's lips.

Actually, Miles sort of has a point. In truth, it is, sort of—definitely—an insane idea.

And yet, here we are, hurtling towards the city. We left in the afternoon, buying ourselves some time with a small white lie. I told my parents I wanted to take Nina home and stay the night, and Miles and Gideon each told their mums they'd be sleeping at the other's house. Ava couldn't miss a schoolday without her mum getting suspicious, so she agreed to stay behind and make sure Mrs Kostakis didn't call Grace at any stage.

During the first hour of the drive, we'd forged the vague beginnings of a plan: we'd arrive at the school in the evening, wait until we were sure it was empty, the neighbouring houses asleep, and then we'd steal the statue and cart it back to Hamilton, reinstating it outside the hospital. What happened after that was up to the town council.

'So. Who wants snacks?' Miles says, jolting me back to the present.

'What have you got?'

'What *don't* I have? Sour chews, chips, Cheesymite scrolls, Turkish delight—'

'Ew,' Nina says. 'That's the worst.'

I stick my hand out, grinning. 'Mine!'

In the end, I get the Turkish delight, Nina gets the sour lollies, and Gideon and Miles share the chips between them. The snacks bring a feeling of cheer back into the car, despite the fact that Gideon and I aren't talking directly to each other, and Nina and Miles are trying to pretend they haven't just made out in my grandmother's house. The car ride mostly consists of Miles and I talking about our biology assessment, while Gideon chimes in with all the English books he hasn't read yet. Nina doesn't let a single song finish before she skips to the next one, and she eventually gets banned from the role of car DJ.

'There's a petrol station up ahead,' Gideon says. 'We'd better stop, it's an hour till the next one.'

The problem with living in small towns is that you have to pass a whole lot of nothing to get anywhere worth going. The drive into the city is four hours, and most of that is eucalypt forest, farming properties and wetlands. At least Gideon's car is roomier than Nina's. We drive with the windows cranked down, hair flying into sticky lips and shirts blowing in the breeze. Nina spends most of the drive with one hand out the window, fingers curling on the wind. I try to get her to sit straight, pulling her arm in, but she refuses. My heart speeds up every time another car passes, but she just smiles, leaning into the sun.

Gideon pulls into a tiny service station—the kind with a weather-beaten sign and two paint-peeled fuel pumps. We give ourselves ten minutes to get out of the car, use the bathroom and stock up on snacks. Miles and Nina make a beeline inside.

I wait until Gideon has the pump locked into the car before I ease the passenger door open, letting my legs hang out the side.

'Who's with your mum today?' I ask quietly.

He looks up, his expression hopeful. I still haven't forgiven him, but I'm tired of pushing him away. 'One of her friends is coming over for the day and staying for dinner, and then the care nurse is coming over.'

Two people, just so he can have a sleepover. 'How's the nurse going?' I wonder how much it costs to have a medical professional living in your house.

'He's cool, I guess. Pretty chill. Mum likes him. Has a Smurf tattoo on his arm that creeps me out though.'

I laugh without meaning to. 'Sorry. The Smurfs creep you out?'

'They're tiny blue anarchists, and they made themselves a lady friend out of clay.'

I raise my eyebrows. 'I didn't realise you were such a… Smurf-pert.'

He groans at my joke as he watches the numbers tick over on the meter. 'Yeah well, the artist was pretty cool. His grandfather was a pirate.' He pauses, eyes flicking to mine for the barest moment. 'Tell your mum thanks, again. She's been really helpful. The grant applications, and the nurse... we really appreciate it.'

'I will.'

The silence between us returns.

'I'm sorry,' he says. 'For everything.'

I shrug, biting my lip. 'Me too.' I wish things were back to normal between us. I wish he'd tell me about the artists he likes, and the comics he follows, and whether the home-care nurse makes Grace's tea the way she likes it. I wish I wasn't still mad at him no matter how much I've tried to forgive him.

Gideon turns away, and I climb out of the car while he's not looking, heading inside the service station. Nina catches my eye and makes her way over from an aisle filled with chewing gum and condoms.

I just lean my head into her shoulder, groaning, and she hugs me. 'You're gonna be okay,' she whispers.

'When?'

'When you're both ready.' Then she squeezes my hand and slaps my butt, and we pile back into the car.

The rest of the trip is quiet. We finally reach civilisation, and plug the school address into Gideon's phone. Nina starts to helpfully point out landmarks to fill the silence. 'Look, we snuck into that bar to watch a band play. And we tried to camp in that park but we got scared and called our mums to come get us. Reece broke her arm falling off that ride in the fun park.'

But as we get closer and closer, even Nina stops talking. She holds my hand in the silence, waiting as we turn down all-too-familiar streets. If she were still narrating, she'd say: *Look, that's where we walked home every day after school. That's the cafe we met at every Saturday. That's where we planned our grand Paris trip.*

We turn a corner. *Here's where she crashed her car.*

I slap my hand on the window. 'Stop. Stop!'

Gideon slams on the brakes, pulling over to one side of the road. Something in my voice makes him turn around. 'Reece? What's wrong, are you okay?'

I unbuckle my seatbelt and fling open the door, my feet on the ground before I know what I'm doing. Nina calls after me, but she doesn't follow.

Willow hated roses. That's the first thing I think. I've never been here. Never to this exact spot. I avoided it in the months after she died. It's nothing special: just a regular street, with little picket fences and street lamps and a guardrail on one side. Her car paint is still stuck to it.

I close my eyes. Take a breath.

Someone has planted a small white cross. She wasn't religious, but I guess it's just what people do. And all these months on, there are roses, roses everywhere, browning in the sun. Some have rotted, sweating in their pretty plastic wraps. But some are new—people still come here, it seems, to remember her. *But this isn't where she lived,* I want to scream. *This is just where she died. It doesn't mean anything.* It's just a random spot, on a random street. Just a place you wouldn't even notice if it weren't for the cross marking the ground she died on.

Someone sits down beside me. 'Are you okay?' It's Gideon.

I shake my head. There's a photo of her framed in glass so it doesn't spoil. It's tilted to one side, so I reach out to set it straight. *Hey Will. I miss you.*

'Let's go,' I whisper.

Gideon holds out his arm. 'Wait, Reece. Do you want to talk about it?'

I sniff, brushing away tears. 'This doesn't mean anything. This wasn't her life.' Then I blink, and the tears are gone. My heart pangs but it keeps beating.

'Let's go.'

We reach the school at dusk. It's late, so no one is there except a single car that we assume belongs to the gardener. Nina insists we do some surveillance, so we park across the street and huddle in our seats. Nina climbs into the boot so we can look through the rear window, and Miles finds a reason to follow. Then she complains that Gideon is too conspicuous sitting in the driver's seat alone so she makes him sit in the back seat with me. 'We can say we're waiting for our parents this way,' she whispers.

'Firstly,' I say, 'you don't have to whisper, no one can hear us. Secondly, who's going to believe we all came from the same parents?'

'I don't know, maybe it's a *Brady Bunch* situation.'

I roll my eyes and sink down further in the seat. Nina and Miles are whispering furiously, and I don't know where to look because Gideon is squished into the tiny space beside me.

'I've never actually sat in my own back seat,' he muses.

'Really?'

'I only got the car this year, when Mum...you know. We sold the old car. It was this tiny hatchback and her walker wouldn't fit in the boot.'

Gideon ducks his head low and a tumble of blonde curls fall into his eyes. 'Hey,' he murmurs after a while. 'I know things are weird right now, but...are you okay? With Willow, and the school...'

The sky has grown darker, and I wonder how long we've sat here. 'I'm okay,' I reply. 'It's weird, being back. But it's not as hard as it was. I keep thinking about our first day this year. It seems like it was forever ago. Will was so happy— she had all these plans. That was the worst part, you know. I didn't just lose *her*, I lost all future possibilities of her. We were supposed to travel. Go to uni. Live in a crappy sharehouse and argue over whose turn it is to take the bins out. She wanted to get a tattoo. She wanted to get married. She wanted all these things, and every day I'd remember something new she'd never have. Never have pink hair like she always wanted. Never camp at a festival. Never...I don't know. Just never anything, ever again.'

'And now?' Gideon asks.

His hand is right next to mine. If I spread my fingers out, I just might feel the brush of warm skin against mine.

It takes everything I have not to sink into his lap and wait for him to hug me tight.

'Now…' I answer, staring out at the school gates. 'Now I think, we played music together and I was so terrible she laughed until strawberry milk came out her nose. And she let me drive her car around an empty car park just for fun. She went to Tokyo with school and gorged herself on custard cake until she was sick. She let Nina cut her fringe and ended up with ear-length curls that took her a year to grow back out. Maybe it wasn't everything she wanted, but it was still a life. And sometimes that's not enough; sometimes I want to scream because it's so unfair. But mostly I'm glad we did so much while we could.'

The grief doesn't suffocate me anymore, I realise. It's there, like a scar, but the edges are no longer raw, just like Ava said. I can touch it without falling apart.

Gideon nods, and I think maybe he understands, just a little. 'I took Mum to the waterhole this week.' I look up in surprise. 'I know it's not the same. But I wanted some good memories. It feels like we've only had bad ones lately.'

'How did you even *get* her there?' I ask.

He grins. 'I sort of *borrowed* one of the Sandcruiser wheel-chairs from work. Carried her when I had to. It was insane, I got halfway there and realised how stupid I'd feel if anything went wrong.'

'But nothing did?'

He shakes his head, leaning back with a contented sigh. 'We had a good day. One good day.'

Then Nina sits bolt upright, smacking the seatbacks.

'Guys! The gardener's leaving!'

Gideon looks in my eyes. 'It's go time.'

The school seems different in the dark. The portables loom in the distance, eerie and abandoned. The gym soars above us, shielding us from the main road. But mostly it's the quiet that's strange—our footsteps echo, bouncing across the open quad.

'Shh!' Nina hisses at Miles. 'Are you wearing iron boots?!'

'They're Docs!'

'They're *loud*!'

We creep through the teachers' car park, and a wash of emotion comes over me. This is where we stood, where we walked, every day. This is where we laughed, and cried, and whispered about boys and complained about home-work. This is where I ran endless laps, trying to appease a cursed statue.

Except it's not cursed, after all. Willow was wrong.

Nina's hand slips around mine, squeezing me in the dark.

'Ready?' she whispers.

And there she is—Queen Mab.

Mary Anne Blackwell. My nan.

I squint in the darkness, trying to make out the panes of her bronzed face. The nose is all wrong—it's squashed and flat. Her hair is too short. And they've given her a strange hat that obscures her eyes. But if I look at her just right, I suppose I can see the resemblance.

I reach out, the way she's reaching for me, and touch my

hand to her outstretched palm. 'Hey, Nan,' I whisper. The bronze is cool and smooth, nothing like her warm, weathered hands would be.

Nina tilts her head. 'Huh.'

'What?' I turn, frowning at her.

'Nothing. I just never noticed before…'

'What?'

She shrugs. 'They gave her weird boobs.'

'Nina! I'm having a moment.'

She gives the statue a fist bump. 'Hey, Nana B. We're here to avenge your spirit. Sorry about the boobs though.'

Gideon and Miles shuffle behind us. 'You guys are so weird,' Miles says.

'I kind of like it,' Gideon adds. 'She looks sort of regal. Like the queen, with less corgis.'

'Do you ever wonder if there's people inside statues?'

'Miles—' Gideon warns.

'Okay, but hear me out—*how would we know?*'

'Miles!'

I slam my hands over my mouth. I can't help it. My shoulders shake uncontrollably. And I laugh, a great, choked, half-crazed noise. I lean into Nina, and she's biting on her lip, trying to keep a straight face, but she can't. 'This is so stupid,' she says. 'Willow would love this.'

I wipe away tears—happy tears that are buried in the corner of my smile. 'Yeah. She would. Remember her weird kleptomaniac phase?'

'Hey! We agreed not to talk about that.'

'We agreed not to talk about that in front of *her parents.*'

'Whatever. Come on, let's steal your grandmother, shove her in the boot and get going.' She's already pulling on a pair of black leather gloves.

'Nina, seven hundred people have touched this statue, and you're worried about fingerprints?'

She shrugs. 'I watch documentaries, I know stuff.'

Miles is looking nervous, and Gideon pokes him in the ribs. 'You okay there, bud?'

Miles has gone pale. 'I didn't know we were meant to bring gloves.'

'You weren't,' I say.

'But what if we get arrested?'

'We won't.'

'But—'

Gideon takes Miles's hands and, before he knows what's happening, forces them flat on the bronze. 'Whoops, you just started a life of crime.'

Miles snatches his hands away. 'How dare you? These are magic hands—'

I snort. Nina giggles.

'—magic *music* hands. My piano hands!'

Gideon gives him a droll look. 'Please say that, and exactly that, when we get arrested.'

'You said we wouldn't get arrested!'

'Boys!' I yell, and it must be too loud because they shush me all at once. 'Can we please get on with the thieving?' I hiss. 'Maybe let's try to *not* get caught?'

'Fine,' Miles grumbles. 'How do we do this?'

We gather around the statue—Nina and I at each arm,

365

Gideon and Miles at the legs. We all look at each other, nervous, until Nina counts us down. 'No pressure or anything, but this is a pretty significant moment for womankind. So don't you dare drop Reece's grandmother. Count of three, everyone ready?'

We all nod.

'Three...'

I clutch a solid bronze elbow.

'Two...'

Gideon ducks low, ready to hoist from the knees.

'One...'

A final glance. I look up, trying to find something in the statue's face. *Sorry, Nan...*

'Go!'

We all lift.

And nothing happens.

I lift with all my might, bending so I'm nearly underneath her arm, pushing up with my entire body weight. The boys are grunting and cursing, and Miles is leaning right into her side, feet scrambling for purchase.

And still, nothing happens.

We sweat and we swear and we all swap positions, sure that we're doing something wrong.

'Nina,' I grunt, leaning so far sideways that I would fall flat on my face if this stupid statue ever did move. 'How much does bronze weigh?'

She peers around Nan's shoulder, eyes wide. 'Why would I know that?'

'You didn't check?!'

'*You* didn't check either! *Hey Siri, how much does bronze weigh?*'

A little automated voice answers, muffled in her pocket. *'I'm sorry, I couldn't find anything matching that description.'*

Gideon frowns. 'It weighs the same as everything else.'

'What?'

'You said "what does it weigh?" A kilo of bronze is still a kilo. You want to know—'

Nina looks up, viciously stabbing at her phone. 'If you try to mansplain this situation to me, I swear...'

He holds up his hands in surrender. She returns to her frantic searching, but her thumbs slow. 'Hypothetically, if I had asked...'

Gideon takes the phone from her, tapping on it and then reciting from the screen: 'Bronze weighs almost two hundred and fifty kilograms per cubic metre.'

'Bro,' Miles says. 'Maths is not my thing. Compute.'

'That's...I don't know, a tonne? Maybe more?'

'So,' I say, 'we're basically trying to lift a car.'

Miles bends at the waist, inspecting the ground. 'A car that's cemented into the ground, by the way.'

'What?' I say, as Nina and I duck at the same time. 'Huh. I...never noticed that before.'

'Like the boobs.' She nods sagely.

We take a few steps back, and stare at each other with a mix of awe and shock.

'It was all for nothing,' I whisper at last. And I don't want to admit that the idea of Hamilton waking up and finding Mary Anne Blackwell once again guarding the gates of the hospital thrilled me but…fine, Nina got to me.

Maybe it felt like the world would be right again, if I could just fix this one thing. I couldn't fix Willow. I couldn't fix Nan. And now I can't fix this.

I blink back tears of frustration, swallowing my disappointment.

'Hey,' Nina says gently. 'We still had fun, didn't we?'

'Nothing went right this year,' I shoot back. I know I'm being childish, but we came all this way for nothing. Gideon had to leave his mum at home and I lied to my parents and Miles looks like he's going to pass out from stress and it was all for *nothing*.

I tip my head into my hands. 'I dragged you all this way. I'm so sorry. This was so stupid, we should have just stayed home. I ruined everything, I'm sorry.'

Nina bumps my shoulder. 'You didn't ruin anything,' she says. 'Right, guys?'

'Right,' Gideon says.

'Right,' Miles echoes.

I look up, blinking through tears. 'Miles, I'm so sorry, you didn't even want to come, and I know the music academy is important, and exams are next week—'

'Reece, it's fine.'

'No, it's not! You wanted to stay home and study and I made you come anyway—'

'Hey, it's fine, we had fun, we had snacks.'

I push to my feet and start to pace. 'We should just start driving back now. We should all be studying for exams, this was a ridiculous idea.'

'Reece,' Miles says, and something in his voice cuts through the night. 'It's fine. I'm not…I'm not going to the academy.'

My mouth drops open. Gideon's eyebrows shoot up.

'What…but you said…all that practice…I don't understand.' I look over at Nina, but she's as shocked as the rest of us.

Miles drops to the gravel, sitting cross-legged, energy spent. 'Look, I don't want to make a big deal about it.'

'It's a huge deal! It's your dream, why are you just giving it all up?'

'That's the thing, isn't it,' he says, kicking at nothing. Refusing to look up. 'It's not *my* dream. It's my dad's. And Mum's. Even Ava expects me to go. And I thought, hey, I'm good at it, right? It's fun, I like playing, don't get me wrong.'

'But…?' We've all gathered close, watching him.

'But I don't love it. And those kids, they're obsessed. I didn't even realise, until I watched Ava play at the exams. She's like—damn, she's like magic, you know? She's good. Not just small-town good, she's *good* good. And she loves it, and it's so easy for her. She just gets it. She hears it, and she plays. I have to practise *all. The. Time.* I don't get a break. I don't get a life. It's not *easy* for me. And I realised, you know, at some point I stopped loving it and maybe I sort of…I don't know, resent it a bit, I guess?'

Gideon's nodding at the sky, letting Miles talk himself out. When he finally slumps down, Gideon shuffles closer and puts one arm around his shoulder. 'What did your mum say?'

Miles shakes his head. 'Nothing, yet. I haven't told her. I haven't told anyone.'

'You could still change your mind,' I say. 'If you wanted to think about it.'

He shakes his head again, wiping the back of his hand across his mouth. 'Nah. It's done. I withdrew my place already. Maybe it's not my dream anymore, but some kid out there is dying to get in. I wasn't gonna take their spot.'

'Miles…' Nina steps forward, hesitating. Then she throws herself in his lap, arms crossing over Gideon's. And then I sit beside them, and my arms lock around theirs too. We must look strange, the four of us, sitting here, joined together. Maybe it's fate. Maybe it's luck. Maybe it's just the way it was meant to be, right now, right here.

'So,' Miles says, sniffling a little. 'Since I don't know what the hell I'm doing with my life next year, and we can't boost this thing, maybe we should get going? I might end up needing these exams after all.'

I stand, exhausted. 'Yeah. Yeah, let's go home.'

'Guess we should give this back to Frank then,' Nina says, handing me the photo from inside her pocket. It's the original from the bookshop, taken when the statue still stood outside the Hamilton Hospital. She took it from our fridge before we left this afternoon, for good luck.

I snatch it out of her hands. 'Wait…' I hold the picture up to the moonlight, looking between the photo and the statue before us. 'You guys,' I whisper. 'There's no hat in this photo.'

Gideon jumps to his feet, rushing to peer over my shoulder. 'Well, shit.' Then he grins, looking between Miles and Nina. 'Sorry Miles, you might still be a criminal yet.'

I race over to the statue, reaching for the hat. I never noticed before, but up close it's a different shade of bronze, almost gold: it's shinier, smoother, like it's newer than the rest. You would never even notice it didn't belong unless your nose was pressed up against the statue like mine is now. I strain, reaching up: my fingers barely graze the rim of the hat, and it's *heavy*. But it shifts, slightly.

Gideon steps forward. 'Here,' he says, grabbing me by the waist and boosting me up.

The hat is awkward and cumbersome and it nearly slips out of my hands. I have to yank it with all my strength, but— suddenly, finally—it comes loose. I grin, staring down at it.

And then something inside the hat moves. I shriek so loudly Gideon nearly drops me. I land with a thud, hands slick with sweat. But I realise it's not a giant bug or curled-up snake, it's…

'Is that…paper?' Gideon's voice is low and close, rumbling in my ear.

I bring it close, the scribble barely legible. And then I look up at them, grinning, twisting the pages so they can see: *Mary Anne Blackwell: a private memoir.*

25

WE WALK BACK to the car in stunned silence. I clutch the manuscript in one hand and the golden hat in the other, and I'm suddenly eager to be back on the road, sheltered safely in the back seat. But Gideon stops at his car.

'Guys. We have a problem.' He's looking down at one tyre, sitting deflated and uneven.

Miles peers over Nina's shoulder. 'Is it...not meant to do that?'

Gideon sighs, Nina swears, and I just sit on the gravel, the stolen hat and hidden papers cradled in my lap. Gideon pops the boot, then he swears too. 'I already used the spare,' he says, voice flat. 'I meant to get another. I just forgot, after everything...' He looks around hopelessly, but the roads are dead quiet, and even if someone came past, they couldn't just jump the car.

'Call roadside assistance,' Nina says, flicking the yellow sticker on his window.

Gideon covers his face, mumbling into his hands. 'I sort

of…didn't pay the bill.'

We call anyway, but we hang up again when the operator says the after-hours call out fee is six hundred dollars.

'We'll just crash here tonight,' he says, lips pressed thin. 'I drove all day anyway, I should probably get some sleep. Can we stay at Nina's?'

Her eyes go wide. 'Two strange boys in my house? You want my mum to disown me?'

'Fine. We can sleep in the car. I'll call again in the morning, fork out the fee.'

'I'll chip in,' Miles says.

Nina nods. 'Me too.'

'We all will.'

Gideon flushes, and I know he's embarrassed that he can't afford it by himself. 'Thanks, guys. Guess we should just…' He waves a hand at the car and starts pushing the seats back so we can lie down.

Nina bats her eyelashes at me, a silent, pleading look on her face. I give a tiny shake of my head and she frowns, telepathically projecting her rage. And even though I don't like what she's suggesting, I also really, really don't want to sleep in a car, with no toothpaste or shower. There aren't even any snacks left.

'I have to pee,' Nina says pointedly.

I groan and relent. 'Fine. I know somewhere we can stay. It's walking distance.'

I spent six months missing this house and now I can't bear to step inside. The spare key is still nestled under a loose step, and the door still squeaks when it opens. The furniture is still covered with sheets, and it still smells like the rosemary my mother planted five years ago.

But it doesn't feel like home anymore.

'Pick a room,' I say, voice full of false cheer. 'Someone can take the old couch. And I don't know if we have hot water. Or power.'

Nina flicks a switch in the kitchen. 'Negative.'

Gideon and Miles are hovering in the doorway, as though they're not even sure they're allowed inside. They're looking at each other with twin expressions of disbelief, but it's Gideon who first breaks the silence. 'Reece, is this...is this your house?'

I turn so he can't see me flinch when I answer. 'Was. Was my house.'

Miles whistles, low and long. He tiptoes through the front room. 'You guys left a lot of stuff behind.'

I shrug like it doesn't bother me. 'Mum didn't want to take everything down to the coast if we weren't going to stay. She said it was a trial run. They come back occasionally, grab more stuff. Plus Dad wanted to re-decorate, so...'

Miles nods, like suddenly all the rattan and white-washed furniture in the Hamilton house makes a lot more sense. Dad once got giddy over a chandelier made of shells, but Mum wouldn't let him hang it.

I point upstairs. 'Theo and I left our old beds here. Someone can sleep in his room. It's a single though.' I swear I see Miles wink at Nina but I choose to ignore it. 'I'll grab the air mattress. And some clean towels.'

I walk calmly to the garage, open the door, and sink onto the cold cement.

This is where we played dodgeball. This is where Mum taught us how to change a bike tyre.

This is where I last saw Willow.

Nina approaches, sitting down beside me and resting her head on my shoulder. 'Sorry. This is weird, isn't it?'

I cross my arms over my torso, leaning forward. 'A little. Actually, a lot.'

'Sorry.'

'It's fine. It didn't make sense to sleep in the car.'

She kisses my cheek, then uses her phone light to find the air mattress. She knows where everything is anyway, so I let her. Then I take a steadying breath, head to the laundry and manage to find some towels—clean, if a little stale-smelling. A quick rummage also reveals some spare blankets stuffed in the back, plus a few pillows that are on the flat side of fluffy, so I bundle everything up and bring it out to the lounge room. Nina has a pump plugged in already, the bed inflating at her feet.

'The water's probably cold, but it's better than nothing,' I say, setting everything down. 'There's a bathroom down here and one at the top of the stairs. Help yourself to whatever you can find. Nina knows where everything is too.'

Nina screws up her nose. 'I'm *so* not sleeping in Theo's bed, by the way. That little deviant has too many cooties. Shotgun the couch.' I smile, because that couch is where we had our first sleepover, sleeping top to tail and watching one of my parents' scary movies.

'I'll sleep on the airbed,' Miles says. 'Gid, you drove all day. Take the bed, get some sleep. And have a shower, you stink.'

'Gee, thanks.'

I give him a thin smile. 'Come on, I'll show you.'

This house is bigger than our Hamilton rental—Mum and Dad's old room is down a long corridor, plus there's a study up here and a little alcove in the bay window. I used to sit there and read, waiting for Willow's car to pull around the corner.

Theo's room is cold and dark, most of the walls bare—he actually packed when Mum told him to. I peel off the sheet that covers his bed, coughing on a cloud of dust. 'Sorry, it's been empty a while.'

Gideon shrugs. I wonder how long this uneasy truce will last, but I'm too tired to care. 'Bathroom's next door,' I add. Then I stand there, quiet, wondering what else I should say, but I can't find the words. 'Um. So. Goodnight, then.'

I start backing out of the room, but his eyes snap up. 'Reece, wait...'

'Yeah?' I squeak.

He shakes his head. 'Just...goodnight.'

I close the door behind me. I think about going downstairs again, but I can hear Nina giggling and Miles whispering and I don't want to interrupt.

Guess there's nothing left to do. I creep down the hallway, hearing the shower tap flick on. I touch the door handle to my old room, and it swings on its hinges.

It's exactly as I left it. Which is to say, it's a mess, and there's a sea of boxes stacked in one corner—mostly half-packed and stuffed with random armfuls of clothes and trinkets. I made a severely underwhelming attempt at packing when we moved. Whatever boxes I managed to fill are the ones that ended up in Hamilton. My wardrobe is still half-full of winter coats and fancy dresses. The bookshelf sags with stacks of novels I never read. My bedside table is littered with the scraps of my old life: my school pass, one earring. And the walls. The walls are covered in photos. Me. Nina. Willow. Some of the other girls from my high school. There's one of Nan, even. One by one, I take them down, easing Blu Tack off the back. I stack them in a neat little pile, and rest them on my bedside table. Time for them to come home with me.

I sit cross-legged on the bed, and pull out Nan's manuscript. I stare down at the title page.

Maybe this is what she wanted. She left me her books. She left me clues. Who else would have known that statue? Who else would have found these pages? I think of Mum's words. *Did you ever think there was a reason she didn't sell them?*

I suspect I'm holding the reason in my hands. *Just listen.* Maybe that's all she wanted, in the end.

There are years of history here. Names of women, of their children. The lies Nan told to give them a new life. Reports of their health, years later, when she went to check on them. There are letters and cards shoved between the pages, thanking her. Even a few photos, snapped of smiling faces.

There are more names, too, of the women she couldn't

help. The ones who were scared, or angry, or who never wanted a baby anyway. She kept everything, just in case. And I know, right then, that this isn't my secret to tell. It's the legacy of a life my grandmother lived in private, and even if she wanted to share it with me, I would never share it with anyone else. These women wanted a new life, and they'll get it.

Finally, I read Alba's story. She couldn't bear the thought of leaving without telling her mother goodbye, so she let her in on the plan. Her father found out when Alba started packing her bags—he didn't even know she was pregnant. He was so ashamed he told everyone she drowned, and bade her and the baby good riddance. Told Alba and Nan never to come back, so long as he lived. Guess it's lucky he died a few years later. Nan moved back to Hamilton when she eventually got tired of the city. She had made Hamilton her home; no one was going to keep her away for very long.

I lean back into the squashed pillows. The apothecary curio was an antique-shop find—it's one of the first stories Nan wrote down. She bought it for herself as a graduation present when she finished med school, taken by the romanticised notion of the original owner: a woman who wore a beard and studied at university in disguise, then travelled to remote towns to help in any way she could. The only mystery remaining is how on earth Nan commissioned a hat to sit atop her statue to hide these papers, but I guess some things will remain secret.

A knock at the door startles me. I shove the papers to one side. 'Nina, it's fine, just come in.'

The door edges open. Gideon sticks his head around the corner, and my traitorous heart flutters.

'Hey,' he says, a little throaty. His hair is wet and dripping down his shirt, and he's wearing boxers instead of his jeans. 'I just wanted...I just wanted to make sure you were okay.'

I spread my hands protectively over the manuscript. 'I'm okay,' I say. 'Kinda overwhelmed. But okay.'

He steals a few more steps into the room, and gives a low whistle. 'You left a lot of stuff behind.'

'Left in a hurry.'

It reminds me so much of when he first came to my house—my *new* house—wandering around the collection of my things, all the trinkets that make a life. He sits on the edge of my mattress and picks up the stack of photos. He laughs at one, then sets them down again.

I watch him, the muscles in my shoulders tense. 'Gideon, what are you doing here?'

He sighs. 'I came to say sorry. Again.'

'Oh.'

He picks up my hand and holds it in his lap. 'I'm sorry I got so angry about art school. And I'm sorry I took the book—I don't know what I was thinking. It just felt like maybe, for once, there was a future I finally wanted, one that finally felt real. And Mum was so sick, I thought maybe I could get her proper help. It was stupid. It was one *stupid* moment, and I ruined everything.'

'You didn't ruin everything,' I say. His thumb traces a circle on the back of my hand, and I shiver. 'I'm sorry I applied without asking you. I didn't realise how cruel it was. I wish I could take it back.'

He gives me an awkward half-smile. 'So you forgive me?'
I nod.

And then because it's quiet, and because he looks broken, and because I *want* to, I lean forward and kiss him. A brush of my lips, soft and questioning. He sits very still, and I start to pull away, thinking I've made a mistake, but then his hands come to my shoulders and he's kissing me back.

He pushes me gently into the mattress, his body half-covering mine, his hands in my hair. I shove his T-shirt up, desperate to feel his warmth again, to catch the scent of the ocean on his skin. His own hands are wandering, emboldened by my recklessness, and just as his fingertips brush my bra he pulls away. 'I have to tell you something,' he says, breath ragged. His lips are only inches from mine, and I think he'll stop talking if I kiss him again.

'Now? Right now?' I reach up, flicking my tongue over his lips. It almost works—his forehead tilts forward, resting against my own.

Then he groans, pushing back, his body heat rushing away all at once.

I sit up, yanking my shirt straight. 'Is this like—a safety thing? Or a diseases thing?' I laugh nervously, but I feel a pit in my stomach. He looks like he's in genuine pain trying to get the words out.

'I just...' he starts, then stops. 'I just don't want you to do this because you feel bad. Or because...I don't know. I just don't want to keep any more secrets.'

I feel my cheeks turn hot. 'God, Gideon. It wasn't a pity pash.'

'Okay.' He's nodding vigorously. 'Okay. Then I still have something to tell you. I have an interview.'

I don't understand. 'A job interview? What about the lifesaving club? I thought it paid well—'

'No,' he says, taking a long breath. 'Art school. I have an interview. The admissions officer called when I didn't reply to the offer. We started talking, and she said I should apply for the scholarship program, and I said I couldn't cover board even if I did get a scholarship and *they* said there were special loans, and then *I* said my mum—'

I slam my hand over his mouth. 'Gideon. You got in?'

'I have an *interview*,' he says, words muffled through my palm.

I squeal, throwing myself in his lap, pressing close. 'You're gonna get in, Gideon. I know it.' His breath hitches, and his hands dig into my side.

If he has hope, he doesn't let it show. 'Might. I *might* get in. Don't tell the others,' he says. 'I don't want to explain... if it doesn't happen. But Mum...it's what *she* wants, too.'

'I promise,' I say, but the words get lost because I'm kissing him again, impatiently tugging his shirt over his shoulders.

And finally he grins, lifting me so I'm straddled across his lap, nuzzling into my neck. His nose traces its way down my throat. 'You know what this means?'

I have no idea what it means, because I have lost all capacity for thought. My world has reduced to the spot above my collarbone, where he's muttering the words between kisses. 'We'll both be in the city next year,' he says.

I freeze. He must notice, because his hands go still. 'What? What did I say?'

'I…have to tell you something too.'

I try to wriggle away but he holds me close. 'It's okay, you can tell me,' he says. 'Whatever it is. Diseases?' he jokes, and I give a strangled laugh.

'No, not that. Gideon…it's just—the thing is—I won't be in the city next year.'

He blinks, not understanding. 'You're not going to uni?'

I shake my head, clinging to his fingers to stop my own from trembling. 'No, I am, eventually. But after Willow, and Nan, my grades kinda…suck. I already talked to Principal Pearson. She helped me apply for special consideration.' I close my eyes and say the words I've been dreading. Not because they're wrong, but because it still stings a little. A future slipping away, if only for a moment. 'I'm not going to uni next year, I'm staying in Hamilton. I'm redoing the year. So is Nina. I mean, not in Hamilton, obviously, she's doing it at our old school, but both of us needed more time—'

His hand comes up to cup my face. 'Hey, Reece.' He kisses my forehead, waiting until I've stopped babbling. 'It's okay. You're gonna be okay.'

'But you and Miles will be gone, and I'll be all alone, *again*…'

'You'll be okay—and you won't be alone. You have Ava, and Nina, and I'll be home on weekends. It's *your* future, Reece. What you're doing sounds smart.'

I lean into his chest. 'I'm going to be the sad senior kid who had to repeat. Everyone's going to think I'm an idiot. Oh *god*, Billy's going to have a field day.'

He chuckles, hands running up and down my spine. 'You're not an idiot. And we'll still see each other. And Miles—who knows what Miles is doing, actually.'

'We're all kind of a mess, huh.'

He kisses me again. 'Nah. I think, for once, we're all where we're meant to be. Besides, it's only a year. You'll be in the city in no time.'

'About that...'

He looks nervous. 'What? What else?'

'I talked to one of Nan's friends. She wrote me a recommendation letter, before Nan died. She said I can intern in Puerto Rico for a semester before I enrol in a university—whenever that is. It's a Doctors Without Borders program. It'll help boost my scores too, if I, um...if I want to apply for medicine.'

And then he grins. 'Dr Blackwell. That sounds pretty cool.'

'You already *knew* a Dr Blackwell, you idiot.'

He wrinkles his nose. 'Let's make a deal, and let's *not* talk about your nan while I'm imagining you naked.'

'*Hey.*'

'Sorry. It's just, the whole genius girlfriend thing is kind of a turn-on.'

'Girlfriend?'

He just grins wider. 'For, like, six weeks. Until exams are over, and I'm wherever I am, and you're back in school.

And after that…if we're lucky…'

I smile, memorising his dimples. I wonder how long I can call them mine. 'Let's not talk about after that,' I say. 'We can make our own luck.'

26

THE MUSEUM DISPLAY is sold out. There's a huge banner, with Nan pictured in her scrubs, and a red sticker plastered in one corner that says *No more tickets*.

I fidget with the edge of my dress. Mum and Dad have dressed up, and even Theo is wearing a suit jacket, but most of the crowd looks pretty casual. Gloria, the curator, came to find me at the start, to thank me again for the loan. I apologised because they had to push back the exhibition while waiting for my paperwork, but she waved it off. She asked what I was going to do with all these books when the exhibition closes, and I just shrugged—I'm not entirely sure, but at least it feels right. Nan's books will stay in the family. The curio, of course, never quite made it to the museum.

'Dude, look at this stuff! Hey, Reece, can I suck your brains out through your nose?'

I smack Theo's hand and a rusted metal contraption drops to the table. 'You're not supposed to touch anything!' I hiss.

Mum sighs, but she doesn't seem to mind. Her eyes are

on the crowd, all the people who huddle together, gathered over the open pages. 'I didn't know so many people would be interested,' she says. A hand flutters over her heart. 'It's like she's here again.' Dad squeezes Mum's hand, and they disappear into the crowd.

'I'm gonna go look at the weird brain shit,' Theo says, leaving me alone.

But not for long. A hand slips into mine, giving an affectionate tug. 'I told you Nana B was badass,' Nina says. 'What did they say when you gave them the bronze hat?'

I laugh. 'They said that although it wasn't a *medical* oddity, they would be delighted to accept the mystery bronze hat. They might even help me figure out where it came from.'

'As they should,' she answers, nodding sagely. The hat glimmers behind the safety of a glass barrier. *This hat protected worthy secrets for many years*, says the plaque beside it. *Mary Blackwell and her family dedicate this exhibition to women everywhere: the ones who came before, those who will come after, and those who are still fighting.*

'How'd first day back go?' Nina asks, nudging me with her shoulder.

'Oh, you know, humiliating. Kinda boring. But, not cursed this time, which is a bonus.'

'You were never cursed.'

'I know,' I admit. 'It was weird, without you two. It didn't feel like the final first day. Again.'

'I think it'll always feel weird without her.'

I remember Willow's easy smile. 'I know. I miss her. I wish she could see this.'

Nina snorts. 'Please, she'd be over with Theo looking at the jars of body parts.'

'Gross,' I say and laugh, because remembering doesn't hurt so much anymore.

Miles, Gideon and Ava manage to wriggle in our direction, precariously holding drinks in each hand. 'Well, it's no paddock party, but this is pretty sweet,' Miles says.

'I'm really glad your nan wasn't a murderer,' Ava says, very earnestly.

Gideon just smiles. He's moving to the city soon—he got into uni after all. I try not to think about it too much. Mum helped Grace get into a residential care program that the hospital is trialling for younger patients. It means she can come and go as she needs, and they can still keep the bungalow for weekend visits. Grace waves at me, laughing beside Mrs Kostakis. Gideon waits until the others are distracted, then whispers in my ear. 'Guess who I just met,' he murmurs.

'Who?'

He points discreetly at an elderly lady leaning against a walking frame, and a man who hovers close beside her. 'That's Alba Thornton, and her son.'

My eyes fly wide and I take half a step forward without meaning to. 'That's Alba?'

He grins, nodding. 'She asked if I knew anything about a nice young lady she'd heard organised all this...'

'Oh my god!' I squeal. 'Can I go meet her? Is it weird? Does her son know? Should I wait?'

Alba's milky eyes land on me from across the crowd. I give a feeble wave, feeling the bizarre urge to curtsey. In a way, she led us all here. Without that first clue, we'd have never known all the answers.

Gideon's still smiling when I look up, his eyes never leaving my face. 'What should I do?' I ask Gideon. 'I'm so nervous, my hands are sweating. Can you tell my hands are sweating?'

He leans against a glass cabinet, taking a sip of his drink. 'What do you want to do?' he asks, in a measured, reasonable tone that I find immediately infuriating.

'I don't know. That's why I asked you.'

He takes me by the shoulder and turns me so I face the room. 'Reece, I think we've determined at this stage that you can do anything you want to.'

So I take a step. And then another. Until the crowd envelops me, and Alba puts a paper-thin hand on my shoulder, and her son introduces himself.

And when I look back, the people I love are there, waiting. Like they have nowhere else to be, and all of the time in the world to be *here*. Because there's no such thing as curses, but there are second chances. And luck. And love. And a life that might not be perfect, but that's made stronger from the cracks.

Acknowledgments

I started writing this manuscript in 2019—needing an escape, nostalgic for summers gone by, wanting to dip into the comfort of a slow beachside town. Little did I know how much that escapism would be needed in the years to come.

The world has changed a lot since I first started writing, and I can't quite believe that this book has survived it all. This journey to publication wouldn't have been possible without the guiding hands of so many, and the below is almost certainly an incomplete list of those who deserve a word of thanks. If I've forgotten your name, please invoice me for the cost of one (1) Aperol spritz, and I promise to make it up to you.

Firstly, a huge thank you to Michael Heyward for offering the Text Prize. Giving debut writers the opportunity to have their work read and considered for publication is an invaluable gift to the Australian literary community. Thank you to Samantha Forge, who first saw promise in this novel, and delivered the news that quite literally changed my life. Thank you to Ian See, for wrangling these words into publishable format and guiding this story towards its final form, and to Emma Schwarcz for catching my (many) typos. A huge thanks also to the entire team at Text Publishing, who worked so hard to get this book into readers' hands, including the incredible marketing, publicity and sales team: Kate Lloyd, Jamila Khodja, Julia Kathro and Madeleine Rebbechi. This gorgeous cover was designed by Imogen Stubbs and illustrated by Adèle Leyris. There are so many invisible hands that bring a book to life—publishing assistants, typesetters, proofreaders, rights managers and many more—and I appreciate your work more than you might ever know, even if we've never had the chance to meet.

This novel wouldn't have been possible without the amazing people I met through RMIT's Professional Writing and Editing program. While this isn't the book I started writing in PWE, I will be forever grateful to the unfailing support and wisdom of Clare Renner, who not only insisted I would love the Young Adult class (good call), but also completely changed the way I thought about writing. In fact, the entire Young Adult class of 2013 were bloody superstars—I still think of you all, and always hope to spot your names on covers at my local bookstore.

To my incredible, kind-hearted, ridiculously talented, supportive and perceptive writing group—there are not enough adjectives in the world to express how much I love you all and value your friendship. You have kept me going, one foot stumbling in front of the other, during the hardest times. Your guidance has shaped this book in every possible way—thank you, a million times, Kate, Sue and Tina. May we always have Wednesdays and potatoes.

This book is dedicated to my mum, but none of it would have been possible without the love and support of two great women in my life—my grandmothers, Jan and Margaret. Throughout my childhood, they gave me many boxes of second-hand books to satiate my love of reading. Those books seemed all the more magical for having had a life of their own—I loved the inscriptions from strangers, the dog-eared pages and underlined words. There is nothing I treasure more, even now, than those battered copies of The Baby-Sitters Club and The Famous Five. I hope they know I think of them every time I sit at my computer: every story I've ever written is woven with pieces of them.

(I would also like to acknowledge my great-grandmother Doris, though she was more likely to lend me a grisly and deeply age-inappropriate murder mystery. I still miss her kicking my butt at Scrabble.)

To my beautiful family: Mum, Glenn and Holly. Thank you for always being there for me; for giving me a sanctuary to escape to when I need it; for your open arms, your pantry stocked full of snacks and your tolerance for my giant garden-stomping dog.

My mum has always believed that this book would happen. She has an incredible ability to be proud of even the smallest achievement ('I bought fancy shampoo!' is met with equal enthusiasm as 'My book got signed!'). I don't think I understood, for a long time, how that support can shape a life: if I ever took bold steps, it's only because I knew she would be there at the end of the day with the kettle on, no matter what.

Glenn, thank you for *always* answering the phone—whether it's to locate my mum, to answer 'how do I fix this' questions, or just for a long chat. I will always be grateful our families found each other, at just the right time. (Not to mention, a big chunk of this book was written at your kitchen counter, which is, quite frankly, a creative oasis.)

Extra-special thanks to my sister for reading not only this book but every book I write, with relatively few complaints. Thanks for answering my FaceTime calls, baking a stress-cake, and listening to me talk my way out of plot holes. May you always be the Amy to my Jo: your wisdom, wit and kindness are things to treasure.

To my dad, who rushed to purchase this book the moment it was available—I may not be able to buy you a car when this is done, but thank you for the support none-theless. You gave me my first 'proper' chapter book, and I still have it on my shelf (in retrospect, 767 pages was perhaps a lofty ambition for a ten-year-old).

Thank you to the entire Morales and Ruiz family, who welcomed me as their own. Your love, support and laughter mean the world to me. Thank you for starting a family-wide debate on my behalf to translate the single line of Spanish in this book.

To Roberto, my partner, best friend, in-house chef and personal cheer squad. Thank you for picking me up when I'm low, for celebrating the highs, and for leading us through the last two years with the stubborn belief that the world would recover. Thank you for making me laugh, for introducing me to *Cobra Kai* and sitting through *The O.C.*, and for every weekend that I've holed myself away upstairs while you kept our house running. I'm so proud of the life we've built together. If we could go back to that Ferris wheel eight years ago, I'd make sure we took a better photo.

(Also, if you happen to be one of Rob's colleagues who was coerced into purchasing this novel through his vigorous sales pitch—thank you and, also, sorry.)

Thank you to Leo—you can't read this, but Rob insisted you deserve a mention. I love your giant head, your zoomie somersaults, and your uncanny ability to know when the coffee machine is switched on. You're a strange dog, now that I think about it.

To my physio, who literally had to tape me together again so I could finish my copy edits. She thought I was joking when I said I'd give her an acknowledgment—I wasn't. Thanks, Aimee.

To my gorgeous friends (you know who you are)—I am finally available for brunch dates! Thank you for your patience all those weekends I spent writing and editing (*always* editing!). Thank you for accommodating my weird schedule, for the messages of support, the funny videos, the hugs, the drop-ins, the laughter and the love. Especially Liz, who has stuck by my side for twenty years, and doesn't seem to be sick of me yet—that's a forever kind of friend. Everyone should have one of those.

And finally, thank *you*, dear reader. I started writing stories when I was six—it's surreal to think that there are now people holding a published book full of my words. Thank you for picking up this book, for supporting bookstores and for deciding to share your time in this fictional world. None of it is possible without you.